Chapter 1

THE SHRILL RINGING in my room is like a five-alarm fire drill. It's six a.m. For a split second, I think it's just another ordinary day—alarm goes off, I get up and make some coffee, and wake up Shay. But today is anything but ordinary.

The disastrous events of the last couple of years roll through my mind as I get dressed. There has to be some small detail I've forgotten. Something that didn't seem important at the time, but might have been a clue about what was going on. But try as I might, nothing stands out. In fact, the more I think about it, the more of a blur the last few years of my life become.

Quietly I sit, sipping my coffee and watching the clock. Every tick closer to nine seems like another inch closer to doomsday. My stomach's in knots, and my heart is ready to burst out of my chest. I can't do anything to stop this. It is what it is, and I have to move on, but it's so damned hard, I can barely breathe. Like it or not, today is the start of my new life. First stop: divorce court.

★ ★ ★

"CONGRATULATIONS ON FINALLY dumping that weight around your ankle!" My best friend, Jenny, sits in my kitchen, watching the coffee I made her go cold. She never fully understood my lifestyle choice. To Jenny, getting married is like a fate worse than death. She claims to love the *'newness'* of relationships. First kisses, stolen glances, the rush of someone new between the sheets. Her personal motto has always been *'once the butterflies disappear, so do I.'* She's my best friend, my confidant, and my polar opposite in every way.

"He isn't an ankle weight, Jenny. Ugh, why am I still defending that horse's ass? What is wrong with me?" I reply, trying to rub out the tension headache that's forming between my eyes.

Regardless of what Jenny thinks, I love my life. *Loved* my life. It was quiet and safe. Bob worked and took care of the bills, while I stayed home with our daughter, Shay. Life was perfect. Until that home-wrecking slut joined our family.

Starting a new dental practice meant long hours for Bob. Keeping the house, Bob's books, and making time for a very active toddler was pushing me to the limit. The answer to all my problems was Cami.

She was young, energetic, and could play games with Shay for hours. She was a godsend. So much so that even when the practice took off, Bob insisted we keep her. I told him if he was home more, it was silly to have the nanny come so often, but he was adamant. Besides, Shay loved her. She'd become part of the family.

As usual, Bob spoke, and I quietly went along.

I was so blind.

"The only thing wrong with you is that you allowed that pompous asshat to run your life for far too long. You earned yourself a scholarship to art school, graduated summa cum laude, then just resigned yourself to a life of servitude to that dictator you called a husband. Once you get out in the real world, you'll see there is way more to live for than life in the suburbs with *Dr. Bob.*"

Easy for her to say. She's pretty and blond and doesn't have

KADE

A SECOND CHANCE ROCK STAR ROMANCE

Jane Anthony

Cover Design by:
Cassy Roop, Pink Ink Designs

Editing by:
Nichole Strauss, Perfectly Publishable

Proofreading by:
Jenny Sims, Editing4Indies

Formatting by:
Christine Borgford, Perfectly Publishable

Steph and Rod Forever

a single stretch mark on her flawless porcelain skin. She practically lives at the gym. I, on the other hand, am short with unruly curls and boring brown eyes. My hourglass figure makes it hard to dress, and my weekly Zumba classes aren't really doing as much as I'd hoped for my post-baby bod. I'm hopeless. I wasted all my pretty years on Bob. He was my first and only everything.

I was just sixteen when we met. He was a senior, captain of the football team, and I couldn't believe someone that popular would actually date me, the shy art nerd. It seemed like all the girls in our school were practically lining up to date him.

When he asked me out, I thought he was joking. Blond, handsome, and built, he could have had anyone he wanted. He was like a teen heartthrob. The kind of guy girls swoon over in *TigerBeat* magazine. And, for some strange reason, he wanted me. Why me? I was a mouse. A dust mite. A piece of cellophane. You could walk right by me and never even know I was there.

In hindsight, that's probably what he liked about me the most. I let him control everything. He made the plans, and I tagged along, happy and content just being in his company. Bob was my world. I would have done anything to make him happy, but he never was. Nothing was ever enough for him. He just wanted more. More money, more things . . . more women.

My eyes well up with tears as the memories wash over me. No matter how hard I try, I can't pinpoint exactly when everything fell apart. I'd been so busy deluding myself into thinking everything was fabulous that I'd overlooked so many things.

Jenny's face softens as the first tear trickles down my cheek. "God, I'm so pathetic," I whine.

"No, you're not, Ains," she says softly, taking my hands in hers. "I'm sorry; I shouldn't be so quick to dismiss Bob when I know how badly you're hurting."

"No, it's not your fault. You're right. I know Bob isn't worth all these tears, it's just . . ." Saying it out loud somehow makes it feel that much more real. Bob and Cami looked so cozy sitting side by side in the courtroom earlier, while I sat there alone feeling fat and depressed. He promised me happily ever after, but he destroyed that vow along with my heart.

Jenny rips a paper towel from the holder near the sink, dabbing my tears the way she'd done a hundred times in the last year. When everything fell to hell, Jenny was the only one in my corner. A true friend like her is a rare commodity. She's always had my back.

★ ★ ★

"GIVE US TWO beers, two shots of tequila, and keep 'em coming!" Jenny shouts. I shoot her a look, and she shoots me one right back. "Your daughter is with your parents, and you're a free woman. Live a little!"

The Blue Stone Bar and Grill is jam packed full of professionals in suits getting their happy hour buzz on. Being out at five o'clock is alien to me. Normally, I'd be rushing around to prepare dinner for my family. Where I belong.

Skipping the shot, I reach for my beer. "Getting hammered isn't going to help my situation, and I have a lot to do tomorrow after I pick up Shay from my parents' house."

"Oh, yeah. The 'Family Vacation,'" replies Jenny, using air quotes, her voice dripping with disdain. Our yearly vacation was always a big event. Bob had it in his head that he was a successful dentist, and as such, we should be taking vacations that "make people jealous." He's so pompous sometimes. Shay and I would have been just as happy at the Jersey Shore, but Bob needed bells and whistles. He needed to travel, see the world.

Last year, we spent three weeks in Egypt. It was hot, and the food was terrible, but Bob loved it. We'd briefly discussed doing a month in Europe this year, and I'd assumed that with everything going on, that plan had left the table. Imagine my surprise when I found out he and Shay still intended to go—with Cami. "How are you holding up with all that?"

"I'm dealing with it." It's a lie. I know it, and Jenny knows it. In reality, I'm hanging on by a thread. Not that I was dying to go, but the thought of being without Shay for a whole month makes me want to crawl in a hole and cover myself with dirt. It's like going a month without water. Impossible. Losing her every other weekend is hard enough. I half considered telling her she couldn't go, but she's so excited. How can I say no?

"Well, what if I told you I might be going on a little extended vacation of my own?" Jenny's Cheshire Cat grin spreads from ear to ear. It always seems unintentionally devious. Or maybe it just seems that way because whenever I see it, I somehow know trouble is lurking around the corner. My mother refers to her as "That Jenny." As in, "What has 'That Jenny' gotten you into this time?"

The idea of her taking a vacation is new information. Jenny doesn't do anything without running it by me first. She's the type of girl who uses the bathroom while talking on the phone. Crude yet hilarious at the same time.

"I couldn't say anything until it was official, but I took on a new client at my PR firm. We'd been in discussions for months, and it was killing me not being able to tell you, but you know how it is."

I nod, but in reality, I have no idea how it is. Jenny is one of the most successful people I know. She started her own public relations firm from the ground up and worked tirelessly until it was a pretty big name in the industry. She represents many famous people and always has the best gossip. I have so much insider information I could probably write a book.

"Brace yourself for this one. It's Black Diamond."

The frosty carbonation lodges in my windpipe, causing a teary-eyed choking fit. She's going to be working with Black Diamond. *Black. Diamond.* Just hearing the band's name makes me want to pump my fists in the air. Black Diamond has been my favorite band since college—a fact I've kept well hidden in my current social circle. I'm not sure poetic lyrics like *'close those eyes and let me love you to death'* fit in with the Coldplay crowd that generally surrounded me.

Every word drips with erotic torment. Not only are they heavy and loud, but their lead singer, Kade Black, is the epitome of hot rocker dude. He's vulgar and cocky with a voice sexy enough to make me break out in a sweat. And the bod on him . . . don't even get me started. It should be illegal for one man to be that hot. It's not fair to the rest of the world. Needless to say, Bob hates Black Diamond.

"So they are starting their East Coast tour in a couple of days, and I'll be going with them to revamp their promotion for it. Kade is apparently a huge hothead, and they want to bring me along to defuse any potential situations right away," she continues, bouncing up and down in her seat with excitement. "Why are you looking at me like that? Aren't you excited?"

My lashes flap as I collect my thoughts and wipe the deadpan expression off my face. I am excited. However, I hate to admit that I'm also a little jealous. It isn't Jenny's fault, but I'm having trouble processing her amazing news while still feeling so overwhelmingly sorry for myself. I'm not ready to end my pity party just yet, but I plaster on a supportive grin anyway. Jenny loves the band as much as I do; I need to stop being so childish. "Yes. Holy crap, that's incredible! Congratulations!"

"Well, there's more. The idea of hanging out alone on some crappy tour bus didn't exactly thrill me. I mean, what if these guys all turn out to be douchebags? That would suck, right? I'm bringing an assistant to help out."

"Oh, that's cool! You guys will have so much fun!" I down

the untouched shot in front of me. I need a solid buzz if I'm going to have to feign happiness all night. "Who are you bringing with you?"

Her grin dazzles so brightly you could probably see it from space. "You."

Clearly, she's had too many shots of tequila. Jenny's manicured fingers close around my arm. "Did you hear me, Ainsley? We're going on tour with Black Diamond!"

"You're nuts! I can't just drop everything and go on tour with a rock band. I'm a grown-up. I have responsibilities," I say, shooing her away with my free hand.

"What responsibilities? Shay is going to be in Europe this summer with Bob—the family trip you are supposed to be on, might I add. You were all geared up to leave town for a month anyway. You're just trading in Europe for a tour bus full of hotties!"

The woman has lost her damn mind.

It's absurd. I'm a thirty-year-old housewife. I can't go on a tour bus full of rock stars . . . can I? It's a once-in-a-lifetime opportunity, for sure. The air in the bar is stagnant and hot, but the mere thought of being in such close quarters with Kade Black causes my skin to prickle.

Overhead, the song fades out, and a low growl bursts through the speakers. I know this song. Title track, "Demon Speedway", Black Diamond's debut album. It's a sign. I've had a shit year, an even worse day, and I deserve this.

Kade's voice belts out the chorus:

Livin' fast and dyin' young,
Our wicked journey's just begun.
Take a ride with me, baby, racing down the demon speedway.

I close my eyes and seal my fate. "When do we leave?"

Chapter 2

P ULLING UP TO my childhood home, I wish I were anywhere else. The dentist? A firing squad, perhaps? Anywhere but here. I just know the second I walk in that house my mother is going to start in on her crap again. She's so old-fashioned. She and my father were married right out of high school, and she spent the last thirty-three years waiting on him hand and foot. With a role model like that, it's no wonder I turned out to be Bob's Stepford Wife.

My mother stands poised at the sink, scrubbing the porcelain basin. "Hey Ma, is Shay up yet?"

"Hi dear, come in. Yeah, she is upstairs packing her bag." Her incessant scrubbing stops as she turns to greet me. "This is the way you leave the house? No wonder he ran off with that young girl. At least put on some makeup. You look exhausted." She pats her damp hands over the tight curls framing her forehead to press down any flyaway strands that may have come loose. I roll my eyes. She has on a full face of makeup just to clean the house. My mother: Mrs. Perfect.

"He didn't leave me because I run errands without makeup, Mom. Can we please not go into this now? I've had a rough night as it is." The corners of my mouth turn down. Her harsh words cut deep. She's right. I feel haggard and old, and it's written all over my face.

As the court date neared, I found it difficult to sleep, the finality of it all hitting me harder every time my head hit the pillow. First Bob left, and now, he's taking Shay with him. To make matters worse, my inner turmoil turns to fear when I consider the possibility that Shay may want to live with her father and Cami instead of me. Shay adores her. Cami is young, pretty, and fun. Everything I know I'm not.

"Well, you obviously weren't doing something right at home. Men just don't up and leave their wives for no reason, Ainsley."

"Why are you always taking his side? You're *my* mother. I would assume you would be more supportive. He is the one who broke my heart and tore our family apart. I'm trying to figure out how you see this as my fault. I wasn't the one screwing around!"

She turns back to the sink and resumes scrubbing the non-existent dirt. "You should have tried harder, that's all I'm saying. You could have forgiven him. When I was younger, you didn't throw away a marriage. You learned to fix it and move on. Vows are forever, Ainsley."

Apparently, Bob hadn't gotten the memo.

The stabbing sting of her words stick in my heart. I can't believe we're having this conversation again. Tears burn my eyes, but I refuse to release them in front of her. There's no point. "I am moving on, Mom, and you need to, too. I don't need you to rub salt in the wound."

"Hey, Mommy!" Shay calls as she bounds into the kitchen, her messy blond ponytail swinging behind her. "Grammy and me painted our nails, and we baked a cake. She even let me eat a piece for breakfast!"

"Oh, did she? Sounds like you two had a great girls' night!" I say, embracing my daughter. She's wearing her Super Girl tee, complete with attached cape. Her fascination with superheroes started as a toddler and never really ended. Bob never got it. He has no sense of whimsy. "We have to go now, though; we have so much to do before you leave for Europe with Daddy."

"And Cami!" Shay adds. Hopefully, no one notices me flinch. The thought of the woman who I paid to watch my daughter going off on our family vacation as some twisted mother figure makes me want to throw up.

"I wish you were coming with us, Mommy."

"You'll have a great time with your daddy!"

"And Cami."

"Yes, and Cami."

Chapter 3

"**I** CAN'T BELIEVE THEY booked all of this for just the two of us."

Jenny's company car picked us up at my house early this morning. A few hours later, we were unpacking our bags in the most luxurious hotel I've ever stepped foot in.

The suite at the Hotel Reginald is nicer than the resort Bob took me to for our honeymoon. Hell, it's nicer than my house. Stunning would be the best way to describe it. Everywhere I look is leather, glass, and fancy fabrics. If this is our suite, I can't begin to imagine what the band's rooms look like.

"This is The Fool's Gold tour. It starts extravagant, but once all the press dies down, and the tour gets underway, it won't be as affluent. We'll be stopping in several cities along the East Coast, so sometimes, we'll be staying in hotels, and other times, we'll be sleeping on the bus."

The bus. My nose wrinkles at the thought. I haven't even gotten there yet, and I'm already dreading it. Sleeping on a bus sounds about as pleasant as a pap smear. Just Jenny, me, and five sweaty, self-centered men stuck in a tin can on wheels.

"What's the matter? What's this face about?" Jenny points her skinny finger, moving it back and forth in front of my face.

"Just wondering what Shay's up to." Dropping her off yesterday was rough. When Cami answered the door, she barely even looked at me. The girl stole my husband. The least she can do is look me in the face like an adult before whisking my kid off to another country.

"I know you worry. But Shay is going to be fine. Bob would never let anything happen to her."

Shay's safety in Bob's care isn't what's upsetting me. As I was hugging her goodbye, she whispered in my ear, "You're gonna be okay, Mom. I'll be back before you know it." Hearing my eight-year-old's consoling words gutted me. I'm setting a piss-poor example for her. It's no wonder she's so obsessed with superheroes—she needs to seek outside influences to teach her how to be a strong, independent woman. I'm a failure.

"It's just the voices in my head playing tricks on me, ya know?"

"Voices, huh? Pretend you're deaf." Jenny's face splits into a grin. "Now, let's get dressed for the meet and greet. Are you ready to come face to face with Kade 'rip my clothes off' Black?"

"Oh jeez, Jenny, you're so embarrassing." I laugh, but the question burns in the back of my mind as I put on the outfit Jenny picked out for me. Am I ready to come face to face with the man I've fantasized about for over a decade? The odds of him turning out to be a pompous jerk are pretty high. I've spent more than enough time with a guy like that already. The last thing I want is to be stuck on a bus with another one.

"I'm not so sure about this outfit," I call out to Jenny as I check myself out in the floor-to-ceiling mirror. "I feel like an old lady trying to be hip."

She saunters into the bathroom, looking flawless as usual. Her silver mini dress hugs her slender curves and shimmers as if she's covered in a thousand mirrors. "You're crazy. You look amazing in that outfit. Those pants look *delicious* on you, I swear." The dramatic lick across her pink lips drives her point home.

Jenny insisted on choosing this outfit herself. The high-waist black leather pants are so tight they fit me like a second skin. The knee boots are great, but the heels are skyscraper high and could probably double as weapons. My usually short legs appear as though they're a mile long. I love a sexy shoe, but these are a bit overkill.

"Stop fidgeting. You look gorgeous."

The beads holding together the strip of silk covering my front clink together as I try to check myself from all angles. This shirt was really nice on the hanger, but I'm not so sure about it on me. It drapes dangerously low in the front. The whole top leaves very little to the imagination. One sudden movement and I'm going to get arrested for indecent exposure.

This is so not me. I'm a basic jeans and T-shirt kind of girl. My normally plain face and yoga pants scream New Jersey housewife and not the glamorous ones you see on TV.

"Well, I feel naked."

A dismissive wave is her response to my cry for help. "Your makeup looks awesome, by the way. Good call on the smoky eye." She tousles my huge bouncy waves, adding an extra oomph of volume. "Come on, we have to go."

A mix of reporters, fans, roadies, and other assorted workers mill about the banquet room, having drinks and picking from the buffet when we arrive. I fiddle with my hands, unsure what to do with myself. "Here," Jenny says, shoving a glass into my hand. "You look like you're ready to jump out of your skin. Have a drink, loosen up."

The smell of Crown Royal wafts out of the glass. "Whiskey and Coke?"

"Yeah, you look like you need something stiff. Thought you could use a cold beverage too."

"I feel weird being here. I have no idea what I'm supposed to do."

"Just stick with me. You don't actually have to do anything."

A short man with stiff hair catches Jenny's eye and walks our way. "Vic, nice to see you again!" she says, extending her hand. "This is my assistant, Ainsley Daniels. Ainsley meet Vic Bellagio, manager of Black Diamond."

"Good to meet you, Ainsley. Welcome to the tour."

Vic's power suit looks like it cost a fortune but doesn't hide the fact he looks beaten down by life. His age is hard to place; somewhere between forty and fifty, I'd say. His face seems young, but the salt and pepper hair and lines around his mouth make him appear older. That, and his eyes are so bloodshot, I'm tired just looking at him.

Before my very eyes, Jenny morphs from party girl to business suit Barbie. She and Vic dive into shoptalk, going back and forth about schedules and appearances, while I stand there having no idea what the hell they are talking about.

Jenny's clout on this trip so far is a real eye opener. When I think of Jenny, visions of keg stands and streaking come to mind. The girl I grew up with is not the powerful woman who stands before me right this moment. She's like the human equivalent of a mullet—business in the front and party in the back.

"Is the band ready to come in? I'd like to do some introductions first, then Rock Show Magazine would like to take some photos for an article they are writing about the tour."

My stomach churns at the very mention of the word *introductions*. The whiskey has done very little to calm my nerves, even though the glass clutched in my hand is nothing but ice now. I'm wound so tight I'm ready to bounce around the room. I don't know if I'm elated or nauseous—probably somewhere in the zone of both.

A ruckus in the bar area calls our attention. "There they are," Vic replies. "Right on time."

Jenny saunters over like she owns the place, while I trail behind wishing I were invisible. "Jennifer Price and Ainsley Daniels, I'd like you to meet Black Diamond. JJ McGarity, Konner Langdon, Lance 'Banger' Allen, and . . ." Vic points out each musician then trails off, narrowing his gaze at the band. "Where the hell is Kade? I thought I instructed you guys to make sure he was here on time? We have a schedule!"

"Don't have an aneurysm, Vic; I'm right here."

The smooth, deep voice that flows in from behind me sucks all the oxygen from the room like a vacuum. My palms grow damp. Actually, everything grows damp. Kade Black is right behind me, and I'm four seconds from hitting the floor.

"Thank God. I don't want another incident like the one in Oklahoma. We need this concert to go off without a hitch, Kade—I mean it."

"Yeah, yeah, yeah, I told you that wasn't my fault. Those two farm girls needed the hick banged out of them. I was doing the world a service, Vic." His voice is deep and rich, the way you'd imagine dark chocolate would sound if it could speak. Sinful, but way too tempting to turn down.

"Well, in the future, provide those kinds of *services* on your own time. Now," Vic starts, replacing his scowl with a plastic grin, "please meet our new public relations manager, Jennifer Price."

I turn to look, then grunt when my face hits a wall. A thick, bulging, lickable wall that smells like heaven. "Whoa, girl," he says, his enormous hand consuming my bare shoulder.

Holy. Crap.

My gaze travels up his body. Way up. He has to be six-five, easy. Even with these stilts on my feet, I'm still just facing his chest. Not that I'm complaining. My mouth waters just looking at him. You'd think I'd just gotten out of an all-women's prison. A simple button-down shirt clings to his sculpted torso in such a way that I want to reach out and touch him to see if he's real. Tattoos peek out beneath rolled up sleeves, black jeans hug him in all the right places, and the scent . . . He's a splendid mix of soap and spice and something else I can't quite place, but it's all man and totally intoxicating.

It takes a whole five beats to catch my breath and find my voice. I'm not just star struck; I'm blown away. He's big and beefy and sexy as hell.

Dark blue eyes stare down at me, half shaded with a wild dark mass of just-woke-up bedhead. "Don't go fallin' for me now," he jokes with a wink and a grin, a hint of Southern charm flowing through his words.

Focus and speak, Ainsley. Stop drooling on yourself like an idiot.

"Uh . . . Hi, I'm Jennifer Price." Jenny stretches her hand out between us, saving me from the most embarrassing moment of my life. All he did was smile, and I may as well be a puddle of goo on the carpet. How am I supposed to go three weeks like this?

He takes her hand, his eyes flitting back and forth between us like a predator, wondering which one he's going to eat first. "This is my assistant, Ainsley Daniels," Jenny continues, completely unaffected by both his presence and the heat that's radiating off him like the sun. *Or maybe it's just me who's hot?* I don't know. But when he looks back in my direction, his eyes scan me from top to bottom, pausing on my cleavage before turning back to his bandmates.

The next hour is a blur. I just can't take my eyes off him as he speaks. That smooth, sexy voice sounds so much better in person than on television. The way he carries himself demands attention. I can feel his presence in the room. Every time I glance in his direction, I'm greeted by piercing eyes that take my breath away. He watches me, his gaze caressing my skin in a way that affects my thoughts and makes me blush. I want to look away, but I can't. He's impossible to ignore.

* * *

THE SCENE STRETCHED out before me is like the last days of Caligula. The dance floor at the nightclub ripples like an orgy. Bodies writhe and grind and touch with wanton disregard like an STD mosh pit. I sit alone at a table in the VIP room just watching. The smell of sweat and sex thickens the oxygen, making it hard to breathe. Or perhaps it's the smell of my own self-doubt causing the stifling air around me. I may look the part tonight, but I'm not sexy or risqué like any of the half-naked girls stalking the club.

A bottle of whiskey and two shot glasses clang on the table in front of me, and the hairs on the back of my neck stand on edge. My gaze travels up a tattooed forearm, past a rippling bicep and a strong shoulder, to lock on a pair of eyes so blue, they are hypnotic. The shade is a color so unique there isn't even a name for it, and I should know. Art is my thing.

Kade flips the chair next to me backward, kicks his leg out, and sits, crossing his forearms over the back of the seat. "You look like you could use a drink." The miniature glass perched on his fingertips shines in the lights like a chocolate diamond. I stare down at the brown liquid without moving. My attempt at being inconspicuous worked against me. In a room dripping with debauchery, I stick out like a sore thumb.

Jenny isn't around to save me now. The disco ball shine of her dress casts shards of light all around her as she moves and sways in my peripheral vision. *At least one of us is comfortable.* She dances freely, while I'm doomed to sit on the sidelines, nursing my two left feet. Another thing making it abundantly clear that I don't belong here.

"Don't you talk?" Kade lifts my hand from my lap, forcing me to take the glass. "Loosen up, princess. It's a party," he drawls, downing his shot, and pouring himself another.

The sardonic way he calls me princess ruffles my feathers. He's patronizing me, and I don't appreciate it. I place the shot on the table and cross my arms over my chest in a huff. "I don't care for whiskey, thank you very much." While I fancy myself more of a Pinot Grigio gal in the comfort of my own home, going out with Jenny all these years has made me quite fond of the occasional whiskey and Coke. But I wasn't going to give Kade Black the satisfaction of knowing that.

The corner of his mouth quirks up into a devastating grin that kicks up my heart rate and hatches another litany of butterflies in my stomach. I try my best to remain annoyed and pretend I'm not drooling into my own cleavage. The man's confidence is locked and loaded. He has the market on sex appeal cornered and takes advantage of it being at his disposal. "Take the shot. Maybe that stick in your ass will fall out all on its own."

My mouth drops open in disbelief. *What did that cocky asshole just say to me?* Laughing at my horrified expression, he swallows his second shot. "I can assure you, Mr. Black, that I do not have a stick up my ass."

Like Eve offering up a sacred apple, he lifts the shot glass again. The arch of his brow and mischief in his eyes dare me to eat my words. I swipe the glass from his fingertips and suck the shot back in one gulp. Tears sting my eyes as the acrid taste of straight whiskey burns its way down my esophagus. "Happy?" I wince.

"Almost." He pours another and slides in front of me. This time, I throw it back without hesitation. I'm completely giving in to peer pressure, I realize, but something about him is so persuasive. I can't figure out what it is that's drawing me in.

Sure, he's handsome, but it's more than that. He has an energy around him. A force field. The more I fight it, the harder I feel the pull.

Jenny's green eyes lock on mine. Yellow circles dapple her skin from the lights reflecting off her sequined top as she saunters over. "Come dance with me!"

Before I can protest, her hands are on mine, pulling me onto the illuminated dance floor. A palette of neon colors drips down her white blond hair. She knocks her slender hip against mine and twirls me in a circle. Heavy bass thumps from the speakers. The spinning and the alcohol combined forces my hips to move. It flows through my body and out my fingertips. I close my eyes and let the beat take over.

The smell of spice and whiskey wafts from behind me and long fingers close around my waist. Only one man in this whole room has hands that big. The booze and music drop my defenses to a manageable level. His hand slides down my back, gently bending me over, and pats my ass before rubbing the sting away. He moves to the beat, grinding against me. I go with it, dancing without a care, while he dry humps me from behind, pressing his growing erection against my backside. The butterflies in my stomach flutter like gangbusters, flapping around and stirring up desires I didn't even know I was capable of having.

I spin around to face him. The neon lights overhead shine on his black hair, filling it with splotches of bright, bold color, but his eyes darken with heated desire. We stop dancing altogether. The heat from his hand encompasses the bare skin on my back, while his knee sits firm between my legs. He leans, pulling my body flush against his and grazing my ear with his fabulous lips, filling it with his husky whisper. "I bet you're just as sweet as sugar." I swallow hard, my entire body quivering.

"I got a shot at the bar with your name on it, Kade."

A girl who doesn't even look old enough to drink stands

next to us, her huge fake boobs pushed up to her throat, and her shorts rammed up her tight behind.

The fire in his eyes fizzles out. He breaks his tight embrace and follows her toward the bar, leaving me standing there alone and stunned. My body still vibrates from his touch, but my self-esteem is shot to hell. What is it with men and younger women?

Chapter 4

DAYLIGHT SLICES THROUGH the windows. The tiny rock concert going on inside my head is unrelenting. With a groan, I crack open my eyes wondering where I am and trying like hell to remember what happened last night. The mattress dips and moves. An arm covered in ebony ink falls over me and pulls me close to the mystery body in my bed. A body that smells too damn delicious for words.

Please don't be who I think it is.

The pounding in my head is unbearable as I struggle to sit up. The last thing I remember is . . . *shit* . . . what *is* the last thing I remember?

Memories of the night before pop in my brain like camera flashes. I remember dancing. And I definitely remember shots. Everything beyond that is still a bit fuzzy.

"Go back to sleep." Pillows muffle the baritone, but I recognize the voice without even having to look.

What the hell did I do?

I poke my fingers into his side with a timid little push. "Uh . . . Mr. Black. Um, wake up."

He doesn't move.

"Mr. Black, I'm going to need you to get up. Now!"

He groans but still doesn't budge.

"Kade!" I yell, wincing at the sound of my own voice.

"What?" he whines, looking up at me with the sexiest sleepy eyes. The pounding in my head rivals the one between my legs in an instant. My thighs rub together, trying their best to extinguish the sudden flames that have taken over the lower half of my body.

Kade Black is in my bed. Naked.

"Can you please enlighten me as to why you're in my bed?" I ask. "What happened last night?"

"You got hammered and were walking aimlessly in the parking lot mumbling to yourself, so I brought you back to the hotel." He grins and flops onto his back. "You're right. Whiskey really isn't your thing. Who's Bob?"

"Oh, God." It's all starting to come back. The dance, the alcohol. I can barely hear over the sound of my own heartbeat. This is quite literally the second worst morning of my entire life. I mentioned Bob? Kill me, now! "He's not important."

"He sure sounded important. You were wishing death upon him and the 'home-wrecking whore he's shacked up with,'" he replies using air quotes.

I suck in a sharp breath, wincing at how shitty the details of my life sound coming from Kade's beautiful mouth. "My ex-husband left me for another woman."

He lets out a long slow whistle. "Well, that sucks."

Could he be more blasé if he tried? What does he know anyway? He doesn't understand anything about reality. He probably has people wipe his ass for him. I should have known better than to expose details of my personal life in front of someone like him.

Shifting in bed, I wish I could rewind back to last night and not drink so much. The sheet rubs against my bare skin, and I realize that I've exposed myself in more ways than one. "Why am I naked? Did we . . . ?"

"Relax, nothing happened. You got sick all over yourself. I

untied your top and put you to bed."

"If I threw up on my top, then where are my pants?"

That wicked smile crosses his lips again as he scratches his forehead with one finger. "Well, that leather looked a little tight. I thought you'd be more comfortable without them."

"How humiliating," I groan. My head throbs even worse now. I bend my knees and hug them to my chest, resting my head on top of them. I can't believe this is happening. I've been on the stupid tour for less than twenty-four hours, and I've already made a fool of myself. It has to be a new record. It's a damn good thing I'm not an actual employee because my ass would be so fired.

"No need to be embarrassed; it's nothing I haven't seen before. I promise I was a perfect gentleman. Now speaking of perfect . . ." He playfully lifts the sheet to take another look, laughing as I cover myself tighter.

"Well, since we're both awake now, why don't we order some room service? I'm starving."

He slips out of bed and walks to the bathroom, wearing nothing but his birthday suit and a smile. *Holy cock!* I avert my gaze, but it's too late. I've seen it all.

"Could you get dressed please?" I close my eyes, but the image of his naked ass won't leave me alone. His back is just as gorgeous as his front. And just as firm. Between my thighs, I'm slick and warm; a reaction I haven't felt in a very long time.

"I ain't shy," Kade says, taking my hand. I squeeze my eyes tighter, afraid of what he plans to do with it, but instead of hot skin against my palm, I feel the chill of cold glass.

My eyes crack open. "Thanks," I mumble, before bringing the glass to my lips and pretending not to watch everything flex as he slips his boxers back on.

"Whoa, small sips, babe. I don't need another exorcist moment from you."

I roll my eyes. "Why are you here anyway? Shouldn't you be with Miss Silicone USA trying to see how many indecency laws you could break?"

"Who?"

"You know . . . big tits, tiny shorts. 'I have a shot for you, Kade,'" I chide in a high-pitched falsetto, batting my lashes for added drama.

"Oh. Her. Don't tell me you're jealous?"

When he smirks, at first I want to kiss it, but then I want to smack it. Goddammit! How is it possible that I still find him this attractive, fully knowing what an egotistical ass he is?

"No, I'm not jealous. I just figured you'd have better taste." He lifts a dark eyebrow, still grinning like this is the most amusing conversation of his life. An exasperated sigh huffs from my lips as my arms cross over my chest. He's the most infuriating man I've ever met. "Is there anything you don't find funny, Mr. Black?"

"Very few things," he says before his expression sobers. "And to answer your question, I'm with you and not her because I prefer women to little girls."

The blood rushes to my face so fast I'm woozy. My mouth opens to say something, anything in response to that, but my brain, for the second time, has completely stopped working.

"C'mon, get up and get dressed. Forget room service, we'll go out to breakfast."

One little compliment and I'm supposed to fall at his feet? It's unbelievable how full of himself he is. "I'm not going anywhere with you."

"Well, it's a good thing you'll be here for the next few weeks then."

"What are you even talking about?"

"When that stick finally comes out, I'm sure it's gonna be a big one." I open my mouth to tell him to go to hell, but he cuts me off and continues. "Come on! Get up and get dressed. You owe me one after last night."

His hotness at this point is irrelevant. The idea of being stuck with him for three weeks sounds less like the fantasy Jenny promised and more like doing hard time. "You're not used to hearing the word no, are you?"

"No."

With a pounding head, I drag myself out of bed, clutching the sheet around my naked body. "Well, get used to it. Goodbye, Mr. Black!" I storm into the bathroom and slam the door behind me.

Reaching into the shower, I turn the handle and step in. The last few days have been bizarre, to say the least. Not that long ago, everything seemed simple. I knew where my life was going, and I was comfortable with that. But now, I'm slugging back whiskey and waking up in swanky hotel rooms with sexy rock stars. *Who am I?*

And Kade Black. What the hell is his deal? He can have his pick of any girl he wants. Why is he so intent on annoying *me*? He's like a large child. Very large. Arousing. Luscious. With abs for days and a mouth that's made for sin.

My stomach grumbles as I step out of the shower. Breakfast sounds like a good idea right about now. I dress quickly and twist my hair into a messy mop of wet curls on top of my head, lacking the energy to make myself up.

A stab of regret sticks in my gut when I walk through the suite and find Kade gone. Not that I expected him to stick around after I told him to leave, but it would have been nice if he'd tried a little harder.

On second thought, no. It's better he left. I already made a jerk of myself once. I don't need him to bear witness as I kill my so-called best friend for ditching me last night.

The lock clicks seconds before the door opens, and Jenny

tiptoes in, shoes in hand, then slides the door closed without making a sound. I stomp into the living room, guns blazing, ready for the showdown of the century. "What the hell, Jenny?"

"Oh! Ainsley! I figured you'd still be asleep." She throws her bag and shoes on the couch and breezes into her room.

I follow, waiting for an explanation that never comes. "Are you at least going to tell me where you were?"

The look on her face is incredulous. As if I'd be thrilled she got me hammered and left me in a strange place to fend for myself. "Are you mad at me for something?"

"I'm not happy! Do you have any idea what my morning was like?"

Jenny turns with a sympathetic grin. "Kade stayed here last night, didn't he? I had a feeling he would do that."

My eyes go as big as saucers. "You knew?"

"Yeah, I knew," she says, pinching her brows together. "Did you think I would just leave you in a night club alone? I tried to get you back here, but you were belligerent. He threw you over his shoulder and carried you up kicking and screaming."

My bottom lip quivers like a toddler. She tried to watch out for me, and I was a drunken idiot. Full of trust issues and untapped anger, I'm a therapist's dream. I have no control over the fury that's slowly bubbling to the surface. It's not Jen's fault, and it's not Bob's. It's mine, and I'm so tired of feeling this way. The weight I carry around with me is backbreaking. It sits on my chest, constricting my lungs until I can barely breathe. It's become such a part of me over the last year that it never occurred to me I am the only one who has the power to let it go. I want nothing more than to just open my arms and let that heavy load fall to the ground and never look back.

Tears stream down my cheeks and fall onto my shirt. I'm sick, embarrassed, and so goddamn angry I can't take it anymore. Falling to the ground, I clutch my head in my hands, sobbing so hard I can't catch my breath. Jenny kneels on the ground next to me, taking me in her arms for the millionth time since this whole thing started. "I just want to be over it, Jen. When am I going to be over it?"

"I don't know when, lovie. But I know you will, and once you are, you'll never look back."

Chapter 5

"**L**ADIES."

The strong voice that filters in from behind us is all too familiar. Jenny and I came to the hotel's pool hoping for a little relaxation before the night's events, but it doesn't look like that's going to happen.

"Morning, gentlemen," Jenny coos. She's all smiles today, while I feel like I've been hit by a truck. A six-foot-five, two-hundred-plus-pound truck full of booze and swagger.

Still reeling from embarrassment, I pretend to be enthralled with the book balancing on my lap. As the morning progresses, images from the night before flash in my mind like Polaroid pictures—fuzzy, yet still able to make out if I try real hard. I don't want to admit it out loud, but I remember more than I let on.

Kade wasn't just a gentleman, he was . . . loving. The memories come in clips and waves, but certain things stand out clear as crystal. Him sitting next to me on the bathroom floor, holding my hair, stroking my back while humming me to sleep; us at the club, before I tossed my cookies, talking, laughing; him whispering in my ear, claiming me as his.

Even now, a blush creeps up my face just thinking about it. His lips grazed against my ear, causing all the hair on the back of my neck to stand at attention, much like it is right now. I mentally chastise myself for allowing him to get under my skin.

We were both drinking. It meant nothing. After all, if he was serious about any of it, he could have had anything he wanted from me last night.

His shirt and sunglasses hit my lounge chair as flashbacks from earlier this morning invade my brain. Tattoos snake around his arms and come up over his chest, twisting around each sinewy muscle with precision. Board shorts hang low on his hips, showcasing his broad chest, slender waist, and *oh my gosh* the Adonis Belt. He's an Adonis, all right. A dark one that's cocky and covered in ink.

The Kindle sits forgotten on my lap while I watch the way the cool blue water ripples around his body and drips down his chest and hair as he comes up for air. Being a voracious reader of romance novels, the irony isn't lost on me that I'm potentially living inside of one at this very moment in time. Kade is the embodiment of a book boyfriend. He's got the three T's cornered—tall, tatted, and tough.

"Wipe your chin, Ainsley." Jenny's voice breaks my concentration. I look over, squinting in the sunlight. "Maybe make it a little less obvious that you're totally eye-fucking the guy right now."

"I'm not," I say, picking my Kindle back up.

Jenny laughs. "It's okay; I know he's like your wet dream come true."

I glance in his direction to make sure he's not within earshot. If he heard us, I'd die. "I can't believe you don't think he's hot."

Her gaze flicks at Kade, sizing him up before settling back on me. "He's too friggin big. He's, like, well over a foot taller than you are. How would you even go to bed with a dude that size? He's probably packin' an anaconda in his shorts."

I suck my lips into my mouth, hiding my knowing grin. It's more like a baby's arm holding an apple. The only man that

I've ever fantasized about that wasn't fictional is Kade. Knowing and dreaming are two very different things.

Drops of water mark the dry patio as Kade pulls himself out of the pool and squats next to my chair. I try my best to act unenthusiastic; meanwhile, my entire body feels like it's about to take flight. His rock hard body glistens in the bright sun, and strands of dark hair stick around his neck as drops roll off onto the ground at his feet. "Feeling better?"

"Yes, thank you." I feel his blue gaze roaming my body, checking me out in the little hot pink bikini I'm wearing, but my eyes stay fixed on the Kindle. It's not fair. Why me? There is nothing special about me that would cause this kind of attention from someone like him. I'm just your average, everyday woman. Plain and boring.

He lingers at my side, watching me with intent, waiting for me to look up and engage him in conversation. I swipe my finger across the screen, changing pages regardless of the fact that I can't focus enough to read a single word.

"The feeling of his calloused fingers on my bare flesh was new and thrilling . . . What are you reading?" He grabs the book from my lap and stands up. Mortified, I jump from the chair and try to get it back, but he holds me back with one hand while holding the book out of my reach with the other. *"My hips bucked into his hand, but he pulled it out too soon, sitting up and sliding my arousal between the tips of his middle finger and thumb . . .* you dirty, dirty bird!" he laughs.

"Give it back to me!" I demand, standing my ground.

"Stretched to capacity, he tongue-fucked me mercilessly . . ." he continues. "Oh man, this is graphic! You like this stuff?"

"You are such a cocky asshole, you know that?"

"Asshole?" He closes the Kindle and chucks it on the chair behind me, sweeping me up in his arms and jumping into the pool.

"Oh, you're a dead man," I sputter, pushing my sopping curls out of my face.

The water is cool, but I feel like I'm boiling with him this close to me. His fingers tighten their grip on my hips as he pushes me to the wall of the pool. "You don't want to kill me. Hating me is far too much fun for you."

Against the backdrop, his eyes stand out, pinning me in his smoldering blue gaze. "Mr. Black, I. . . ."

"Kade."

"Excuse me?"

"Cut the Mr. Black shit. My name is Kade, and I want to hear it bleed from your lips the way you said it last night."

Unfortunately, the hours between dancing and vomit are still a complete blur. I could have literally said anything to him, and I have zero memory of it. "How was that?"

His lips move close to my ear again, his masculine smell seeping through the overpowering scent of chlorine. "It rolled off your tongue in a breathy purr when you asked me to fuck you."

Could I possibly have been that drunk? His thumb roams across my cheek, caressing the pink circle that I feel growing larger by the second. "Surely, you're mistaken," I say, trying to keep up the shield I've placed over myself, and hoping he doesn't hear the waver in my voice. "I don't purr."

Kade shakes his head, with a wicked smirk curling up along the corners of his mouth. "Oh, there's no way I misunderstood that, princess."

This morning's embarrassment comes flooding back in waves. Like a car accident, I don't want to know, but I can't look away from the disaster. I have to know every gruesome detail, every humiliating syllable I said to this man who both irritates and arouses me like no one I've ever met. "What did I say, exactly?"

"Your exact words?" I nod, and Kade moves in closer, his lips grazing gently across my ear as he speaks. "You said, 'I'm a grown woman who's never had an orgasm. Please, just fuck me out of my misery already.'"

My mouth drops open, but I force it closed, still trying to remain unflappable. It's true. Bob was never able to give me an orgasm. Whenever we had sex, I'd lie there, waiting for it to be over. It's an embarrassing revelation, but surely, I'm broken. "And your response was?" The question turns my stomach inside out, but I have to know the answer. What is it about me that's so repulsive that I can't even get a man into bed when I'm begging for it?

His tongue darts between his lips, catching a rogue drop of water that's broken free from the raven strand of hair hanging over his forehead. My stomach roils as I wait for his answer for what seems like an absurd length of time. "When I finally fuck you, I want to make sure you remember it."

That is not the answer I was expecting.

"When?" I whisper, dropping the tough act. My heart is beating so fast, I'm certain he can hear it anyway. "You mean if."

"Are we still playing coy?" His hands rest on the tile ledge, caging me in. "There is a scorching energy between us, A. Don't deny it. It floats off you so thick I could practically taste it. So how about this? I scratch the itch I've felt ever since last night, and you get back at big bad Bob. Two birds, one stone."

I can't deny the energy. I feel it, too, but I'm not a one-night-stand kind of girl. I'm the epitome of a good girl. Nice to a fault. Bob waited years for me to finally come around. He used to tell me I'm "the marrying kind." Back then, I never really understood what that meant, but now I realize it's not a compliment. Girls like me are doomed to be stepped on and taken for granted. We're only good enough to cook meals and keep house. There's a reason I'm here, and it's not to take in the scenic sights of the East Coast. It's to let loose and find myself.

Taking a deep, calming breath, I lift my arms from the water and drape them over Kade's shoulders, threading my fingers together to keep the shaking in my hands at bay. "You think one night with you will help me forget all my troubles, huh?"

Kade's smirk grows into a full on grin. His hands slip off the ledge, and disappear under the water, using my ass as a handle to pull me against him. "There's only one way to find out."

Chapter 6

"JEN, WHAT DO you think of this outfit?" I stroll into the doorway doing a model twirl for Jenny's inspection. In a couple of hours, we'll be whisked off to another show at the Arts Center, and after that, Kade and I are scheduled to fulfill our agreement.

One night. No Rules. No strings.

She pokes the swell of my breast with her bony finger. "Damn girl, your tits are fierce in that top!" If anyone ever spied on us in private, they would think she and I were either lovers or crazy. Jenny suffers from what she likes to call "boob envy." Basically, she's jealous because I have them, and she doesn't.

I swing back toward the mirror to double check my look. She's right; my boobs are practically in my throat. He's already laid his cards down on the table. I don't need to try so hard. I start loosening the ties on the red corset top to tuck the girls back inside, but Jenny stops me. "No, leave it the way it is! When you got it, flaunt it!"

Sitting at the edge of the bed, I pull on the same tall stiletto boots I wore last night. The sky-high heels do little to match Kade's towering stature, but at least they give me enough lift to give off the illusion of height. The shaking in my hands makes it difficult to lift the zipper. The bravado I had this afternoon has deflated, making me wish I hadn't opened my big mouth.

Kade Black's list of lovers is miles long, and those are the ones I know about. Mine is a lonely list of one. I talk a good game, but when push comes to shove, I'm going to end up disappointing Kade just like I disappointed Bob.

Jenny sits on the bed next to me, taking my trembling hand in hers. "Are you sure you're going to be able to go through with this?"

"Yeah. I'll be fine. It's just . . . what if I'm bad at it?"

Jenny looks at me as if I have lobsters crawling out of my ears. "Bad at it? Lovie, it's not like you're a virgin."

"I know. But if I were good at it, Bob wouldn't have had to look elsewhere."

Jenny rolls her eyes. "That's ridiculous, Ainsley. He didn't cheat because you're bad in bed. He's an asshole who has no idea how good he had it."

I wish I could agree, but I still can't help but think if he were satisfied at home, he wouldn't have strayed. The adjective I'd use to describe our sex life is *nice*. Not that I had any basis for comparison, but I wasn't unhappy.

Real life isn't like a romance novel. I'd pore over the pages of filth, drooling over the fictitious lives of the characters in my books, and try to emulate them, but Bob liked things his way. There are certain things men just don't do with their wives. Or so I'm told.

★ ★ ★

I'M A HUNTER you're my prey,

I'll chase you down and make you stay . . .

The lyrics ooze out of Kade's mouth, seducing the crowd with a menacing mix of snarls and wails. They swarm the stage and soak up every word with an energy that buzzes like a team of wasps. He stalks back and forth, pausing only when a distinctly evil note causes him to double over to pull the intimidating growl from deep within.

Standing backstage and watching him move with the grace of a panther, I'm drawn to the edge like a lamb to the slaughter. He strokes me with his words and devours me with every note. His screams arc over the crowd and come back like a boomerang, twisting around me and holding me in their grasp. He's magic.

By the end of the show, I'm panting. The guys walk off the stage and saunter past me, talking about where the next after party is going to be. Jenny glances in my direction as I stand off to the side wringing my hands together.

Maybe this was all a big joke. Kade doesn't really want me; he just wanted to mess with me. Get my hopes up, see how far he could push me until I finally gave in to his advances. I look away from the crowd, hiding my feelings from sight, when I feel a presence behind me. Heat hits my back, a spicy, masculine scent fills my nostrils, and the breath I didn't realize I was holding trickles out. "That shirt . . ."

"What about it?" I look down at the corset then back up at him.

Kade's glare drops to my cleavage as his finger traces the zigzag strand of string holding my top together, leaving a trail of tingles following close behind. "I'm gonna tear it off with my teeth."

My stomach does a somersault. Unnerved by his bluntness, I nod like a jackass. I'm so out of my league, it's not even funny.

"Have fun guys, I'm out." Kade offers a wave as he walks away from his band.

Assorted expletives float through the space in the mocking baritones of the other three members, but Kade just keeps walking toward the exit, with me following quietly like a Geisha. Surely, he's told his buddies about our arrangement. Kade is like Genghis Khan. The type of man who gets to eat first, while the rest of the guys dine on crumbs. The mental image makes me chuckle until I realize the main course on tonight's menu is me.

Kade has his hands planted firmly in his pockets as we stroll over to the hotel side by side. There are no sexual undertones, no smug looks, no snarky one-liners. He's got me in his pocket, too, and he knows it.

The little light on the door handle turns from red to green as it accepts my keycard with a click. His presence fills the space behind me, close enough to feel his warmth without actually touching. Kade's a man who knows what he wants, and he wastes no time going after it. Hot breath caresses my skin. His lips searing my neck, his fist in my hair, his hand on my stomach—it's all too much. I don't think I can go through with this. I thought I was brave. I thought I'd be able to handle it, but I'm suddenly having a change of heart. Or maybe just a heart attack.

I shouldn't do this.

I can't do this.

"Kade . . . I . . . it's been a while . . ."

"How long?"

I turn to face him, but the carnal lust in his eyes makes my gaze drop to the floor. "About a year." My own confession rattles me. Has it really been that long?

His fingers catch under my chin, forcing me to look at him. "We made a deal, Ainsley. I'm going to fuck you so hard that by the time I'm done, you'll ache for my cock to be inside you."

Kade licks his chops like a lion preparing to feast on his most recent kill. Taking hold of the string with his teeth, he pulls, loosening the tie, and the strapless corset flutters to the floor. Cold air caresses my bare skin; my nipples stand at attention. A gentle tug at my hair exposes my throat to his waiting mouth. His luscious lips move slowly, each kiss exploding on my skin like cherry bombs. Forget my morals, I want him.

No, I *need* him.

"Lie down." It's not a request. It's an order. Breathless and nervous, I do as I'm told. I'm nothing if not obedient.

He kneels over me, continuing his slow descent down my chest, teasing one nipple with his tongue before moving to the next, while I squirm and pant beneath him. *I can't believe this is happening.* Kade Black is seducing the skirt off me, and I'm loving every second of it. Me, the deserted housewife, is being worshiped by the Stone Cold God of Rock 'n' Roll in a hotel suite that probably costs as much as my ex-husband makes in a week.

My body goes rigid as he comes closer to uncovering my midsection, and my hands subconsciously spring to my belly, shielding the cesarean scar on my lower abdomen. I've never been embarrassed by it before, wearing it proudly as a badge of honor, but next to the chiseled perfection above me, my imperfections make me feel less than worthy. "Maybe we should turn off the light."

Grabbing my wrists, he forces my hands above my head. "Hands stay up, Ainsley. I call the shots." The sound of my name followed by his stern demand stirs something deep inside me. Try as I might to deny it, his control turns me on.

His eyes flare as he takes in the sight of me in my black lace thong and stiletto boots. "You look fucking good enough to eat," he groans, sweeping his tongue over the troublesome scar then slithering up from my navel to my neck. Everything about it is hot. His mouth, his breath, his skin, it all consumes me like fire.

"You're going to come so hard, you'll forget his name. And when you're wasted, clinging to the edge of sanity and begging me to stop, I'm going to make sure you do it again until my name is the last one on your lips." He tears off the tiny strip of lace and buries his face between my legs. My body bows at the sudden intrusion as he parts my folds and moves his tongue slowly, tasting me like ice cream.

"Juicy as a peach." The low growl rumbles deep inside when he talks. Flashes pop behind my eyelids, and another moan rips from my throat, erratic and loud. He goes harder and deeper than I ever thought possible. I can't see. I can't think. All I can do is feel.

He grabs my thighs and forces them apart in a savage and powerful move that reminds me he's in charge. A thick finger slips inside, stroking me from deep within as my hips rotate, finding a rhythm that threatens to tear me in two. Pleasure twists in my gut like a tornado. Every nerve in my body pulsates. His tongue finds my throbbing clit, tonguing, whirling, and sucking until I plummet over the edge.

A surge of energy rockets through my body, and my back vaults off the bed. The sound that rips from my diaphragm can't possibly be mine. A guttural howl comes from deep within that I'd never heard before.

Kade's fingers bite into my hips, pinning me to the mattress. "That didn't sound like my name . . ." The vibration of his voice against me is almost too much. The assault with his tongue continues without mercy, so delicious and aching, I can't take it. Still reeling and dizzy from the first orgasm, I scream without hesitation as he swirls his tongue around my still swollen nub a second time. "Kade . . . Kade . . . Kade," I chant, jamming my eyes closed as my body writhes like a snake while squeezing his head between my thighs.

His presence hovers above me. "That's my girl."

Aftershocks rock my body as I tremble lifelessly on the bed, assuming that's the end. I came twice for him. Surely, that's enough.

The rustling of clothes and the crinkling of foil are the only sounds in the room, other than the noise of the blood rushing my ears. The bed dips all around me, and a strong knee knocks my legs apart again. My eyes drift open and look at him with bemusement. "Don't pass out yet, sweets. We're nowhere near finished."

When his mouth lands on mine, his kiss is soft and tender, the complete opposite of the tongue-lashing I'd received just moments before. My body hums with renewed life. I feel him pressed against me, and I want more. I want it all.

"It's gonna hurt at first, but you'll get used to it."

He fastens his hands to my forearms above my head, locking his gaze on mine as he eases himself inside my body. The combination of pain and pleasure causes me to bite down on my lip as my body stretches around him. I squeak like a high school girl losing her virginity. The monster between his legs should be registered as a lethal weapon. I moan and whimper, but he only chuckles in my ear. Fuck, he's big.

With him buried deep inside, my inner walls clamp tight. A groan rumbles in his chest. "You tryin' to make me come?"

"I can't help it. You feel so good."

I finally get what the fuss is about. Once with him won't be enough. All my pain, all my sadness, all the bullshit built up from over the years is being washed away, pulled under the tide of ecstasy that I've never had the satisfaction of experiencing before. Kade's a dealer, his body a drug. He's not even done, yet I still want more.

My swiveling hips rise up to match each thrust. He sits back on his haunches, grabbing my hips and tilting them just so. The move seems so basic; I almost wonder what he's doing, until his shaft rubs against the spot. *Oh, that spot!* The precise spot that heats and throbs with each rhythmic plunge. "I'm gonna come again," I whine, my fingers digging into the edge of the mattress above my head.

A hulking growl rivals my exhausted squeals. Corded muscles flex in his neck and shoulders as he throws his head back and fills the condom with his release. He collapses onto my chest, our sweat-slicked bodies sticking to one another. I'm drained to the point of exhaustion yet still buzzing with excitement.

That was definitely a first, in more ways than one. All my life I thought I was the problem. Turns out my inability to orgasm wasn't me. Kade proved it with flying colors. Bold, beautiful, vivacious colors still pouring out of me in a rainbow of satisfaction.

Propping himself up on an elbow, he strokes the crumpled curls back from my forehead. "You okay, sweets?" he whispers low in my ear.

I grunt something in response, and his musical chuckle tickles my ear. Kicking off my boots, I roll to my side and get comfortable, as he gets up to discard the condom. With the terms of our deal carried out, I expect him to get dressed and leave, but the bed shifts behind me as he settles back in. "I knew that guy was a loser," he says, so quietly it's almost to himself. He nuzzles my shoulder with feather-light kisses, holding me in his art-covered arms.

Kade's a cuddler. Who knew?

Reeling in the memory of what just happened, I lie awake listening to his breathing and feeling the rise and fall of his chest against my back. My body is tired and sore but so, so happy. I've been fucked out of my mind by *Kade Black*. I have no idea how the hell it happened, but it ranks number one on my list of most awesome things ever.

Chapter 7

K ADE IS GONE when I sit up in bed. Conflicting thoughts bounce around inside my head like a pinball game. Everything happened so fast. We've only just met, yet here I am basking in the memory of the most mind-blowing sex of my life.

"Oh hey, sweets, you're up."

The deep sound of his voice startles me. I didn't anticipate him coming back, yet here he is looking downright edible in my doorway holding two mugs in his expert hands. A sexy guy bringing me coffee in bed is definitely something I could get used to.

The very sight of him sends a ball of excitement straight through my core. His body is flawless, as if it were chiseled from stone. Every muscle is sculpted, curved, and rippling from his chest, all the way down to the defined V that disappears beneath his jeans. For a split second, I consider jumping from this bed to see how far down it goes, cursing myself for being too nervous to traverse his body the way I should have when I had the chance.

He sits on the edge of the mattress and hands me the steaming mug. The coffee burns hot on my tongue as I think of something to say. My experience with one-night stands is nil, but I'm pretty sure afterward, the guy's supposed to leave in order to avoid awkward situations like this. They didn't coin the term 'walk of shame' for nothing, right? Then again, maybe he's just being cordial. After all, in a few hours, we'll be stuck together on a tour bus for the next three weeks.

"You didn't tell me you had kids."

"Kid. Just one, and I didn't think it was relevant," I say, lifting the mug to my lips again. Bringing Shay into this fantasy changes things. Kade and I agreed on one night. It was sex, not an interview for my autobiography.

His blue eyes soften as he sits there, one hand gripping the mug, the other resting gently on my leg. This is weird. It's too much like a relationship. He's drifting into my personal space, and it freaks me out how comfortable it feels. "Of course it's relevant. What's his name?"

"*Her* name. Shay. She's eight."

Again, he stays perched at my bedside, waiting for me to elaborate, but I don't. Why bother? He doesn't really care about me or my daughter. Sharing the intimate details of my life with him only cheapens what we had, but the silence is deafening. I want to change the subject, say something cool and confident, but I'm neither of those things. "So . . . should we get breakfast or something?"

I roll my eyes at my own idiotic question. He doesn't want breakfast. We are checking out in few hours. He probably has a hundred things to do. But the corners of his mouth tug up in a wicked grin that sends pink spreading all over my skin. "Oh, I could definitely eat," he says, letting the tip of his tongue slide across his bottom lip.

The coffee cup still hovers next to my mouth. He plucks the half-empty mug from my hand and sets it on the nightstand then jerks my hips until my back hits the mattress and tucks his messy bedhead under the sheet.

He's not actually going to . . . oh, my gosh, he is . . .
Oh hell, breakfast can wait.

★ ★ ★

KADE QUIETLY SLIPS out of the hotel room just as Jenny's bedroom door opens. The fat, mischievous grin splitting her face tells me she was waiting for him to leave. "Hey girl, how was your night?" I say, acting breezy on purpose just to watch her sweat. After years of enthralling me with salacious stories of single life and getting nothing from me in return, she's about ready to spontaneously combust from this one.

"Dish. I want details." Wasting no time, she plops down on the couch and gets comfortable.

"There aren't words to describe it."

"Exceptional? Marvelous? Tremendous? Give me an adjective here, I'm dying!"

Staring into space, I try to think. What's the best way to sum up the most erotic experience of my life? "Orgasmically mind-boggling."

"So I guess this means you came."

"Like he's the vagina whisperer."

"Did he . . . you know . . ." She waggles her eyebrows while sliding her tongue back and forth across her top lip. I could feel the blush rising to my cheeks again. "Heck yeah!" she exclaims, not waiting for my response.

"Oh my God, I'm a slut!" I bury my face in my hands.

"Well, you know what I always say." Jenny laughs. "The best way to get over someone is to get under someone else. Now, come on. Let's get packed."

★ ★ ★

THE BUS DEPOT looms ahead as we approach, and I crane

my neck to get a better view of where I'll be spending the next few weeks of my life. The cacophony of thousands of fans beyond the gate resonates as I step out of the limo.

The enormous bus embellished with the Black Diamond logo on the side is certainly not what I expected. When they said "bus," I assumed we'd be taking something like the New Jersey Transit, but this is more like a house on wheels.

A small kitchenette equipped with a refrigerator and microwave greets me upon entry. There's even a small dining table with a bench seat. A Keurig on the counter with a box of assorted coffees next to it catches my eye, and I give myself a mental high five at the sight of it. Being stuck on a bus for hours on end is one thing, but being stuck on the bus with no coffee is a recipe for disaster as far as I'm concerned.

I look around, wondering how the sleeping arrangements work. The bus is large, but surely not large enough for seven people. Walking in further, I get my answer. Four pods line each wall—two up and two down. Each pod contains a bed with a curtain that could be closed for privacy. The maximization of the space is impressive. It all seems so futuristic.

With the crew in another bus that will trail behind this one, Vic and the band pile on. All those extra bodies make the open space feel tight. JJ, Banger, and Konner fall into pods, and Vic follows in behind them. "Yes, we're leaving here shortly, and we'll be right on schedule. Okay, excellent." He disconnects the call and turns his attention to me. "Oh, Ms. Daniels, nice to see you again. I hope you and Ms. Price are getting along well with everyone."

"Oh hey, Vic. Everyone's been wonderful, thank you." Jenny snorts, and I shoot her a look. "So how does this all work? Do we just grab any bunk, or are they assigned? Should I wait until Kade gets on to make sure he gets his pick first?"

"The prima-donna never sleeps in a bunk," grumbles

Konner.

"Doesn't he take the bus?"

"Yes, of course, Ms. Daniels, the band always travels together, but Kade feels . . . more comfortable sleeping on the pull-out couch in the lounge room." He points to another room at the far end of the bus. It looks like a little "hangout" spot with a large couch, some chairs, and a coffee table.

Jenny's already settled into the bunk right next to Banger, their matching blond heads bent together in deep conversation. Of the four, he's the hardest one to pinpoint. Tattoos cover his upper body right down to his fingers. His flaxen hair hangs long past his shoulders, which he always covers with a beanie regardless of the summer heat. As far as rocker stereotypes go, Banger lives up to every one, but he's so quiet, almost reserved. Much like Kade is to me, he's the polar opposite of Jenny. I guess it's true—opposites do attract.

The scraping sound of heavy boots shuffle down the walkway of the bus. The delightful mixture of leather, spice, and man assaults my senses before he even makes himself known. It's the very same fragrance he left on my sheets after leaving the hotel this morning. His large stature fills every available space as he comes into view. Looking at him against the row of pods, I can see why he sleeps on the pullout. I don't think he'd fit in there.

"Nice of you to join us, Mr. Black," Vic snaps.

"Get off my case, Vic. I made it, didn't I?"

Vic purses his lips then claps his hands together. "Well, now that everyone is here, the bus leaves in five minutes!" The Diamonds grumble and go about their business as Vic joins the driver up front.

I turn away to claim my bunk. Kade's hand runs down my bare arm, evoking an army of goose bumps to arise. "You're not sleeping in one of these coffins on wheels. You're with me,

A."

He walks ahead, his hand settling into mine, pulling me into the lounge room with him and closing the accordion door. "Won't the guys want to hang out in here?" The leather jacket slides off his shoulders, exposing his bare arms and a T-shirt with the phrase *Singers Do It With Their Mouths* written across his broad chest in bold letters. It feels like baby birds are hatching in my chest. I'm intimidated and intrigued both at once. Turned on and terrified beyond belief.

"I don't care." He glides onto the couch, pulling me down onto his lap. "I'm not real big on sharing," he whispers, nipping at my ear. "And I usually get what I want."

Holy crap.

"Yeah, but there isn't really a lot to do on the bus."

His teeth release my ear then scrape against my neck in a pinching sting that elicits an unexpected reaction. Arousal. So much so, I'm sure he can feel it on his legs. "I can think of a few things to do."

His hand burns hot on my bare thigh as he spreads my legs and swipes his nimble fingers across my slit without venturing inside. My hips buck. He laughs at my distress and does it again. I mewl and whine and writhe on his lap, but he isn't curing the ache that's slowly building, threatening to split me in two. "Are you sore?"

I shake my head. "I thought we agreed on one night." Turns out, I do purr. I barely recognize the breathy sound of my own voice. It's wanton and needy—two things I've never felt before.

"Does that mean you want me to stop?"

"No!" My hand closes around his thick forearm to keep him from pulling away, and his lips twist into a devilish grin. Clearly, he gets off on tormenting me. "Please."

"You're a big girl, Ainsley," he croons, swirling his middle finger around my opening, giving me a glimpse of relief while still keeping it far from reach. "If you want something, you'll have to ask for it."

"Please . . . make me come."

He slips inside my slick heat, and my head falls back with a gasp. Everything about him is larger than life. His personality, his talent, his cock, his hands. All of them are bits and pieces of a man that's opening me up to new pleasures unnumbered.

A second finger joins the first, crooking, bending, teasing my inner walls and drawing out a cry I'm sure can be heard through the thin plastic accordion door. His mouth covers mine, stifling my bliss-induced moans as his fingers fuck me to the brink of insanity.

"I'll make you come, sweets. Then I'm gonna lick it off my fingers when you do."

His thumb presses against my sensitive nub in small wicked circles, as his fingers continue slithering in and out. My nails dig into the soft flesh of his arm. He's about to get his wish. The climax swirling in my gut rages inside of me, grabbing hold and not letting go until I do.

I come apart. Ripped in half, shuddering and whimpering, soaking his hand with my release. The moment his fingers slide out of me, he sucks them into his mouth like he said he would. His tongue dips between them and down his palm like a tiger cleaning his paws, lapping up every last drop like its candy. "Damn, sweets, that was fucking hot," he murmurs, adding a breathy "mmmm" for effect.

"You keep calling me that. Why?"

He finishes his snack and crudely wipes his hand on the couch. "I thought that was obvious." A hint of my own flavor lingers on his lips as they brush against mine. "You have the sweetest pussy I've ever tasted."

"Oh."

Caught off guard by his vulgar answer, I slide off his lap

and onto the couch, keeping my legs draped over his. This kind of attention is unsettling. Earlier this year, the love of my life threw me away like trash. Now, I have the world's hottest rock star indulging in me like I'm his own personal piece of dessert.

Whatever this is between Kade and me isn't just a one-night stand. His ravenous need to please me is primal and obscene; two qualities I never thought would turn me on this much. The tingling in my skin hasn't subsided since last night. Every time Kade touches me, I feel more alive. Like a lethal narcotic, I need more to sate my hunger but know it's ultimately going to kill me in the end.

Chapter 8

K ADE SITS IN the corner with a guitar on his knee.
Skilled fingers move deftly across the frets on the neck
as his pick hand plucks the strings. He hums along
with it, pausing to write, then continues.

He rarely plays the instrument on stage. Only when a specific song requires a second guitar line does he strap it on and work the strings. The baritone of his voice calls to me from across the room. My gaze keeps wandering in his direction as I absentmindedly doodle on a magazine on the table.

"Wow, did you just draw all that?" Konner and JJ are engaged in an Xbox battle on the couch next to me. Konner's eyes flicker back and forth between the magazine and the screen as his thumbs click rapidly around the game controller in his hands.

"Yeah, I guess I did. It's nothing, just doodles."

I'm forever drawing little pictures on everything. It's something I do to relax. Peering down at the magazine on my lap, I see the entire page is covered in ink. The band's logo starts in the center, and the picture works outward from there. In the distance is a face, with a snake for a tongue that wraps around a hand. The snake writhes down the arm and back around, biting the face. Beyond that, a series of vines and leaves litter the rest of the page. It's not my best work.

Konner's on-screen character erupts in a splatter of red as some unknown assailant blows him away with an assault rifle. "No way, that's pretty good. JJ, check this shit out." He snags the magazine out from under me and chucks it at his friend. His appreciation for my artwork has me flustered. I haven't created anything real since college, and even then, I was shy about sharing it.

"Hey, that is a seriously kick-ass picture. You drew all that in ten minutes?"

The controller sits in JJ's lap as he runs his fingers over his shaved head. He and Konner seem attached at the hip. The two play like children and bicker over everything.

Reaching over Konner's camouflage-covered legs, I grab the magazine from JJ's hands. "It's no big deal." I shrug. "You guys are all artists too, right?" I stuff the magazine under the couch, hoping they'll forget about it.

A flashback comes to mind. Memories of Bob telling me art school was a waste of time. I spent my whole life working toward something, only to allow my husband's lack of support to murder it like the pixelated soldiers on the television ahead. Art was in every fiber of my being. I lived it. Breathed it. But I set it aside to raise my daughter and play Stepford Wife to a man who never appreciated me.

"Well, yeah. I can play guitar, and I can screw, but I can't draw worth a shit." JJ drains his beer with a belch.

"Dude," Konner mumbles in a drawn out lilt. "That's fuckin' gross. There are ladies here. Have some respect." Konner's attempt at chivalry makes me smile. Burping is offensive, but dropping F-bombs seems quite acceptable.

"Here, you play. I need another beer." The game remote lands in my lap as JJ heads for the kitchen.

"Bring me one too, ass-face." JJ flips Konner the middle finger as he backs out of the room.

Day turns to evening, and the playful fighting gets more riotous as the beer supply dwindles. Kade stays focused on his guitar, locked in the zone as he continues to write. Laughing, Jenny flips her hair while she and Banger sit in the corner huddled together in yet another deep conversation.

"Ah, shit," JJ's voice rings out from the front of the bus. "We're out of beer! I'm fuckin' starving, too. When do we stop to eat?" His Southern drawl turns from slight to pronounced the more he drinks. The guys are from somewhere around Georgia, but their accents have diminished from years of living on the West Coast. Kade doesn't seem to have one at all anymore, but every so often, a random word will come out, and I'll catch it like a foul ball.

My stomach growls at the first mention of food. Jenny and I had eaten a quick breakfast before we left, but that was the last meal I had.

"Yo, Vic! Tell the driver to stop at the next pizza joint he sees!" shouts JJ, walking back to the room. "And a liquor store!"

Kade looks up from the guitar on his knee and peers into the night sky as if he's surprised to see it. "Relax, JJ. You're not going to combust if you have to wait ten minutes between beers, bro."

JJ scowls and drops onto the couch, pouting like a child and putting his feet up on the table. "Whatever, dude."

When the bus finally stops, Vic insists we get our food to go, but the guys run off, ignoring his attempts to keep us on schedule. The members of Black Diamond are like Vic's wayward sons. He works so hard to keep some semblance of order, yet all his attempts fall on deaf ears. He's a nice guy, but they disregard him as the annoying killjoy he is.

The Pizza Castle is anything but majestic, as the name would suggest. It's a dive in the middle of God's country West Virginia, nestled not far beyond the outskirts of a trailer park.

Kade's hand rests possessively on the small of my back as he leads me through the parking lot. I like it. In his hands, I feel protected and safe. The dimly lit pizza place is half pub, half restaurant. A huge bar runs the length of the room opposite rows of tables with booths in the back. A handful of drunks loiters about, making inappropriate comments as we pass. They leer at us, and Kade's grip on me tightens.

We pile into a secluded booth in the back, hoping for some privacy away from the public, and a frazzled looking woman with a leopard print shirt under a white apron comes out to take our order. "What can I get ya?"

"I'll take a pitcher of beer and your phone number." JJ waggles his brows, flashing an adorable grin while a flush creeps up the woman's cheeks. Considering the classy folk we encountered when we came in, and by classy I mean completely disgusting, it's highly doubtful that she ever gets hit on by cuties like JJ.

"Bring out a few pizzas and, like, three orders of wings, too, sweetheart," adds Konner. He winks and tucks a strand of blue hair behind his ear. His tongue stud clinks against his teeth, and JJ shoots him a scathing look. I'm not really sure why. The woman looks like she's about fifty and is missing her front tooth.

A jack-o-lantern grin flashes on her face as she jots the order down on her pad. "Anything else?"

"Can I get an order of chicken fingers, please?" I add.

"You got it." The waitress nods and leaves to put in our order.

"Wow, fried food? Don't let Bob see you eating that."

My death stare wipes the smile off Jenny's face, but it's too late. Her big mouth aired that tiny piece of my dirty laundry, and I can't reel it back. My weight was a frequent topic of conversation between Bob and me. Before Shay was born, I was waifish and gaunt, but afterward, my body was never the same. Once skin and bones, I became curvy and voluptuous. I'm only a hundred and twenty pounds, but it may as well be two hundred. Every time food came near my mouth, he would ask me if I really needed that last bite, or roll his eyes if I dared to mention I was hungry. Bob had a clear-cut picture of how he wanted his life to be, and nothing was going to veer from that.

The beer goes down smooth, and the urge to pee hits like a lightning bolt. When I stand up from the table, I sway on my feet, and Jenny grabs my arm to steady me. "You all right, babe?"

"Yeah I'm fine. I just have to pee."

"You want me to go with you?" The look of concern on her face is sweet but unnecessary. I'm fine. Besides, from where I stand, I can see that the bathroom is only a one-person stall. I don't need her to wait for me in the hallway and risk being accosted by one of the skanky-looking locals hanging at the bar.

"Nah, I'll be back."

On wobbly legs, I walk past the bar and the leering eyes of the drunken old men. The five-inch platforms on my wedged sandals do nothing for my ability to get there in a straight line. I avoid eye contact at all costs, hoping not to disrupt the herd and wishing I'd changed into jeans before going out. A couple of harmless whistles ring out as I pass, but I make it to the bathroom unscathed.

The lights in the tiny room flicker as they come to life. The place is dank, and the lock on the door is busted. I hover over the toilet to do my business, holding onto the sink to keep from falling over.

Drinking before I ate was not a smart idea. I only had a beer and a half, but with my stomach so empty, the alcohol went straight to my head in a bad way.

I stand up, still clutching the sink for support. The beer

sloshes around inside my belly, and my reflection swims in front of me. I splash some cold water on my face hoping to revive myself a little before making the trek back to the booth. My hands blindly feel around the room looking for a paper towel, when I hear the door click open and shut.

"Jen, I said I'm fine. You don't need to hold my hand."

"I'm hoping to do a lot more than hold your hand, darlin'."

The gravelly voice strikes a chord of fear deep in the recesses of my gut. Too frozen to turn around, I raise my head toward the filthy mirror in front of me. The man's hair is greasy and combed straight back off his red forehead. He's more than a few days past shaving, the silvery strands of wiry hair standing out bold against the remaining black ones on his muddy face. The whites of his eyes are yellow, and his teeth are gray with rot.

"I saw you lookin' at me, darlin'. I was watchin' you in that cute lil' mini dress, shakin' your way up here." The way he slurs the word "darling" makes my skin crawl. It reminds me of something you'd hear on *Dateline*. His back is against the door. My desperate mind races, trying to think of a way to get past him, but he advances upon me too quickly.

His hand runs up the back of my leg, and I cower, cringing from the odor of bourbon and decay on his breath. "I'm sorry if you thought I was looking at you, but I'm really not interested. Please just leave me alone."

My voice trembles. He blocks me in on either side, gripping the edge of the sink in front of me. My plea does nothing to halt his attempt to seduce me. He buries his nose in my neck, smelling me like a flower.

With my shoes on, we're the same height, but he's stocky and thick. The man looks like he's spent a lifetime poisoning his body with God knows what. He grinds his pelvis into my backside, and I whimper with fear. "Yeah, you like that."

"Get away from me!" I want to scream for help, but I'm buzzed and terrified beyond the capacity for rational thought. The only thing running through my foggy brain is fight or flight, and flight isn't an option.

With all my might, I elbow the drunk in the side. He winces and stumbles, but his grasp on the sink tightens. I'm still trapped, only now I pissed him off.

"Oh, you like it rough? It's your lucky day, darlin', so do I!"

My back and head smash against the dirty tile with a heavy thud as he swings me against the wall. Tears stream down my face both from the pain and sheer terror that this man is going to rape me in this disgusting bathroom while my friends sit fifty feet away.

He locks my wrists above my head. I kick and cry, but his hold on me is strong and unyielding. Finally finding my voice, I scream, "Let me go!" I'm stuck here. My only hope is that someone notices I've been gone a while and comes looking for me.

His knees are braced against the wall, holding mine open as grimy fingers inch up my skirt to the waistband of my panties. There's a knock on the door, followed by a low voice saying my name. *Salvation!* "Kade! Help me!"

The door flies open, and I hit the ground. The next few minutes are a blur of arms and fists, and the sickening sound of cracking bones and skin smacking against skin. Blood splatters across my face as I lie helpless on the floor, crying in a heap. Water shoots from pipes where the sink once hung, now on the floor next to the guy's lifeless body. I don't know if my attacker is alive or dead. All I see is a crumpled mess lying in a pool of his own blood.

Kade lifts me off the filthy tile, cradling me in his strong arms, and runs out of the bathroom. He carries me through the restaurant, out the door, and onto the bus, finally sitting me down on the counter in the bathroom. "Are you hurt? Do you need a hospital?" His hands skim my skin looking for signs of damage, but the only thing marred is my psyche. I'm covered in blood, but none of it is mine.

A knock raps against the door, and I leap into Kade's arms, shaking like a frightened puppy. "Kade! What the hell happened? Where's Ainsley?" Jenny's shrill voice is more piercing than I've ever heard it. Kade literally carried me out of the restaurant without a word to the others still sitting in the booth in the back. The mess in the bathroom must have scared the hell out of her.

"She's fine, Jen. I got it." The voice rumbling in his chest vibrates across my cheek. I cling to him for dear life as his protective hands stroke my crud-covered curls. I don't even want to think about what would have happened if he hadn't been there.

"Ainsley, are you okay?" Jen's voice is thick with concern. There's no way she's going to leave me unless she's heard from me directly, and I don't want to worry her any more than I already have.

My breath stutters in a failed attempt to sound collected before answering her back. "Yeah, Jen. I'm okay."

"All right, lovie. I'm right here if you need me."

Her footsteps wander from the door, and the sound of sirens in the distance bring my worst nightmare back to the forefront of my mind. The feel of his blood on my skin is just as foul as his breath. I need to get every trace of that man off me.

Kade steps away long enough to start the shower but comes right back. Steam clouds up the tiny bathroom as he hikes the dress over my head and drops it into the wastebasket next to the toilet. Even if it weren't splattered in blood, I'd never wear it again. He lifts me off the counter, places my feet on the tile, and then removes my bra and underwear.

When he looks up from his position on the floor, he doesn't

have the same lust-filled eyes I've grown accustomed to. Right now, I see worry staring back at me in his soulful gaze. This isn't about sex for him, not this time.

Rising from the cool tile, he takes my hand in his, helping me into the shower. The water pelts my skin but doesn't ease my wounded soul. It runs off my body in pink trails that disappear down the drain. I huddle under the spray, holding myself, quivering despite the scalding temperature. I have nothing more to fear, but I don't want to be alone.

Kade fills the space in the tiny stall shower. I recoil at first, still skittish over the feeling of a presence behind me. Fresh tears begin to fall, and I melt into his body, allowing his warmth and strength to wash over me like the water from the nozzle above. "I'm sorry, Ainsley. I should have gotten there sooner."

"It's not your fault, Kade. You saved me."

"As long as I'm around, no one is ever going to hurt you again."

Chapter 9

"**K**ADE." VIC'S HUMMINGBIRD rap on the accordion door is more irate than usual. "There are police everywhere, Kade. You need to come out."

The word police causes me to spring up like a Weeble. This is bad. Jenny and I are supposed to be here to keep Kade *out* of trouble, but I've done the exact opposite. I *caused* trouble.

Kade's lips drop to my head as he pushes himself off the edge of the bed. "Try to get some sleep. This might take a while."

"I'm going with you," I argue, standing up with him.

"No. You're staying here. I'll handle this."

I continue pulling on my shoes and throw a sweatshirt on over my T-shirt. "Kade, be serious. You're in a butt-load of trouble because of me. Besides, the police are going to want my statement anyway."

"A, I don't get in trouble. I *make* the trouble. The cops aren't gonna do shit to me."

And the cocky asshole returns.

"Whatever. I'm going with you anyway." I roll my eyes as I open the accordion door and walk out.

My pulse races as I make my way past the row of pods and into the cool night air. Being wrapped in Kade's embrace on the bus offered a false sense of comfort, but out here in the parking lot, surrounded by police and a gaggle of onlookers, my inner wounds begin to fester. I feel vulnerable, like any one of those people could come out of nowhere and hurt me again. Just like *he* did.

A hand grabs mine, and I practically jump out of my skin. "Relax, sweets. It's just me."

Kade's presence outside kicks the lifeless mob into a frenzy. Policemen guard the lines of yellow tape that now barricade the area, keeping the crowd from rushing the crime scene. *Oh my God, I've created a crime scene!*

"Mr. Black, Ms. Daniels." Two men in blue uniforms approach us as we stand together in the lot. "I'm Officer Stranz, and this is Officer Fairchild. We need to ask you a few questions." Officer Stranz opens up his little notepad and continues. "In your own words, can you tell me what happened here tonight?"

I swallow hard, trying my best to keep my composure before rehashing the whole terrifying story. The officers make notes and nod along as I tell them in gruesome detail the events that occurred earlier that night. Kade's hand squeezes mine as I recall the way the man talked to me and how he reacted to my telling him no.

"Okay, so just to reiterate: Butch Robinson followed you into the bathroom, made an unwanted advance, and then proceeded to become aggressive when you told him no."

Hearing the slimeball's name for the first time gets my hackles up. It's just as sleazy as the man himself. "Yes, that's right."

"At what point did Mr. Black intervene?"

"I guess I was gone a while. Kade came to see if I was okay . . ." *Maybe I should let him handle this. I don't want to implicate him and make things worse.* My gaze rolls in his direction. His jaw's clenched tight, and his nostrils are flared. Hearing the recounted tale of what happened returns his murderous scowl with a vengeance. His hand holds mine so tight, I start to lose feeling in my fingers.

"Ms. Daniels?" the policeman urges.

"And I did what I had to do," Kade counters.

The policeman looks up from his notepad without moving his head. "So you admit to having assaulted Mr. Robinson in retaliation?"

"I did what I had to do," Kade reiterates.

Officer Stranz stands straight, crossing his arms over his chest trying to look oppressive. If I wasn't scared out of my mind, I might have laughed. Kade wins in the intimidation competition by leaps and bounds. He's built like a brick wall. The sleeves on his T-shirt threaten to tear each time his arms flex. Not only that but, considering his erratic behavior, he probably has lawyers on standby in every city he ventures into. "If you aren't going to cooperate, Mr. Black, I'm going to have to bring you into the station."

The corner of Kade's mouth curves into an arrogant grin. "You gonna cuff me, too? I love the feel of cold metal against my skin."

What's he doing? He's actually goading the cop into arresting him! I stand there stunned as the cop grabs Kade by the arm and attempts to pull him toward the squad car.

Kade stands firm and drops a kiss on my mouth that sends my thighs up in flames. "Tell Vic to take care of this. I'll see you in an hour," he whispers before allowing himself to be escorted to the black and white vehicle.

The crowd goes berserk. I'm rooted to the spot as he ducks into the backseat. Camera flashes pop, the red and blue lights blink, blinding me as I watch the car drive away. I turn and run back to the bus to talk to Vic as Kade instructed.

Later that night, I lie in bed alone waiting for Kade to return.

Vic seemed little more than annoyed that Kade had been arrested, giving me hope that he would be able to take care of it just like Kade said. Vic may be a total harpy, but I'm beginning to see why the band keeps him on. It seems like he has connections in every state.

The creaking sound of the accordion door startles me awake. "It's me, A. Don't be afraid."

He pulls off his clothes and slides into bed next to me. "It took you longer than an hour."

His rich chuckle comforts me in a way I haven't felt all night. It's smooth, carefree. I love the sound of it. "Yeah, well, a few of the guys downtown were fans."

Snuggling in next to him, I breathe in the spicy scent of his skin and twist my leg up over his. "Is everything going to be okay?"

"Yeah, sweets. It's all good. No worries."

His arms wrap around me as I melt into his warm body. He always feels hot. As if his blood is rocketing through his veins at a furious pace at all times. It's cozy, like cuddling up next to a fire that smells divine.

"So what happens now?"

"Now we go about our business as if it never happened."

I let out an inadvertent sigh of relief. Forgetting it ever happened sounds excellent to me.

Chapter 10

DESPITE MY LATE night, I wake up early, finding it hard to sleep on a moving bus. Kade lies next to me sleeping like a log. I watch for a few minutes, taking in the tiny parts of his face that usually go unnoticed. Long, beautiful eyelashes rest along a little row of freckles that sweep across his cheeks and onto his straight nose. Dark stubble grows along his chiseled jawline. His tatted up muscles seem less severe as he rests there peacefully, but the bloody scrapes on his knuckles are a stark reminder of what he's capable of.

I climb out of bed and slip from the room, closing the door behind me. The bus is quiet, save for Jenny on her cell phone with what seems like a business call in the kitchenette. She spots me coming toward her and greets me with the raise of her index finger.

"Okay, thank you so much. Yes, I'll be in touch with details."

She trades in the call for a series of swipes. "Mornin, Ains. How ya feeling?" Her distracted tone is questionable. The clicking of her nails against the screen of her phone continues with the rapid movement of her thumbs.

"I'm better, thanks. Busy morning?" I move about the tiny space preparing myself a cup of coffee from the Keurig machine as the relentless click-click-click of Jenny's nails continues behind me.

"You betcha." She finally stops her incessant texting and places her phone on the table face up. She stretches, releasing a groan that leads me to believe she's been sitting there a while. "I'm trying to spin this crazy story to work in your favor instead of Kade looking like a crazed baboon."

The lights on the coffeemaker flash when I close the lid with the pod inside. I smack the middle button, having no idea what size my cup is, and hope for the best. "What story? What do you mean?" I tear my eyes from the trail of brown liquid filling the mug to see Jenny back on her phone.

"Seems you and Kade are trending today." With the simple nudge of her finger, the phone glides over the smooth tabletop toward me. Top story today: Kade Black, Hero or Heavyweight?

"Oh, no! Jenny, this can't be good." I flop onto the bench seat, my coffee long forgotten and no longer needed. My eyes are so wide as I scroll through the articles that they actually start to hurt. I anticipated a little news coverage, but nothing like this. There's so much.

Some articles paint him out to be a hotshot who came to the rescue in my hour of need, while others just claim he's a maniacal monster who beat the guy up for fun. When I come across one that actually has my name in it, I almost choke on my own tongue. "How did they get this information so quickly?"

"From a lot of places. People at the restaurant, or onlookers that were crowding around as he was arrested. It's more likely the information came from a mole, though."

I look up from the phone. "Mole?"

"Yeah, a mole. You know, a rodent, a rat . . . someone at the police station probably leaked the story. Reporters pay top dollar for stuff like this."

She slides off the bench and saunters up to the Keurig for another cup of coffee. How can she be so calm? This is a disaster! My name is plastered all over the internet, and no one even knows I'm here! I can just see Bob sitting down over croissants in Europe, poring over the news and seeing grainy cell phone images of my face staring back at him. Standing next to Kade Black of all people! I'm going to be sick.

"My personal favorite is the article that claims you're a tranny Kade picked up on a street corner."

I fling the phone back to her side of the table not wanting to look at it anymore. "So what's your plan?" Jenny places my coffee in front of me as she scooches into her side of the bench at the table, but the thought of drinking it now makes me want to hurl.

"I've been on the phone all morning. *Music Buzz* is squeezing Kade in tonight for an interview to tell the real story about what happened. He's going to need a red cape and friggin' set of tights by the time I'm done spinning this shit in his favor."

So much for forgetting this ever happened.

Music Buzz is the number one celeb news show. I'll be humiliated on national television when Kade tells the world he had to save my drunk ass from getting raped in a dirty bar bathroom. Everyone is going to know my business. Bob . . . my parents . . .

Shay.

How am I going to look my innocent daughter in the face and explain to her what happened to me and what it means? This is worse than a disaster. This is life altering.

"Ainsley, lovie, you look like you're going to faint."

Jenny's calmness exacerbates the situation, only making me feel worse. She's about to destroy my life, and she's so damn composed. "Does he have to do this? Can't we just let this go? It was bad enough I had to live through it once, why would you make me do it again? Where's your sense of loyalty?" My voice grows progressively more earsplitting as I come to the end of my rant. I'm having a mini panic attack right here in the kitchen.

"Hey, my loyalty lies with my company. I have to do what's best for it, and that means keeping the client happy. I'm sorry if you don't like that, but it's business."

She's tactful and professional—you have to give her props for that. This is business, and I screwed with it from the start by sleeping with Kade in the first place. I'm the one who drank too much, and I'm the one who declined her offer for the buddy system in the bathroom. The only person here to blame for this mess I'm in is myself. Jenny has a job to do, and she's doing it, much to my chagrin.

"So it will go like this," she continues. "Turns out this Butch Robinson guy was a small time drug dealer with a rap sheet a mile long, full of misdemeanors and assault charges. You just happened to be in the wrong place at the wrong time. Kade heard your cries and selflessly came to the rescue of the woman he loves. It's pure gold."

"But he doesn't love me." Far as I know, I'm just his piece of road tail. He's never going to go for that. I'll be willing to acquiesce that he likes me—and I stress the word *like*—but love? No way. There might be something brewing beneath the surface of that gorgeous head of his, but love definitely is not it.

Famous rock stars just don't fall in love with boring housewives. Period. They have tumultuous relationships with models and actresses. The thought of Kade sitting through a family dinner with my parents would have me rolling on the floor with laughter if I wasn't so unbelievably nauseated from having this conversation.

"Ainsley, be serious. Have you seen the way that man looks at you?"

"Yeah, like I'm his own personal sex toy."

She snorts and takes a sip of her coffee. "No. Like you're the Mona Lisa."

"Great, so I'm an ugly woman from the fifteen hundreds.

Comforting, thanks."

"No, you ass." She laughs. "I mean there's something about you that draws him in. He can't quite figure out what it is, but he can't look away either. He's had the same look in his eyes since the day those baby blues landed on you."

I don't bother honoring her crazy insinuation with a response. There is no use talking about it anymore. There is little, if nothing, between us. I'm a fun distraction from the tour, and that's it. No matter how she chooses to spin this incident, that's all it is. Nothing more, nothing less.

The click-click-clicking of her nails on her phone is the only sound between us until my name is bellowed from the back. Our heads whip in the direction of the lounge room then back at each other. The Cheshire Cat smile grows on her face like stop motion footage of a blooming flower. "Well Mona, it seems your services are being requested in the boudoir."

★ ★ ★

"WHERE DID YOU fling my underwear?"

I hang over the edge of the bed, peering underneath for the garment Kade couldn't seem to get off me fast enough. He was hesitant at first, handling me with kid gloves. I think he was worried that I would freak out because of last night—what I'm now referring to as "the incident"—but the second he got my approval, it was on.

"I honestly don't know. Maybe I ate them in the throes of passion."

Laughing, I keep looking. The last thing I need is for someone else to find them. I'd shit twice and die. It's bad enough this interview is hanging over my head. That's gearing up to be mortifying enough as it is.

The light blue strip of lace peeks out from under the wooden slats of the mini blind. I kneel on the bed attempting to snatch my underwear free, but Kade sidles up behind me, emancipating them before I get the chance. "Hey, give those back!"

"Finders keepers." He crumples them in his fist, holding them over my head in a pathetic game of keep away. "I prefer you naked anyway."

Jenny's voice saying there's something about me pops into my mind. Yeah, there's something about me all right. I'm a nice warm body meant to sate his gluttonous needs. Whenever we're alone together, he doesn't talk feelings, he talks sex.

He's carnivorous.

He's profane.

But most of all, he's insatiable.

"So Jenny is planning on having you meet with *Music Buzz* tonight," I say, as he pulls me down onto the bed next to him.

"Mmmhmm," he replies, his lips vibrating against my throat.

"She's going to try to spin it, you know, like you went all ape trying to protect me . . ." A sharp breath hits my lungs as his tongue trails down my chest and flicks my nipple. " . . . she wants to make it seem like we're together, you know . . ." His mouth coasts to my other nipple and graces it with the same flip of the tongue. My eyes roll back, but I keep going, attempting to get my point across. " . . . but, like, I don't really know how you feel about that, so I don't know what you're going to say . . ." My breathy mumbling continues as he kisses down my body and lifts my legs onto his shoulders. "So what are you gonna say?"

My body conceals the bottom half of his face, leaving only two brilliant sapphire orbs visible. They lock with mine as I finish my insane rambling. "I'm gonna say whatever the fuck I wanna say. Now, stop talking."

⋆ ⋆ ⋆

A CHILL RUNS up my spine as I knock on Kade's door. The meeting's going to be held via computer from his hotel room. I'm nervous about this whole thing. I tried to talk to him about it a few times, but he's so stubborn. I have no idea what Kade's going to say and, while Jenny seems to think it's fine, I would feel a lot more comfortable had he and I worked out some kind of game plan for how this was going to go down.

The host of the news show appears on the monitor and begins to talk. The buxom blonde explains this segment will be pre-recorded, and to just act natural. She primps as she stares at herself in the little square in the bottom of the screen. "Okay, on me in three, two, one . . ."

"Hiiii!" the host starts in her bubbly on-air personality voice. "Candy Conners coming back at ya with special guest, Kade Black from Black Diamond! Say hi, Kade!"

Kade smiles and waves. "Hey Candy, thanks for having me."

"Y'all are out on tour promoting your new album *Fool's Gold*, right? How's that working out for ya, Kade?"

The way she says his name pisses me off. She mewls it like a desperate feline in heat. I'm thankful that I'm not in front of the screen, because if looks could kill, I'd be facing life in prison.

Is this jealousy?

"Good! The shows have been great. The fans have been real cool. Sure you heard all about the trouble we had in West Virginia last night."

I roll my eyes at her flirty giggle. I've seen *Music Buzz* about a million times. How have I never noticed how obnoxious and fake the hostess is?

"Oh yes, I'm pretty sure we all did. There's a lot of, shall we say, *buzz* . . ." she pauses for a split second allowing her unamusing joke to resonate with the viewers. " . . . going around about that. Why don't you let us all know what really happened?"

Kade's gaze flickers in my direction so quick I almost miss it. Before I even have time to register it, his eyes are back on the screen focusing on the most tasteless Candy I've ever come in contact with. *See? I can make jokes, too, bitch.*

"A friend of mine was assaulted in the bathroom by a known drug dealer in the Virginia area. The guy didn't want to take no for an answer, so I had to step in."

"The reports say you did a little more than step in. The man, Butch Robinson, is in critical condition. This Ainsley Daniels must be someone very special to you to generate that kind of reaction."

Another lightning-fast flicker of the eyes is all he offers me. She's spoon-feeding it to him. I sit in the chair wringing my hands together waiting to hear what he's going to say. He looks into the camera, his lips curling into a flirty, lopsided grin. "You jealous, kitten? Don't worry, she hasn't managed to tame the beast yet."

I sit there dumbfounded, trying to keep my emotions in check. Hearing Kade call me out as nothing stings more than I care to admit. Not only that, but is he *flirting* with that despicable host right in front of me? I'm not dumb enough to believe he's my boyfriend, but I expected a little more class than this.

Jenny glances at me, nibbling her thumbnail and trying to ignore the obvious slap in the face I just received. Even Banger grimaces on my behalf. I'm too stunned to be embarrassed by the incident because I'm humiliated by Kade. The very same man who lapped me up like a saucer of milk not six hours ago.

The host asks a few more questions while I seethe with anger. As soon as the meeting's over, I excuse myself and run from the room as fast as I can gracefully go. But Kade darts after me, reaching me before I can get to my door. "Where are you going? What is your problem?"

"I should ask you the same thing," I shoot back. "You didn't have to pretend to like me, Kade, I would have fucked you anyway."

His face contorts into a bewildered scowl at my outburst. "What are you talking about? Where did this come from?"

"She hasn't tamed the beast yet? Seriously? I didn't expect a public admission of love, but I think I deserved a little more than that bullshit." As the words fly out of my mouth, I realize how insane I sound. I'm acting like a jealous girlfriend. I don't want to have feelings for him. I want this to remain casual. My insides are at war, and he's the only person for me to take it out on, which is fine since he's the cause.

He winces as if I'd struck him. "You know what's bullshit? You are. Don't stand there and make bogus accusations at me. It's part of the job. Flirting with the hosts is a way to guarantee I get invited back. It's part of the game. That scum bag really did a number on your self-esteem, didn't he?" His finger pokes me in the chest as he speaks, but I smack it away. "What goes on between you and me is my private business. I don't fuckin' share. That goes for women, spotlight, and personal information. If that makes you feel used and dirty, that's your baggage to carry, not mine." His eyes turn from brilliant blue to dark as he stares down at me, his anger swirling around me like a storm. He crosses his arms over his massive chest.

Now, it makes sense. He got himself arrested in order to take the emphasis off me. He'd rather go to jail than have to discuss who I am with people.

"So what's it gonna be, sweets? You want to let some nasty blond bitch come between us? That's fine with me. But once I've moved on, I don't come back."

We stand there for a moment, chests puffed out, both of us unwilling to break first. I can't believe I fell for his nice guy routine. He actually made me think I was wrong about him. All of his "no one will ever hurt you" nonsense was a nice touch. He's good.

A loud crack stops me from walking off, and I whip my head back around toward Kade, toward the direction of the noise, to find him pulling his arm back and storming in the opposite direction. He punched a hole clear through the wall of the hotel's hallway.

Screw the show, screw the tour, and definitely screw Kade Black.

Chapter 11

I TOSS AND turn all night, unable to sleep. It's late, but I'm wired. I refused to attend tonight's show but told Jenny she should go. My foul mood was best kept to myself. The last thing I wanted was another fight. She returned to the room hours ago and is currently snoring on the bed next to mine.

All those hours alone left me with a lot of time to think. I overreacted. Jenny's words implanted themselves in my brain, and I lost my cool when the exact thing I knew would happen happened. Kade and I are having fun. I could choose to either continue it or end it.

I'd be insane to want to end it. The sex is face-meltingly hot. Who knows when I'll meet a guy who could curl my toes the way he does again?

Then again, I do have my pride. Do I have what it takes to keep this up for the next few weeks, knowing he could throw me away at any time? Then there's the possibility of him sleeping with someone else . . .

I'm not going to be able to sleep until I've gotten this off my chest.

A three and two zeros blink on the digital clock. Getting out of bed, I throw on my robe and pad across the dark room. I've made a decision, and I have to see him.

My palms shake and sweat as I let myself out of the door

and make my way to Kade's room. The light glows from underneath his door. I lift my fist to knock but stop short when the realization hits me that he may not be alone. What if he brought some groupie back to his room with him? I'd deserve that after the way I stormed away this evening.

I swallow past the lump in my throat and knock. If he's with someone else, so be it. Shadows dance underneath the door as he approaches. He answers and leans against the frame, shirtless in pajama bottoms and bare feet, his hair mussed up in such a way that looks like he'd been running his hands through it all night. My heart continues to hammer in my chest, but now, it's for another reason.

"Can we talk?"

His arm waves across the room, inviting me inside. "How was the show tonight?"

"Fine."

"That's good," I say, trying my best to seem casual, while inside I'm dying. I toy with the terrycloth ties, trying to distract myself from the awkward situation, but the new bandage on his hand speaks volumes about my behavior.

"A, why are you here?"

"I couldn't sleep."

"And you felt the need to come tell me about it?" The muscles in his forearms strain under the thick black ink on his skin as he pretzels his arms across his chest in a defensive stance.

"Okay, I deserve that. Look, I'm sorry about what happened earlier. You were right, and I'm a jealous idiot. I've never dabbled in casual sex before, and that's my baggage, not yours." My voice hitches, but I clear my throat and continue. "The only man I'd ever been with before you was my husband, and he cheated on me. My heart is broken. I couldn't give it to you even if you wanted it, so it's better that you don't."

He thoughtfully scratches the back of his head as he walks

through the room and sits on the bed. "What makes you think I don't?"

The question detonates a bomb in my mind. My midsection is suffocating, strangled by the ties on my robe pulled so tight I'm asphyxiating myself. "Well . . . I don't know . . . I just . . . I thought . . ." Is he messing with me again, or is he serious? I'm having a hard time trying to figure it out.

He grabs hold of my lapels and pulls me toward him, bringing my asinine stammering to an end. "I like you, sweets." The poor mangled robe ties loosen as he takes them in his hands. "I like you watching me from backstage." His hands work the twist at my waist, causing the robe to fall open. "I like you pissed off and stewing over something outrageous I said." His eyes flare, raking over my body in the baby blue nightie as he pushes the robe off my shoulders. "I especially like the way you breathe my name when you're in my bed."

His smoldering gaze dares me to make the next move. "And you like me naked, too, right?" I slip his hand between my legs, and his brows shoot up to his hairline.

"No panties?"

I shrug. "Someone stole them earlier today."

His lips meet mine in a searing kiss that throws the Earth off its axis. Whether singing, kissing, or tonguing, Kade's mouth is an endless bounty of pleasure I can't resist. He lies back on the bed, taking me with him. Wild, honey-colored curls fall in a curtain around our faces as I feast on his lips.

Skilled hands roam my bare ass, slipping under my nightie. "Settle down, rock star," I say with a gentle hip jerk, bucking him off then slinking backward on all fours, moving down his body with catlike grace. My nails rake down his stomach, causing all the muscles to ripple like ocean waves as my fingers reach the band of his pants. His cock springs out, thick, hard, and all for me, but for some reason, I hesitate.

"It ain't gonna bite."

Two pink circles heat my cheeks. "Are you clean?"

"As a whistle."

Appeased, I languidly lick him from base to tip. A low-pitched groan escapes his lips. His fingers tangle in my hair, and my head pops up. "No hands."

The demand seems to catch him off guard. "What?"

"You may be used to calling the shots, big man, but this time, I'm headlining the show." I stare him down, making no move to start the task at hand. Kade isn't the only one with tricks up his sleeve. Two can play his little games.

He threads his hands behind his head, biceps straining under his tattooed skin. My leisurely licking starts over, tracing the thick ridges and swirling around the velvet tip with my tongue. A salty trickle beads around the slit. I lap it up before drawing him into my mouth.

The breath leaves his lungs. My palms grip his solid thighs, bracing myself for support as my lips slide down the shaft. His pelvis thrusts, knocking my head back. I sit up defiantly. "Nu-uh-uh," I tease, waggling my pointer finger at him and shaking my head.

Darkened eyes glare at me. "You're begging for trouble."

"Promise?"

Dipping my head again, I suck hard, swallowing him down the back of my throat. The sound of my name tumbling gruffly off his lips is a beautiful thing. Every visceral groan arouses me. A boiling, throbbing pang radiates between my legs just knowing I please him. In life, I'm not the kind of woman who takes control. Demanding and courageous aren't attributes I possess, but Kade relinquishes his power to me, making me feel seductive and brave.

He pulses in my mouth, and my lips slide all the way up, suckling the tip before letting go completely. He lets out a disgruntled grumble. The sight of his glorious cock, thick and purple from the suction of my mouth, instills a sense of urgency that I can't control. A slick swollen ache I feel deep inside that only he could soothe.

Gliding up his body, I grab his length and position it at my entrance and ease down slowly, inch by thrilling inch until I'm full, stretched to capacity with the tiniest bite of decadent pain.

With my hands planted on his chest, my hips move in slow, methodical circles, building up a rhythm all my own, and take back control of my own body. I clench him tight, ride him hard, and wring every ounce of pleasure I can until I'm on the brink of gasping for breath, crying out from the sheer ecstasy of it.

Pure bliss swirls and rolls and threatens to tear me apart. I'm almost there.

Almost there . . .

Oh, God, almost . . .

His body moves faster than my lust-addled brain can keep up. My back hits the bed. Rough, strong hands flip me to my stomach and hoist my backside in the air.

In one fierce stroke, he sinks back in from behind. I yelp, my body trembling from the shock and crying out from the lost release. He holds me firm, not moving, torturing me with his stillness. "I was close, you asshole."

"Yeah, I know." He chuckles.

I jerk and buck, needing to feel him and attempting to steal back control, but all my efforts are in vain. His hold is unyielding. One hand clutches at my hip, while the other fists my hair, snapping my head up to catch our reflection in the mirror ahead. He's enjoying this, and he wants me to know it.

A cocky grin splits his face as he watches my irritation simmer. Rose flush sits on my cheeks; my eyes flare like burning embers. "Kade, please," I beg. Oh, how he loves to hear me beg. He gets off on it.

Small jerky movements are all he offers. I bury my face in the bed, frustrated and whimpering, needing more and hating him for keeping it from me. He forces my head up again, catching my gaze in the mirror. "Eyes on me, sweets. I want to see those beautiful browns when I finally let you come."

His hips move in long, steady strokes, smacking against my ass cheeks. "I own your orgasm, Ainsley. You come for *me*."

The head of his cock reaches all the way to the end of my canal and sends an electric current slithering up my tailbone with each dynamic thrust. Blue-black eyes lock on mine, his jaw set in grim determination, lips curled into a devilish little sneer. A sheen of sweat breaks out along his heaving chest and rippling abs.

"Do not close your eyes," he warns.

Euphoria sweeps through me like a tidal wave, consuming me whole, and drowning me in a sea of pleasure, leaving nothing left in its wake but deep gasping sobs. My arms and legs quiver. My body trembles.

Kade's grip goes from strong to monolithic. Fingers bite into my skin so hard, I'm sure they're leaving bruises. He curses and groans and growls my name, causing the sweet ache to resurface a second time. Determined eyes stay trained on me, watching me pant and struggle to stay centered on all fours. The thick muscles in his neck and shoulders tense as I clench around him, but he pulls out suddenly, taking himself into his own hand and shooting pearls of hot cum on my ass and back.

We topple over like dominoes, his large body collapsing first, knocking my smaller one to the bed beneath him. He rolls to the side and rains kisses down my neck and shoulders, covering me with tenderness.

"Don't move."

The sound of running water filters from the bathroom as

Kade disappears inside. He returns with a washcloth and lovingly wipes his remains off my back, dipping between my legs until I'm clean.

He fucks like a beast but loves like a puppy. The ideal mix of hard and soft, reading my mind and giving me everything I need. I don't want to wonder how many other women have seen this side of him. If he was gentle and kind to them, the way he is with me. It's absurd, but I still want to believe that, on some level, I'm held in higher regard than all the others are.

"I'm on the pill." That information would probably have been a little more useful to him before I slid onto his bare cock. Better late than never, I guess.

"It doesn't matter. I like how you look wearing my cum." Chucking the soiled cloth on the carpet, he climbs back into bed and pulls me against his chest. His fingertips trace the lines of my body. I sigh, burying my face in the crook of his neck, my favorite part of him.

His chest rises and falls with each deep, contented breath he takes. "I can't remember the last time I felt this comfortable with a woman."

"Really?" It's difficult to imagine Kade being uncomfortable around anyone, much less a member of the opposite sex.

"Women are usually more interested in what I can give them than who I am. They get off on the rock star fantasy. Thing is, getting them off is the easy part. It's this that I have trouble with." He glides his hand down my arm, slipping it under mine and threads our fingers together.

"What's that?"

"The intimacy."

The vulnerability in his voice stirs something inside me. His unwavering confidence was what drew me to him in the first place, but as he slowly allows me inside, I'm seeing his brazen behavior is nothing more than an act. Underneath the brawn and temperament is a lonely man looking for someone to love him.

"You seem to do it effortlessly."

Raising our joined hands, he skims his nose and cheek along my knuckles. "Because being with you is effortless," he whispers against my skin.

The emotion comes on so strong I feel dizzy. I've kept my heart locked up tightly in a box, but little by little, Kade peels the tape off and the lid cracks open. Somehow, I need to find a way to slap the lid back on before it's too late.

"Can I ask you what happened with your ex-husband?"

Talking about Bob while resting this comfortably in Kade's bed seems wrong. It's like putting sardines on ice cream. Even after you've picked the nasty fish out, the foul taste lingers. It's too late; your dessert is ruined.

"It's a touchy subject, I get it. I just can't seem to wrap my brain around what kind of man would let a woman like you go."

"A woman like me?"

"Yeah." His fingertips continue to roll up and down my back, causing chills to break out along my skin. "Beautiful, sexy, confident, strong . . ."

I rest my fingers over his lips. "I'm none of those things, Kade. I'm timid and scared of my own shadow."

A breathy chuckle blows against my fingertips. He takes my hand in his, lowering it to finish his statement. "You're stronger than you give yourself credit for."

I lower my gaze. This outpouring of compliments and affection isn't something I'm used to. Growing up, my family was stoic and cold, and my husband followed suit. To be revered in such a manner is alien to me. "But I'm not. I found my husband in bed with our twenty-four-year-old nanny, and I did nothing."

I'll never forget that day as long as I live. It had been a busy afternoon. I had cleaning to do and a PTA meeting to attend, plus I refused to miss another Zumba class at the gym. In addition to that, I had to get to the bank, the dry cleaner, and buy all the supplies for the school fundraiser.

Getting all of that done left me with so little time. I rushed home to make a quick dinner then had to run back out to the school with Shay for the poster committee. Somehow, between all of that running around, I'd lost the glitter. I knew I'd bought it; it must have fallen out of the bag when I brought it inside.

The garage door was unlocked. I entered the house, assuming it would be on the kitchen counter where I'd left the bags that afternoon, but rifling through all the crap on the counter, I cursed myself when I came up empty-handed. The whole thing seems so trivial now. I was upset. Over lost glitter.

I racked my brain trying to think about where it could have fallen, when I remembered Shay had some in her room. A noise wafted from my bedroom as I ran upstairs to get it, but oddly, the door was closed. A sinking feeling fell into my stomach. I told myself Bob was in there working out. The wind must have closed the door. Any lie that was believable enough to keep me from turning that knob and walking inside.

A soft female moan drifted through the door and punched me in the chest. My heart hammered, and my palms grew damp. I swallowed hard and opened the door to my nightmare.

The first thing I saw was sleek strawberry hair and a slender back sitting up in my bed. Her gyrating hips drew my eyes to the mattress and the person below her. The rapid beating of my heart drowned out any other sound. My feet moved with their own agenda because my brain had gone into overdrive and stopped working.

Flashes of recognition burned into my mind: A manicured hand on her back. A gold wedding ring. A wrist watch

I remembered buying. All these things bled together into a blinding whirlwind of emotions I couldn't even begin to communicate.

My mouth opened, and they both jumped, their looks of horror and regret replacing the looks of agonizing pleasure from minutes before. I have no idea what I said. I was floating above my body looking down at the scene, paralyzed by betrayal.

Tears filled Cami's eyes, and Bob took her hand, comforting her. He was comforting *her*. She was getting her fucking tears on my three-hundred dollar sheets.

"I didn't expect you home."

A thousand different words and phrases Bob could have come up with, and that was what he chose.

He didn't expect me home? *Thank you, Captain Obvious.*

My mouth was agape with no sound coming out. I just stood there like an idiot. A million thoughts rushed through my mind too fast to choose. The questions eventually slowed down like the spinning wheel at the end of the *Price is Right*, and I was finally able to squeak out a single phrase. "Tell me this is the first time, Bob." He lowered his eyes in shame, unable to answer the question, while Cami just sat there blubbering like the child she is.

"I should have told them to get out. I should have screamed and yelled and threw things like those women you see on those horrible daytime talk shows where they fight over the loser they're both screwing. But I'm a coward. I walked out of my own bedroom, closed the door behind me, grabbed the glitter, and drove back to the school." I shiver, and Kade gives me a squeeze as if inadvertently bracing me for the contact of the memory.

"I found out later it had been going on for a couple of years, right under my nose. I was so busy with Shay and taking care of everything that I never even noticed. A piece of me died right there at the foot of that bed. He told me the next day that he was glad I'd found out. He was in love with her and wanted a divorce."

Kade doesn't speak after that. He doesn't tell me Bob's a jerk, or that I can do better. He just sits there in heavy silence, holding me, and proving once again he knows exactly what I need.

Chapter 12

"YOU LOOK EXHAUSTED."

"Thanks, friend." I take the venti iced latte from Jenny's hand, regretting having stayed up all night. I feel like death, and I look even worse. The minute we get back on the bus, I'm taking a nap.

"This shouldn't take much longer. We just need some promo shots for social media and the band's website."

"Sure," I grumble, falling into a chair and pressing the coffee to my warm cheek, letting its coolness revive me. We've already been here an hour, and I'm fading fast.

The constant tour coverage is the worst part. It's funny how natural their photos look online compared to how forced they are in real life. It's all smoke and mirrors. An illusion set up to appear as if they are having the time of their lives when, really, they're just going about the motions because the label is making them. It's work.

"Okay, guys. Just be cool and do what you'd normally do. Pretend you're just hanging out," the photographer, a girl who calls herself Joy, instructs, raising her camera to her eye again. Her hair is the same brilliant shade of gold as Shay's, and the freckles dotting her heart-shaped face make my chest hurt. The resemblance is uncanny. I can't take my eyes off her.

JJ grabs his privates and sticks his tongue out with a sneer.

Vic shoots him a stern look. Joy is completely unfazed by the whole thing. In fact, she snaps about twelve pictures of it, also making sure she gets photographic evidence of Konner slapping him right in the bull's-eye tattooed on his head. Banger leans up against a tree smoking a cigarette, and Kade just stands there looking miserable.

"All right guys, take five."

Joy drops her camera, letting it dangle around her neck. The sun glints off the ring in her eyebrow as she approaches JJ and Konner, who are now brawling on the grass. When she smiles, the tiny space between her two front teeth is enough to send me over the edge. Shay and I have been playing phone tag. I miss her voice, and I long for her adorable face and gap-toothed grin. Every second I'm away from her is torture, in spite of how much fun I'm having here.

A shadow passes across my closed eyes like an eclipse blocking the sun. I look up, and Kade's towering over me with a grin. "Having fun?"

"You know it." I yawn.

Kade's lucky the unkempt look works for him. His raven hair sticks off his head in every direction in shining black spikes. Stubble covers his normally clean-shaven jaw, and his shirt isn't even buttoned all the way. He looks like he literally rolled out of bed and came here. Which he did.

"I do have one question, though," I say, rising to my feet. "How is it that I look like hell, but you look even sexier when you haven't slept?"

Kade slides his hands behind my back, threading his fingers and pulling me against him. "I'd like to say it's a gift from God, but that would be giving the man upstairs too much credit. This is all natural, baby." I stand on tiptoes, meeting him halfway as he drops a kiss to my nose.

"Super cute guys, let's see some more." Joy stands off to the side, camera in hand, capturing our private moment on film.

"Ainsley isn't part of this shoot," Kade drawls, turning toward the photographer. "You don't have her permission to use her image."

"Actually, we do, Kade," Vic adds. "She's part of the tour. She signed a waiver before stepping foot on the bus giving us rights to use her image any way we see fit."

"Who authorized that?" Kade's loud voice is carried on the breeze. All eyes turn to us as he sidesteps in front of me, blocking Joy from being able to take my picture again.

"The same people who set up this tour, and the ones who pay your salary," replies Vic. "RatBird Records. They love the bad boy gone soft angle."

Still standing behind him, I see Kade's arms cross over his chest. The other members of the band have congregated around to see what's going on. "I ain't fuckin' soft, Vic. And my private life will remain private."

I can't see his face, but his voice is low and laced with warning. He still insists on keeping me a secret. Possibly for my benefit but, more likely, for his own. Kade wears his rock star persona proudly on his sleeve but buries what's inside under a mountain of arrogance and attitude. He feels something for me, I'm sure of it, but whatever it is, he doesn't want to advertise.

"Give me the camera." He gingerly holds out his hand, but no one moves. "Joy, is it?"

"Yeah." Joy grips the camera to her chest, protecting it as if it were a young child.

"Kade." I step to the side, making my presence known, but he doesn't acknowledge me.

He stares the photographer down, his upturned palm waiting for her to hand over the camera. "I'm not going to hurt it. I just want that picture gone."

"Kade," I say again. The tension in the park is thick and intense. He's not going to lay a hand on that girl, that much I know for certain, but I have no idea what will happen if he doesn't get his way.

"Stay out of this, Ainsley."

"Excuse me?" I step between him and Joy. He's blowing this entire thing out of proportion. It's a silly photograph. "First of all, don't ever tell me what to do. Second, leave the poor girl alone." I turn toward Joy, who's still clutching the camera against her body. "It's hot, I'm tired, and I just wanna get the hell out of here. So please, for the love of God, delete the photo, and let's get on with our lives, k?"

Joy's eyes glitter in the sunlight, and I notice she has one brown eye and one blue one. It's interesting and strange, much like this entire situation. Her eyes drop to the camera, and her thumbs roam over a series of buttons before looking back up again. "Done."

"Thank you." Without looking back, I walk away from the whole debacle, sandals clacking on the pavement below me. Kade likes his privacy—believe me, I get it—but that doesn't give him an excuse to act this way.

He stops me next to the van, his hand closing around my arm with a tender grip. "We need to talk."

"What about?"

"I don't want you tainted by my life." Kade swallows hard. His eyes soften, losing the razor-sharp edge that leaves me bleeding with want every time he looks at me.

"You don't owe me an explanation, Kade. I understand. This thing between us . . . no strings, no rules. Right?"

"No, you don't understand. Ever since I saw you in that banquet room, I've wanted you. It's more than physical. You've gotten to me." He points at his chest as he talks, still warming my arm with his gentle grasp. "I don't want to announce to the world that you're mine, because no matter how much I delude myself into thinking it, and how much I want it, you aren't. You leaving hangs over my head like a guillotine. I can't stop it from coming down, no matter how hard I struggle."

An unfair ache blossoms in my chest. This fantasy seems so real at times, I forget that it's not. Kade's become such a part of me over the last few weeks. The thought of never again hearing the way my name falls from his lips, feeling his kiss on my body, or seeing the way his eyes burn with desire every time he looks at me, hits so hard it borders on the side of pain.

"Let's not think about it, Kade. Let's live for the day and love for the moment."

His lips touch mine in a tender caress, so painstakingly sweet, I can't breathe. It wasn't supposed to be this way. He was supposed to fuck me raw and throw me away. That was the deal. Now, I'm drowning in his embrace and acting like someone else completely. He's changed me, and deep down, I know I've changed him, too.

* * *

CURLED UP LIKE a kitten in the corner of the couch with my Kindle on my lap, I'm enthralled in the forbidden love affair of the couple gracing the electronic pages. During the day, everyone hangs out in the lounge room, but I managed to secure my own private spot in the corner of the bus, where a tiny loveseat sits off the side of the kitchenette. Sometimes, it's so loud in there I can barely think.

"What are you doing in here?"

Startled at the sound of Kade's voice, my eyes snap up from the device. I'd immersed myself in the story, blocking out all the other noises around me. I never even heard him coming.

"Nothing. Which is what I have planned for the whole night."

The break in the show schedule left the guys scrambling for something fun to do. I don't even know what city we're in, but I can't think of a thing I want to do more than just sit on this couch and read. Believe it or not, there is such a thing as too much fun, and I think I've reached my limit. I've ingested so much booze and cheap takeout over the last couple of weeks, I'm starting to wish I'd packed my fat pants.

Kade sits on the loveseat next to me. I untangle my legs, stretching them out onto his waiting lap. "This is what you plan to do tonight?" He trails his finger down the tip of each of my toes as if it's tumbling down the steps. The tiny bit of intimacy makes all the hair on the back of my neck rise to attention.

"Unless you have any other more exciting offers, yes."

His thumbs press into the arch of my foot then he rolls each toe, working his hands down naturally before trading in one foot for the other. I respond with an appreciative sigh. Is there anything he's not good at? "Let me take you out."

My gaze slides from the black and white screen to Kade's waiting blue eyes. Ever since we had that fight, he's been a little less arrogant and a little more affectionate. He's still a cocky asshole—it is his defining characteristic, after all—but little things here and there make me question his sanity. Case in point: his hands mauling my feet at this very moment.

"Why, Mr. Black, are you attempting to make an honest woman of me?" I grin at the ridiculous notion of being wooed by the guy I've already been having dirty sex with. He really doesn't need to put forth the extra effort. I'm quite fine to read here alone while the rest of them go out looking for trouble.

He flashes his panty-dropping grin, and my pulse kicks up a notch. "I don't wanna marry ya, sweets; I just wanna buy you dinner before I fuck you for a change."

I feign outrage, but I've grown so used to his crassness at this point that it falls on deaf ears. There was a time when I would have found this kind of profanity highly offensive, but now I'm not only used to it, I find it charming. Like the boy on the playground who's mean to you for the sole purpose of getting your attention, Kade's a big child who's always looking for ways to horrify me. Besides, he's not that far off. I'm pretty much a sure thing. "How can I say no when you make it sound so romantic?"

"What can I say? Romance is my specialty. Be ready at seven."

★ ★ ★

"SO WHAT ARE the plans for the night?" Jenny kicked the guys out of the lounge room so she can help me get ready. I don't really need her help, but playing dress-up with me is something she thoroughly enjoys.

"I'm not sure. You know Kade; he doesn't give more information than necessary."

Jenny circles her finger, and I twirl for her on demand. "You look hot. He's going to love that dress."

Standing in front of the hanging door mirror, I turn at all angles to make sure everything is where it should be. The simple one shoulder dress fits like it was made for me. It's conservative with a sexy flair. More my style than any of the other clothes I've worn on this tour. And it's all black—Kade's favorite color. "What are you guys doing tonight?"

"There's a bar downtown. Tweedle Dee and Tweedle Dum have some stupid bet going about who could go the longest without showering and still get laid." She tugs on one of my curls and watches it spring back up. "Lucky for them, they are good musicians because those two are idiots."

"Unhygienic idiots at that."

I refresh my berry lipstick and compulsively look at myself again. "I think this is as good as it's gonna get." A nervous rock sits in the pit of my stomach. I've already slept with him. A lot. We've spent almost every moment together since the day we met, but slapping the word "date" on it makes it feel less casual. Not only that, but this will be my first date since I was sixteen. I'm not sure I even know what to do.

The accordion door squeezes open, and Kade walks in. "Hey A, you re—" He stops short. His smoldering gaze starts at my feet and rises up my body slowly, drinking me in like he's just come from the desert and I'm a tall glass of water. "Damn."

He doesn't look so bad himself. The gray dress shirt he wears hugs every hard curve of his body, and his black jeans fit just enough to showcase his strong thighs without being too tight. Don't even get me started on his cologne. I could live for days on his scent alone.

"Don't just stand there, Romeo, say something nice. 'Damn' isn't a compliment," Jenny spits.

Shooting her my signature death look, I grab his extend-ed hand and gasp when he jerks me against him and leans in close. "You're gorgeous." The tickle of his breath on my ear combined with the velvety sound of his voice turns my nervous rock into a horde of butterflies. I take a deep breath in an effort to relax before I pass out from the stress of it all.

We leave the bus hand in hand, and he leads me to a car idling in the lot. "You rented a car?"

"I want this to be a real date. I can't pick you up at your house, but I can pretend."

He opens the passenger side door, helps me in, and then closes it behind me. The night is just starting, but I already know it's going to be my favorite part of the tour so far. He's starting to let me in. To show me the real him, not just the Kade the rest of the world gets to see.

Twinkling lights strung overhead illuminate the worn cob-blestone patio in the tiny Italian restaurant. Kade's hand settles into the small of my back as we follow the hostess to a secluded table in the corner. It's both possessive and natural, and I love the way it feels.

The light from a candle highlights his eyes in a way that gives them a bright, ethereal glow as he sits across from me. "I thought the terrace would be better than sitting inside. More privacy. You aren't cold, are you?"

"It's wonderful, Kade."

My heart flutters as he flashes me 'the grin' for the second time. He's obviously pleased with himself. He should be; he's earned it. So far.

"So," he starts, "what do you like?"

I peer across the table as he looks down at his menu, the realization striking hard that what I like is sitting across from me at this very moment. I'm into him. Hardcore.

He feels my stare and looks up as I drop my gaze to my own menu, feeling the flush, and finding it hard to catch my breath. My skin feels hot and clammy. I chastise myself for feeling something I know I shouldn't. I'm only going to end up getting hurt again.

"I don't know. Everything looks so good."

The waiter pours our wine and takes our orders, and Kade raises his glass in a toast. "To starting over."

"To starting over," I repeat with a clink of his glass.

"So," I say, after taking a sip. "You know all the sordid details of my crazy life, tell me something about you. Something I wouldn't have already read in the tabloids."

"What do you want to know? Ask away."

"Tell me what the great Kade Black was like as a boy."

"Believe it or not, I was kind of shy as a boy. I was a military brat who traveled around a lot."

"So that explains it." He arches an eyebrow at my cryptic conclusion. "Those guys have a drawl that you don't really have. Your accent is indistinguishable."

"Oh, right. Yeah, the rest of the band was raised in Georgia. I only lived there for a few years. Prior to that, I was all over.

"Any siblings?"

"No. Just me and my folks."

"You must be close with them. I bet they are really proud of you."

Talking about his parents makes him visibly uncomfortable. He shifts in his seat, fingering the stem of his wine glass. "They aren't around anymore. They've been gone since I was a teenager." The sparkle in his eyes dims, and his mouth turns down.

The sudden urge to sweep him into my arms comes on strong. I want to hold him against me, kiss his pain away, and soothe the sad look that's taken over his face merely mentioning his family.

Kade Black is a beautiful, damaged soul with more depth than I gave him credit for. Unfortunately, he's also six-foot-five inches of nothing but heartbreak. He's testosterone and swagger eighty percent of the time, but the rare occasions that he's allowed me to peek at the man behind the curtain have led me down a path I don't know how to come back from. My body craves the cocky asshole side of him, but my heart is completely smitten with the man hiding underneath.

Chapter 13

EVERY DAY BLEEDS into the one before it in a monotonous string of concerts and highway. I'm so sick of the road. It feels like I haven't slept in weeks. We're heading back toward the direction of New Jersey now. Soon, we'll be in Pittsburgh then, after that, the summer festival in Tuxedo, New York. It's our last stop before splitting with Black Diamond. They'll continue the tour out West, and I'll go home.

I roll over to grab my phone and send off a quick "Good Morning" text to Shay, like I've done every morning, before lying back in bed. Kade stirs next to me, slipping his hand around my waist, keeping me tethered to him. This bed is our haven. Our private sanctuary away from everyone else. It's the only place where we can be us. In here, we aren't a cocky rock star and a single mother. We're Kade and Ainsley. No one has expectations of us. No one is watching, judging. He's mine, and I'm his, in a lovely delusion that ends the second our feet hit the floor and reality sinks in. He and I only have a couple of more days together, and all of this will be over.

"Where'd you go?"

The deep, quiet sound of his voice cuts through my thoughts and pulls me back to him. The closer I get to our expiration date, the more I find myself daydreaming about what could have been if we met in another life. One where he isn't famous and I'm not broken, and we can try to have a real relationship like a normal couple.

"Just wondering what Shay's doing."

Shay's my first priority, the only thing that matters to me, and the biggest reason I can't let myself continue on this path I'm headed down. She's not just a part of my life, she *is* my life, and I let her down. Her father left us, and I shattered into a hundred pieces instead of being strong for her. It's another reason on the list of many that I should never have gotten involved in this. She needs a mother more than I need a mate.

"You miss her." Kade props himself up on his elbow so he can look at me. He's always focused. His mind never wanders; his eyes never leave mine. A few weeks ago, his intense gaze made me uncomfortable. I thought this was his way of being in control, but I was wrong. He just cares about what I have to say.

"More than you can imagine."

"I can imagine, A," he says, sweeping his fingertips across my cheek. Kade and I haven't really discussed our imminent demise, but the air between us gets heavier as time closes in on us. I can feel his rapid heartbeat against my palm. The wheels are turning in his head; I can see it in his eyes. "I don't want you to go."

"I have to."

His spine curls as he sits up and rests his arms on his knees. "You don't have to. You can stay on the tour, come back to California with me. We can do this, Ainsley. I want to do this."

I sit up in bed and kick my legs over the side, turning away from him. I've grown used to him demanding my body, but right now, he's asking for my heart. Any normal woman would jump at this chance, but I'm not other women. I'm me. Irreparably broken and unwilling to give myself to another person like that again. "We shouldn't be having this conversation."

"No," he says turning me to face him. "We should have had

this conversation weeks ago. The second I felt myself falling for you, I should have laid it out on the table. I'm a man who gets what he wants, and what I want is you."

"Well, you can't have me!" Jumping from the bed, I start throwing on my clothes. "My life is in New Jersey with my daughter! My feelings for you are irrelevant. You have no right to even ask me to move across the country with you!"

Kade stands up, pulling on pajama pants and a T-shirt. "So you admit you have feelings for me. Why are you being so obtuse about this? You'll still be Shay's mother in California!"

"You don't get it! I can't take Shay from Bob, and I wouldn't want to. She needs us both."

Bob may be a cheating ass, but he's the only father Shay has. Even if I wanted to go, he would never allow me to move her three thousand miles away from him.

"Ah, fuck Bob!" he shouts, backhanding the air in front of him.

He's too arrogant for his own good. A caveman. An ornery toddler expecting people to bend to his will. I'm not his assistant, his lackey, or his friend. After this, I'm not even sure I'm a fan of his anymore. "No. Fuck you! If given the choice between my family and you, my family wins. Every time."

Something comes over Kade. A veil falls over his eyes, darkening them from blue to black. Hands shake at his sides, and his trembling lips turn into a scowl. "After everything he put you through, you still love him," he seethes, his chest rising and falling with shallow breaths.

It sickens me, but I do. I can't just turn it off like a faucet. Love doesn't work that way. But that doesn't lessen my feelings for Kade. I'm so confused I just want to cry. "I don't know who I love."

He takes a step forward, his fingers twitch like a methadone patient, and his nostrils flare. A rumbling growl comes from deep inside his chest. I've seen him mad a dozen times, but I've never seen him like this. If it were anyone else, I might be afraid. I've witnessed how Kade's temper could spiral out of control. I half expect him to turn green and start tearing the entire place apart, but I know he'd never hurt me. He stomps past me, throws open the door, and disappears at the front of the bus.

Jenny peeks her head in the room. "I could hear you two yelling all the way in the kitchen. What's going on?"

I grab her hand, pull her in, and close the door behind her. "He broke the rules, Jen!" I explode, pacing the room. "He's such a cocky son of a bitch sometimes; I want to wring his neck!"

Jen and I both lurch forward as the bus comes to an abrupt stop. "We can't possibly be in Pittsburgh already. We just left Baltimore," Jenny says, changing the subject.

She pokes her head out the door to see what's going on. Vic is buzzing back and forth like an angry hornet about to sting. "Band meeting! Everyone off the bus!"

Jen backs up, sliding the door closed again and leans against it. "So what are you going to do?"

"What kind of question is that? I'm going home." I grab a duffel bag from the closet and start stuffing my clothes in it. "I can't stay here anymore."

"Wait." She grabs my arm. "You can't leave right now. We're in the middle of nowhere."

Kade's words run through my head. *I always get what I want.* I fall onto the edge of the bed, tears flooding my eyes. Three weeks after my divorce, here I am crying over yet another man. I'm pathetic. The minute Kade realizes that fact, he'll only turn around and leave me too. It's inevitable. "How am I supposed to face him now?"

The bed bounces as Jenny plops next to me. "Do you love him?"

"I don't know." I shrug. Starting a new relationship so quickly after the last one ends is a recipe for disaster. I'll never know if my feelings for him are real or not until it's too late, and I don't have the luxury of taking that risk. There's too much at stake for me to chase down a rebound. "I'm just so confused."

"Of course you are. Everyone saw this coming but you, Ains. I warned you he was falling for you. How could he not?"

Voices filter through the bus as the guys pile back on. "Jen, you in there?" Banger's drawl is soft spoken as usual.

"What's going on?" she says, as she opens the door.

Banger's beanie is missing. It's so rare to see him without it that it almost doesn't look like him at all. His blond hair falls past his chin, covering a portion of his face. He swipes his overly tattooed hand across his forehead and pushes it back behind his ear. "We're makin' a change to the schedule."

"Why?" I ask.

Banger's aqua eyes are tired and bloodshot. He's always so kind and quiet, the type of guy who prefers animals to humans, and watching a movie over having a party. He's the calm one in the group. The center. But judging by the tight set of his jaw, I can tell that whatever happened outside wasn't good. "Kade wants to work on new material."

"Where's he now?"

"He's sitting up front. Give him some time, Ainsley."

Blame is written all over his face. I'm causing a problem. Our private life is leaking into his professional one, and it's all my fault. For fifteen years, the band has played together in flawless harmony. Until I showed up. I'm throwing off the balance, and I can't be here anymore.

* * *

IT'S STILL DARK out as I sit in the kitchenette sipping my coffee. Kade and I are barely speaking. The band is giving me the cold shoulder. I've made a disaster of everything. I can't stay here, but there's no way I'll be able to say goodbye. The decision weighs heavily on me, and I know what I have to do.

Sneaking down the quiet corridor, I pull back the curtain on Jenny's bunk and gently shake her awake. Her eyes flutter open. "Ains, it's five a.m. What the hell?"

"I'm leaving."

"Thank you for sharing. I'll talk to you when you get back." She pulls her covers up over her shoulder and rolls over.

"No. I mean, I'm leaving the tour. I just called the car service. Troy should be here in twenty minutes."

Jenny pushes herself up on her elbow. "What do you mean you're *leaving* the tour? What happened? Did Kade do something? I'll kill the son of a bitch."

"No, no. It's nothing like that. It's just . . ." I blow out a breath, collecting my thoughts. I'm a coward for sneaking out, but this fantasy can't last forever. It's best to make a clean exit before I make everything worse. Kade is fun and hot, but I'm too much of a realist. I tried living the dream once, and it turned into a nightmare. "You don't have to leave with me. Stay the last couple of days and enjoy the festival. I just didn't want you to wake up and find me gone."

Jenny sucks her bottom lip between her teeth. "Banger asked me to stay. I told him yes."

My eyes turn as wide as saucers. "Really?" I raise an eyebrow in disbelief.

"He did. I have no idea where this is going, but I really like him. He's quiet, but he's sweet and funny. I have nothing to go back to. No family, no home. I live in an apartment, and I'm self-employed. I can do my job from anywhere. I'm sorry I didn't tell you earlier. I just didn't know how."

"Have you even slept together yet?"

She lowers her gaze then looks back up at me through her light lashes. "A few times."

"Wow. We really are a couple of sluts, aren't we?" I say with a grin.

"Are you going to be okay, Ains?"

Pressing my lips together, I consider it for a moment. "You know what, Jen? I am."

With tears in my eyes, I hug my best friend goodbye. Everything's changing, but it's just a part of life. I swallow the lump in my throat and get out of the bunk. I can do this. For the first time in my life, I'm completely alone yet unafraid.

In our room, Kade lies asleep on his stomach with the sheets tangled around his body. I resist the urge to get back into that bed next to him because I know if I did, I'd never want to get up again. When he wakes up, he'll breathe a sigh of relief that I'm not there. A nice clean break and we'll both continue with our lives as if we never met.

As I walk out the accordion door for the last time, I look back, burning the image into my memory. I'll never forget the time we shared. Kade gave me more than multiple orgasms. He gave me the confidence to stand on my own two feet. He showed me Bob hadn't broken me completely, and that I will love again. Jenny was right in more ways than she knew. This experience was exactly what I needed—it helped me get myself back again.

The crunch of gravel outside alerts me to Troy's presence. Giving my surroundings one last long look, I send a silent "thank you" into the atmosphere before disappearing into the morning air.

It's funny how leaving home feels like an endless journey

but returning seems to take no time at all. As the car pulls onto my street, I brace myself. The last time I was here, I felt like my life was crumbling, but today, a piece of me feels like it's coming back together again. Strange to believe it was only three weeks ago. So much has changed, and I'm not the same Ainsley I was then. A storm of emotions rages within me, but within them is the feeling of hope. I vow that from this moment on, I am going to be the superhero Shay looks up to.

The house is dark and silent. I welcome it, happy to be home. When I walk upstairs to my bedroom—the bedroom I shared with Bob for nine years—I don't cringe when I walk through the door. It's no longer the scene of the crime. It's my refuge.

I send a quick text message to Shay letting her know I'm home, drop my bags, and climb into my own bed. There's no warm body, no spicy scent, no sweet embrace. It's just me and the new life that's waiting to start.

Chapter 14

STARTLED AWAKE BY a loud banging downstairs, I sit up, rubbing the sleep from my eyes.

Who the hell knows I'm even home?

The glass panel in front of the door makes a distorted picture of the person standing on my porch as I creep down the steps. The pounding starts again, and I hear his voice.

"Ainsley, open this door!"

Kade came after me.

I peer in the mirror at the bottom of my stairs and gasp at the hot mess staring back at me. The side of my face is creased from sleeping, and my hair is flat on one side. I try my best to smooth my crumpled tendrils when he knocks again. "A, please open the door."

His muffled voice sounds less severe this time. The touch of desperation in it constricts my chest, making it hard to breathe. Through the thick glass, I can see his forehead resting against the door. I was stupid to think this was going to be easy. I should have known better.

The midday sun cascades through the open doorway, highlighting the broken man in black on my doorstep. His eyes rage in bold swirls of cerulean and sapphire as they rake over me standing in the foyer in my rumpled blue sundress covered with nautical anchors.

Why do they have to be so impossibly blue?

Why does he have to look at me with that intense gaze that slices me open, leaving oozing gashes on my already tender heart?

"Did I forget something?" My voice trembles, but my stance remains strong, although my knees are ready to give out at any moment.

"Yes. You did. This." He rushes through my front door and crushes his lips against mine. A low growl radiates from his chest. His hands circle around my waist as he presses us against the wall in the entryway.

The heat between my legs threatens to incinerate me to ash. His lips, his smell, even the taste of his tongue are as intoxicating as whiskey. I'm dizzy. His hand slides up my thigh, disappearing under my skirt and tracing the line of my hip. The fiery touch of his fingertips burns my skin, creating a dull ache that's insurmountable.

My traitorous hands find their way around his neck, pulling him in closer, pressing the hard lines of his body against mine. His hands, both of them now, cup my ass, digging into my cheeks and pressing me into him even closer. "Get in the car."

His usually smooth voice is rough and gravelly. His husky demand clears the fog from my brain. My hands find Kade's chest and push, causing him to stagger back, surprised. "I already told you I can't go with you. You need to leave."

"I'm not going anywhere without you." His chest heaves and the swirling colors of his eyes roll like a kaleidoscope. "We're not done."

My heart somersaults in my chest; the way he growls that we're not done both thrills and terrifies me at the same time. I take a deep breath, trying to control the lecherous hormones that rage through me every time he comes too close. Just like he is now. "You need to get back to the concert and let me get on with my life."

"Fuck the concert." He pushes on the door, and it swings closed with a bang. "Why did you run out this morning? Do you have any idea what it was like waking up and finding you gone?"

The pain reflected in his eyes twists the knife deeper in my gut. He gave me all of him, and I took it and ran like a thief in the night, instead of dealing with it like an adult. I'm a coward, and he deserves better.

I lower my face to the floor, ashamed and embarrassed over my hasty actions this morning. Heat creeps up my neck and face like a rolling cloud of lethal fumes. I ball my hands into fists, digging my nails into my palms to force back the tears building beneath my eyelids. This is the exact reason I ran. I don't want us to end this way. How can I look at his face and break his heart?

He lifts my chin with his fingers, but I continue to look away, refusing to catch his liquid blue gaze. I can feel his eyes burning through me, searing my soul. "I can't go with you. This has to end, and you need to go," I repeat. This time, it's weary and weak. My sense of empowerment is hanging on by a thread, my resolve crumbling to dust.

A single tear escapes my lashes, taking with it a flood of others. His thumb pads across my cheek, swiping it away but more follow. My heart feels like it's shattered into shards, leaving my insides hollow. Every second he stays is another tear in the fabric of my being. Soon, I'll be completely unwound, an untethered pile of my former self laid out on the hardwood floor.

His lips caress my wet face, kissing my tears, my chin, my jaw. Salty wetness burns my eyes as his mouth finds mine, tenderly kissing away my pain and breathing new life into me. We can't continue. He knows it, and I know it. He'll only break my heart. We are a bird and fish wanting to be together, but sharing no commonality with which to live. His chaotic life is in California, and my quiet one is, and always will be, here. With Shay.

"A woman like you should be cherished. Loved. Let me love you."

He brushes my curls back and finds my neck again. I close my eyes, reveling in the feeling of his lips on my skin. As a couple, Kade and I would never work, but throughout the course of our whirlwind romance, there is one common denominator that will always hold us together.

This time, when he lifts me in his arms again, I don't fight it. I wrap my legs around his waist, giving in to the want, knowing it will be the last time. One last hit before quitting him cold turkey.

Untied boots scuffle down the hall. I'm wrapped around him completely, clinging tight with my arms and legs like we're attached at the torso. When my ass hits the granite, I know he's found his destination.

I tear off his shirt and run my tongue across the thick lines of ink, taking delight in the taste of his skin. My hands spring to his belt next, but he grabs my wrists and jerks them above my head in his tight grasp. "Not yet."

He inches up my dress, using his finger to push aside my underwear, and then slips it inside. My head falls, resting on my arm. "I need to hear you say you want me." He touches me. Teases me. Nothing with him is ever easy. He works me up until every nerve in my body is humming with life and aching for more. Each time, he takes me further, seeing how far he can push me until I'm ready to break down, begging him to take me.

"I want you, Kade."

He slips in a second finger, pushing them both in knuckle deep, and I gasp. "What do you want me to do?"

"Make me come."

"Not good enough," he growls, slapping my clit with his fingertips before diving back inside me again. "Tell me how."

My backside slithers across the granite counter, moving against his hand between my legs, but the grip around my wrists tightens. "Look at me, Ainsley." I do as I'm told. The blue flame in his eye serves as a warning. He'll keep this up until I talk.

"With your mouth."

"Then?" A mewling cat sound escapes my throat when he slides his fingers over my throbbing clit again.

"With your cock."

"Good girl."

He releases my wrists, then grasps my hips hard, yanking me to the edge of the counter as he drops onto the stool and buries his head between my legs like a starving dog to a bone. My panties aren't even off yet. He presses his mouth against the damp cotton, his breath hot, his tongue wet. I lean on my hands, lifting my ass as he pulls them down my legs. The dress goes next, flying over my head, flung God knows where with little care.

Kade's hands catch under my knees and bring them up, resting my feet on the edge of the island. I'm spread wide open. A buffet for his enjoyment. His fingers wrap around my thighs holding them apart, as his tongue rakes across my opening from bottom to top. My head falls back as my entire body buzzes with a scorching sensation.

Already teased to the point of madness, I fall hard and fast, unraveling like yarn. A trembling ball of energy slithers across my tailbone, exploding in my gut and blossoming throughout my body. Kade's touch affects me this way. He's the only one who makes me feel mighty and powerless all at once. Like I'm floating and drowning, a death wish I never want to be saved from.

My body's light but my legs feel heavy. My feet slide from their position on the counter, falling down, and hitting the cabinet below it with a thud. I sit up. His lips devour mine as the buckle of his belt grazes my flesh. Heavy breathing and the tinkling of metal are the only sounds as I pull open his belt and drop his pants to the floor.

"Where's your bedroom?" he growls, stepping from his boots and the confines of denim shackling his feet.

"Upstairs."

His arms tighten around my back, carrying me to the stairs as if he's afraid to take his hands off me for a second, kicking the table in the foyer in the process. We drop like a sack of bricks. Kade takes a knee, my butt hits the hardwood, and the vase of fake flowers smashes to the ground as the table skids into the corner. "That was graceful." I laugh.

I feel his smile against my mouth. "Are you okay?"

"I'll live."

Again, his grip around my body tightens as he lifts me off the floor, continuing his mad dash to my bedroom and falling into my bed. He pushes into me without hesitation, both of us groaning at once. So many feelings bubble to the surface; I'm having trouble containing them. He owned me from the moment I met him, and not because of the fame or his looks, but because of him. He's my other half. The missing part of me that exists outside my body but makes me whole. No matter what the future holds, a piece of me will always belong to him.

Chapter 15

KADE LIES BEHIND me, holding me tight against his naked body and caressing my shoulder with his lips. "I wish you'd reconsider finishing the tour with me."

"You know I can't." I turn and face him, placing my hand on his cheek. "Being with you has meant so much to me. You're a good man, Kade. In another time, another life, maybe we could have been something. I'll never forget you, but I can't live a fantasy."

Kade's lips land on the corner of my mouth. "Will you at least come back to the festival with me?"

"We had an amazing afternoon. Let's not spoil it."

He rolls onto his back taking me with him. My fingertips graze the soft skin of his chest and the tattoos that cover his shoulder. "I'm in love with you, Ainsley. "

A fresh wave of tears pool in my eyes and my lids close to keep them at bay. Just when I thought my life was over, Kade burst into it kicking and screaming, mending my broken heart with his gentle hands. He fought for me up until the end, but I can't keep him. Shay needs stability. A firm foundation. Kade's life is not what I want for her, and going back to the festival with him would only further complicate things. "And that's the exact reason I can't go back with you."

There's nothing left to say. The rhythmic sound of his heart thumps in my ear, thrumming my name with every beat. I close my eyes, listening to the sound, melting into his warm skin, and breathing in his spicy fragrance for the last time. Kade Black loves me. I have no idea why, or how it happened, but he does. And I'm pretty sure I love him too.

The click of the door downstairs disturbs my moment of Zen. "Did you hear that?" I ask, sitting up.

"Hear what?"

"Ainsley!" A deep voice floats up the stairs, followed by loud, heavy footsteps.

"Oh crap, it's Bob!" Considering the scene downstairs, I can only imagine the horrifying thoughts going through Bob's head.

I jump from the bed and throw on yoga pants and a tank top, seconds before he bursts in the doorway in a frenzy. "Ainsley! Oh my god, are you all right?" His eyes, wild with worry at first, take in the scene and fill with contempt. It's all too familiar. Except in the alternate version, I'm the one standing dumbstruck in the doorway, while Bob is the one with the guilty look on his face.

His lips curl into a sneer. "Oh. I see," he chides.

"What are you doing here, Bob? You're not supposed to be home until the end of the week. Where's Shay? Is she okay?"

"Shay's fine; she's at the house with Cami. You and I need to talk. Maybe your little *boyfriend* can show himself out while we discuss a few things."

"Hey man, watch it."

Kade rises from my bed. More than half a foot taller than Bob, with fifty extra pounds of muscle, he's intimidating even wrapped up in my floral bed sheet. From the corner of my eye, I see Bob wince. He's thick and stocky, tough in his own right, but Kade's a powerhouse.

"Kade, it's okay. I can handle this," I say, raising both palms, calming the beast I see beginning to take over Kade's demeanor. "Give me a couple of minutes. I'll meet you downstairs."

His glare shifts past Bob and lands on me. Puffing out his chest, he stalks toward the door, knocking into Bob's shoulder as he passes. "I'll be right downstairs if you need me." The testosterone in the room is so thick I can smell it. He stands aggressively over my ex-husband, addressing me, but making sure Bob knows he won't be far away.

Turning toward Bob, I cross my arms over my chest, annoyed. "Okay. We're alone. Talk." He walks to the bed, sitting down and giving the seat next to him a suggestive pat. "I'll stand, thank you." Even if I wanted to sit, I wouldn't. Bob is never going to tell me what to do ever again.

"Europe was a bust. As soon as I heard about what happened in West Virginia, I couldn't concentrate on anything else. I followed every move Black Diamond made in the last few weeks. I saw every kiss, every article, and every tiny blurb that had your name connected with his." I stand in the room waiting for the harsh words I'm sure are on their way, but Bob takes a breath and continues. "I never should have left you, Ainsley. I made a mistake, and I want to come home."

The blood in my veins turns to ice. "You what?"

"I thought I loved Cami. I thought I'd made the right choice, but seeing you with *him*. You're different now. I can't explain it. I guess it took you moving on for me to realize that I'd made a mistake. I want to be with you, always. I want you and Shay and me to be a family again. I know we can work it out."

I say nothing; just stand there in open-mouthed shock. All I wanted since this entire thing started was for Bob to come home. Now here he is, begging for my forgiveness, asking for another chance.

"Say something, Ainsley. Don't leave me hanging. You want me on my knees, look . . ." He falls from the bed to his knees, offering himself up as a sacrificial rite. "Say you'll come back to me. Say this thing with him is nothing. I love you, and I want you to be my wife again."

Tears spring to my eyes. Bob is groveling. He's on the floor, admitting he was wrong and telling me he loves me. We can be a family again. All I have to do is say yes.

"I've wanted to hear you say that for the last year. Whenever I thought about living in this house without you, about not being your wife anymore, it made me physically ill. This family was the most important thing in my life." I pause, collecting my thoughts, refusing to let the emotion building up inside to boil over. "But it's over. I've not only accepted it, I've grown accustomed to it. The truth is, you leaving is the best thing that ever happened to me. You didn't make my life better; you stunted it. You kept me under your thumb for far too long, and now, it's my time to shine." With Bob still on his knees, I walk toward the door of the bedroom. "You broke up this family, and you need to live with that." I turn my back on Bob for good.

A shiver slithers up my spine when I find Kade sitting at the island. Thoughts of earlier spring to my mind. My body reacts, but I force myself to ignore the tingling in my stomach and between my legs that always comes from being near him. "Is everything okay?" he asks as I approach.

"Everything is great," I reply with a reassuring grin. It's far from it, but it will be. I just need time.

Kade reaches for me. I take his hand, moving closer to where he sits on the barstool. The midday sun sends a ray of light shooting through the window blinds. It catches his eyes just right, making the deep blue pop bold and bright in the sterile white room.

Movement in the corner of the kitchen catches my eye. Bob runs out of nowhere. His face is pinched in an angry knot, and his hands are balled into fists. "You wife-stealing son of a bitch!"

he barks, lashing out and catching Kade in the chin.

Kade's head whips around. Red shoots from his mouth, dappling the tile at his feet. When he wipes his lips and sees the blood, his face contorts into at murderous scowl. "Oh, you're fucking fucked, bro. I will end you, you sorry excuse for a human being."

Kade's thick finger pokes Bob in the chest, as Bob backs away frantic and scared. His back hits the wall, and Kade's hand wraps around his throat, lifting him off the floor as Bob clutches his forearm, kicking and gasping. "You want a piece of me, asshole? Try hitting me now that my back's not turned the other way," Kade seethes. A frame falls off the wall, smashing to the ground. Bob flails around like a fish out of water. He isn't a small guy, but next to Kade's massive form heaving against him, he looks like a child.

"Kade!" I squeak. The sound of my voice softens him instantly. He loosens his grip, and Bob falls to the ground in the pile of glass, grasping his throat, red faced and sucking wind.

"Get the fuck out of here," he snarls, grabbing Bob by the back of the shirt and hauling him to the door. "Next time you want to come in this house, you ring the damn bell."

The door opens, and Bob's gone. Kade stands close by, his chest heaving and hands twitching by his side, just like they were when we fought on the bus. "Come here," he growls.

The look in his eyes has gone from soft to vicious. Anger still drives through his veins like a motocross rider. He needs an outlet to work through it. He needs me. No matter how large and powerful a man is, at some point, he needs a woman strong enough to embrace the beast and soothe it out. Or bend over and absorb it. I'm not doing either.

"You're too much of a loose cannon, Kade." His eyes blink rapidly, as his breathing finally begins to slow.

"I know I'm moody and impulsive. It's something I live with

every day." His boots scuff on the hardwood with each gentle step he takes toward me. "But you humble me. You bring with you a sense of calm I can't explain. I need it. I need you."

I drop my gaze to the ground between us, unable to look into his beautiful face as I formulate the best way to get him to understand. "I can't love you, Kade. Not the way you need me to. I'm not strong enough to deal with your emotional wreckage when I still have so much of my own." Lifting my face to his, I see nothing but bleakness in his eyes. "It's time for me to be an adult, take ownership of my life, and be the mother I should have been from the start. The positive role model Shay needs, not the broken shell of a woman I've been. I'll never achieve that with you. You're too consuming. I need to focus on her now."

Kade offers me his hand, but I don't take it. I can't bear to touch him anymore, not when it hurts this bad to make him go. His blue gaze burns into me as he backs to the door. "I may be leaving, Ainsley, but this isn't goodbye. Go ahead. Get your shit together. Do what you feel you need to do, but mark my words: when that day happens, I'm coming back for you."

Chapter 16

SKYPE'S MUSICAL JINGLE plays from my laptop as I pop the cork on my wine. I hit accept, and Jenny's smiling face pops on the screen. "Hey, lovie! What's going on? Miss you, girl!"

My own smiling face shows in the little box in the corner. Dark hair is piled on top of my head in my usual messy bun with curls spiraling out around my ears. "Hey, Jen! I miss you more! Where are you?" I take a sip of my wine and see movement on the screen behind Jenny.

Having to schedule these Skype dates instead of meeting for real kind of sucks. I understand that life takes us in different directions, and I'm happy for her, but I miss her so much it hurts sometimes.

"We're at Banger's house in California now." Light blond hair cascades off her shoulders as she turns her head. "Banger, say hi to Ainsley!" she calls out behind her.

"Hey, Ainsley!" I hear from somewhere in the background.

"Hey, Banger!" I wave, not knowing if he can actually see me or not.

"So what's new, chica? How's work? How's Aaron doing?"

I roll my eyes at my friend. She knows damn well what his name is. We've been dating three months already. "*Eric* and work are both good." I put emphasis on my boyfriend's name on purpose. Leaving the tour early last year caused a backlash of shit that, unfortunately, she had to clean up. In addition to that, I think deep down she was secretly hoping I'd change my mind and go back.

"He asked about you, again. Why won't you at least talk to him?"

Dark blue eyes, severe as a summer storm, flash in my mind, but I shake them away, taking a giant gulp of my wine. Just the mention of *him* causes my pulse to pick up to the speed of a Formula One racer.

She's found a way to bring him into every conversation we've had over the last year, but I shoot her down each time. The memory is just too painful to discuss. He told me he loved me, that he'd be back for me, but a month or so after he left, talk of him and that slut Misti Rain trickled into the airwaves.

The porn star turned pop star showed up on his arm for every big event from the Grammys to the MTV Music Awards. Their relationship was never confirmed by either of them, but Kade keeps his privacy so heavily guarded, he wouldn't have been seen with her if it wasn't something serious.

To add insult to injury, she's only twenty-two. And tall. In heels, she's almost as big as he is. With her blond hair and tight body, they look great together. Every time I think about his stupid come on, I don't know whether to laugh or cry. He prefers women to little girls. *Sure he does.*

"We both want different things. There isn't much else to say." Jenny sighs as I pour myself another glass of Pinot.

I shouldn't have let him in. At the time, I was sure our love would eventually run its course, but all these months later, it's still there, sitting in my heart and dying to get out.

"Mommy, did Aunt Jen call yet?"

My nine-year-old daughter comes bounding down the stairs like a herd of buffalo. Amazing how one little person can make such a ruckus. She slides into the kitchen on her socks and lands right next to where I'm sitting.

Perfect timing!

"Oh my gosh, that can't possibly be Shay! Shay is just a little girl. Who's that gorgeous woman standing next to you?"

The grin on Shay's freckled face is a mile wide as she waves at the screen. Jenny wasn't just a constant in my life, but in Shay's as well. She hasn't said too much about it, but every now and then, a comment will slip that tells me just how much Jen's move cross country has affected her.

"Aunt Jenny! It is me! Grammy says I'm growing like a weed! I'll probably be as big as you by the time you come home again! Did Mommy tell you I'm going to be a big sister?" Her words tumble over one another like dominoes. I've told her a hundred times to slow down when she talks, but sometimes her excitement gets the best of her.

"Yep, Mommy told me all about the twins. Bet your daddy's so excited for that. When are they coming?" Sarcasm drips off her voice. Jenny would never say it in front of Shay, but I know exactly what she's thinking. My ex-husband is a cold-hearted schmuck.

"Cami still has a while I think, but you should see her. She's huuuuge!"

Jenny's cackle fills the kitchen, and I press my lips together trying not to follow suit. "Shay, honey, it's not nice to say people are huge. Why don't you run along now and let me finish my visit with Aunt Jen, okay?"

"All right," she grumbles. "Bye, Aunt Jenny. I miss you, love you!"

"Miss you, love you, too, sweetheart." Jenny waves as Shay scrambles out of the kitchen and back up the steps to her room. "How huge is she exactly?" The grin stays plastered on her face as I make sure Shay is out of earshot.

Without Shay watching, I feel free to smile. When it comes to Cami and Bob, Jenny and I are like the cast of *Mean Girls*. As over it as I am, I still have a nasty, resentful streak regarding the whole situation. "Violet Beauregarde, Jen. I'm going to leave you with that image and move on."

She slaps the desk and laughs so hard she snorts. "You fuckin' kill me, Ains! I swear!"

"All right, enough about me. What's going on with you? How's life on the road?"

Jenny's life was glamorous before she ended up connected to one of the biggest names in rock 'n' roll to date. Now, she's practically royalty. She spends all her time partying at the swankiest clubs and hanging backstage at the coolest concerts.

"To be quite honest, I'm a little tired." She bops her left hand over her exaggerated yawn, and my chin practically hits the counter when I'm blinded by the enormous rock on her delicate ring finger.

"Holy. Crap," I deadpan. Jenny's face lights up like a jack-o'-lantern, while I sit there in open-mouth shock. "Is that what I think it is?"

"It is!" she squeals and bounces around in her seat.

Her excitement draws me in, and before I realize it, I'm bouncing too. "Oh my gosh, congratulations! Tell me everything! Hold it up again, let me see it!"

Her delicate hand dangles in front of the camera so I can check out her new bling. The lamp in the room catches the emerald-cut diamond at just the right angle and fragments of light seem to shoot out of it on all sides. The dazzling sparkle is hypnotic. "Damn, girl. Banger's got some taste."

"Fuckin'-A, he does!"

She pulls her hand back and looks so happy that my chest overflows with emotion. Banger's great, and I'm thrilled that she's finally met someone who makes her happy, but it pretty much seals the deal of her ever coming back home.

"You're going to be my maid of honor, right? You have to be. I won't take no for an answer."

"Absolutely! Why would I say no?"

She chews the corner of her lip raising both eyebrows. "Well. . . ." She pauses, twirling a piece of her snow-white hair. "Kade is going to be the best man."

I feel like I've been punched in the stomach. I've only had two glasses of wine, but the room is spinning so fast I might throw up in my own lap. Jenny's unexpected announcement must have momentarily stopped my brain from functioning at full capacity. Of course Kade is going to be best man. He's Banger's best friend.

"Ainsley?" I hear Jen's voice, but I'm lost in my own head.

Kade Black.

"Hey, Ainsley, wake up." The snap of Jenny's fingers brings me back to the present. My eyes focus and she's looking at me, her brows creased together and her lips pinched to the side. "You all right? You look like you're about to pass out."

"Yeah. Yeah, I'm fine. I just . . . I don't know, got lost for a second."

My tongue darts across my dry lips trying to wet them. After all this time, Kade Black is still the one who got away. Some may argue that it's more accurate to say he's the one I pushed away. Tom-ay-to, tom-ah-to.

I was hoping to continue my blissful state of ignorance, pretending what we had didn't teeter on the edge of something great. It was only supposed to be a fling, a steppingstone, an ineffectual nothing on my path to moving past my ex-husband and onto my new life. But as hard as I try, I can't simply forget how sweet his words were, how amazing his lips felt, and how quick his eyes could cut me to the bone with one little look.

"Are you going to be able to do this, lovie? All I did was say the man's name and you look like you've seen a ghost."

Jenny is quite astute. Ghost is quite possibly the perfect way to put it. He may be physically gone, but his presence still lingers all around me. I can still feel him devouring me on this very counter, and the rumbling vibration of his voice telling me I'm the sweetest thing he's ever tasted. Every so often, I even smell him. That delicious blend of spice and masculinity that was all-consuming, making me drunk with desire.

I will my heart to slow down; I command it, but it doesn't listen. "Yeah. No worries. Between Shay and the gallery, I can't stay for any real length of time. Do you have a date yet? I can look at flights tonight."

Jenny's face turns slightly to the left, and her gaze follows. She nods and looks back at the screen. "About that. Banger and I decided it would be better to get married in New Jersey. All my family is there, and it's just easier for the handful of us to travel than it is for all of you. We really don't want it to be a big deal, you know?"

I stare at the screen blank-faced. Going to California was one thing—I could fly in, hide in my hotel, and fly out with minimal damage. Kade is going to be in New Jersey. With her.

"Okay," I manage to grumble out. "Sounds like a plan."

This was bound to happen sooner or later, but I'd hoped for later. Way later. Like maybe after my lady parts had dried up into unusable prunes. Even then, I have no doubt that Kade would be able to breathe new life into them. I hate that he still has this effect on me after all this time, but he just isn't someone you can shake that easily. Because he's either imprinted himself onto your heart or simply wouldn't allow it. In our case, it's both.

The day I left him was one of the most difficult of my life, and not a day has passed since that I don't think of him at least once. My hands may be shaking right now, but I need to get my shit together before the zoo comes to town. Especially now that I have Eric.

Eric! Shit!

My brain is screaming at me. Eric is calm and quiet, everything I should want in a partner. We met in the gallery where I work. He approached me, asking if he could record a piece in the gallery for an indie film he was working on. We hit it off, and he asked me out for coffee. Coffee turned to dinner, and the rest is history. It's not serious, but I feel guilty thinking of Kade just the same.

Eric is nice and super sweet, but he doesn't make my pulse race. He doesn't light my skin on fire or send me into agonizing oblivion when we're in bed together. It's a real relationship. Fire eventually fizzles. It's best not to have it to begin with.

"Banger! I think Ainsley is having a stroke!"

"Jenny!" She giggles, but I don't return the pleasantry. "I'm fine, really. It's going to be awesome. I can't wait to see you guys." Meanwhile, all the dogs in the neighborhood are barking from the shrillness of my voice. I take a deep breath and get myself in check. "So when are you coming?" My voice is normal again, thank God, but my cheeks are flushed, and my brown eyes are almost black.

"Well, I hired a great planner, so I have a lot of stuff covered. I've already called in a few favors, lined up the hall, and the photographer. Banger, of course, is in charge of the music . . ."

I plaster on a supportive smile as Jenny rattles off her to-do list, but I'm having trouble concentrating on anything besides the vision of rock hard abs in my face.

" . . . the shorter the engagement the better, you know, because once the press finds out about it, all hell's gonna break loose. I'm planning to come home next month so you and I can dress shop together and look at flowers. Oh, my gosh, I have so much to do! Okay, lovie, I gotta go. But I'll text you my travel itinerary, and I'll see you next month. Love you!"

"Love you too, bye!"

Jenny disappears, leaving me staring at the Skype homepage. My mind flips through all the possible scenarios like a Rolodex. Kade Black wasn't just the star of every erotic fantasy I've had since my twenties, he was the most arrogant man I ever met. It's a lethal combination that equals nothing but pain. That's what he is—a walking heartbreak just waiting to happen.

Thinking about this is crazy. It was a year ago, and he's moved on. We both have. I'm not the same woman I was then. I've risen from the ashes of my tattered past life and evolved into the strong independent being I am today. A little of that is because of him, and I'll always be grateful, but while I have changed, our situation has not. Kade's colors shine too bright in my pastel universe. He blazes like the sun in brilliant hues of red and gold. For one scorching minute, I held him in my grasp, but I had to let go before his fire surrounded me and left me charred and smoldering.

Kade is not a safe choice. A man like that can't possibly be held in the palm of one woman's hand. He's a gift to the world and needs to be free. Being with him only complicated things, and I can't make that mistake twice. My heart won't be strong enough to let him go a second time.

Chapter 17

Kade

THE SPOT NEXT to me where she belongs is cold. I sit up in bed and find myself alone. My lashes flap like butterfly wings trying to blink the sleep away. Tomorrow evening, we'll be back in New Jersey, and I'll have to say goodbye to her. I have one more day to convince her to stay with me, and I intend to make the most of it. The guys and I practiced the song I wrote for her until my voice was hoarse. It's going to be amazing. Just like she is.

I lift my arms and stretch. It's too damn early to be awake. Today is the first day of the festival, and we have so much shit we gotta do, but the first thing on my list is to drag her from her coffee gab fest with Jen and bring her back to our bed.

I'm still half-asleep as I saunter through the bus expecting to see my girl in the kitchenette. Jen and Vic are sitting at the table, white-faced and silent as I approach. "Mornin'," I garble through a yawn. My confused gaze darts around the space. It's not big enough to have missed her on my trek from the back.

"Kade, have a seat." Vic's voice is even more annoying this morning than it usually is.

Grumbling, I start to leave. I never listen to Vic. I don't listen to anyone. I do what I want, and right now, all I want is my girl.

"You're not going to find her. She's gone."

I turn, glaring daggers at my manager. "What do you mean she's gone?" My heart rate kicks up, but I'm certain I misunderstood. I feel my chest tighten. My fists clench and unclench, trying to work through the adrenaline-infused twitch that has sprung up out of nowhere. She can't be gone.

"Kade, listen to me." Jen slides out of the bench seat and creeps my way like one would approach a rabid dog. Her voice is soft as cotton, but her body language is rigid. "Her time here was up. She was ready to go home and get back to her life."

"What's her address, Jen?"

Panic begins to seep into every pore. The blood is heating under the surface of my skin, and my heart slams against my ribcage. How could she do this? How could she just leave without a word?

"No. You need to let her go." She moves to where the kitchenette meets the sleeping pods then stops. "It's over."

The word 'over' runs through my mind on a high-speed loop. We're not fucking over. "Jen. Her address." I'm trying my best to stay cool, but I'm about four seconds from tearing this entire place apart. I don't give a damn about anything else right now but her.

"I'm not going to give it to you, Kade! Stop asking me! She's gone. Get over it!" The pitch of her voice goes up an octave but cracks as her attempt to be stern falls flat. It rouses the guys from their bunks, and they come out one by one like onlookers watching an accident unfold.

The walls close in all around me. My teeth grind so hard my jaw hurts. My eyes burn. Outlines, once crisp and clear, become wavy and blurred. "Give me her fucking address, Jen!"

My roar booms through the bus like gunfire. Banger's skinny arms wrap around her as she cowers into him and buries her face in his chest. The sight of her trembling throws cold water on the fiery inferno of rage burning inside. I don't want to scare her; I just need her to listen to me.

I crumple to the floor of the bus in a puddle of self-disgust. I lost my girl, and now, I've lost my mind. "Jen. Please."

My anger has fizzled into a painful ball of regret and anguish *bouncing around in my gut. My head hangs in my hands as my back rests against the cabinet, and I feel my face and palms grow damp.*

"I can't let her go."

* * *

THANK GOD THIS tour is over. Spending almost a year on the road is starting to wear thin. I'm too old for this shit. I know it's part of the job, but somewhere along the line, touring went from exciting to just damn exhausting. Different cities, different faces—they all blur together into a sea of nothingness. When I look back at the last thirty-three years of my life, that's all I see. Nothing.

Sure, my career is the stuff of legends. I am the Stone Cold God of Rock-n-Roll. *Rock Show Magazine* crowned me with that title over a decade ago, and I've lived up to that name every day of my life since. I've defended it with blood and sweat, never resting until the world knew I was the king. I sat atop my musical empire, squashing anyone who had the misfortune of climbing anywhere near my level. I was un-fucking-touchable. Then, in the blink of an eye, everything changed.

Ainsley Daniels.

Her name is like a symphony. It rolls off my tongue so fluidly; it's almost like the letters are dancing. The memories of her are so vivid in my mind; if I close my eyes, it's almost like she's still here. As if she didn't disappear like the fog, while the rest of the world was sleeping. I went ballistic and ran after her, but it was too late. She was over it.

My entire kingdom came crashing down around me. The walls I'd built within cracked and crumbled and fell to the floor in shattered shards of the life I'd worked so hard to achieve.

Fucking Ainsley Daniels. She is a typhoon. A tidal wave. A goddamned wrecking ball. She burst into my world unannounced and left nothing but destruction in her wake. The worst part about it: I can't get her out of my head.

She is the kind of woman who sneaks into your heart unde-tected. Her smile is poison, and her eyes are a razor. You won't even realize you've been cut until your blood hits the floor.

At first glance, I believed she was the damaged soul who needed fixing. It wasn't until she left that I knew it was the oth-er way around. She didn't need me—I needed her. I still need her.

Our single, "In Ainsley's Eyes", went platinum almost over-night. It was our biggest success story to date, and the last thing I've successfully written. After the much-needed break, we're supposed to start work on the new album. The label is breath-ing hard down my neck to continue this hot streak we were on, but I'm in way over my head. I have a notebook full of ran-dom lines scrawled on various pages, but nothing even close to a song. It's all lover's lament bullshit. I'm so fucked.

I've spent the last year searching for answers in the bottom of a bottle. The stomach-scorching burn of whiskey does noth-ing to fill the emptiness I feel, knowing she made her choice and it wasn't me. I should have fought harder to keep her. Instead, she told me to go, and I went.

The front door creaks open then slams shut, but I don't make a move to see who came in. Heavy footsteps trudge into the room, and my drummer's drawl cuts through the quiet. "Jesus, Kade, you look like shit. It's three o'clock in the after-noon. Are you drunk already?"

Banger's holier-than-thou attitude does nothing for my al-ready dark mood. He walks over to the blinds and twists them open. The brilliant California sun filters in through the window blinding me with its yellow shafts of light.

"What do you want, *Lance*?" It's been so long since I've talk-ed to another person, that my voice comes out like I've been gargling sawdust.

Banger scowls at the sound of his real name and rocks the couch cushions with his boot-laden foot. "Get up, man. I got something to tell you, and I don't want to have to stare at your ass while I'm saying it."

A bottle of Gatorade lands next to me as I push myself up to a sitting position. I swipe a hard hand down my face and stare at it for a second, my foggy brain wondering if it appeared there by magic. I look up at Banger, grunt some kind of thank you, and pour the sweet red fluid down my dry throat.

"You're losin' it, dude. What is going on with you?"

My oldest friend sits on the couch opposite me with his elbows resting on his knees. The beanie he always wears sits low on his forehead, and his scraggly blond hair jets out from underneath. He stares at me, waiting for an answer. When I don't give one, he rolls his eyes and continues. "You are hitting rock bottom, man. This shit's gotta stop."

"What shit? I'm a rock star, am I not? Partying comes with the territory."

I drain the Gatorade and chuck the bottle to the floor. The plastic makes a hollow sound when it connects with the hardwood and rolls over to the couch where Banger is sitting.

His concerned glare pisses me off. Twenty years ago, I showed up on his doorstep, a scared, lonely boy seeking solace from my messed-up life and needing a place to crash. I'm a man now. The last thing I need is another father. The one I had was enough.

"Partying?" Banger turns his head from side to side, surveying the messy room around us. "I don't see a party, dude. I see a lonely guy drinking his blues away in the middle of the afternoon."

I feel my mouth curl into a sneer. "Did you come here just to fucking annoy me, man? If that's the case, you can show yourself out."

Getting off the couch, I wave my hand in the direction of the door as I head toward the kitchen, catching my own reflection in the mirror across the way in the process. My skin is gray, and I haven't shaved in a week. He's right. I look like death warmed over.

"I asked Jen to marry me."

"Congratulations. I hope you guys are very happy," I grumble without breaking stride. I'm being a dick, I realize, but I'm not in the right state of mind to be happy for anyone right now. I feel like shit, and my mouth tastes like artificially flavored gym socks. Banger is getting his happy ending. Some guys get all the breaks.

"Are you going to be able to dry out long enough to come out to New Jersey for this wedding or what?" That stops me in my tracks. Did he say New Jersey?

"Come again?" I turn slowly, glaring at my friend.

He stands up and crosses his tattoo-covered arms over his chest. "We're getting married in Jen's home state. You happen to know anyone special in New Jersey?" He arches his brow while chucking me the side eye. The skinny bastard is screwing with me. He knows as well as I do who lives in New Jersey.

Her face materializes before my very eyes. Her doe eyes locked on mine with her plump bottom lip stuck between her teeth. I want to reach out and touch it, but I know it's a mirage. A side effect from a broken heart and a drunken bender. If Ainsley could see me now, she'd be disgusted by me.

"I need a best man. What do ya say? You ready for this?"

My eyes snap up to his, and I'm suddenly sober as a judge. Hell yes, I'm ready for this. I'm going to go back to the East Coast and reclaim what's mine.

A smile spreads across my face for the first time in days. "When do we leave?"

Chapter 18

Ainsley

J ENNY'S FLIGHT SHOULD be landing any minute. I'm
so excited to see her that I'm one step away from piddling
on the floor like a Pomeranian. My eyes keep dropping to
the watch on my wrist as if stalking the time is going to make it
move any quicker.

People from all walks of life come and go. I witness joyous
greetings and tearful goodbyes, and I wonder where everyone
is going or where they've been. I spend the time making up stories for them in my mind to appease my own curiosity.

I'm lost in thought when a Barbie doll blond comes strut-
ting through the crowd like she's on a mission. Jenny's pin-
straight hair flies behind her as she pulls her rolling suitcase.
She's flawless in pink skinny jeans, a white V-neck tee, and her
Gucci handbag dangling from the crook of her elbow. "Ains-
leyyyyyy!" Louboutin heels clack along the tile floor as she runs
up to me, throwing her slender arms around my neck.

"Oh, my gosh, I missed you so much! You look awesome!
California really agrees with you!" I hug my friend and can feel
the wetness in my eyes threatening to ruin my mascara. Pulling
back, I stop to look at her again. Her face exudes happiness.
She's practically glowing.

"So do you! I love your hair!" Last time we were face to

face, my hair was a voluminous mop of bouncy curls in various shades of browns and honey. It's still long, but darker now, and today it's much sleeker. "That blond streak in the front is fierce!"

The bags spin along the carousel as we watch them all go by. The black and pink cases finally emerge, and we snatch them off the belt then navigate the airport arm in arm.

"So where to?" I ask after we load her bags in my Jeep Cherokee.

"They are holding a dress for me at Kleinfeld's. Let's go there first!" Jenny slides her Prada sunglasses up her nose and climbs into the cab. She has always been stylish, but being in California has kicked that up a notch, turning her into a full-fledged fashionista.

I pull out of the parking lot and maneuver around the airport's winding roads toward New York City. "I can't believe you're throwing a wedding together in two months. Why the rush?" I weave in and out of the lanes, bypassing cars until the road opens up, allowing me to coast toward the exit ramp.

Jenny snorts and plays with the radio. "Banger has his heart set on a Halloween wedding. Besides, I'm not getting any younger. It's best to lock someone down before my tits hit the floor and my resting bitch face is no longer adorbs."

I snort, unable to argue with her logic. Jenny's bluntness is probably what I miss most about her. She is straight up no bullshit, and you can't help but respect her for it.

She clicks through the presets and stops on her favorite rock station. A deep raunchy growl filters through the speakers, and the tortured wail of my name bellows out right behind it. My finger jabs the station control on the steering wheel before I can hear any more.

The song is just another memory I can't seem to escape. Every time I hear it, my heart catches in my throat. The agonizing way he grinds out my name hollows me out. He seems to spit it through clenched teeth when he's not crying it out in anguish. It's a contorted mix of desire and resentment that hangs me out to dry; a constant reminder that he offered me his heart, and I handed it back to him because I was too afraid to take it.

Jenny pushes her sunglasses up on her head, creating a blond lion's mane effect with her hair. "You can't just pretend it didn't happen. It wasn't some insignificant fling. Not to him."

It wasn't insignificant to me either. Things between us got hot and heavy really fast. *Hot* being the operative word. It was too intense, too passionate. I wasn't ready to feel so much so quickly. I'm still not ready. "We had a good time. It ran its course."

"You're deluding yourself. You weren't there to see the panic in his eyes the morning he woke up and found out you were gone. It broke him, Ains."

That's where she's wrong. The painful memory seeps its way into my mind like venom. Clear as glass and just as sharp, living with it is my constant punishment for the way I behaved.

My eyes stay trained on the road, hiding the overpowering feelings behind them from sight. Pushing him away was the hardest thing I'd ever had to do, but it was for the best. There's no way intensity like that could have lasted, and once it fizzled, he would have only gotten bored of me. Losing him would not only have destroyed me but would have been too confusing for Shay. I can't get her involved in my love life unless I know it's forever. "Whatever we had was over before it started."

Jenny sighs and flips her shades back down. "So is Eric meeting us for dinner tonight or what? I need to put my stamp of approval on this new dude of yours before he makes an honest woman of you."

I cast a sidelong glance at my friend. "We are nowhere near

that level in our relationship, but yes, he'll be there, and you can meet him."

I'm nervous about what these next few months will mean for Eric and me. Eric is the epitome of the life I've worked so hard to achieve this last year. He's artistic and peaceful; everything I should want in a companion. As a result, I've kept so many things hidden from sight, but bits and pieces of my past cling to the outskirts of my present like dust. As much as I would love to wipe it away, I can't. It's a piece of me. It's the reason I am who I am, and I need that constant reminder in order to stay true to myself.

Jenny's wedding descended like a tornado, kicking things into its spinning cyclone that have laid dormant for all these months. Before long, I'll be forced to face the demon that I've cast aside in order to create my new world. When that day comes, I'm unsure if my relationship with Eric will be strong enough to withstand it.

* * *

THE CITY STREETS buzz with life. Yellow cabs dot the concrete landscape and commuters walk briskly down the busy sidewalks, but I'm drowning in a sea of white organza as Jenny tries on her gown. The shop is busy for midday. Salespeople in nice suits move in and out of the tiny rooms carrying dresses of all sizes and colors. The smell of fresh flowers lingers in the air from the oversized arrangement in the corner.

"Ains. You need to come in here. I can't come out." Jenny's voice comes through the door of the dressing room, wavering like the ocean tide.

"What do you mean, you can't come out? Just open the door. Come on."

I hear shuffling inside the small dressing room. The swooshing of fabric and Jenny's light footsteps make their way to the door, but it doesn't open. "I'm in a wedding dress, Ainsley."

"Yeah, honey. I know. Now, come out so I can see you." I pause for a beat, but she doesn't emerge from the room. "Is something wrong with the dress? I'm sure they can fix it."

Her muffled voice is quiet, but I can hear the nerves wrapped around each word. "I'm getting married. Banger is going to be my husband. I'm in a friggin' white gown. How did this happen?"

"You and Banger are good together, and you're going to live happily ever after. I promise."

"But how do you know?" The sound of her worry hurts my heart. I have no business making that promise. I *don't* know. In fact, I'm living proof that there is no guarantee. I thought I'd found my happily ever after with Bob. My knight in shining armor turned out to be a turd wearing tinfoil.

I lean against the door, pressing my hand to the white painted wood. I can hear her whimpering on the other side. "Well. I guess I don't. Love is a gamble. Sometimes you win big, sometimes you don't, but that shouldn't stop you from wanting to play. You love him, right?"

"More than I love myself," she whispers.

As the knob starts to turn, I step back to give my friend space to come out of the dressing room. The breath catches in my throat and tears fill my eyes as she comes fully into view. "Is it that bad?"

Her green eyes are damp with unfallen tears, and her mouth is pulled into a thin line, but I've never seen Jenny look more beautiful than she looks standing in front of me right now. "You're stunning."

She walks toward the three-angle mirror next to the dressing room to look at herself again. "You think he'll like it?" She turns from side to side, smoothing out the material and checking it out as best she can.

"He's going to love it."

The dress is as elegant and unique as the woman wearing it is. The white satin clings to Jenny's slim body like Saran Wrap. A chiffon overlay follows her slender curves from the sweetheart neckline all the way down and flows into a long train in the back. Black butterflies drift up from the bottom and appear ready to take flight off the sheer lightweight fabric as she moves.

When she looks back at me, her Cheshire Cat smile returns. "I'm a sexy bitch!" A laugh bubbles up from my chest. That sad, unsure woman from a few minutes ago has vanished like a cloud of smoke, and the confident one I grew up with has returned full-force.

Once upon a time, that was me on the opposite side of the dressing room door. Only I wasn't nervous, despite Shay already growing like a tiny pea in my belly. I was so sure that Bob was the one. Perhaps that should have been my first clue that he wasn't.

* * *

JENNY IS BEAMING over margaritas at Jose Tejas while we finalize the details for her upcoming wedding. "Banger and the guys should be coming in to meet us in two weeks. Are you sure you can't stay at the hotel with us? It would be so much fun."

"Yeah, I'm sure. Shay will be doing a lot of shuffling back and forth between Bob and me, and I'd rather just sleep in my own bed."

I'm not being one-hundred percent honest. The truth is I don't trust myself staying in a hotel so close to Kade again. I have no control over myself when I'm around him. His ability to rock my world with a single look was uncanny. How one tiny smile has such an effect on my lady parts, I have no idea, but one glimpse at his heart-stopping grin, and I'm a goner.

The man is a friggin' magician—every time he entered a room, my clothes disappeared.

I glance at my watch. Eric will be here any minute. "Listen, Jen, there's something I didn't tell you about Eric."

A look of horror registers on her face. "Oh God, he doesn't have, like, a lazy eye or something, does he?"

"No, it's nothing like that." I laugh. "It's just . . ." I trail off, trying to come up with the right words for my thoughts. "Eric doesn't exactly know about my history with Kade."

Jenny's eyebrows disappear behind her bangs. I feel my ears grow hot under her green-eyed glare. "What do you mean he doesn't know? Was he living under a rock last summer?"

She has a point. Black Diamond isn't just some shoddy garage band. They are practically a household name. As a result, for a short time, so was I. Kade and I made big headlines over those three weeks we were together. Grainy images of Kade being shoved into a squad car while I watch in horror pop into my mind. The sickening sound of cracking bones and skin hitting broken tile and the penny smell of some guy's blood on my face . . . I force myself to remember these things on purpose. I can't allow the countless wonderful memories I have to overshadow his Jekyll and Hyde temperament.

"No, he's just . . . artistic."

To this day, whenever I tell anyone my name, the usual response I get is, "Oh! Like the song!" After all, Ainsley isn't exactly a name you hear every day. I assumed Eric would eventually connect the dots, but he never did. As time passed, I figured why bother telling him at all?

"He's heard of them, but he doesn't listen to mainstream rock music, and he definitely doesn't pay any mind to pop culture. He doesn't even have a Facebook page. I mean I had no idea who Adele was until you pointed her out. Same thing, I guess."

"He still wants you, you know." She blurts it out so quickly, I'm not sure I heard her correctly. "He's miserable, Ainsley. You have no idea what you did to him."

"Oh yeah, he looked pretty devastated with Misti Rain on his arm." I've purposely avoided this conversation for a reason. He may have her fooled but not me. I know him far too well. Kade's not a lover; he's a hunter. A feral beast who craves the chase and thrill of the kill. He doesn't want *me*; he wants what I represent. A challenge. I sit upon the pedestal he's placed me on because I'm the one person who dared to do what no one else ever has. Tell him no.

"Hey," she says, her voice soft. "Misti was nothing to him."

"Was? She's not coming to the wedding?"

Jenny snorts. "Oh, God no! I told you a dozen times. He doesn't want her. You're the one he loves." She covers my hand with hers. "Lovie, if you really want to be with Eric, then you need to be honest with him. In a few weeks, the two of you are going to be face to face with the big man himself. Rip off that Band-Aid and get it over with."

I know she's right, but at this point, I feel like a jackass. After all these months, what do I even say? *Hey, remember that singer I said I dated? He's actually the badass frontman for the most notorious hard rock band in the world. Oh, and he gave me multiple earth-shattering orgasms.* Yeah, no, that wouldn't go over well at all.

"Hey, honey. Sorry, I'm late." Eric's sweet voice startles me, and a blush creeps up my cheeks. I shift uncomfortably in my chair, trying to extinguish the burning arousal I feel from just thinking about Kade. Our lips meet in a chaste kiss as he takes the seat next to mine. "I see you gals started without me."

"Hi!" My voice has taken on that annoying overcompensating, high-pitched tone that goes along with the guilt I feel. Eric is such a good man. He deserves a woman who is able to give him all of herself. I feel like the worst human being on the planet. "Eric, this is Jenny. Jenny, Eric." I volley my hands between the two of them as I make introductions.

I don't want to notice the way Eric has to lift off the seat to reach across and shake Jenny's hand. He's not a big guy, and that's okay. "It's nice to finally meet you, Jenny. Ainsley has told me so much about you."

My eyes immediately roll past Eric and settle onto Jenny. Her eyebrow twitches, and I can feel what she's thinking even before she even opens her mouth.

"Likewise, but she failed to mention you were . . . English?"

Jenny's eyes lock on mine, reiterating everything I already know. Eric is the complete and utter opposite of Kade Black. Kade is massive, all parts of his anatomy included. He's a mountain of a man with fuck-me eyes and a messy mass of unkempt black hair. He's temperamental and cocky, and you can practically smell the danger emanating off him. Eric is lanky and thin. His neatly styled light brown hair fades into a trim beard framing his face. He's handsome and gentle, but he's certainly not the six-foot-five inches of inked rock god I've had the pleasure of getting up close and personal with.

"Australian, actually. I guess I'm just so used to it now, I didn't think to mention it." I flash Jen a tight-lipped smile and open my menu. I didn't mention it because I knew what she'd say. *Why are you fighting so hard against your heart that you go from one obvious extreme to the other?* Tough guys like Kade are not dependable. I should know; I was married to one. Seems I have a type.

Eric, ever the gentleman, attempts to make polite conversation with my friend. "So, Jenny, Ainsley tells me you're marrying a musician."

"I am! He actually plays the drums for Black Diamond."

The look on Eric's face is devoid of emotion. Jenny's brows crinkle together, and my mouth goes dry. I reach for my margarita, hoping the frozen concoction soothes the sudden desert in my throat. "You know, Black Diamond? They have a bunch of hits. Let's see . . ."Soul Crusher", "War Cry" . . ." She looks into space as if she's giving the topic some serious thought, but I know she's full of it because she can probably rattle off every song in album order. "They had a really big one recently. What was it called? Ainsley, I bet you'd know."

Bitch!

She casts an innocent smile, batting her eyelashes. "I don't recall right now." My eyes meet hers in a silent warning. I am not amused.

She reads me loud and clear and drops her eyes to her menu. "I'm so hungry. I wonder what's good to order."

Jenny's motives are understandable. Now that they are all going to be here, this isn't something I can continue to ignore. I will tell Eric everything eventually, just not today. Eric is a great guy, and I'm sure he'll understand. I just need to come up with a good way to tell him, before New Jersey gets leveled by Hurricane Kade.

Chapter 19

Kade

WE ALL LURCH forward as the bus comes to an abrupt stop. "Band meeting, everyone off!" Vic's nasally whine is more irate than usual. The bedroom door flings open, and Jenny pokes her head out. From the corner of my eye, I see Banger give her the "kill" signal, and she backs into the doorway again. For once in his life, Vic's hysteria is justified. Five minutes ago, I walked to the front and announced I'm done with this tour.

The four of us stagger through the doors like a herd of cows. I told Ainsley I wanted her to continue the tour and come back to California with me. She looked me in the face and told me no. If she isn't staying, then neither am I.

"What's this about, Vic?" Konner asks, pushing his blue hair out of his eyes with his ringed hand. The strands get caught in the wind and only blow back toward his face again.

"Your fearless leader has decided to trade in fifteen years of blood and sweat for a woman he's known for three weeks," Vic spits.

Four sets of eyes settle on me waiting for the punch line. There isn't one.

"Ainsley and Jen are scheduled to leave the tour in a few days," I start. "When they leave, so am I."

"What the fuck are you talkin' about, man?" JJ asks in his smothered drawl. Tired and hungover, his lilt is extended and slow, taking *far too long for the question to roll off his mumbling lips.*

"I'm talking about Ainsley. She's gotten in my head, bro."

JJ's bloodshot eyes narrow. "You're bailing on us for some piece of ass you've only known for three weeks?"

"Watch it, man," I warn, stepping into JJ's personal space. "Your skinny ass has been begging to be kicked for years. Don't make me have to be the one to provide it, Junior."

"No, you watch it, asshole!" JJ shouts, poking his finger into my chest. I feel the anger beginning to roil in my gut. I don't wanna beat JJ's ass, but I will if he provokes me. "We let you get away with your sanctimonious shit, but this toes the line. Your decisions affect the rest of us. You're not allowed to up and walk away because some bitch decides she's done with you."

One minute, he's yelling at me, and the next, JJ's back is pressed up against the side of the bus with my hand around his throat. "Keep talking and watch what happens. I fucking dare you," I seethe. His fingers close around my forearm, but I'm not squeezing hard enough to do any real damage. Yet.

"Whoa, whoa. Kade, calm the fuck down," Banger runs to JJ's aid, pushing us apart. "You need to control your anger, bro."

I drop my arm. JJ doubles over, panting and grasping his neck. "I don't need to control my anger. Everyone around me needs to control their habit of pissing me off."

Banger walks to the back of the bus and paces back and forth, his tattooed fingers threaded behind his head. I follow, leaving the other three guys behind. He exhales a slow, deep breath. "Jen's not leaving the tour. When Ainsley goes, she's going alone."

"But she's only contracted for the first leg," I say, confused.

Banger's freaky-as-shit eyes land on mine. "I asked her to stay, and she said yes. Looks like we both had the same plan."

My first reaction is to punch something, but I stand rooted to the floor slack-jawed, unable to move, unable to speak. I'm in the Twilight Zone. Any second, that Rod Serling fucker is going to march out from behind the bus and that creepy ass music is going to start playing in the background.

I should have known. Most people assume his nickname comes from being a drummer, but it came long before that. Banger is a chick magnet. Even when we were gangly teens, Banger laid more pipe than a plumber. He has that quiet cool that babes just go nuts over. The guy barely speaks, but whenever he does, it's usually to spout insightful shit that changes your life.

"What exactly did you say to Ainsley?" he continues.

I eye up my friend, wondering what he's getting at. "Just the truth. I think I'm falling in love with her."

He quietly nods, allowing what I said to sink in. "You think, or you know?"

"I know it. She's it."

"You can't force her to love you back, bro. Ditching everything you've worked for is not going to change anything."

Ainsley does love me, though. I can see it in her eyes. The way they burn fierce and bright, pulling me within them. I can feel it every time she kisses me. It's not just lust; it's passion and fire. "So what do you suggest, Obi-Wan?"

For the majority of my adult life, Banger's been holding onto my strings and keeping me grounded. I have a tendency to make irrational decisions and lose my shit at the most inopportune moments. This dude is my conscience. "Make a statement, bro."

And sometimes, he says lame shit, too.

Yeah, I'll make a statement. I'll chain her to the bus and refuse to let her go.

The thought of Ainsley in chains excites me a little more than it should, and my dick twitches in my pants. "What kind of statement?"

"I dunno, but it should be big enough to prove to her that your feelings aren't bullshit. Up until now, you've been treating her like your dirty little secret. A girl like Ainsley isn't going to just believe that you like her. You need to show her."

I fall back against the bus, crossing one ankle over the other. A statement. My gaze wanders around the deserted parking lot while I consider what the hell would possibly make Ainsley want to stay with me. Matters of the heart aren't my forte. The only things on this planet that I know are music and fighting. My eyes shoot up to Banger's. "What if I wrote a song and played it for her at the festival?"

"Couldn't hurt."

★ ★ ★

MY MUSCLES ACHE and my hands are on fire. Sweat drips off my hair and into my eyes, but I can't stop punching.

The bag hangs in front of me in my home gym. Grunting like a beast with every hit, my knuckles mutilate the black leather with a loud slap. I have aggression I need to work out before I get on that plane. I've managed to stay sober, which is a feat in and of itself, but regulating my temper is not as easy.

Two days.

That's how much longer until I'm staring into the beautiful brown eyes of the girl who torments my dreams. Banger said she is seeing some guy. Whenever I imagine his hands on her body and her legs wrapped around him, the thought causes a blind rage that stirs up the urge to kill. The bag jerks hard as my fist slams into it with the driving force of a team of Clydesdales.

I have to get my shit together. I cannot go ballistic at this wedding when I see her there with someone else. Somehow, I need to prove to her that I'm not the violent asshole she thinks I am. I have to formulate a plan. If I don't play this cool, I'll lose her forever. Banger didn't say anything about this guy, other than they've been seeing each other a few months already. It would be a lot easier if I knew what I was up against.

When I finally give the bag a rest, my arms are Jell-O, and my hands are numb. My chest is heaving like a madman as I stand there catching my breath. I suck down some water and crush the empty bottle in my fist, but my insides are still teeming with acid. I drop to the floor and start banging out sit-ups with fury.

Ainsley Daniels.

She belongs to me. I beat on my chest like the caveman I am to drive that point home and continue my workout, but I don't count my reps. The word *mine* blinks inside my head in pink neon with each move.

Mine.

Mine.

Mine.

The last guy who touched her now eats his food through a straw. Ainsley's deer in headlights look is the only reason the guy doesn't have a size thirteen Doc Marten imprint on his forehead right now. I'd be willing to concede that maybe I overreacted just a tad, but whatever, the guy had it coming. I don't fucking share.

My body is wrecked by the time my workout is complete. I'm sore all over. It hurts to move, but I peel myself off the floor and head to the shower.

Blasting hot water scalds my skin. My throbbing hands press against the tile and my head hangs down, letting the steaming water beat on my back. The spray relaxes my weary muscles, but raw, animal testosterone continues to pump through my veins, plumping up my dick as I think about her. I close my eyes to will my obnoxious erection away, but all I see is her face.

Taking matters into my own hands, literally, I grab the base of my cock and pump my fist upward. My eyes pinch shut, imagining that my hand is her body wrapped around me, soaking and hot. A groan bounces off the clean white tile as my forehead rests against it while pummeling my own dick with my furiously flying fist. Her name slides off my tongue. An eruption of cum shoots out of the tip then trickles down my hand like lava. This is what I'm reduced to—a grown man jerking off in the shower.

Ainsley is special. She's not some groupie who just wants to hang around rock stars and party. She never cared about any of that shit. She's the kind of woman you want to curl up with on the couch and hold in your arms until the sun comes up. The kind you want to kiss in the morning and make love to at night. If given the chance, I fully intend to spend the rest of my life doing all of those things and more.

Chapter 20

Ainsley

MY STOMACH IS in knots. I finish my makeup, which is a feat since my hands are shaking like a detox patient, and walk back into my messy bedroom. Discarded dresses and shoes lie haphazardly around my room as I try to figure out what to wear to Jenny and Banger's rehearsal. Eric will be here in half an hour, and I'm still standing in my bra and panties. It shouldn't be this difficult, but I'm nervous. I want to look good but not *too* good. My conservative side and my wild side are fighting for control and wreaking havoc inside my brain. I wish Jenny were here to pick for me.

There has to be something else I missed. Ugh, I'm being ridiculous. I walk over to a little black dress in the corner and slide it on before I change my mind again. There, I'm done. Except . . .

I do a little turn in the mirror. The one-shouldered dress fits me like a glove, but something about it turns my stomach into stew. This dress is what I was wearing at the exact moment my relationship with Kade turned from casual sex into something more.

Wearing it is a bad idea. It sends the wrong message. I should take this dress off and get rid of it. But instead of throwing it in the fireplace and never looking at it again, I step into tall red and black leopard print heels and walk back toward the full-length mirror.

My hands slide down my body, smoothing the fabric flat against my skin. After all this time, I can still detect the faint scent of his aftershave in the soft fabric. It's comforting, like coming home after a long journey.

The doorbell rings right on time. "You look nice," Eric says taking in my outfit, but his eyes linger a little too long on my shoes. Ever since we started dating, I've tried my best to wear smaller heels, usually in boring colors like black and nude. I can't tell if the fact that the four-inch heels make us eye to eye is what bothers him, or if he just doesn't like them. Either way, I don't bother to ask. The realization comes far too late that I didn't wear them for Eric. I wore them for someone else.

"You look nice too." Eric's trim suit looks tailored just for him. As usual, he's pristinely put together, not a hair out of place. I like that he's neat and tidy all the time. He balances out my mess. We look good together.

He kisses my cheek and opens the car door for me. The weird indie music he listens to fills the space as we pull out of the driveway. I don't even know how you'd categorize it. The haunted voice of the woman singing is melodic and ethereal. It's too delicate for the way I feel. I need something loud to drown out the sound of my thrashing heartbeat.

Ignoring the awful song, I take a deep breath and go for broke. "Eric, there's something I've been meaning to tell you."

He turns the volume down on his radio and glances in my direction intently. "Well, I'm right here, love. What is it?"

Just like ripping off a Band-Aid.

"The man I was with before you is going to be here tonight. I should have told you sooner. I'm sorry. I just don't want you to think I was purposely keeping it from you or anything." My heart and lungs feel like I've been running in place. I'm warm, overly so for the balmy evening it is.

His caramel-colored eyes soften and crinkle in the corners. They are pretty and kind, but they don't hold any heat. There's no fire, no longing. Nothing in them that stirs me up and renders me paralyzed. "Is this a bloke I need to be worried about?"

Sand fills my throat and turns my tongue to cotton. Ending things was my decision, and it's still the right one, but my body has a mind of its own. Especially around Kade. "No." My response is as hollow as the woman's singing. "I just thought you should know."

The car pulls up, and the valet opens the door for me. Lights dot the hardscape, casting a soft glow along the rows of evergreen shrubs that line the walkway. A red-vested attendant holds open the heavy door to the hall as I pass through. The floor is an endless ocean of marble that leads to a set of winding staircases on either side. My eyes follow them and land directly on the dazzling display of glimmering crystal that hangs from the ceiling. The place is simply breathtaking.

"Shall I check your wrap?" I unwrap the shawl from my shoulders, and Eric lays it over his forearm.

"Ainsley! Up here!" Jenny's shrill voice echoes through the lobby from the top of the stairs. She leans against the railing and looks down at me standing next to a centerpiece of twigs and brightly colored fall leaves, waving to catch my eye. The chandelier creates a halo effect around her platinum hair, making her even more striking than she normally is.

I wave up as Banger materializes next to her. "Get your ass up here, girl!"

He makes me smile. Jenny is dressed to the nines in a white Dolce & Gabbana lace sheath dress, while Banger is rocking a tuxedo T-shirt and black Dockers. Hey, at least he took his beanie off. It's progress.

Catching Eric's eye at coat check, I point at the overhang. He gives me a supportive thumbs-up, and I ascend the massive staircase to meet my friends. I'm assaulted by chin scruff as Banger grabs me in a bear hug that lifts my feet off the floor. "Hey, you!" I say as my shoes clink against the marble. "I see you dressed for the occasion."

Vibrant fingers slide his long hair out of his face. Whenever I imagined Jenny settling down, it was always with someone super professional like her. I envisioned lawyers, bankers, or CEOs. Never in a million years would I have expected her to be standing at the altar next to a guy like Banger.

It isn't that he's not good looking; he is just the opposite of her in every way. A kaleidoscope of colors strategically covers both sinewy arms right down to his fingers. The swirling patterns continue onto his lean chest and back as well. He has the same long, white-blond hair she does, but his ghostly eyes are what you notice first. His light aqua irises are so pale; you'd think they were fake.

"Psh, I make this look good." He drapes a colorful arm over Jenny's shoulders, and her fingers immediately lace with his. It's a simple move, but one that shows their level of intimacy. They can't help but touch. It's second nature.

"Don't worry, Ains. Tomorrow, he'll be clean-shaven and dressed to impress." She looks up at him, the adoration as obvious as the button nose on her face. "Right, baby?"

Banger scrunches up his nose and makes a face, and Jenny makes one right back. These two are so in love, it's sickening. "Come on, let's get started. The rest of the guys are here already."

She untangles from Banger and takes my hand in hers. As I'm led into the room, a thrill waves through my body like spectators in a stadium. It starts in my stomach and ripples up through my chest and down my arms. I pretend not to notice, but he's impossible to miss. Standing at the bar, larger than life and burning a hole clear through me, fuck-me eyes and all, is Kade Black.

Chapter 21

Kade

A INSLEY FLOATS INTO the room like the angel of death coming to collect what's left of my heart. Fuck, she's beautiful. I can't tear my eyes away. I watch her from across the room as she greets everyone with smiles and hugs. She pretends she doesn't see me standing here, but her gaze drifts in my direction more than once.

Her hair is different, but I'm struck by the feeling of déjà vû. It's almost identical to the day we first met. She was standing with Vic and the boys, decked out in black dominatrix leather like a sultry sex kitten. That purple thing she was wearing as a shirt barely covered her, but she didn't need to try so hard. She was gorgeous anyway. I was a moth, and Ainsley was the flame. She drew me to her without so much as a look. She owned me before either of us even realized it.

I've waited for this moment for over year, and now that it's here, I'm rooted to this floor, unable to propel myself forward. I just watch like a fucking stalker and drink in every inch of her from head to leopard-printed toe.

She turns toward the doorway and smiles. Some scrawny bastard with a beard sidles up next to her. He extends his hand as she introduces him to everyone. My heart is jackhammering like a quarterback on prom night. My hand squeezes my glass so tight, I'm afraid it might shatter. I can actually feel the veins bulging out of my neck.

Finally, my feet decide to move, and my long strides put me in front of her in an instant. The smell of her perfume floats around me. She wore the same heady fragrance the last time we were together. There's no eloquent way to describe the scent. It's like angels dancing in an enchanted forest full of sweet shit. Everything about this woman is sweet—her skin, her lips, and that little slice of pie hidden between her legs.

Her eyes drift up my body and stop at my mouth, same as they did the day she first saw me. When my tongue slides along my dry lips, her eyes flare with hunger. I know what she's thinking. Any man can fuck, but oral is an art. Licking isn't enough. You have to get intimate. Nibble, slurp, suck, and eat it like it's the last meal you'll ever have. Kiss it like you love it. Which I do. Saliva builds on my tongue just thinking about all the times I buried my face between her creamy thighs. Ainsley would tremble with orgasms like a leaf in the wind, begging me to stop before I'd even come up for air.

"Been a long time, sweets."

"Kade." Her weight shifts from foot to foot. "Good to see you." She blinks her long lashes as her eyes study my face. I recognize the look in them right away. It's the same one she had when I came after her. That rebellious desire she can't hide, even when she tries.

"Eric Struthers. Nice to meet you, mate." Her boyfriend extends his puny hand, and my first instinct is to crush it. His other hand reaches across her back and clamps around her side, a desperate attempt to mark his territory.

Fuck that. He's *trespassing* on *my* territory.

I play nice and shake the guy's hand. He has to look up at me, way up, and I like that. "Kade Black. Likewise."

The guy looks nervous. He should be. Her gaze penetrates

my flesh, but I don't look her way. *Squirm for me, baby. You know how much I love it.*

"Okay, since everyone is here, let's do this!" Jenny's sharp voice cuts through the moment and draws Ainsley's attention from me to her. I don't doubt she did it on purpose. These girls all stick together.

After spending the next forty-five minutes learning how to friggin' walk, we meet in the hotel's restaurant for dinner. I watch and wait to get her alone, but the boyfriend never leaves her side. When he leans in to talk to her, she listens and smiles, but I can tell she's not all that enthralled by him. Her body language screams it. There's too much space between them. Her hands hang at her sides, and her brown eyes don't flare with excitement when she looks at him the way they do when they fall on me. I'm her tightrope, but he's her safety net.

Her eye catches mine just before she walks alone toward the exit. I give her a two-second head start then I make my move, following her down the hall toward the ladies' room. "Ainsley!"

She stops and spins on her giant fuck-me heels as I saunter over to where she's standing. She inches backward as I invade her personal space and rest my hands beside her head on the wall. The pulse in her neck begins to throb. "Why so cagey, sweets? Do I make you nervous?"

"No." She swallows and chucks a brief glance down the hall. "But I'd appreciate it if you backed up a skosh, big man."

I call her bluff and lean in closer. "Is that really what you want? Because that dress tells me otherwise."

She's wearing the exact dress she wore on our first and only date. I can only assume that she did it on purpose to torture me. It's not overly revealing, but it hugs her hourglass figure, accentuating every appetizing curve.

Back then, my hands roamed every inch of that fabric before peeling it off and owning her. I can see that memory in her eyes, flashing hot and bright. She remembers it just as clearly as I do.

"It's just a dress, Kade." The breathy way my name rolls off her tongue makes all the blood in my body rush to my lower half. Her trembling lips beg to be kissed, but I hold back. We're not there yet.

My fingertip traces the crooked neckline, testing the waters to gauge her reaction. Her chest rises as I graze over the exposed swell of her breasts. Her sparkling eyes dance and her fingers twitch. This is the most alive I've seen her all night, and I love that I still have this kind of effect on her.

"You can act coy all you want, sweets, but I know you still want me."

"Awfully sure of yourself, aren't you?" Her eyes challenge me, but the quiver in her voice gives her away.

"Mmmhmm." I nod and the corner of my mouth quirks up into a cocky grin. The shallowness of her panting breath becomes more apparent as I come in close to her ear. "I know my way around your body, Ainsley, and I can smell your arousal from here."

Her eyes go wide. She parts her burgundy lips to say something, but only a breathless hitch in her throat comes out. "And it is sweeter than ever," I add, taking a step back. Her palms splay flat against the wall, and her knees press together.

I shove my hands in my pockets and walk toward the exit, whistling as I go. My need for her is intense. The woman brings out a beast in me that's hard to control. I don't just want to fuck her; I want to possess her. Hurl her over my shoulder, drag her ass to the hotel with me, and claim every inch of her in my bed, but I came on too strong last time and she ran away from me. It won't happen a second time. This time, I will do everything in my power to make her mine. I'm not walking away from her again.

Chapter 22

Ainsley

ERIC LIGHTLY SNORES next to me as I lie in my bed looking up at the ceiling. I made love to one man while thinking about another. I'm no better than Bob was. Eric and I haven't been together that long, and we've never discussed the possibility of a future, but I'm still doing wrong by him. The hold Kade continues to have over me is so much stronger than I thought.

My run-in with him in the hallway left me shameless with need. His lips singed my ear as he leaned in close, and his clean masculine scent scrambled my brain, sending bolts of lightning to all of my erogenous zones. Once the feeling in my knees returned, I stalked into the restaurant and told Eric it was time to go. My tongue was in his ear before he even pulled out of the parking lot, but the relief I was hoping for wasn't found. I don't know what makes Kade so special that he can pull orgasms out of me with the snap of his fingers, but as of now, I'm one for three.

Kade was able to read my body, and being with him was exhilarating. He was the perfect mix of savage and sweet, looking into my eyes, seeing what I needed, and giving me everything. He sent me to the edge of madness over and over until I'd beg for mercy, only to laugh at my pleas and go harder. It was raw. It was primal. It was like nothing I'd ever experienced.

I look over at Eric sleeping in my bed. His slender back peeks out from the covers, and his wiry arm disappears under the pillow. Seeing Kade couldn't have been easy for him. Kade Black is an intimidating man. He's big and brawny and sexy as hell. He carries himself like a panther, full of confidence and grace.

I was amazed at how well he acted around Eric. He said hello, shook his hand, and maintained his distance, but I saw the lethal look in his eyes. The Kade I knew last summer would have ripped through that restaurant like a freight train destroying everything in its path. But last night, he laid in wait, stalking his prey only to pounce the moment I was alone.

Light breaks over the horizon, and it's time for me to get up. I have to meet Jenny and the other girls at the hotel to get ready for the big day. I push myself out of bed and into the shower, drained from lack of sleep, but thrumming with unresolved sexual energy. The hot shower spray cascades down my body. The room fills with steam, and I stay there, allowing the scalding water to beat down on my weary muscles.

Eric is still asleep as I quietly dress in yoga pants and a tee shirt. I kiss him goodbye and let myself out. Tomorrow morning, he's leaving for New Zealand to film a documentary. He has so much work to do, but he's still going to try his best to meet me later at the hall. If only he wasn't so damned nice.

My mind races with heavy thoughts as I drive back to the hotel. One more day and they all go back to California. I need to put as much space between Kade and me as possible. My body aches for him, but I won't act on it. I've been down that road before.

I maneuver through the hotel to Jenny's room and knock. Her cousin opens the door and waves me in. "Hey, Kelly. What's up?" I've known Kelly for years. She and Jenny were always close growing up, so I spent a lot of time with her as a kid. It's been years since I've heard a word from her, and I'm actually happy to see her.

"Oh good, you're here." She hugs me hello and closes the door behind me. "The bride has been asking for you. She's in the bathroom."

The massive bridal suite has been converted to a salon, with separate sections for hair and makeup. I meander to the bathroom, waving hello to bridesmaids and guests on the way. "Jen? You all right in there?"

The bathroom door whooshes open. A slender hand pulls me inside, and the door clicks behind me. Vanity lights catch on the bedazzled word 'Bride' on Jenny's shorty robe as she stands with her back to the door. "I need your underpants."

"My what?" My brows furrow together.

"Ains. You're the only one I know who wears white panties. Give 'em." She extends her upturned palm. "I forgot to pack them, and I need my undies to be white."

I roll my eyes. "That's gross. No one is going to see your underwear, Jen, just wear what you have."

"No! Everything needs to be perfect. Banger and I haven't had sex in weeks. When he takes my dress off later, I need everything to be white underneath. We're going for this whole fake virgin thing."

"Ew. Spare me the details."

I sigh. Jenny knows me all too well. I wish I could say she was wrong, but my panties are most definitely white. This is one of those details they leave off the maid of honor duties checklist. "Turn around." She turns her back to me while I lose both my undies and a little piece of my dignity. I pull my yoga pants back up and hand her the white bikinis. "You owe me big time for this one."

"You are the greatest! I'll be sure to give you a shout out

while Banger's eating them off me." She plucks the underwear from my hand and slides them up her slim legs.

"A simple thank you is enough, really." I laugh. "You can keep them."

Jenny turns to leave the bathroom, and I follow her out. "You left in quite a hurry last night," she says as I park myself in the hairdresser's seat.

"Did I?" I wince as the stylist begins to tame the curly rat's nest that sits atop my head. I always envied people like Jenny with their poker-straight locks. When left to its own devices, my hair could rival most clown wigs. It's no wonder I've adapted the messy bun as my go-to hairstyle.

Jenny sits on the edge of the bed, crossing her long tan legs. "You did." She examines her nails as if they are the most interesting thing she's seen in days. "You and Kade have a nice chat in the hallway?"

I look down, absentmindedly picking at the hem of my tank top with my thumbnail. "You saw us?"

"Honey, I could practically smell the smoke from the fire between your legs in the banquet room." She runs her hand through her smooth hair and re-crosses her legs. "You guys eye-fucked each other throughout the entire rehearsal. Bet Eric got some extra dirty last night."

My eyes widen and my mouth drops open. The stylist remains professional, but I can only imagine what she's thinking. "I'm sorry to disappoint, but nothing happened between Kade and me, and nothing will happen."

Jenny stands up from the bed and snorts. "Yeah. Sure it won't." The makeup artist waves her over, and she walks away. I should know by now that hiding anything from Jenny is futile. She just knows me too damn well.

Chapter 23

Kade

I FEEL LIKE a gorilla in this tuxedo. The shirt is stretched so tight across my chest that the buttons are threatening to pop. At least my pants are long enough. Silver linings.

The rest of the band is lined up next me in matching monkey suits, sweating like we're preparing to face a firing squad. Konner's hair is purple today. He changes the color every few weeks or so, and chose this particular shade to match his tie. JJ compulsively tongues the rings in his lip. It's his tell. He must have found a chick in the crowd that he likes. We are a motley crew of misfits for sure.

I glance at Banger standing to my right. He's fidgeting. His hair's all combed back nice and neat, and his face is shaved clean. Jen definitely has this dude wrapped around her bony finger. It's crazy to think of one of us having a wife. We may be in our thirties, but we're still a bunch of immature idiots. I'm happy for him, though. Jen's a pain in the ass, but she's a great girl.

The music starts, and a line of bridesmaids start filing in. I should love this. I should be cataloging which broad I'm going to bang first, rather than pining for the one who crumpled my heart in her tiny fist like tissue paper. My life was like an all-you-can-eat buffet. I'd get my fill of one woman then move on to the next just as quick. There was always one waiting, sometimes two, but it wasn't until I met Ainsley that I realized how awesome it is waking up next to the woman you love. Reaching out with closed eyes, pulling her against me in those early morning hours . . . the scent of her hair, the softness of her body. It's Utopia. The sex was molten, but I keep coming back to those moments.

Girls at a wedding are especially easy pickings, but I have my sights on only one. She comes down the aisle in the same purple dress as the other three girls, but they can't hold a candle to her. She floats like an angel. The material moves with the gentle sway of her hips as she makes her way to the front. She's exquisite. My eyes stay fixed on her as Banger and Jen exchange their vows and are pronounced man and wife.

The ceremony was nice, but I'm glad when it's over. Strands of tiny lights twinkle in the purple and black banquet room. The holiday theme is so dramatically overdone; I'm shocked Jen didn't ask us to come in costumes. Thank God for that.

JJ and Konner are sitting next to me arguing over which chick they're going to screw, as if they can't have their pick of literally any broad in this joint. Well, every one except mine. These guys are like the idiot brothers I never had. Everything's a competition with these two knuckleheads. On the last tour, they actually made a bet to see who could go the longest without showering and still score. The funk on the bus was foul, but it didn't deter the chicks starving for a piece of a rock star meat at any cost. Women are messed up. Most of them, anyway.

"You guys are barking up the wrong tree with that girl."

Ainsley's sweet voice gives me chills as it filters in from behind me. That Jersey Girl accent makes me want to do a fist pump every time I hear it. "She has no interest in what you're packin'," she adds, gesturing to the black-haired bridesmaid Dumb and Dumber have set their sights on.

"Whatever, Ainsley. I got everything that girl needs right here." JJ grabs his junk, giving it an exaggerated shake and curling his lips into a fake sneer.

I roll my eyes, embarrassed for a split second to be associated with the man-child sitting next to me, but Ainsley just wrinkles her nose and shakes her head, taking their bull in stride. After three weeks on a tour bus, she's as numb to his crap as the rest of us are. I'd love to say it's all rock star attitude, but sadly JJ's been this way since I met him. "Never gonna happen, JJ."

"Fifty bucks says I get that girl on her knees before the night is over," he bets, scratching at the bull's-eye tattoo on the side of his shaved head. Why someone who's as big an asshole as JJ would get a fucking bull's-eye tattooed on his head, I have no idea. It just goes with the territory. Guy's always been a mouthy moron with a death wish.

"You got yourself a bet!"

She takes the seat next to me, and we all watch as a short-haired chick in a pants suit comes up and kisses Black Hair dead on the mouth. Ainsley's smile spreads from ear to ear, as she looks back at both guys.

JJ's eyebrow shoots up in shock. "Well played, sister," Konner says, joining Ainsley's hand in a high five. I just sit back and smile. *That's my girl.*

Defeated, JJ throws three twenties on the table. "Keep the change."

Ainsley grabs the cash and deposits it into the top of her strapless dress. *Andrew Jackson, you lucky bastard.*

"If you're looking to score, I'm pretty sure little orphan Annie over there has some serious daddy issues." She points at a girl with flame red hair and a black mini dress shaking her ass on the dance floor. JJ and Konner continue their juvenile arguing as they leave the table.

"Flying solo tonight, huh? Crocodile Dundee ditch you to

go walkabout?"

Her eyes narrow and she scowls. "No, he didn't ditch me." Her petite fingers nervously tangle in my discarded tie on the table. "He had a problem at work. He'll be here later."

"Maybe it's none of my business, but any man who puts you second isn't worth your time." She doesn't say anything in response, and she doesn't have to. Ainsley's ex-husband is a grade-A douchebag. I had the displeasure of meeting him once. That asshole actually had the balls to sucker punch me. I would have squeezed his head off like a balloon if Ainsley hadn't stopped me. I swear the dude almost pissed himself. Anyway, my point is, she is so used to being put on a shelf that it's second nature at this point. She's strong and independent—both qualities I love about her—but that doesn't mean she shouldn't insist on being number one.

The band changes gears, and the music switches to a slow song. I extend my hand out to her. She looks at it for a second, letting her gaze fall to me before allowing me to pull her out onto the dance floor. Her arms ring around my neck, and my hands wrap around her back. The entire world disappears the instant her tight body presses against mine. Her head rests near my shoulder. Hot breath blows on my throat. My eyes drift closed as I bring my face as close to hers as I can and get drunk on her spellbinding fragrance. It's a better high than any drink or drug.

As we move to the rhythm of the music, my thumb caresses small circles into the soft skin on her back, and her wild hair tickles my knuckles. I can't say what happens when we die, but if there is a heaven, this would be mine.

I want to hold her like this forever. She fits me like a missing puzzle piece. Without her, I'm jagged and rough. Too misshapen and angular to fit quite right into this world. She makes me whole. She must feel it too. My heart pounds against my ribcage, ready to burst from all the things I want to say. Things I should have said a year ago but was too macho to let out. Instead, I did what I always do—fuck instead of feel. Sex is easy. Why is love so complicated?

My arms wrap tighter, and a soft sigh passes her lips. We're barely moving now, just holding each other on the dance floor. I'm dying to kiss her, but the second my lips touch hers, I know it won't be enough. I'll want more. Her body stretches, pushing against me as her nose grazes my collarbone. She wants me as much as I want her; I know it.

"Can I cut in?" Her head bolts off my shoulder, and our magic moment goes up in smoke.

"Eric, you made it!" She drops her arms and smiles, but it isn't genuine. Her entire demeanor changes the second she hears his voice. Her docile body becomes as rigid as stone.

I step back, and he comes between us. "Thanks for keepin' an eye on my girl, mate. I got it from here." His voice is casual, but his words are dripping with warning. It's bro code for stay the hell away. I'm impressed. The bearded bastard is ballsier than I thought.

He scoops her up in his scrawny arms, and I see red. Testosterone shoots through my veins like a bullet. I wasn't graced with a fight or flight mentality. I only have one switch. Right now, it's turned up to eleven, and I want to kill this motherfucker.

You're too much of a loose cannon. . . .

Ainsley's words hold me in a vise grip and keep the avalanche of rage from crushing what's-his-name's smug face into dust. My arms hang at my sides, muscles tense and fists balled. He twirls her around, and her eyes plead with me to be civil. Her gaze lingers on me longer than it should. Is that longing? Or pity? Either way, I can't stand to look at her right now.

In the distance, I see Banger staring daggers at me. I inhale sharply through my nose and make eye contact with my friend. He mouths something at me from across the room. *Walk away.*

Acting like a primate now would be detrimental to my band, my friendship, and my future with Ainsley. Banger is right; I need to calm down and deal with this shit without violence. I take one last look at my girl then turn around and walk out of the room.

Chapter 24

Ainsley

"EXCUSE US, ERIC." Jenny grabs my hand and pulls me to the bar at the edge of the dance floor. "Ainsley. My love. Do me a favor." She threads her fingers together in front of her like she's praying. "Stop messing with Kade's head. Either fuck him or tell him to fuck off. I don't care. But defuse this situation now."

Her jade glare tears me a new one. I press my fingers to my forehead. When we were on tour, Jenny cleaned up every mess I made, but that was business. This is her wedding. I'm allowing Kade to seep into my brain and stomp on the cognizant parts that tell me right from wrong, and I'm messing up her moment in the sun.

"I don't know what I'm doing! Why is this so goddamned difficult?"

"It doesn't have to be. You just need to ask yourself which man you really want." She catches the bartender's eye from the other end and holds up two fingers. "You know the answer. I think we all do."

I shake my head. "No, it's not that simple. Kade and Shay . . . Eric is the smart choice."

The bartender comes back down to our end and leaves two identical drinks in front of us. The ice inside the black liquid is shaped like mini skull heads.

Jenny slides one glass in front of me. "Shay will love who- ever you love. Eric may be the smart choice, but is he the one who makes you the happiest?"

That's the problem right there. Shay would love Kade. How could she not? He's a big child who looks like Superman. But she currently has a man who flies in and out of her life when- ever he feels like it. She doesn't need another. Kade already proved how easily he can jump from my bed to someone else's. Before I choose to share my life with anyone, I need to believe in my heart that he plans to stick around.

I pick up my drink and suck hard on the straw, draining half the glass in one gulp. Whiskey and coke. That's right. Jen's li- quor of choice happens to be the same as Kade's. "I'm happy."

Her head cocks to the side, and she plasters on her signature know-it-all grin. "You're content. It's not the same thing. Look, Eric is super nice, and the accent is sexy as hell, but come on. There is zero chemistry between you two."

My eyes glance at the table where Eric is sitting alone. I guess I never really thought about it before. Being with Eric was comfortable right from the start. He's easy to talk to, and we have so much in common. "I guess he's a little stiff."

The bartender takes my empty glass, and Jenny pushes hers in front of me. "Stiff? The guy barely touches you. Even when you were dancing, it looked like rigor mortis was about to set in." She laughs, and I drop my face to my palm. "I'll support whatever you decide, but if it screws up my wedding, I'm go- ing to go Bridezilla on your ass, and I don't want to have to do that," she says with a wink. "Finish that drink first. A little liquid courage will do you some good." She gives my hand a supportive squeeze and leaves me standing alone at the bar.

Doing as I'm told, I suck back the second drink. The whiskey burns as it travels down my esophagus and leaves a warmness in my belly. My fingers tingle, and my nose feels numb. I look back at the table and see Jenny chatting up Eric. She's creating a diversion so I can slip out quietly, reminding me, yet again, that she is so much better of a friend than I am.

I take a deep breath and exhale slowly. I have no idea what I want, but I have to at least coerce him to come back inside. He's the best man; he needs to be in here.

Walking around the dance floor, I exit the room undetected and lean against the railing to search the room below. Kade sits against the wall with bent knees on the bottom step of one of the expansive staircases. His shirt is unbuttoned down to his stomach, exposing a white ribbed tank underneath. I stay and watch him for a moment. He's as close to physical perfection as a person can get, but underneath that chiseled jaw and strong physique is a man who's as flawed as the rest of us.

Whiskey, stilettos, and stairs are a dangerous combination. I move down the steps carefully, catching his eye when he hears me coming. "You lost?"

He shifts his long legs, giving me space to sit on the bottom step next to him. "I am. I'm completely and utterly lost." I rest my head against his thick arm and sigh. "I lose myself in you every time you come near me. You scramble my brain and leave me dizzy." His pinky skims my exposed thigh. The tiny amount of skin-to-skin contact sparks like a flint. The intimacy of the moment is too great. I sit up and lean against the balusters on the railing instead. "I'm too old for dizzy. I want more. You and I just don't work."

"That's some bullshit." He turns to face me.

I blow out an exasperated breath and push myself up straighter on the steps. Nothing that involves Kade is ever easy.

"Mind-blowing sex isn't a relationship. It's the illusion of one." I hear the words coming out of my mouth, and even I don't believe them. I downplay what we had as nothing but physical, but it was so much more than that. My feelings for him terrify me. I pushed him out of my life over a year ago, but I was never truly free.

His sarcastic laughter burns me up and makes me want to smack the cocky smirk off his face. I don't have time to dwell on it long. His mouth crashes onto mine, and my mind goes completely blank. His full lips are as strong as I remember, as they've been in every dream and every fantasy I've had since we've been apart. My lips part allowing his tongue to slide inside, and my hands find their way around his neck, slipping through the silky hair at the nape.

Memories grab me, reminding me how good it feels being wrapped in his strong arms and losing myself in him. A growl escapes his chest. I reply with a soft whimper of my own, echoing off the sterile marble all around us. He takes hold of my bottom lip with his teeth, letting it slide between them before letting it go completely. Our chests heave with ragged breaths. I can't help but stare at the sheen on his lips, a combination of our saliva mingling together just so.

My heart flaps against my ribs like a bat. He grabs my hand and rests it on my chest, his bigger hand on top. "This is not an illusion." His hand is hot on my skin, clouding my brain with lust too thick to think clearly. He tastes exactly the same—like whiskey with a chaser of trouble—and the desire for more is so strong it crushes me like a weight. "Now cut the holier-than-thou shit, ditch Dundee, and come upstairs with me."

His sudden demand clears the fog from my brain, separating the clouds of desire, and leaving nothing but rays of anger shooting through. "You're a cocky son of a bitch, you know that? I'm here with someone else." I smack his hand away like a spider. My blood is boiling. With one kiss, he managed to both prove me wrong and bump me down to Bob's level. I rise, standing on the bottom step holding onto the railing for support. "You think you know me? You don't know shit!"

"I know enough to know you still want me."

He jumps to his feet on the floor. Between the massive heels on my shoes and the height of the step, we're nose to nose, and he uses that to his advantage, stepping as far into my personal space as humanly possible. Our chests are so close I can feel the heat radiating off him in waves. His hands cup my face. Long fingers splay around my head and disappear in my hair, holding my gaze locked on his. Neon shades of blue flow out from the center of his eyes to the navy outer rim like electric charges through a plasma sphere.

"You look me in the eye, Ainsley, and you tell me you feel a fraction for him what you feel for me. Tell me he's the one, and I'll walk away right now and never bother you again."

He pauses, waiting for my answer, but I don't give one. I can't because it would be a lie. "Yeah, that's what I thought," he finishes.

"Ainsley."

My head whips around as a thick Australian accent floats down from the landing above. My stomach coils as Eric trots down the stairs and stops a few steps from where we're standing. "Should I go?"

"No!"

"Yes!"

Kade and I both answer simultaneously.

Kade drapes a possessive arm over my shoulders. I glare at him, pushing him off me and take a step up, hoping that putting more space between us would calm my nerves and cool the warmth I still feel from him being so close. "No, Eric. Kade was just leaving."

"Unless you're coming with me, sweets, I'm not going anywhere," he says with another cocky laugh, crossing his thick arms over his chest. Even in a tuxedo, he looks menacing, but

I know he won't dare swing unless provoked. I also know Eric isn't going to be that stupid.

My chest feels so tight it's like breathing through mud. Jenny's shrill voice echoes in my head, *defuse this situation.* "You know what? Forget this. *I'm* leaving."

Turning on the staircase, my own gracelessness ruins my dramatic exit as my heel catches on the step. I buckle and fall backward. Right into Kade's arms.

Eric stands idly by, watching as Kade immediately springs to action, setting me on the step and removing my shoe. Gentle hands stroke my ankle and twist my foot softly to the right then the left in a thorough examination. "I think you're gonna live," he says, still brushing his fingertip up and down my naked foot resting on his bended knee. His touch, no matter how small, sends an immediate reaction to the pleasure centers of my brain making me woozy.

"I'm just gonna go then," Eric finally says, brushing past us down the stairs.

"Eric, wait!" I call out as he reaches the door.

He turns, my pathetic hobble on one sky-high heel and one bare foot doing nothing to help me. His caramel eyes are creased in the corners, and his mouth is turned down. Hurting him was the last thing I wanted to do, but I still managed to do it anyway. "I'm sorry, Eric. I can only imagine what you must think of me right now, but you have to believe me when I say whatever he and I had is over."

Eric's hand strokes my cheek. I lean into it hoping to catch a glimpse of the same tiny spark that's ignited whenever Kade and I touch. There's nothing. "You're kidding yourself, Ainsley. What's between you two is clearly unfinished."

He makes a move for the door, but I grab his forearm. "Eric, don't go." My eyes plead with him to stay. I can't let our relationship end like this.

"Why do you want me to stay?" The question is simple. At least, it should be, but I can't think of a single good reason for him not to leave. I've been awful. I used him as a distraction to shield my heart from a man I fear will only take it and run. I settled for Eric because he was safe. I still long for the shelter of that safety, but I don't know how to spin it in a way that doesn't sound completely selfish.

"You're important to me."

"Important? We've been together nearly half a year, and I have yet to meet your daughter. I told myself that it's because you're new to dating, but I've been kidding myself all along. It's because your heart already belonged to someone else." The truth slices deep, leaving an oozing gash on my pride. "You need to figure out what you want, love. When you do, maybe I'll still be waiting." His lips meet my cheek, and before I can protest, he's gone.

I slip my foot out of my other shoe and wrench the high heel still dangling from Kade's fingers as I pass. "You had no right to do that."

"He's not the guy for you, Ainsley," he calls as I stomp up the staircase.

I turn and look down at him, furious at my own pulse for reacting to his cocky grin. "Maybe not. But neither are you."

Chapter 25

Kade

I ALWAYS MANAGE to piss her off. I'm so damned good at it. She's sitting at the table alone, looking like a feral cat about to scratch my eyes out. Perhaps I overstepped a boundary by kissing her, but fuck that. It was the only way to get her to shut up. The rapid-fire beating of her heart told me everything I already know. This isn't over for either of us.

Do I feel guilty about running the guy off? Not one fuckin' bit. Yeah, I'm an arrogant ass, and I don't give two shits about it. She doesn't belong with him; she belongs to me. I just need to make her see it.

Banger and Jen are leaving for their honeymoon in the morning, and the guys are going to head back to California. Shortly after, they'll scatter to their respective families for the holidays. That's usually when I get the most work done, but something tells me I won't be able to string together two sentences after this trip.

The night wears thin, and I see Ainsley circulate the room. I stay where I am next to the bar, pretending to have a blast, when really I've been nursing the same skeleton-filled Crown and Coke for the last hour. Her hips sway to the beat of my heart as she comes toward me. I down my drink and slide the glass to the edge of the bar. "Can I have a water please?" she says as the bartender approaches.

"Water, huh? I almost forgot how much of a party animal you are." She glares at me through brown slits but doesn't say a word. The morbid ice clinks against the edge of the glass as she tilts the water to her lips. I watch her throat move as she swallows, and my mouth becomes bone dry. "Silent treatment. Mature."

Her brow arches as I remove the glass from her hand and take a sip. "I'm not giving you the silent treatment. I just have nothing to add to the conversation."

I love this side of her. Her icy glare, her trembling lips, the gentle flare of her nostrils. Anger and sex go hand in hand. They are the only two emotions that tear us open enough to remind us we're alive. "What do you want me to say, sweets?"

"How about I'm sorry? I know a Kade Black apology is like the equivalent of finding Bigfoot, but maybe just this once, you can admit to being a selfish asshole and take blame when you've done something wrong." A rosy flush grows on her cheeks. She is seething with anger, and I'm so turned on I can barely see straight.

Pushing her hair back with both hands, I rest them on her shoulders and bend to her level, nose to nose. "I'm sorry about Dundee, but I'm not going to apologize for the way I feel about you." The pissed off inferno within her soulful brown eyes dissipates into a minuscule candle flame. "If lovin' you is wrong, baby, I don't wanna be right." I flash my million-dollar grin and stand to my full height again.

Rolling her eyes, she leans against the bar in a huff. "Were you this much of an arrogant ass last year?"

"Probably more. You level me out."

She takes another sip of her water. Her brows crinkle together, and she winces as the coldness slides down her throat. "I can't win with you, can I?"

"Nope," I say with a grin. "By the way, I wasn't kidding when I said I wasn't leaving." There is nothing for me in California. Just an enormous house full of empty rooms. I have everything I'll ever need there, but without someone to help fill the space, it's all bullshit.

"We've been through this."

I shrug. "Yeah and? We can't do any work on the album until Banger gets back from Hawaii anyway. What's wrong with wanting to spend more time with you?"

She rolls her eyes and leans her elbows on the bar behind her. I try not to notice the way her tits press against her dress and instead concentrate on her attempt to hide her excitement at the notion that I'm sticking around. "You really want this, Kade?" Her hands skim across her waist and rest on her hips.

"Fuck yes, I do," I groan.

"Well, this . . ." Her hands leave her hips, and circle the air in front of her. " . . . comes with a nine-year-old daughter, a vindictive ex-husband, and a New Jersey area code. You think about that long and hard, buddy. I'm going home."

"I don't have to think about it. I'm sure about it."

Her mouth opens then closes as an onslaught of emotions roll over her face. "Ains, we're heading out to the bar at the hotel. You coming or what?" Jenny calls out, cutting through the tension and inadvertently taking Ainsley off the hook.

Ainsley glances toward her friend then back at me. "Yeah, I'll follow you guys over." She walks away, leaving me standing at the bar with my heart in my hands like a total loser.

"Ainsley!" I call after her, persistent as ever.

She stops halfway and glances over her shoulder, her lips curling into the most dazzling come-hither grin I've ever seen. "You coming?"

"Abso-fucking-lutely!"

Chapter 26

Ainsley

I 'M DREAMING. I think. In those early morning hours, while you're wavering between sleep and awake, it's hard to tell what's real and what isn't. Twilight dreaming, my mother used to call it. I've had this dream at least a dozen times. I roll over in bed and feel him next to me. His body is warm and strong. I cuddle into the nook of his shoulder, a spot that fits me so well I'm sure I was made for it. It's my favorite dream. It even beats out the sexy ones, although it's close.

A low deep sigh rumbles against my cheek and fingers slide through my hair. Muscles ripple under my hand. My lashes flutter, but my eyes stay closed. I'm not dreaming. I'm in my bed, but I'm not alone.

"Good morning, sweets," Kade says in a thick and gravelly baritone.

"Hey." Somewhere between the wedding and the after party, I forgot all about how angry I was at Kade's impulsive behavior. I got a little tipsy, and he ended up driving me home in my car. "Waking up next to you after one too many drinks is starting to become a bad habit." His rich laugh vibrates in his chest as I stretch out next to him.

Back then, I wanted to crawl into a hole and die, but right now, I never want to leave this bed. His arms wrap around me, and my icy façade melts against the warmness of his body.

"You're right. This is way more comfortable than your couch."

I manage a sleepy smile and breathe a laugh out of my nose. "You wouldn't have fit on my couch, Paul Bunyan." While that is the absolute truth, I didn't want him on the couch. I wanted him here with me. It totally goes against his badass image, but Kade is the best cuddler ever. He's so much bigger than I am. His body practically consumes mine every time we embrace.

"Anytime you wanna see my big blue ox, Tinkerbell, you just let me know."

We lie there for a little while longer in our twilight haze. He needs to get back to his hotel before Shay gets home, but I'm too comfortable to move.

Nuzzling against his chest, I bask in his spicy scent one last time then push myself up to sitting. Kade looks at me through sleepy blue slits. Those sexy as hell hooded bedroom eyes make my soul quiver. "I forgot how beautiful you are in the morning."

Oh, he's good. I can guarantee my hair rivals Medusa's in the front and is probably flat in the back. I also have no recollection of removing my makeup. I'm sure I look like an extra on the *Walking Dead*. "Yeah, my Frankie Says Relax T-shirt is a real turn-on, I'm sure."

"I feel relaxed."

He slides his hand under his head, and the muscles in his arm strain and flex under the thick webs of his tattoos. I was doing an excellent job of not checking him out until now.

Somehow, during the night, he broke my co-sleeping rule—that we both remain dressed—and discarded his tank top. His generous frame fills my queen-sized bed, making it look much smaller than it is. His body is a glorious display of peaks and valleys, covered with splashes of deep onyx. Once upon a time, I played Magellan along the vast landscape, discovering him like new exotic lands; every rippling muscle more exciting than the one before it.

I tear my gaze away and stand, stretching to the sky before disappearing into the bathroom. I gasp at my reflection. *Beautiful, my ass.* He wakes up in the morning like a Grecian God, and I look like Beetlejuice. I wash my face and brush my teeth then search the vanity for a tie to tame the beast that is my hair. Appeased that I halfway resemble a living human again, I open the door, stricken with sadness when I see my bed empty.

His tank is on again, and he's back in his signature dark jeans, having changed when we got to the hotel last night. He was handsome in the tux, but it doesn't suit him. He's a basic guy. Sexy in jeans and a tee. "I'll head downstairs so you can change." He lets himself out the door and closes it behind him. I pull on skinny jeans and a clean V-neck tee before joining him downstairs.

Glancing at the watch on my wrist, my eyes go wide. We slept so late. I can't risk leaving now; Shay will be back any minute. This isn't ideal. Bob walking in on Kade and me in bed together last year was bad enough, but I am adamant about sheltering my daughter from meeting men until it's something serious. Kade's presence here is too temporary. She doesn't need that kind of confusion. She's had enough of that already.

Kade stands at the end of the island with his hand resting on the smooth black granite where my back once laid. Seeing him there causes a dull pang between my thighs. I push the memory out of my mind immediately. Thinking of the past could only complicate things. "Are you in a rush to get back?"

He turns when I enter the room. "Nope. What's on your mind?"

"Well." I can feel the blush on my cheeks. My shaky hands start measuring out grounds as I speak. I'm nervous and I'm not exactly sure why. "Bob said he's dropping off Shay around ten. Which is now . . ." I trail off as tap water splashes into the carafe.

"That's fine."

I pour the water into the machine and turn to face him. "I mean, if that's too weird, I can probably just call Bob and tell him to come later. I know meeting my kid isn't high on your list of priorities or anything." Whenever I'm nervous, I ramble. It's a habit I can't seem to shake even though I'm a grown adult. The shy girl in me always rears her ugly head whenever my self-confidence takes a hit, regardless of how minor. Standing in my kitchen with Kade this close to me is not only messing with my hormones, but my mind as well.

My body tenses as I feel him approach and press against me just enough as he grabs two mugs from the shelf behind my head and sets them on the counter. "I can't wait to meet her." The possessive way he grips my hip turns my dull pang into a throbbing ache. When his thumb finds its way under my shirt and grazes the skin just above my jeans, my heart skips a beat. I swallow hard, trying my best to ignore the heat in his stare.

The shuffling at the front door is a welcome break from the awkwardness of the moment. Our slumber party has caused weirdness in our newfound friendship. Last night was light and friendly, but this morning, you can cut the tension with a knife. The set of his jaw tells me he feels it too. I think we both liked it a little too much. "Wait here."

"Hey, Mommy!" Shay runs into the house, wrapping her arms around my middle. I smooth back the thick blond curtain that always seems to hang in her face. It's amazing to me how I can love someone so much who so closely resembles someone I hate.

I push the door closed only to have it bounce open again as Bob walks in behind her. It drives me nuts that he just walks in here as if he still lives here, but without his financial help, Shay and I wouldn't be able to keep the house. I don't have much of a leg to stand on. "Oh, sorry. Thank you again for being open to switching weekends with me. It was a huge help."

He drops her bag on the bench and hovers in the doorway. "Well, one of us had to be a parent."

"What the hell is that supposed to mean? I went to a *wedding,* not Woodstock." I feel my face get hot. Bob always manages to push my buttons, even when I'm trying to be nice. I don't understand why he's so hostile toward me all the time. *He* left *me.* If anything, I should be the one pissing vinegar every time he comes around.

"A wedding that took you away from your daughter on *Halloween.* Maybe someday, you'll stop making Jenny a priority and start being a mother."

I hate when he acts this way, but I loathe it when he does it in front of our daughter. I feel like scratching his eyes out, but I just stand there with my arms crossed over my chest, deflecting his nasty comment. Stooping to his level isn't going to help matters. "Whatever, Bob," I say through gritted teeth. I grab the door and hold it open for him. "Thanks for dropping Shay off. You know the way out." He scowls, grumbling under his breath as he walks out.

He's always looking for a fight, but he won't get one from me. Keeping my cool when he tries to pull the rug out from me only burns him up more. Why exert the energy to fight back when pissing him off is this easy?

Bob isn't someone who's easy to talk to. I can't remember if he was always that way, or if somewhere along the line, he just evolved into this intellectual elitist who was never wrong. Arguing with him is like running on a Stairmaster. It wastes so much breath, but ultimately, it never goes anywhere. It doesn't matter if I have charts and scientific evidence to back up my claims, Bob will never admit when he's wrong, but it doesn't matter. I'll never let Bob get the best of me ever again.

Chapter 27

Kade

HEARING THAT MOTHERFUCKER use that tone on her makes my blood boil. I beat his ass once, and I'll gladly do it again, but for now, I sit tight and listen, sipping my coffee and hoping Doctor Douchebag doesn't give me a reason to walk out there. When Ainsley shoots his ass right down, I smile. *Good for her.*

Footsteps echo on the hardwood floor and get louder as they approach the kitchen. Ainsley comes in with the cutest little Cabbage Patch Doll right at her heels. Her golden hair cuts across her forehead in a thick wave that highlights her enormous brown eyes. Ainsley's eyes. My heart flutters in my chest. She is just as gorgeous as her mother.

"Hey there." I try to keep my voice gentle. I can only imagine what I must look like to her. Most kids look at me like I'm Frankenstein.

"It's okay, sweetie. Don't be shy." Ainsley squats down to her daughter's level. "Shay, this is mommy's friend, Mr. Black. What do we do when we meet new people?"

The kid eyes her mother like she's a mental patient, but she takes a step forward and extends her hand. "Hi, Mr. Black, I'm Shay. It's nice to meet you."

Holy crap, that is the cutest thing I've ever seen in my entire life.

I take her tiny hand in mine and shake it. It's like a doll hand compared to my bear paw. "Hi, Shay. It's nice to meet you, too, but you can call me Kade if it's okay with your mom."

Shay looks at her mom for approval, and Ainsley nods. She goes to the fridge, grabs a mini carton of milk, and climbs up on the stool next to me. "I've seen you before. My mom has pictures of you." Her teensy fingers tear at the carton but can't seem to get it open.

"I might have a few pictures of your mom lying around too." I wink. "May I?" I take the carton from her hands, bending the flimsy cardboard back and forth until the lip pops open. She smiles, showing off an adorable row of gappy white Chiclets I bet drive her perfectionist father crazy.

Ainsley pours herself some coffee then comes around to the other side of the island in front of us, leaning forward on her forearms and holding the mug between her petite hands. It's not until she lifts it to her lips that I notice the bleeding black diamond on the front. "Shay, did Daddy make you breakfast?"

Shay shrugs and sips her milk. "I had a Snickers bar." I can't help but snort even though it's not my place. Her dad blows as a human being and a dentist. Who lets a kid eat candy for breakfast?

Ainsley rolls her eyes. She's thinking the same thing I am, apparently. "A Snickers bar isn't breakfast." She walks to the fridge and tugs the heavy door open. "You want some eggs or something?"

"Gross, no." Shay wrinkles up her nose and knots her little mouth. Her flaxen ponytail flies back and forth with her exaggerated headshake. "Can we go to Dunkin Donuts?"

"No, you're going to overdose on sugar." Ainsley lets the fridge door close and goes to the pantry instead. Boxes of noodles shake like maracas and glass bottles ding against each other as she rifles through the shelves. "This is useless. I have to take

Kade somewhere anyway. Why don't we just stop at the diner on our way back?"

"Yes!" Shay jumps off the stool and throws her milk in the trashcan. "Can Kade come with us?" She slides around the tile floor in her socks like an excited little Chihuahua.

"Maybe next time. I'm sure he has plenty of other things to do today."

What things? I'm supposed to be on a flight home right now, but I'm blowing off everything to hang out in the suburbs. It seems so absurd, but waking up with her this morning was like seeing the ocean for the first time. It was powerful and magnetic. I pulled her in like the tide and held her close.

I've never been in bed with a woman when sex wasn't involved. Not that the thought didn't cross my mind. If she gave me the go-ahead, I would have happily pleased her several times over, but taking it off the table and just lying with her in my arms was still the best feeling I've had in over a year. We may no longer be in bed, but I'm still unwilling to let her go. "I don't mind tagging along. I have nothing planned."

A shadow passes across her face, and for a split second, I feel like I've overstepped my boundaries. Considering how shell-shocked she seemed over me meeting her kid in the first place, she probably doesn't want me tagging along on a family breakfast, but I inadvertently backed her into a corner.

The girls go off in search of their shoes while I hover in the doorway waiting. Halloween decorations still adorn the neighborhood. Pumpkins and mums embellish all the porches, Ainsley's included. A few houses have tombstones and various other décor meant to scare the kids as they go door to door.

A gust of wind blows outside. A whirlwind of red and orange leaves comes to life and pirouette in the crisp, clean air. I inhale and hold it in my lungs before blowing it out. You don't find natural beauty like this in L.A.

Ainsley and Shay meet me outside and immediately wave to the old guy next door raking his yard. Living in California for fifteen years, and I've never even seen my neighbors, let alone waved to one. "Devils versus Rangers tomorrow night. I got five dollars says Rangers crush it," the old man shouts.

"You got yourself a bet, Walt! My money's on the Devils! Rangers are going down!" Ainsley shouts back.

He cackles and slaps his knee. "You see 'em wipe up the ice with Anaheim last week? Cammalleri took a stick to the face, and they still won. Game was brutal!" He stretches out the last word so it comes out more like "broo-tul."

The exchange between Ainsley and her neighbor continues as I stand there in awe. "Sure was! It's that lucky number thirteen! See ya, Walt!"

The man waves again as Ainsley climbs into the front seat of her car. I drop into the passenger side, gawking at her as if I'm seeing her for the very first time.

"You're an ice hockey fan?" I'm shocked. I would never have guessed that in a million years. Then again, her Dance Mom bumper sticker doesn't exactly scream hard rock freak either, so I guess the woman is full of secrets.

"Go Devils." She pumps her little fist with a shy smile.

Loud music blasts through the car when Ainsley turns the key. She turns it to a manageable volume and waits until Shay has safely buckled into her seat before backing out of the driveway.

"Mom shouts at the TV screen. It's so embarrassing," Shay adds.

The mental picture of itty-bitty Ainsley yelling at a ref for a bad call is kind of hot. It reminds me of all the times she's yelled at me for being a cocky asshole—her words, not mine. She's feisty. I like that. "You guys ever go to the games?"

Ainsley whips out of the driveway, cutting the steering

wheel with the palm of her hand. "Nah. Bob isn't a fan, and Jenny prefers concerts. It's cool, though. Whatever."

She pulls onto the highway and rides the bumper of a wood wall station wagon, jerks around it at high speed the second she sees an opening, then glides across all three lanes, making a hard right and following it around, gunning it through a yellow light. By the time we hit the diner, I'm gripping the door handle in a white-knuckle grasp and sweating, despite the cool November day. She whips into a parking spot and kills the engine. "You all right?"

I rub a hand down my face and slide it to the back of my neck. "I'm happy to be alive."

"What do you mean?" She smiles.

From the day I met her, I was sure she was perfect in every way. She's smart, funny, beautiful—the list goes on and on. I spent three weeks with her day and night with no reprieve, and I never found one flaw. Until now.

"Sweets, your driving is terrifying."

"Get the hell outta here!" She swings the car door open with a laugh. "I'm an awesome driver."

"Yeah, okay Evel Knievel." I open the door and get out. "I'm driving us home."

She gives me a dismissive wave and steps out of the car. Shay runs ahead as Ainsley and I walk side by side up to the path. Clutching my heart with one hand, I hold the door open for the girls to walk through. My stay in New Jersey has been super eye opening so far, but something tells me my wild ride is just beginning.

Chapter 28

Ainsley

EXCITEMENT ROLLS THROUGH my stomach at the sight of Kade's rental car waiting in front of my house. Music booms from the speakers. His hands pound imaginary drums, and his deep voice bellows through the car windows. I can't help but smile. I'm getting a private rock concert in my own driveway.

His eyes open, and he immediately stops when he sees me watching, a stupid grin spreading across his face. Do I detect a slight flush on his cheeks? I didn't think embarrassment was an emotion in his repertoire.

"Don't stop on my account. Please continue." I laugh as he gets out.

Pressing against me, he scoops me up in his arms and begins singing the song I've been avoiding for the past fifteen or so months.

Her eyes, they cut me to the bone,
I'm weak and dying, all alone.
Drown me in your deep abyss,
Save me with your poison kiss

This time, rather than running from it, I close my eyes and

feel his words wash over me. No growling and no angst-ridden cries, just the rich melodic sound of his voice, his hot breath on my ear, and the enticing smell of his cologne creating a sensory overload I can feel all the way down to my toes.

She tears me open, loves me rotten, puts me back together new.
Embeds herself within my heart,
Bleeds me like a new tattoo

I'm reminded of the first time I saw him on the stage, stalking it, owning it. His thundering howl pierced through the arena, his razor-sharp voice tore me open, leaving me bound and bloody, but wanting more.

Always more.

The music was nothing. It was background noise compared to the man who was pulling me in with his gravitational energy. He crouched like a tiger, pushed back a sweaty swatch of raven hair as he glanced at me from the stage, and I was done.

He finishes his song and whispers hoarsely in my ear, "I finally got my wish."

"What wish is that?" I reply, threading my hands behind his back, and looking up at him in the dim light of the evening.

"To sing you the song I wrote for you."

My heart jumps, and for a split second, I feel dizzy, but I hide the emotion from sight, not wanting him to know how those few little lines have affected me. "In Ainsley's Eyes" was supposed to be his tribute to me at the festival, and if I hadn't fled back home with my tail between my legs, I would have heard it that day.

I slip away from his grasp and walk up to the door. Kade follows close behind, his eyes fixed on me so hard I can feel the fibers of my shirt starting to singe. We're suspended in this weird limbo between friends and something else. In pure Kade fashion, he's not minced words about his intentions, while I continue to walk a fine line between telling him to go home and climbing him like a tree.

The smell of pot roast in the slow cooker wafts in from the kitchen as I open the door, filling the entire house with its savory aroma. "You cooked for me?"

"It's really nothing special," I say, preparing to set the table. "When I invited you to dinner, what did you expect?"

He smiles, taking the plates, forks, and knives from my hands and setting them out side by side on the island. "I guess I planned on taking you out."

We move about the kitchen in seamless synchronicity, as if this mindless routine is something we do every day, and I'm a little stunned by how relaxed it feels.

"You eat out all the time. Thought you'd appreciate a home-cooked meal for once," I reply as I slide a bottle of red from the wine rack then search the drawer for a corkscrew.

Kade's hands land on my shoulders, and I freeze. When his thumbs begin rubbing in small, firm circles, a quiet moan escapes my lips. "I do," he says in my ear. My head falls to the side as his lips find my neck. "But I really love eating out, too." The innuendo doesn't go unnoticed. Hormones stifle my breath and hold me rigid, filling my center with wetness and haunting memories of Kade's mouth on my body.

My palms press into the counter, leaving droplets of moisture on the cool granite. I force myself to stay upright and not melt into the awesome heat of his body. "Let me handle this, and go relax." His hands slide off my shoulders and trail down each of my arms, leaving a field of goose bumps in their wake.

With the bottle in one hand and corkscrew in the other, he takes a step back. My skin is instantly cold, but my blood boils like lava. I can barely hear him pouring the wine over the sound of my drumming heartbeat. On second thought, wine might be a bad idea. My head is spinning enough without it.

I turn and catch his gaze as he pushes out the stool and pats the seat. Complying with his silent demand, I park my butt. "It's all good, sweets. You worked. You cooked. I'll serve."

His hands cup my face. The hanging pendant lights glint off his sapphire eyes, causing them to sparkle as he leans in close. I wet my lips, expecting him to press his mouth against mine, but it drops to my forehead, and he walks away to fill the serving dish on the counter.

The breath I was holding flows from my lungs as I deflate. *I'm an idiot.* Less than a week ago, he kissed me and I chewed his ass out. Today, the guy barely touches me, and I'm ready to jump off the stool and mount him in my kitchen. My libido is an out of control roller coaster with Sybil at the switch.

He comes back to the table carrying the dish and sets it down in front of me. The meat, potatoes, and vegetables are separated into neat little piles on the platter. The sight of it combined with my raging hormones causes a bubble of nervous laughter to rise up out of nowhere.

"What's so funny?"

"It's just . . . this. All of this." I wave my palms over the entire scene at the island. He looks at me as if I've lost my mind. "I guess I just realized how insane this is. I'm being served pot roast by Kade Black. In my own house!"

"I'm just a man, A. An ordinary guy with an extraordinary job. That's all." His mouth sets in a thin line.

I cover his hand with mine, worried that I touched a nerve. "You are far more extraordinary than you think. The job is insignificant."

"It's not, though. No one is interested in who I am. They only care about what I do or how I look." He pulls his hand away and drops it to his lap. "I want you to see me, Ainsley. The real me."

It never occurred to me how difficult being him must be. He's always in the public eye, forced to act a certain way because that's what people expect. I understand what he means when he says he's "just a man," but he must know he's more than that to me. "You stopped being that guy a long time ago. But I'll never see you as ordinary. You're too special for that." I touch his cheek and his hand covers mine.

His long fingers wrap around my wrist, pulling me off the stool. "I think you're pretty special, too, sweets."

My body sags against his and curls into his embrace, allowing his warmth to surround me like a blanket. He feels so damn good, and I don't want him to let go, but I pull away anyway. It's all too much. He still overwhelms me. Over a year has passed and nothing has changed for me. The tiniest slip up and I'll be right back there again.

I settle into my seat, missing his strong arms already. "C'mon, let's eat."

Chapter 29

Kade

I RING AINSLEY'S doorbell and my heart somersaults into my throat when she answers. A crown of curls adorns her head, and a thin white sweater clings to her figure in all the right places. I'm at a loss for words, and that never happens.

"Is something wrong?"

I blink and shake some blood back into my brain. "You're gorgeous."

She rolls her eyes at me and clicks her tongue. "You're crazy! Come in." Taking my hand, she pulls me over the threshold. "I had no idea what to wear since you insist on being so secretive."

When I told Ainsley I had a surprise for her, she spent the next few days trying to figure out what it is. I could have just told her, but watching her sweat it out was far too much fun.

I wait patiently while she pulls her tall black boots over her skinny jeans. The same ones she had on the night we met. Images of her wearing nothing but those boots assault my brain. Her legs wrapped so tight around me I still feel the soft leather rubbing against my ass and the heels scratching at my skin.

"Well, now I'm almost sorry I brought you this." I raise my hand letting the white plastic bag dangle from my fingertips. With an arched brow, she pokes a finger in the bag and peeks inside.

The bold red fabric unfolds in her petite hands as she holds it up in front of her. "It's a Devils Jersey." She looks at it then back at me with pinched brows and puckered lips, trying to decipher what my unusual gift means. I can see the wheels turning in her mind. Her mouth drops into a little 'O' of surprise when she finally gets the hint. "Do you have tickets to the game?"

"Sure do, babe," I reply, my goofy grin stretched ear to ear. Her electric smile is only slightly less amusing than her squeal of delight. That's right. She actually fucking squeals and jumps into my arms.

This was the second best idea I ever had.

"Excited?"

"Ya think?" Her fingers trace the thick white lettering over the back of the Jersey as if it's a major award.

"I wasn't sure who you liked, but I remembered you saying something about thirteen to your neighbor."

"Mike Cammalleri. Lucky number thirteen." Her wide smile fades a bit. "This is awesome, Kade, but are you sure you want to take this risk? I mean they are going to go ballistic at The Rock when they see us."

"Nah, I got it covered. Vic got us seats in the box." My fingertips touch her cheek. "Besides, anything that lights up your face like this would be worth the risk."

She stands on her tiptoes, pulling me down to her level and planting a kiss on my cheek. "Thank you. This means so much to me." I hold her against me, drinking in the sweet smell of her hair against my chest and loving how small she is compared to me. I'm starved for her affection like a lovesick puppy. Lack of sex is affecting my brain. I'm starting to get all mushy.

She slips the jersey over her head, resting a hand on her jutted out hip. The red fabric envelops her little body, hiding it from sight, but the elation on her face makes it worth it. I reply with a thumbs-up and a waggle of my eyebrows and lead her out into the cool November night.

We get to the stadium early and park by the private VIP entrance. Once inside, a guard ushers us through a labyrinth of tunnels under the stadium to get to the luxury box to watch the game in protected solitude. Ainsley's face is expressionless as the guard excuses himself and leaves us alone. I feel like one of those pretentious dicks who think they are above everyone and can't mix with the common folk. That's not me at all. Usually, I try my best to avoid situations like this altogether. "I know this isn't how you envisioned seeing the game. It's weird, I get it."

A hesitant smile spreads across her face as she looks down at the ice from the box above. "This is weird, it's true. But it's also pretty friggin' amazing." She turns to face me, her ass resting against the railing and her legs crossed at the ankles. "I love it. And I love that you put all this together just for me."

"I'd do anything for you."

It's the truth. I wish I could tell her just how much she means to me, but no words could explain how I feel. This is the reason I can't write. There's just too much fighting for control inside my heart and mind, and I'm having trouble categorizing it all.

"You know," she says, changing the subject, "the Prudential Center added a hot new 3D projection system not that long ago. Watch the ice." The entire place goes dark, save for the glowing red pitchfork being carried by the team's mascot. The arena's ice suddenly transforms into a bubbling cauldron of animated lava then morphs into a shelf of cracking blue ice. High-resolution Devils highlights dance across what becomes a giant interactive movie screen. "Pretty cool, huh?"

I nod, impressed by the game's intro, even though I've never really been a big sports guy. I'm aggressive enough without adding more testosterone-fueled hobbies to the mix. That being said, I can watch Ainsley watch this shit all day.

The players skate with grace as they chase the puck with skill and speed. The action on the ice holds her captive. "Skate! Skate! Skate!" she chants as someone from her team takes control and flies toward the goal at the end of the ice. She's wired and animated. The player slaps the puck. The other team's goalie dives in its way, but the tiny black dot sails into the net. A loud air horn blasts through the arena, the crowd below erupts into a discord of cheers, and Ainsley is on her feet in an instant. "Yeah!" Her fist pounds the air, and she claps her hands. "Wooo!"

The ice clears. Neither of us bothers to acknowledge that a Black Diamond song, her song, begins playing as the players take the bench for intermission. With racing breath and shining eyes, she sits back down. Her awestruck grin turns into a scorching smile when she catches me watching. "You're staring."

"Sorry. It's just I'm still kind of in shock that you're an ice hockey fan."

She takes a gulp of her Miller Light and wipes the corner of her mouth with a shrug. The irony doesn't escape me that she chooses to follow such a hostile sport. One of the few that not only allows the players to fight but actually encourages it. Hiding inside her calm exterior is a little badass who gets off on the action.

By the time the game is over, Ainsley is so electrified she's practically glowing. The Devils win, and she's still buzzing with excitement all the way back to her house. We pull into her driveway, but neither of us moves from the car. "Why are you really here?" she asks after a short while.

I turn to look at her in the dark. The lights from the dash illuminate her face, highlighting her cheekbones with a delicate glow. A halo of untamed curls slipped from her messy ponytail and coil sporadically around her hairline. I've always found her beautiful, but I've never seen her quite like this. She captivates me. "I told you, sweets. I'm here for you."

Her gaze drops to her lap, and her mouth turns down. "But you can have your pick of any woman you want."

That may be true, but none of them makes me feel the way she does. Women have been throwing themselves at me since I was still living on the base, but when the band took off, the pussy was unstoppable. I lived in whiskey-fueled, hard rock excess for more years than I care to admit. Women were a disposable commodity, a means to an end, and a nice way to satisfy the itch. Ainsley is different. I don't just want her in my bed; I want her in my life. My finger catches under her chin and her eyes meet mine. "The only one I want is you."

"And Misti Rain." Her lashes flutter, blinking back tears I see building in her dark eyes.

"Misti Rain and I are friends. I never touched her," I reply, taken aback by her comment. Has she been holding on to this the whole time?

"You know what? It doesn't matter," she says, shaking her head. "I've worked too hard, and I finally have my life together. Taking this step back would be illogical."

"Forget logic. What's in your heart?"

She doesn't answer. She just looks away, eyes fixed on the yellow glow of the headlights highlighting the garage door in front of us. "Don't look away. Look at me," I demand, bringing her face back toward mine. "Can't you see I'm crazy about you?" She swallows hard but still doesn't speak. "You have to know that, Ainsley. I've been crazy about you since the day you walked into that fucking banquet hall."

My thumb runs across her cheek and up over her ear. She leans into my hand, nuzzling her soft skin against my rough palm. The movement is subtle, an intimate gesture that shows she may be hearing what I'm trying to say with far too many words. I write for a living, but staring into the eyes of the woman who holds my heart, I'm at a complete loss. "I know you feel the same way, Ainsley. I can see it in your eyes, the way they shine like the sun when you look at me. You're holding me at arm's length because you're afraid to get hurt."

"Seeing you with her tore my heart from my chest, Kade!" She jerks her face away, sitting forward and throwing her shields back up.

"And you think seeing you with *him* was easy for me? *You* forced me to go! *You* needed space to get your shit together! I gave it to you." The blood simmers under the surface of my skin as she continues to stare out the window. She's so goddamned stubborn.

"I just . . . expected you sooner."

When her eyes snap to mine, I see what I've been looking for. That swirling mixture of love and lust, fear and anger. A montage of feelings that culminate our messed-up relationship rolling across her face as I cup the nape of her neck and pull her mouth to mine. Her tongue brushes my lips. I follow her lead, breathing her in, her soft moan filling my lungs and undoing any restraint I was desperately attempting to maintain. "Invite me in, Ainsley," I growl.

"Come in," she says, trailing kisses across my face and down my neck. "Come in my house, come in my bed, come in me."

Her words light me on fire. "Once I get you in that bed, sweets, I'm not holding anything back." My fingers tangle in her hair, jerking her head back and biting her neck as a warning. It elicits a sharp cry that makes my dick jump to attention.

"I'm counting on it," she whispers breathlessly. Her hands fist my hair and bring my face to hers, crushing our lips together in a furious frenzy and melting away her self-control. It's hungry and feral, the kind of kiss that rips you apart and puts you back together again all twisted and crooked. It's pouring out of her. The emotion—the fire, the lust, the longing, all the feelings she'd bottled up and tried to ignore—comes rushing out from her lips and fingertips, in a scalding, biting kiss that completely takes me over.

The soft feel of her body, the taste of her mouth, and the smell of her perfume in the confined space turn me into a man possessed. I grab her rough—too rough—and drag her over the console onto my lap. Ainsley moans, not put off by the harsh move one bit. She grinds her hips, pressing herself against me and biting my ear, still fisting my hair like a madwoman.

I pull open the button on her skinny jeans and wiggle my hand inside. The second my finger grazes her sweet little cunt she slams back on the steering wheel. The horn bounces off the garage doors ahead and echoes into the night. She shifts again to silence it, causing a fraction of space between us just large enough for me to slip my finger past her lips and push inside. "Fuck, baby, you're soaked," I groan.

The idea of pulling myself away from her long enough to get inside the house is agonizing. For a split second, I consider having my way with her right here in the car, but the idea leaves my head as quickly as it entered. This isn't the time for a quickie. When I finally get her upstairs, I'm going to destroy her, and I'm not going to stop until she's a sticky, screaming mess.

"Make me come," she whines. "Don't tease me." Her eyes jam shut as she searches out my lips, devouring them as my fingers dip in and out, each time drawing the wetness up to circle her clit before diving back in again. Urgent moans vibrate against my mouth. She bucks and bites and rides my hand hard. Tremors ripple through her. Her head falls back, exposing her creamy neck as all her muscles tighten and squeeze the life out of my hand. Another horn blast rips into the quiet night, but all I hear is the keening cry ripping from her lungs as she comes apart.

"Out of the car, Ainsley. Now," I growl, flinging the door open and practically pushing her off my lap. She flies out of the car and doesn't wait for me as she unlocks the door.

I'm behind her in an instant, taking her in my arms and throwing her over my shoulder with a smack on her ass. "Kade!" she squeals and kicks her legs as her feet leave the ground. That tiny taste of her only made me more ravenous. I need to hear her scream again, to feel her body go rigid then slack in my arms over and over.

This cat and mouse game has lasted long enough.

Kicking open the bedroom door, I fumble for the lights in the dark then hurl her onto the bed like a side of beef. We tear at each other's clothes, eagerly undressing like horny teenagers getting laid for the first time.

Every moment we've been apart, I've fantasized about this. Thoughts of sinking into her deep and hard, feeling her shatter around me until she can't think straight, have kept me awake at night. But here we are, and I'm the one who can't get a grip on my own thoughts.

Tearing my mouth away, I sit up on my knees. I have to slow down. The spinning in my head rivals the throbbing of my cock, and if I don't relax, I'm going to end up finishing way too fast. Can't have that. No, what I have planned is going to take all night.

She looks up at me from the bed, chewing on her lips and tracing the thick outline in my shorts with blazing eyes. I can't say I blame her. He's quite impressive. Women are either usually fascinated or frightened by the enormity of it, but he and Ainsley are well acquainted.

"What are you waiting for?"

A deep growl rumbles in my chest as the light scratch of her fingernail trails from base to tip. She's toying with me and loving every second of it. "I know what you want, baby. But first,

I'm gonna lick that sweet pussy until you're begging to have me inside you."

I taste her skin from neck to navel, and notice for the first time since I got her clothes off that her panties match her bra. My lips curl into a devious smile. Matching lingerie is a clear-cut sign: she expected this.

The lacy fabric is drenched with her arousal. I peel it off her hips and bring the tiny scrap to my face, inhaling the sweet smell of nectar, salt, and citrus all mingled with the scent of her hair, skin, and sweat. It's intoxicating and heady in all the best ways, and I'm starved for it.

Licking my lips, I drop my mouth between her legs. Her back bows, and the throaty satisfied sound she makes nearly rips me in two. I groan against her, close to coming in my boxer briefs from her taste and the view of her bared open in front of me. My tongue swirls inside her as I spread her wide with my thumbs, slow at first, relishing every whimper, every mewl that's uttered from her incredible lips.

" . . . Kade . . . oh, my God . . . your mouth . . . uuh-hh . . . Harderharderharder . . ." Her words jumble together in one long, ragged sentence. She's hot and wet, gyrating against my face as my finger pierces her decadent flesh again. Her body sucks it in, clenching tight as a fist. So fucking tight. My cock pulses with the anticipation of plunging into her, feeling her constrict around it, but my mouth is too greedy.

" . . . so fucking sweet . . ."

I tease her swollen clit; tonguing it, sucking it, nipping it with my lips until my name falls from her mouth in thick raspy gasps. Her legs clamp around my head and her hands tear at my hair, damn near pulling it out in giant clumps, but I don't want to stop. She's pure sugar. I could eat her out for days and never get enough.

"Kade. . . . please . . ." Her breathy plea turns my already hard dick to molten rock.

"Please what?" I say, adding a second finger and crooking them both deep inside her. A flush creeps across her skin in a gorgeous shade of pink, and her dark eyes flare like two orbs of smoldering charcoal.

"Please fuck me."

Chapter 30

Ainsley

THIS SHOULDN'T BE happening, but blinding need makes it hard to think. Partly because I came so hard the earth stopped rotating, but mostly because Kade is the one who made it happen. Consequences be damned, this feels too damn good to stop.

I'm dying inside. Torn in half by Kade's mouth and hands. The taste of myself on his tongue drives me mad, and I just want more. I need more.

He stalls at my opening. I grasp the firm muscles of his ass in a desperate attempt to pull him in, but he holds firm, teasing my cleft with just the tip as he rains an avalanche of kisses down my neck and chest in the most loving manner possible. "I need to hear you say it, Ainsley. Tell me I'm the only man you want."

"Only you, Kade. It's only ever been you." At least, I think that's what I said. My words come out breathy and incoherent as I allow myself to fall under his spell, giving in to temptation and begging him to take me. I have no idea what tomorrow has in store for us, but right now, it's him and me and this delirious thirst hanging between us that will never be fully quenched.

It's all so familiar. The feel of him pressed between my legs, giving me just a taste, and prolonging the moment until I'm trembling with need. He penetrates me in one slow stretching thrust. The delicious bite of pain from his size and strength causes me to cry out from the utter perfection of it. Tomorrow, I'll be sore. Every move I make will be a reminder of where he's been and how good it was. The steady rhythm of his pelvis moves in time with the cadence of my beating heart.

"Fuck, sweets, I'm broken. You shatter me; you own me."

Dirty talk is nothing new, but this is more than I can handle. I expected a savage animal. A hard bestial pounding that would render me senseless, making me lose myself in the mindless pleasure only he knows how to give. But I find myself lost in his eyes and the possessive feeling of his arms holding me. Each languid thrust pushes to the surface all the feelings I'd buried deep inside.

I feel born again. My skin is charged with energy so profound I can hear it humming all around me. I'm putty in Kade's hands. A ragdoll, soft and pliant, easily controlled and manipulated. He sits up on his knees. Strong arms snake around my back, holding me effortlessly as my fingers clench around his bicep steadying myself on his lap. His hot mouth attacks my breast, flicking my nipple with his tongue and causing it to pebble to an agonizing point before closing his teeth around it.

The pleasure grips hold of my insides and works its way around me like a vine. My world explodes with a cannon shot of bold colorful lightning. I bounce hard on the bed, realizing only then that he's dropped me as I writhe and pant through the most brilliant eruption of my life.

Kade's hand slams against the mattress as he falls forward. I feel his body go rigid. " . . . I love hearing you scream . . ." he grinds out through ragged, urgent breaths.

Satisfaction rolls over me in giant waves of ecstasy, rippling up my spine and drowning me in his embrace as the sound of his voice fucks my ear.

I whimper as he removes himself from me, my oversensitive body feeling the emptiness immediately. Then . . .

The cuddles.

Tears well in my eyes the second his big body lovingly curls around mine. I missed this. His hugs, his kisses, his warmth, his love. All of it. I spent so long pushing him away, and for what? He loves me. We may not have a future, but we have right now, and maybe that's enough.

★ ★ ★

THE ROOM IS pitch black as I rub the sleep from my eyes. Kade's side of the bed is empty. A pang of abandonment hits me in the chest. The fear that he left the moment I fell asleep causes me to sit straight up. Relief washes over me as my eyes adjust to the dark, and I see his clothes are still on the floor. But the sheets are so cold, my curiosity gets the best of me. Slipping out of bed, I wrap myself in a blanket and pad down the stairs.

A single light shining from my dining room draws me in, but seeing him stops me in my tracks. His head rests in his large hand. Thick tufts of black hair poke haphazardly through his long fingers. The elegant curve of his back showcases every sturdy muscle, and his broad shoulder ripples as his forearm glides over the dark wood.

I take a few tentative steps forward, careful not to make a sound and spook the magnificent creature hunched over my table. His body becomes still, and a deep hum fills the quiet house. It's melodic and graceful. It pulls me in closer, until the humming stops and his arm starts its furious pace over. Over his shoulder, I spot a corner of white and realize he's writing. Line after line of scrawling blue ink fills the page in front of him in handwriting that's as wild and chaotic as he is.

Unwilling to disturb his process, I turn to retreat back to my room, but he lifts his head and catches me before I can make a quick escape. "Did I wake you?"

The sound of his voice brings me back. The bright light from above creates an angelic effect, making him look almost ghostly. His tattoos appear gray, and his brilliant blue irises shine against his whited-out skin. He reaches for me, and for a moment, I'm afraid. Going to him now would tug the tiny thread of restraint I have left, sealing me to him forever and sending my soul along with him when he returns to his life. But turning away from him isn't something I'm capable of doing twice.

My fingers thread with his as he pulls me into the space between his legs. "No, you didn't wake me," I say, pushing the hair off his forehead. His eyes drift closed, his long lashes casting a shadow over the tiny freckles on his cheekbones. My thumb caresses the dark eyebrows that frame his gorgeous eyes and skims down the straight slope of his nose. It traces the outline of his mouth, dipping into the perfect Cupid's bow I love so much, and circles around under his plump bottom lip, finally coming to rest on his angular jaw. The day-old stubble is a reminder that he's all man, but hiding just beneath the surface is a strange boy-like feature you wouldn't normally see unless he's let his guard down enough to show it.

His eyes flutter open. Wild curls bounce down my back and over my bare shoulders when he pulls out the band that was holding my tresses at bay. His hand glides down my messy tendrils past the line of my neck and disappears inside the blanket. Chills break out on my skin as his fingertips roll down my bare back. Lips sweep over my collarbone and up my neck soft and slow.

Every encounter we've had was hurried and intense. We usually tear into each other in a frenzied rush, clawing and biting in a sweaty mass of slapping skin on skin. This is something completely different. We explore each other with our hands and mouths, enjoying one another instead of racing to climax like animals. This slow-paced, erotic intimacy is unexpected and satisfying in a way I never dreamed possible.

He lifts me in his arms and carries me upstairs. The view of the sky through my bedroom window changes from black to blue as the sun begins to rise. My hands roam his torso, reading every peak and valley of his chest and stomach like braille, committing them to memory and savoring the feel of his warmth under my trembling palms.

Light sluices through the blinds, adding a third dimension to the tattoos that run the length of his arms and pecs, bold swirling patterns shrouded in darkness against smooth skin. His body isn't just beautiful; it's a work of art.

Nagging thoughts of him with other women float from the recesses of my mind. The angel on one shoulder is cooing in post-coital bliss, but that nasty little devil on the other keeps telling me that rock stars are notorious for sleeping around. "How are we gonna do this, Kade?"

He rolls over and sits up on the edge of the bed. "We'll make it work."

I sit up under the sheet, pulling my knees to my chest. Last night was amazing and surreal. Having a normal life with Kade by my side would be my greatest fantasy, but I'm too much of a realist to hold onto the hope of that. It's a fairy tale, and fairy tales aren't real.

Jealousy still sits in my gut like a third person in the room. Kade's a good man, but my heart is still too brittle to be able to handle a guy like him. I'll always be wondering what he's doing in California, and who he's doing it with. I can't help it. Bob's affair has jaded me to the point of no return. "But your life is three thousand miles away."

He twists around to face me. "My life is with you," he says, his knuckles raking across my cheek. "I'll find a way. I promise."

Chapter 31

Kade

I BANG AROUND the kitchen looking in various cabinets for the things I need. Everything in this house is just so . . . her. The plain white cabinets are a stark contrast to the sleek onyx granite. The curtain above the small window adds bold splashes of lime green, bright pink, and yellow. She even has a green teakettle on the stove. The room is a unique juxtaposition of her personality—simple, sexy, and fun.

After assembling my ingredients, I get to work. Last night was unbelievable. Her body responded to my touch as if no time had passed at all. She was uninhibited and free, but this morning her walls went up, and she was guarded again. I don't know what else to do to ease her mind about us. Being here only confirmed what I already know. Ainsley's it. The last woman I want for the rest of my life.

I throw freshly chopped peppers into a bowl, and then begin cracking eggs one after another as the pan heats in front of me. Growing up, I was taught that hard work is the key to a successful life, even though my father's idea of hard work bordered on slave labor. He got me a job working at the mess hall before school when I was thirteen. Breakfast is the only food I ever learned how to make, but I can make one good enough to feed an army. Literally.

Ainsley's quiet footsteps pad down the stairs. From this spot, I can see her as she comes down the hall toward me. Her wild hair is wet from a shower, framing the shy smile on her gorgeous face. A shuffling at the front door turns her attention, and Shay comes bursting through like the noisy little pixie she is. "Hey, Mom!"

"Hey, sweetie! You're early! You okay?" Ainsley asks, greeting her daughter with a hug and a kiss.

"Yep! Cami's sick. Hey, Kade!" Shay waves in my direction on the way up to her room as the ex-husband pushes his way through the front door right behind her.

"Cami has another migraine. You know Shay. She's so . . ."

Dr. Douchebag spots me in the kitchen, and the Wonder Woman backpack in his meaty fist falls to the floor. "What the hell is he doing here?" He stomps further into the house, pointing his stubby finger, unsuccessfully trying to intimidate me with his bulldog sneer.

"Bob, the company I keep is none of your concern."

Ainsley steps into the space between the hall and the kitchen, blocking the path that leads directly to where I'm standing. I watch in slow motion as his arm sweeps her aside; she loses her footing and her back smacks hard into the wall.

I see red. My blood burns with testosterone-fueled fire. The last time I came face to face with this fucker I almost killed him, and I'm thirty seconds from being a repeat offender. My fingers grip the counter to keep myself from charging in there and ripping him apart limb from limb.

If I lose my shit now, I'll lose her for good.

My heart hammers against my ribcage. My teeth are clenched and my nostrils flared, but I stay fixed to the floor, knowing once I get my hands on him, there's no turning back.

"Not my concern?" he growls at her, red faced. "It's absolutely my concern! He's in *my* house! Around *my* daughter! I pay the mortgage. I make the decisions about what goes on inside!" She's pinned to the wall as he hovers over her, exerting his dominance and signing his own death warrant. "It was only a matter of time before you became a dirty slut, just like your friend Jenny!"

My arm moves on its own, needing something to break. A puddle of yellow and green splatters across the clean tile floor as the bowl flies off the counter and smashes to the ground. I stand poised in the doorway, my hands balled into twitching fists of fury. My muscles are tense; my chest is heaving. There's a target on this guy's face, but I'm still holding back. His outline becomes fuzzy as my vision blurs with unmitigated rage. I can feel my pulse pounding in my temples, right above where my jaw is clenched so tight I could grind my teeth to powder if I moved them just a fraction. He thinks he's tough, but he has no idea who he's messing with.

A little blond head comes bouncing into view, calming my bloodlust immediately. "Mommy?" Shay's eyes are saucers of surprise as she stands in the hallway watching the horrifying scene unfold.

"Go on up to your room, Shay. Mommy and Daddy are having a grown-up conversation."

Ainsley's shaky voice instills little confidence in her daughter. Shay stays where she is, frowning at her father. The fucktard has the decency to back away from his cowering ex-wife, but he doesn't have enough sense to comfort his scared kid.

I walk past Bob and Ainsley and squat down to Shay's level. "Why don't we go play out back? Give Mom and Dad some privacy?" I hold out my hand and wait for her to take it, offering up the most reassuring smile I can muster. She glances at her mother for approval then back at me before her tiny fingers close around my thumb. Grabbing her jacket from the bench, I follow her lead out the back door. Bob's barking continues as the glass slides closed, putting a wall between Shay and her parents.

She walks through the yard kicking the dirt, and I realize that I have no idea what to do with her. "You wanna go on the swings or something?"

"I'm almost ten; I'm too old for swings," she says plopping down in a chair by the patio set with a frown. "I know you just brought me out here because my dad is yelling at my mom again." Her use of the word *again* makes me openly cringe. Ainsley has told me a few stories about how controlling her ex-husband was, but I had no idea her situation was this bad. No wonder she's afraid of falling in love again.

"Okay, I'll admit there's some truth to that." I push myself off the wall of the house and take a seat next to her, leaning my elbows on my knees. Next to her elfin frame, I feel like a giant. This kid could star in Keebler commercials. She's nine, but she's no bigger than a six-year-old. "But I also thought maybe we could be friends."

A gust of wind blows through the yard, kicking up a pile of fallen leaves and lifting Shay's hair off her forehead. "I don't know you well enough to be your friend."

She's right. Shay doesn't know me from Adam. She's probably taken all kinds of classes in school about stranger danger and shit. I'd love to get to know her better, but at this point, I'm pretty much just the creepy old dude who hangs out with her mom.

"Okay then. Let's get to know each other. Ever play Rock, Paper, Scissors, Truth?" I ask, thinking on my feet.

"No," she replies with a dramatic shake of her head. "How do you play?"

"It's really easy." A tiny crease forms between her barely visible brows as I explain the rules of the only game I remember from my childhood, adding one small caveat. " . . . and every time you win, I'll let you ask me a question. But if you lose, I ask you one. Deal?"

She eyes me suspiciously, no doubt seeing right through me. Kids are like dogs—they can smell your fear. "Deal."

"Okay, now hold up your fist like this." I raise my fist out in front of me, and she follows my action. "Rock, paper, scissors, shoot!" She holds up two little fingers in a V formation, while my palm lies flat. "Scissors beats paper, kiddo. You win."

"You like my mom." It's not a question; it's a statement. She's direct. Gotta give her props for that.

"Your mom is very likable," I say truthfully, holding up my fist a second time. This time, she throws paper, and I throw rock. Her turn to ask another question.

Shay sits back in her chair, cocking her head. "She's pretty, right?"

"Very pretty."

This line of questioning is headed in a direction I hadn't anticipated. I assumed she was going to ask me kid-type questions, like what my favorite color was. Digging into my relationship with her mother seems so out of character for a kid her age. Then again, as she so aptly pointed out, she *is* almost ten.

Without missing a beat, she lifts her fist, and I follow suit, throwing out scissors to her rock. She's kicking my ass.

"Are you my mom's boyfriend?" And there it is. The question she's been dying to ask.

She looks up at me with the biggest eyes I've ever seen on another person in my life. Her facial expression is one I've seen on Ainsley a bunch of times. She wants an answer, and she isn't going to back down until she gets it.

In hindsight, I should have expected this. She's a smart girl. It's a natural assumption, but I still wasn't prepared for her to ask. "That's tough to answer, kiddo. You might wanna talk to your mom about that." I raise my fist hoping it's enough to end the inquisition, but her hands remain in her lap. "Do you want to be?"

"That's two questions."

"Yeah, but you passed the buck on the first one."

Dammit.

I purse my lips to the side, considering what to say. Aren't little girls supposed to talk about ponies and rainbows and shit? Forget commercials, she's headed straight to the FBI.

I'm sweating under the hot lights of her stare, but I don't want to blow her off. Her opinion of me is too important. "Honestly? Yes, I do."

"You should ask her. I bet she would say yes."

"I'm not sure it's that easy, kid. Maybe you can put in a good word for me?" I say with a wink. Her ponytail flaps behind her head when she nods. I mentally wipe my brow preparing for her next attack. In my wildest dreams, I never would have anticipated sweating while being interrogated by a fourth grader.

"Seeing my mom lonely makes me sad. I don't want her to be alone anymore."

Goose bumps rise on my arms. There's no way for me to respond to that. I don't want Ainsley to be alone anymore either, but I can't force her to be with me. She needs to come to that decision on her own.

We play a few more rounds before the door slides open, and Ainsley walks out looking like she's been hit by a bus. "You guys having fun out here?"

"Yeah! I'm beating Kade's butt in Rock, Paper, Scissors, Truth! It's an educational game."

"That's awesome, babe. Why don't you go on in now and unpack your bag upstairs, okay?"

Shay waves to me and bounds back into the house. The second she's inside, Ainsley falls against me, unloading a river of tears onto my shirt. "I'm so embarrassed."

"You have nothing to be embarrassed about, A. You did nothing wrong."

She shakes like a leaf in my arms, and I can't tell if it's because she's cold or afraid. I assume it's both and hold her tighter against me.

"I did everything wrong!" she cries, pulling away and wiping her face with her sleeve-covered hands. "I married that jerkoff. I produced a child who has to be raised in this fucked-up situation, and I'm powerless to protect her from it." She flops down into the patio chair Shay was sitting in, dropping her head into her hands. "I'm the worst mother ever."

"Hey, hey!" I kneel in front of her and take her freezing hands in mine. "I never want to hear you say that again. You are an amazing mother, and Shay adores you. This fucked-up situation is not your doing, it's his. Don't ever forget that."

She sucks in a stuttering breath and nods. "He doesn't always act this way. Your presence threatens him."

"No. Stop defending him. His reaction was completely uncalled for."

Hearing her give him the benefit of the doubt makes my skin crawl. He practically assaulted her right in front of me. Hitting me was one thing, but pushing her around is pathetic. "There is no excuse for him ever putting his hands on you. I can't be held accountable for my actions if it happens again."

She covers her face with her hands and sighs. "He came to tell me he wanted me back."

I pull her hands away, unsure I heard her correctly. "Come again?"

"The day of the festival in Tuxedo, the day you came after me. The reason he came over was to tell me he wanted me back." Another cold gust of wind blows through the yard, tossing her hair around her face. She runs her hands through it, securing it behind her ears, but the defiant curls pop right back out again. "He didn't expect to find you in my bed, and he certainly didn't expect me to tell him no."

It makes sense. He realized too late what he lost and assumed I was to blame. I think about how much it hurt seeing Ainsley dancing with that puny Australian dude, and I almost feel bad for the guy. Almost. "Turns out you broke both our hearts that day."

Today started with such high hopes and fell to hell in the blink of an eye. The intense buzz I felt earlier is completely gone, replaced by the nagging feeling that my presence here is making her life harder than it has to be. "Should I go?"

"No," she says, resting her hands on my jaw. "But you should clean up the mess you made in my kitchen." She smiles through her tears, and I hug her against me. Her body is warm against mine, despite the freezing November morning, and restores my faith that everything is going to work out.

Chapter 32

Ainsley

THE DOORBELL STARTLES me as I sit hunched over the open netbook on my counter, wheedling away at the huge pile of bills next to me. "Come in!" I shout, plugging numbers into my bank's website at a furious pace.

I'd casually mentioned to Kade that Wednesdays was scheduled weekly visitation for Bob and Shay, and before he left on Sunday afternoon, he kissed me and said, "See you Wednesday." In hindsight, I should have seen that one coming.

It's been three days, and my embarrassment over Bob's behavior hasn't subsided one bit. I hate myself for letting him treat me that way for so many years. Throughout my marriage, I tiptoed around him, always afraid anything I said or did would send him into a flying rampage of insults and condescension. A stupid naïve fool, I meekly carried out every order my husband gave, took every criticism, every putdown, and every push, shove, and dismissive eye roll for fear that his wrath would be much worse if I didn't. Kade had a front-row seat to the whole gamut, and he handled it with such dignity instead of hulking out like I knew he wanted to.

"Honey, I'm home!" he jokes, closing the door behind him. The sound of heavy footsteps thumps on the floor as he walks toward the kitchen. My gaze stays fixed on the mini laptop until his presence fills my peripheral vision. It tears my attention from the screen to the mouthwatering man leaning against the doorframe.

I focus first on his boots. Steel toe, military-edition shit kickers that are so big they could probably house a litter of kittens when they aren't covering his huge feet. Then I draw my eyes up past his jeans, loose around the ankles but deliciously snug around his powerful thighs and ass. A black T-shirt stretches across his broad chest, and a bottle of Pinot hangs at his side, clutched between two long fingers. His raven hair is wild and messy, like he took a shower and forgot to comb it. A look that most people couldn't get away with but for some reason looks sexy as hell on him. He's like the poster child for debauchery and, after last weekend's nonsense, is the man of my dreams right now.

After Bob stormed out of the house, I watched Kade and Shay through the window in the kitchen. It's amazing how a man so big and intimidating, a man who can cause so much destruction and harm using nothing but his fists, can be so gentle and sweet with my little girl. He stayed hunched down to her level, as if not wanting to frighten her with his size, comforting her, trying to help her forget that her father was inside foaming at the mouth like a rabid animal. Whenever my mind drifts back to his easy smile and her excitement over their silly little game, tiny chills break out on my skin.

Kade sets the bottle on the counter next to me, nuzzling my neck and breathing me in. "How was your day, sweets?"

"It's getting better."

I swivel the stool around to face him, tangling my fist in the neck of his shirt, and pulling his lips to mine. Hormones assault my body like a home invasion. His tongue edges along my lips, and I don't bother to fight it, accepting it into my mouth and hooking my leg around him as he leans over me. Saturday night hasn't been far from my thoughts in days, but seeing him now brings the memory front and center.

He pulls me to the edge of the stool and trails his hand down my cotton-covered thigh, making me squirm under the teasing touch of his fingers. I moan against his mouth. Warmth spreads from my belly to the area he's fondling between my legs. "Forget the takeout. Let me eat you for dinner instead."

"Deal." My leg falls, and I sit up straighter on the stool. "But I have to pay these bills first," I add, spinning back around to the stack of envelopes and snatching the top one. If I don't get this done now, I'll never come back to it later.

Kade glides around the kitchen unassisted, grabbing a wine glass from the cabinet, heaping it full of ice just the way I like, then filling it with a heavy-handed pour. People don't generally drink wine with ice. I'm impressed he remembered. The corners of my mouth kick up in a knowing grin as he slides it in front of me. If I didn't know better, I'd say he was trying to get me tipsy.

He grabs a beer from the fridge next, popping the top and sitting on the stool in front of me. My entire body reacts as I watch him bring the bottle to his lips and take a sip. His Adam's apple bobs as the cold liquid goes down his throat.

"It's getting cold out there. You ever light that fireplace in the family room?" He shivers and licks some residual foam off his luscious bottom lip.

I reply with a snort. It's only November and California boy is already cold. "Yeah, I do. There's a pile of wood out back that needs to be split. I keep forgetting to hire someone to do it."

He leans back on the stool, holding the edge of the counter and craning his neck as he peers out the glass slider. There are giant logs piled up by the shed, the remnants of a fallen tree from last summer's storm. "Don't pay someone for that. I'll take care of it."

A sheen of sweat breaks out on my chest just thinking about Kade in a flannel shirt wielding an ax. It definitely brings new meaning to the term *lumbersexual.*

Everything about him is sexual.

My fingers clack along the keyboard, pushing the thought from my lust-addled mind as I make the payment for my electric bill then move on to the next one. We can play Lumberjack later. Right now, I have adult business to take care of. I tear it open without reading the address on the front, dying to get through this monotonous task and onto more pressing matters. I read the letter and feel like I'm going to pass out.

"You all right?" Kade's brows clip together with worry, but the typewritten words begin dancing on the page, making them impossible to read. I'm suffocating, trying to find breath that's virtually disappeared from my lungs. My hands are shaking so hard, the letter slides from my fingers and flutters to my lap. "A. What's going on? You're scaring me."

"He's suing me," I croak out over my dry throat.

"What?" Kade's face twists up in confusion. "Who?"

The severity of the situation finally sinks in. I grab the letter from my lap and slam it down on the countertop. "The bastard is suing me!" I shout, leaping off the stool and stomping back and forth through the kitchen. "That jealous, petty, spiteful, piece of shit, scumbag, asshole . . ."

Kade jumps off the stool to grab the letter from the counter. "Who's suing you?" His eyes skim the paper as I continue my furious pacing, choking an imaginary throat in midair. "That motherfucker!" He turns and latches on to my forearm. "He can't do this, can he? This is ridiculous."

"He can, and he is."

My anger instantly switches to fear. Tears shoot out of my eyes and cascade down my face as I slide down the fridge and crumple into a ball on the cold tile floor. Gasping for breath, I bury my face in my hands. "He can't take her from me, Kade. I can't let him take her."

Kade sits next to me, pulling me close and resting my head against his chest. "He's not going take to Shay from you. He'll never win this case. It's absurd," he says, gently stroking my hair and back with both hands.

When Bob left me, I was a mess. There were days when I found it hard to even get out of bed, leaving Shay to mill about the house watching cartoons alone. Just a few days after the divorce was final, I ran off tour with a rock band and started a steamy love affair with the temperamental lead singer—the very one I am currently having casual sex with under the very same roof Shay resides in. I dropped the ball on all her after-school activities, choosing to focus on my career, a job that keeps me away from home long hours commuting back and forth to the city. He has plenty to build a case on, and any lawyer will be able to spin it to prove Shay's best interest doesn't lie with me. "I am an unfit mother. Just like he says."

"Ainsley, listen to me," Kade says, drying my tears with the pads of his thumbs. "Bob doesn't want Shay. He wants to hurt you." Kade swings his arm up, grabbing a napkin from the holder. "He can't touch you with his hands. All he's done is find a legal way to beat you up this time."

My body sags against his arm as we sit together on the floor. I have no more tears left. I feel empty. As usual, Bob got the last word. If I lose Shay, I lose everything.

Chapter 33

Kade

"THIS IS SILLY. I can't see how this is going to make me feel any better."

Ainsley stands in front of the black hanging bag at the hotel gym. I held her on the floor of her kitchen for a while, but a man can only handle so much crying before he feels the need to fix it. I know exactly what she needs—a jolt of adrenaline.

"It's not silly, A. Trust me." I take her slim shoulders in my hands and turn her toward the bag. "Give it a whack."

She gives the bag a girlie little punch and looks back at me defeated. "Happy?"

"No, do it again," I say rolling my eyes. "Hard, with all your might. Pretend the bag is Bob. What do you want to do to him right now?" I slam my fist against the bag, growling like a bear and letting out a tiny piece of aggression to show her what to do. It jerks hard, and I steady it with my hands waiting for her to follow my instruction. Ainsley turns back toward it and looks it up and down while rubbing her palms together. She curls them into balls and gives the bag a hard jab. "Better! Do it again!"

She throws a second punch then a third and a fourth. The bag barely moves at first, but then I see it. The look.

Determination. The anger starts emanating off her in droves. A high-pitched grunt follows each punch as she unleashes everything into the bag with all her might.

I stand back, holding it tight. Watching the transformation from babe to beast take hold, I'm loving every second of it.

She kicks it, stomps it with the bottom of her little Nike sneaker with a loud *thwap* like she wants to annihilate it, while cursing at it again and again.

"You suck!" *Thwap!*

"Screw you!" *Thwap!*

"I hate you!" *Thwap!*

Sucking in sharp, wheezing breaths, she stops, her volatile eyes roiling with wild, brutish abandon. "Kade," she rasps, licking her dry lips.

I let go of the bag and scoop her up in my arms, smashing her up against the wall in a kiss as hard and ardent as her vehement punching was a few minutes prior. Her legs wrap around my back, holding herself against me as our teeth grate together.

She lost control. She surrendered to her primal instincts. And it's the hottest thing I've seen in my entire life. Ainsley is an animal. Just like I am.

A moan fills my mouth. The entire length of her body is pressed against me so tight I can feel every crevice of her skin through our clothes. "Letting go feels good, doesn't it?" I say against her lips.

"I gotta get one of these bags."

* * *

I'M SORRY I didn't kill that asshole when I had the chance. Bob suing for custody of Shay is a joke. The guy doesn't even feed her breakfast. He's a piece of garbage.

The antiseptic smelling lobby pumps in top forty hits while I sit and wait for my name to be called. My hat is pulled low, and

I purposely didn't shave. I can't let this happen. The notion that this is all my fault festers in my mind like a plague. If I hadn't been at her house on Sunday, would he still be doing this? If I think for one minute that he'll drop this lawsuit, I'll get on the first plane back to California, no matter how my heart breaks.

The door opens, and a squatty woman in pink scrubs comes out. "Jack Mehoff?" The sound of the fake name I gave releases me from my thoughts, and I follow her into the little room. My knee bounces, and my foot taps on the linoleum while I wait. I'm taking a huge risk being here, but I have to try.

"Well, Mr. Mehoff, what seems to be the trouble?"

Bob comes in wearing his little white lab coat and carrying a clipboard. In this professional atmosphere, he looks less like the asshole I know and more like a regular guy. Somewhere deep inside him has to be something good. Something must be there that Ainsley saw and fell in love with. If I can somehow channel that part of him and show him he's wrong about everything, I can fix this situation.

"The only one I see causing trouble around here is you." I pull the hat off my head and clutch it in my fist. His eyes widen when he sees me then narrow into slits. He chucks the clipboard on the counter and crosses his arms over his chest. For a dentist, he's a pretty big guy, but he's short. If I had to guess, I'd say five-foot-seven on a good day. His false bravado is endearing but unnecessary. I'm not here to fight with him. "It's time we had a talk, Bob. Man to man."

"We have nothing to say to one another. Unless you've come here to thank me for not pressing charges last year when you assaulted me."

Everything about this guy makes my skin crawl, from his Ken doll haircut to his fake Malibu tan. Having obviously peaked in college, he's nothing more than an aging frat boy with a Napoleon complex.

"Let's get one thing straight, bro. *You* hit *me* first. I had no beef with you." I take a step forward trying my best to keep my voice calm. "This lawsuit against Ainsley is bogus. What do I have to do to get you to call the dogs off?"

His humorless laugh makes my hands twitch, and I imagine knocking his veneers down his throat. He's baiting me. My lungs fill with air as I count to ten in my head. "There's nothing you can do. It's done. Shay needs a good influence in her life, not some poor starving artist."

I push my fist against my palm and crack my knuckles to keep from hurling it into his smug face. "Would you really call divorcing your wife to screw around with the nanny a good influence?" He opens his mouth to speak, but I raise my palm to silence him. "We can go tit for tat on this all day, but I'll get right to the point. Ainsley doesn't deserve to be dragged through the ringer because of some hang-up you have with me. She's a good woman, and you've hurt her enough." I swallow the bile rising in my throat as I prepare for what I have to say next. "I'm sorry about the way things went down last year. You and I are not all that different, Bob. We're both hot-blooded men who want what we want." I can't believe I'm standing here kissing this guy's ass. The shit we do for love.

"Don't compare yourself to me. You're a pretty face and a set of vocal cords. Without them, you'd be swinging a hammer in a construction site somewhere like the uneducated loser you are." He swipes the clipboard off the counter and tucks it under his arm. "Now, if you'll excuse me, I have *patients* waiting for me."

My long strides put me in front of the door in two steps. I push it closed without taking my eyes off him. His face turns five shades of red as I step into his personal space. "I've been real nice to you, man. I gave you a chance to do the right thing. You get one more shot to show me that you're not a total asshole and drop this lawsuit."

"Or what?"

"I may be an uneducated loser, but the team of lawyers I have at my beck and call are not. I have the power to drag your ass into so much legal dirt, you'll never get yourself out," I seethe. "Every secret you've ever had since preschool will be uncovered and aired. Every filthy piece of dirty laundry you think you've kept hidden will be brought out, and I will not stop until you are completely destroyed."

A drop of saliva shoots through my gritted teeth and lands on his cheek, but he makes no move to wipe it away. "And as for me thanking you for not pressing charges against me? Maybe you should be thanking your lucky stars that I don't march over to your house and tell your pregnant girlfriend the reason you were at Ainsley's house to begin with." Bob's chin falls as I open the door and walk out, leaving him standing in the room.

"I won't need another appointment," I say to the girl at the desk as I breeze past.

Before the glass door behind me is even closed, my phone is out and I've already started dialing. "Vic? I need you to work your magic, bro."

Chapter 34

Ainsley

T ALKED TO BOB. *The guy's a dick. Expect a phone call.*

I peer down at the text message wondering what the hell Kade is talking about.

A phone call from who?

Before I get a response that explains Kade's bizarre message, the phone rings in my hand. "Hello?"

"Hello, this is Maxwell Stein's office calling for Ainsley Daniels," says the pleasant voice on the other end.

"This is Ainsley Daniels."

"Please hold." I wait while the line goes quiet, wondering what this is all about.

Before long, I hear a click, and a quick-talking voice comes through the phone. "Ms. Daniels, Maxwell Stein from Berghammer and Stein, thanks for your patience. I received a call this morning from an associate of mine who represents Black Diamond. I was instructed to give your case special treatment and to handle it personally."

My mouth drops open. *Kade.*

I spent all morning talking to lawyers. Their fees are out of control. I do okay at the gallery but not well enough for a monetary commitment of this magnitude. I thought about asking my parents for a loan, and while it's not completely off the table, I'd rather not have to subject myself to another degrading game of *Ainsley Needs a Husband* with my mother.

"I appreciate that, but I'm not sure I could afford you."

Saying it out loud makes me feel like crap. I'm a grown woman with a child and very little savings. Starting over at thirty was no easy task, and up until now, I've been so proud of the way I've overcome the odds. Leave it to Bob to always know how to make me feel worthless.

"It's all set, Ms. Daniels. My fee has already been taken care of. You have a tentative court date of December ninth. I'd like to meet with you to go over a few things in my office . . ." My mind wanders, and I stop listening. Kade paid my lawyer fee. Why would he do that? I can't possibly accept this from him. " . . . does that work for you?"

"Sure," I blurt out, even though I have no idea what the man just said to me.

"Excellent. We will see you this afternoon at two p.m. Have a good day, Ms. Daniels."

The line disconnects, and I sit there stunned, still gripping the phone in my hand. Kade really is full of surprises, and this one takes the cake. Various parts of my brain play tug of war with each other. The independent side is immediately angered at his assumption that I need his help, but the logical side wants to cry because, as humiliating as it is, he's right. I can't let my pride get in the way. This is an amazing gift, and I'd be a fool to refuse it.

I go outside to collect my thoughts. The city sidewalk is lively with people bustling about. I lift my face to the sky, letting the midday sun shine down on me. The wind is cold, but it's unusually warm for this time of year. I'll never be able to repay Kade for his generosity. He never ceases to amaze me with his kind and giving nature.

A familiar voice stops me as I turn to go back into the

gallery. "A?"

As if I conjured him out of thin air, Kade emerges from the crowd. He's a day past shaving. A ball cap shields his face and giant aviators mask his brilliant eyes, but his massive height and confident stance are a dead giveaway. "You stalkin' me now or what?"

His face splits into a smile. "Not yet. I have an appointment downtown. Is this where you work?"

"It sure is."

"I'll have to come back when I have more time. You can show me some art." He pokes me in the stomach, and I coil back. Even when I feel this low, Kade always manages to put a smile on my face.

"After the phone call I got today, I'm going to owe you more than an art tour. I might have to give you a kidney." I cross my arms around me as the wind blows through my hair. It's sleek and straight today. A piece gets tangled in my eyelashes, and Kade runs his finger down the side of my face, freeing it and tucking it behind my ear as I continue. "You're incredible. Thank you."

"Keep the kidney. I'll settle for love slave." His arms come around me, his body shielding me from another gust of wind. "Don't thank me. Just win this thing and put it behind us."

Us. Hearing him lump our names together as one unit fills my heart with unnerving hope. "I'm going to try my best." I stand on my toes and press a kiss to his lips. "I'll call you later."

The next few hours are spent immersed in work, organizing the latest exhibit at the gallery. I work through lunch, and before I know it, it's time to go.

My stomach is in knots as I hail a cab to the Times Square office. The Law Offices of Berghammer and Stein reside at the top of an enormous professional building. The glass-encased structure gleams as it stretches high into the sky. I feel small inside the law firm's tremendous reception area. The desk extends the length of the room. Beyond it, in large bold letters, reads the names of the partners. On the opposite wall is a serene tropical fish tank recessed inside. My gaze darts around the room, drinking it all in. The monthly rent for an office like this probably equals what I earn in a year.

The receptionist looks about my age, but her Chanel dress and flawless makeup put her on a different level than me. "Ainsley Daniels. I have an appointment with Mr. Stein."

She picks up the phone to alert the office of my presence. "Just one moment. Please have a seat."

I sit on the couch near the tank, feeling insecure in my Liz Claiborne suit. My purse rests on my lap clutched in my hand as I watch the neon-colored fish swim through the water without a care in the world. They float past each other, small fish in a big space, not bothering to acknowledge the other's presence. It's a metaphor for my life. Even with so many people around me, I still feel so utterly alone.

"Ms. Daniels?" The same pleasant voice from the call this morning interrupts my thoughts. "Mr. Stein will see you now. Follow me." She's tall and thin. Her black hair falls into an elegant bob at her shoulders, and her red lipstick is an exact match to her shirt. The lilt in her voice tells me she's not native to the northeast, but from somewhere down south. It's not a slow Georgia drawl like Banger, more of creole twang.

She leads me into the wood-paneled office. It's masculine and modern. The floor-to-ceiling windows showcase a spectacular view of the busy city below. "Right this way."

Maxwell Stein's office is as clean and streamlined as the rest of the place. The rich mahogany desk sits in front of the same floor-to-ceiling windows as the area out front and sitting on a leather chair next to it is Kade. Warmness spreads throughout my chest. I didn't realize how much I wanted him here until I saw him waiting for me.

"Ms. Daniels, come in." Maxwell Stein stands from behind his desk and motions to the empty chair beside Kade. He waits for me to sit then smooths his pink tie down and returns to his seat. "I've been on the phone with Greg Warner, the attorney representing Robert Daniels in the custody case involving the minor Shay Lee Daniels." He opens the manila folder in front of him and peruses the notes inside. "Mr. Daniels is suing you for full custody on the grounds of unfit parenting." A deep crease forms on his forehead as his dark, bushy brows pinch together. He's silent for a moment as he reads the file in front of him. "Ms. Daniels, I'm going to ask you a few questions, and I want them answered honestly."

He threads his fingers together on top of the large desk. "Are you an alcoholic?"

"No."

"Are you a drug addict?"

"No."

"Are you prostituting the streets at night for money?"

An uneasy bubble of nervous laughter escapes my throat. Is this guy for real? "Of course not."

He untangles his fingers and runs them down his goateed face. "These questions are as ridiculous as the case itself, Ms. Daniels. Unfit parenting is extremely difficult to prove unless there are glaring circumstances that can back it up." He waves his hands over the open file on his desk. "All I'm really seeing here is a domestic issue."

I close my eyes and exhale. His words relieve the tension I've been holding in my shoulders since I first read the letter last night. Kade smiles and gives my hand a squeeze, reminding me that I don't have to face this alone.

"Now, that being said, there does seem to be a small issue

between Mr. Daniels and Mr. Black."

Kade drops my hand and bolts up in his seat, his fingers creating divots on the smooth leather arms. "What issue?"

"According to the notes from Mr. Warner, you and Mr. Daniels engaged in a physical altercation in July of last year. In addition, you allegedly came to his place of business and threatened him just this morning."

"That's horseshit!"

Maxwell lifts his hand to silence Kade's outburst. "No charges have been filed, nor are there any witnesses to back up his claims, so at this point, it's all hearsay. But I do need to remind you that your erratic behavior has been making headlines for years. A quick Google search uncovered a recent arrest for assault just last summer." He lifts his hands to make quotes with his fingers. "Your 'bad boy' reputation doesn't bode well for you."

Stricken with the urge to vomit, my hand springs to my mouth. "His arrest last summer was because of me," I whisper.

Memories of that night weigh on my chest to this very day. Initially, Kade's behavior seemed romantic and endearing, but the settling of the dust added a sense of clarity to my otherwise fear-induced mind. Of the multitude of ways he could have handled that situation, fighting and getting arrested hung somewhere close to the bottom.

To say he was a pit bull was an understatement. He defended me like a bear protects her baby cub. Brutal and bloodthirsty. It wasn't enough to simply stop the attack; he had to incapacitate the man within an inch of his life. The thing is, those savage hands that battered a person unconscious are the same ones that are so tender with me and so gentle with my daughter. That maniac in the media isn't him.

Kade is sitting on the edge of his seat now, leaning so far

over he's hovering above Maxwell's desk. "My actions in that scenario were warranted. I will do whatever it takes to protect them."

"Well, in the meantime, maybe it's best if the two of you maintain some distance from each other. At least in public," Maxwell continues. "And don't worry, Ms. Daniels. I'm going to do everything in my power to ensure Shay stays where she belongs."

Chapter 35

Kade

"**A** PRETTY FACE AND a set of vocal cords? He really said that?" Ainsley sits huddled in the booth, warming her hands with her mug as if she's freezing in spite of the broiling heat blowing in the overcrowded diner. I resist the urge to go to her side, to wrap my arm around her and hold her until the tension in her back eases, and her shoulders drop from her ears.

"Yeah." I nod. "Told me without them I'd be a construction worker." I laugh even though the situation is anything but funny. "Am I supposed to find that insulting? I don't get it." I pick up the tiny white cups of creamer and pour them into my coffee one by one while rehashing the whole conversation with Bob down to the very last detail, leaving out the part where he called her a starving artist. That shit is just downright mean. The spoon clangs against the ceramic cup as the color swirls from brown to beige.

"I appreciate you trying, but I could have told you that conversation would have gotten you nowhere. Once Bob digs his heels in, that's it. End of story." She rests her cheek in her hand and leans on the table. The lawyer assured us that everything is going to be fine, but she still looks unconvinced.

I hook my finger into the question mark shaped handle and

lift the cup to my lips. "Yeah, well, figured it was worth a shot." Putting the mug down, I take her hand. "I'm sorry, A. My presence has done nothing but cause issues for you since day one."

I have a bad temper and a worse way of dealing with it. My brawl at the Pizza Castle threw an unwanted spotlight on her overnight. Never stopping to consider the consequences of my actions, I threw a violent tantrum like I always do. I did the same thing with Bob, and I would have gladly pummeled the boyfriend, as well, if given the opportunity.

She shrugs and her mouth turns down in a sad pout. Seeing how badly she's hurting makes me want to go to Bob's house and throttle the shit out of him. I remind myself for the hundredth time that fighting isn't the answer. Maybe if I used my words more and my fists less, we wouldn't be in this nightmare to begin with.

I sigh. It's insane how things can go from great to crap in the blink of an eye. A few days ago, I was on top of the world, but now, I feel like the weight of it is crushing me.

"So tell me more about this event you're putting together at work," I say, changing the subject on purpose. She's been excited about the charity fundraiser. Hopefully, talking about something she likes can distract her from focusing on Dr. Douchebag for a little while.

"The Indie Artist Exhibit. The gallery does it every year. We give a bunch of local artists the opportunity to showcase their work, and in exchange, the proceeds from anything that sells go to charity."

Our waitress comes by and refills Ainsley's empty coffee cup. Buttons with the chubby smiling faces of her grandkids litter her uniform, and her graying hair frays around her face. She drops a handful of creamer cups on the table with a tight-lipped smile before moving on to her next round of customers. "We have a ton of artists signed up so far. It's going to be a great turnout."

"That sounds like a pretty cool event. When is it?"

"The day after Thanksgiving." Ainsley rips open a little blue packet of sweetener and flicks its contents into her cup with her middle finger. She doesn't elaborate, just twirls her spoon around the cup and watches the mini spiral spin in circles.

The air is thick with pensiveness. We sit in uncomfortable silence for what feels like an eternity but is probably only about five minutes before she finally says what I knew was coming. "This isn't going to work, Kade." Her gaze remains fixed on her cup, avoiding eye contact as she rips the heart from my chest while it's still beating.

"We can still see each other. We'll just have to do it on the down low like Max suggested."

"No. We can't see each other anymore. Period."

She's freaking out again. "Don't do this. We're going to fight him, and we're going to win." The desperate sound of my own voice makes my skin crawl. I can't believe what a pussy I've turned into. The label is right. I have gone soft.

Her eyes snap up to mine. "There is no *we* Kade. This is *my* fight, for *my* daughter. You have your own glamorous life in Los Angeles, but mine is here." The ceramic mugs clatter in their saucers as her hands slam down on the table. "Shay is my life, and whatever this is between us is not worth the risk of losing her."

Pieces of my heart flake off in tiny shards around the gaping wound her spiteful words create within me. We're back in the same place we were a year and a half ago. I'm so sick of her using Shay as an excuse to push me away. This isn't about Shay; it's about her fear of letting anyone inside, and I'm done begging her to be with me. I'm Kade *fucking* Black. I could find at least a dozen women in this very diner who would kill to have a piece of me. "At least you have the balls to say it to my face this time. Do I get another fuck for the road too?"

Her eyes narrow into brown slits. "You really are a cocky asshole." She jabs her arm in the strap of her purse and stands from the table. "Go to hell."

She turns on her heel and stomps away, taking the best parts of me with her. I watch her disappear from sight, regretting every word and every arrogant feeling I had over the course of the last ten minutes. My asinine remark hangs in the atmosphere above the table, and I wish that I could grab it with my hands and take it back. Shay may be her life, but she is mine, and I can't let this be the end of us.

Chapter 36

Ainsley

FAT TEARDROPS ROLL relentlessly down my cheeks as I try to think of the best way to break my seven-year-old daughter's heart. I hate Bob for what he's doing, and I hate myself for blindly trusting him. Shay deserves so much better than this.

The shrill alarm rings out on my phone, alerting me that Shay will be here any minute. I wash my face and run outside to greet her. The big yellow bus screeches to a stop, and my heart begins to pound. The warm afternoon sun beats down on the sidewalk. The rhinestones on Shay's shirt blind me as she skips off the bus.

Once inside, I sit her down at the table with a plate of cookies. My hands shake so badly as I pour the milk that I'm worried I'll spill it everywhere. I set the glass down, take the seat next to her, and try to think of a way to explain it in the simplest terms. We agreed to do this together but, as usual, Bob had better things to do.

"Shay. Mommy has something to talk to you about." She munches on her cookies and listens as I speak. "Daddy and Cami aren't going to be here at the house anymore. They are going to a new house together, and you'll visit and see them, but your home is going to be here with me." I reach across the table and take her little hand in mine. "Do you understand, sweetie? Are you okay?"

I expected questions and crying, but none of that occurs. Instead, her answer is something I'll remember for the rest of my life. "It's *okay, Mommy. At least we still have each other."*

★ ★ ★

"MOMMY, CAN WE have pizza tonight?" I look over at my cute little Shay and see my own giant brown eyes staring back at me. Usually, Bob's traits come through fast and strong, overpowering any sign of me that might be hiding inside, but every so often, she makes a face that reminds me so much of myself it's scary.

"Sure, sweetie. That's a great idea." I open the drawer and pull out the stack of takeout menus I keep hidden inside. "Why don't you pick a movie for us while I call it in?"

She runs off into the family room as I reach for the phone. Maxwell has told me to remain positive, so I am. I'm trying to, anyway. He called Bob's lawyer and arranged it so that Bob is no longer granted access to this house without my permission. From now on, when he drops off Shay, he is to wait in the car and allow her to come up to the house alone. This isn't his weekend, so we'll have to wait and see how that works out.

After ordering our food, I go off to the family room to find her. "Did you find something good to watch?"

"Yep! *Spiderman* is coming on in thirty minutes!" Shay is a big girl now, but ever since she was a toddler, she's been obsessed with superheroes. *All* superheroes—Batman, Super Girl, X-Men, The Avengers. Even the bad guys like The Violator and Lex Luther. While all her little friends played with baby dolls and Barbies, Shay would tie a tablecloth to her back and pretend to rescue them from certain doom. It drove Bob nuts, but I love that she marches to the beat of her own drum.

She's always been different from kids her age. More mature. It never occurred to me to question it, but sometimes, I wonder if Bob made her that way. He lacks the patience it takes to deal with a child, always snapping at her for doing normal kid things like talking loud in the house or leaving her toys out. It wasn't enough that we enrolled her in dance at three-years-old; she had to be the best. Only after Bob moved out did she admit she hated it. For four years, she took dance classes with the sole purpose of making her father happy. It's hard to fit into some-one's perfect mold. I speak from experience.

Pulling the blanket off the back of the couch, I plop into the seat next to her. She pulls a corner over her short legs and curls them under her, a mirror image of my preferred sitting position.

Shay may have been graced with Bob's face and hair, but her tiny frame is all me. She's little. There was a time when her small stature worried the hell out of me, but the doctor assured me it's just the way she is. Smaller than everyone, but with a larger than life personality that more than makes up for it. I say she's nine going on nineteen, and it's the absolute truth. Sometimes, she seems so grown up that I forget how young she really is.

I surf the channels looking for something to watch for the next half hour while Shay cuddles up next to me. "Am I going to live with Daddy and Cami?"

A shot hits me straight through the heart, and a slow burn radiates throughout my chest. I've never discussed the case in front of her. She must have heard something at Bob's house. *Goddamn him and his big mouth.*

"Is that what you want?" I suck in a deep breath, preparing myself for the blow of her saying yes. The fear that she'd be happier there than here is one that I've always held onto. She and Cami have always been so close. It's only a matter of time before she decides she likes her better than she likes me.

"I want to stay here. Daddy isn't really around much, and Cami will be too busy with the babies to play with me. Besides, they fight a lot."

The breath I'd been holding trickles out as I tuck her under my arm. "Don't worry. You're staying right here with me." I give her a squeeze, hiding the wetness in my eyes. Potentially lying to my daughter causes a piece of me to feel like it's dying inside. I've never been anything but honest with her, but this trial is not her cross to bear. She doesn't deserve to be saddled with my worries.

My phone chimes on the couch next to me. Kade's face flashes on the screen then disappears in an instant. "You can invite Kade over if you want. I don't mind."

I look over at my daughter with surprise. "Why would I do that?"

Shay shrugs her petite shoulders. "He's nice, and you're always happy when he's around."

Her candor shocks me, and I'm not sure how I'm supposed to take it. "Am I usually grumpy?" I laugh, trying to make it seem like a joke. I never really considered myself an unhappy person, but it worries me that I'm giving off that vibe to my impressionable daughter.

"No! He just makes you seem. . . ." She stares into space, her forehead creasing and her lips pinched together as she thinks of the right words to say. " . . . less sad." She turns back toward the television and continues watching whatever tween show I stopped at.

"It's okay to be sad sometimes."

Even after Bob moved out, Shay remained stoic about the whole thing. He wasn't home that often to begin with, and Cami had been a constant presence in her life since she was a baby. At the time, I just assumed she just didn't understand.

"Yeah. I guess," she replied.

My phone chimes a second time, and, again, I ignore it. After our fight the other day, Kade's been hounding me to talk to him, but I can't. All it will take is one look in those enthralling blue eyes, and he'll end up in my bed like he always does, but there's too much at stake now. Maybe once the case is over, we can pick up where we left off, but for now, I need to keep my distance. Like Maxwell suggested.

I know he cares for me. I see it in every look, feel it in every kiss. He wouldn't still be here if he didn't, but a choice between him and Shay is a no-brainer. She's everything to me, and I can't live without her.

★ ★ ★

"WOW, THAT'S LOW, even for Bob."

Jenny's scowl doesn't detract from the gorgeous sun-kissed glow on her cheeks. After two weeks in Hawaii with her handsome new husband, I'm sure the last thing she wants is to hear more drama about my suburban life.

"Yeah, tell me about it."

My phone is shoved between my bent knees like a channel set diamond as I rest back on the headboard. From this angle, I look like a pig, all chins and nostrils, but it seems fitting to look as shitty as I feel. "Why is Bob doing this to me?"

"Because he's jealous, and Shay is the only thing he has to use against you at this point. You know as well as I do that this is all about control." It's true. Bob has always managed to control every aspect of my life from the day I met him—down to my hair color. My natural color is dark brown with an auburn hue. Bob liked it light, so I kept it light, even though I was never that big of a fan of it.

"You sound like Kade. He pretty much told me the same thing." My chest tightens at the mention of his name. He still hasn't stopped trying to get in touch with me. I keep expecting him to randomly show up. Again.

Jenny chews on the edge of her thumbnail. "Since you brought him up, I feel like I need to tell you that he's been blowing up Banger's phone over you. Why are you shutting him out?"

I throw my arms over my face in dramatic exasperation then fling them off again. "I have to, Jen. Shay is the only thing that matters to me. I can't be with Kade if it means I lose her."

"Lovie, we all get it. Shay is priority one but ignoring him like he's not even there isn't right."

"Well, a few more days of this crap will have him running for the hills." My life is a Lifetime movie of the week. It's either dramatic as hell, or boring enough to make you want to off yourself. There is no in between.

"Ainsley, be serious. The bigger they are, the harder they fall, and that good old boy has fallen hard as hell for you."

Jenny pauses to throw her hair up in a messy ponytail that looks like it belongs on a magazine cover. Meanwhile, the tiny curls around my hairline are foinking all over the place like I've been electrocuted. Yes, I said *foinking,* and I know it's not a word, but it's the best way to describe what I have going on right now. "Speaking of hard, how was he? As good as you remember?"

My cheeks flush so bright I can see them turning red in the tiny square at the bottom of the screen. "It was better than I remember, Jen." I roll to my side, leaning the phone against the headboard and cuddling next to the pillow that still holds the faint smell of him. Just his spicy masculine scent alone stirs up thoughts of our night together. My hands roaming the hard planes of his abs, the rough yet tender way he kissed me, and the passionate look in his eyes when his body finally invaded mine. For one heavenly night, we belonged to each other, and nothing can ever take that away from me. "He must have learned some new tricks in the last year."

"Ains, Kade hasn't been with other women. The last person he slept with was you."

"Oh, please. You really expect me to believe Kade hasn't had sex in . . ." I count the months on my fingers and continue. " . . . sixteen months? The man could barely keep it in his pants for twenty-four hours." Kade admitted he never slept with Misti, but as much as it makes me want to hurl, I imagined there had to be at least a few random women here and there.

"It's true, Ainsley. I'm shocked he didn't blow his load the second you took your pants off." Banger's voice cuts through the room, shocking the hell out of me.

I sit up straight, knocking the pillow to the floor in secret shame. "Jenny, you aren't seriously talking about my sex life in front of Banger."

Light aqua eyes fill the tiny screen on my phone as Banger steps behind Jenny. "Please, like I haven't heard it in person, like, a hundred times. Kade's a complicated guy. That God's gift to the world thing he's got goin' on is an act." I swallow hard and listen as Kade's oldest friend and confidant spills his secrets to me over the World Wide Web. "Inside that big dude is a little boy who's scared, unloved, and unwanted. You ignoring him like this is doing messed-up things to his mind."

Unloved and unwanted? My brows knit together. "What kind of messed-up things?"

"He's not torturing kittens or anything." Banger laughs. "He's torturing himself, though. Big time. I've never seen him like this. He doesn't know how to control this powder keg of emotions piling up inside him, and eventually, it's just going to explode. Trust me when I tell you, the man loves you more than you give him credit for, and that love is as strong and loyal as the man himself."

"I know he does," I whisper, afraid that if I speak full volume, the tears pricking my eyes will spill over. I never meant to hurt Kade, but he doesn't understand. He can't possibly comprehend the pain I've felt every day since that stupid letter showed up. Maybe Bob is just trying to hurt me because he's angry, but what kind of mother would I be if I said "hell with it" and kept seeing Kade knowing that Shay might end up living with a man who only wants her to hurt me? A man who never wanted her to begin with?

As a parent, I would do anything for my child. I'd go hungry, thirsty, or without shelter if it meant one second of happiness for her. I'd take a bullet, even jump in front of a moving train if I knew it would protect her. I love Kade, but I love Shay more.

Chapter 37

Kade

THE CAP ON my head shields me from the cold. I lift the collar on my flannel coat and shove my hands in my pockets as I barrel through the crowded city sidewalk. I had an appointment with some financial people this morning, but all I'm thinking about now is Ainsley.

I didn't hear from her all week. I've apologized to her a hundred times, but she's avoiding me, and I'm losing my mind without her. I sit in my room like a rat in a cage, compulsively fixating on shit that I can't change.

What if I was standing in a different spot the day Bob came barging in her house?

What if I never hit Bob in the first place?

What if I didn't pop off that hateful comment at the diner?

The what-ifs are driving me insane, and I can't take it anymore. I need to see her and make this right. I can't go another second without laying eyes on her face or smelling her skin.

The shrill ringing of the phone startles me out of my thoughts, and I bark into it more gruffly than I intend to. Banger always has a habit of calling me when I'm aggravated. "What?"

"Nice to hear from you, too, dick. I got your messages. What's up?"

The entire story pours out of my mouth start to finish. I'm

not the type of guy who talks feelings with other guys, but I need Banger's backup. Bob's bullshit has thrown a wrench in the works, but I've already set the wheels in motion, and I can't pull back now. "I'm in sad shape dude. I have one song written for the album. I'm letting everyone around me down because I can't get my shit together."

"And you really think keeping Ainsley is going to make everything right for you?"

"Without a doubt, bro."

Being with her the other night flipped a switch in my closed-off mind, and the lyrics burst out of me like a rocket. Since everything fell to hell, I haven't been able to think of a single thing. Some artists need booze or drugs to get their creative juices flowing, but all I need is her. She turns me into a better version of myself.

"She's got a kid, dude. You really ready for that dose of reality?"

I swallow hard. Kids. The word alone is enough to strike fear in the hearts of men like me everywhere. The very idea of being called "daddy" made my skin crawl. I think back to the day I asked Ainsley to give up everything to come back to California to be with me. Being here with her and Shay, seeing how they interact and how special their bond is, made me realize what I was truly asking Ainsley to give up. I only wanted her. Shay wasn't part of the deal. "Yeah. Ready and willing."

"All right. You don't need me telling you this plan is lunacy. I'm sure you already know it. But if you think it'll work, I'm with ya."

Banger always has my back. He, JJ, and Konner. My brothers. We've been through it all together. Everyone told us we were crazy when we dropped out of school and moved to Los Angeles, but we jumped in Konner's shitty old Winnebago and hit the highway. We made the trip cross-country from Georgia to California and never looked back. The four of us lived on a steady diet of dreams, sweat, and determination. Not making it was never an option, and when we hit the strip, our blackened souls shined like diamonds. Our entire foundation was built on risks. What I'm proposing is huge, but I know they'll be on board.

"Thanks, bro. Make sure that wife of yours keeps her yap shut. Just for now."

I stand at the corner watching the countdown on the pedestrian crosswalk sign. The second the electric sign turns from a hand to a person, hordes of people move across the road like locusts.

My brisk pace slows as I approach the gallery, wiping my sweaty palms on my jacket before reaching for the door. I'm jonesing for her like a dope addict who needs a fix. A blast of warm air hits me in the face as I enter. It's larger than it appears from the outside. The natural hardwood floors are buffed to a high gloss shine, and track lighting stretches across the parameters of the ceiling, highlighting the framed works of art that line the soothing off-white walls. It's peaceful and so quiet you can hear a pin drop. It's the antithesis of my chaotic world. No wonder she hated being on tour.

I pull off my hat and run my fingers through my hair as I walk around. My knowledge of art is nil, but I'm mesmerized as I follow the path, drinking it all in as I go. There's so much beauty; it's awe-inspiring.

Turning the corner, I see her in the glass-enclosed room at the end of the hall. She's wearing a charcoal gray dress that hugs her curves all the way down to her knees. A belt surrounds her tiny waist, and her tights are so black I can't tell where they end and where her shoes begin. Her dark hair is swept up in a neat twist behind her head, and the sexy blonde streak is combed across her forehead and tucked behind her ear.

She fits in among the art like she's part of it. Classy and sophisticated. Watching her, surrounded by all this, I feel unworthy. I'm overcome by the notion that she's too good for me. I finally understand what Bob meant by his jab. I'm ignorant trash who has no place in her educated world.

She peers down at the binder in her hands then looks back up. I see her pointing, delegating a task to someone in the room. She turns her head and smiles as someone else grabs her attention. I watch a slender man embrace her. He lingers too long, his hands brushing her bare arm. My mouth goes dry as my fingers mindlessly wring the hat in my hand.

The beard catches my eye. *The Aussie fuck.*

Still smiling at whatever it is he's saying, she points at things around the room as he nods and gestures, all the while his hand is on her back. The urge to do harm explodes through my gut like a bomb. I count to ten in my head, willing myself to calm the hell down, but I can't. The jealous monster inside me is eating its way out, and I need to remove myself from this situation.

My eyes stay fixed on them as I back up slowly. Squeezing my lids shut, my head whips around like I've just witnessed a horror movie as I turn and glide out of the gallery. The dynamic city seems to move in slow motion. Trails appear to lag behind as people pass by. I'm almost running as I make my way to the parking garage, desperately wanting to get off the street and get to a place where I can work off this surge of aggression in solitude.

I drive back to New Jersey on autopilot. When the car finally stops, I take in my surroundings and realize I'm not where I'm supposed to be.

The wind rustles through the leaves in Ainsley's quiet neighborhood. I shouldn't be here, but my hands twitch with inactivity, and I cannot get back in that car without releasing this bottled-up energy.

I wonder if she has an ax.

She's not due home for a few hours. I'll get my mind straight then go back to the hotel.

Chapter 38

Ainsley

ALL I WANT is a glass of wine and my butt on the couch in front of the E! network. I feel like I spent eight solid hours on my feet getting the gallery organized for the fundraiser, and I'm so glad this day is over.

The view of Kade's car in the driveway causes a minor panic attack. He can't be here. I step out of my Jeep, but he's nowhere to be found. A repeated cracking noise rings through the air as I unlock the door and wander through the house, rehearsing in my head various ways to tell him to leave. But the continuous noise calls to me from the backyard.

Kade's back is to me as he stands wide-legged and poised over a log. Powerful thighs tense under his faded dark jeans. A flannel jacket is thrown to the side and lays forgotten on the ground. Biceps bulge and back muscles ripple under his shirt as the ax he holds over his head comes crashing down, sending two chunks of wood falling on either side with a plink.

With little effort, he grabs another piece and wields the ax forcefully again, grunting as it makes contact. He picks up the freshly cut pieces, hurls them into a neat pile next to my shed, and the entire process repeats.

Grunt, crack, plink
Grunt, crack, plink

His strength is mesmerizing. I can't take my eyes off him. Sweat glistens on his arms and drips off his hair onto the damp shirt clinging to his body. He's all man and pure sex wrapped up in one tantalizing package that's all mine for the taking.

The images that swamp my mind aren't just dirty; they're downright pornographic. Every grunt launches an all-out blitzkrieg in my already throbbing core. Forget throwing him out. I'd rather him throw me down and have his way with me.

I saunter through the yard closer to him. "Whatcha doin' here, lumberjack?"

The ax falls from his grasp to the mulch-covered ground by his feet. Black boots crunch on the shards of bark underneath them as he makes a slow turn to face me. His chest expands and contracts, a white cloud blowing from his mouth with every heavy breath he takes. Protruding veins slither around his rigid forearms as the blood pumps through them. Manic eyes, dark as midnight, flash as his gaze penetrates me so hard I can feel it. I've witnessed this look a dozen times. He's morphed from my gentle giant into Crazy Kade.

A low growl rumbles in the back of his throat as a sneer waves across his delicious lips. They crash against mine so fast I lose my balance, but his rough grasp catches me. Our teeth gnash together; his tongue darts into my mouth, kissing my lips like he's punishing them. A heady mix of sweat, wood, and spice cling to his shirt as he holds me tight against him in his burning embrace. I can feel the thick ridge of his erection press against my stomach, and I want it. No, I need it. Bad.

As usual, he reads my thoughts, tearing his mouth from mine and bending me over the enormous pile of lumber while ripping at my already damp tights and pulling them down with my help. He barely has his pants down before plunging every inch into me with one swift movement. I mewl out a mangled mix of sounds from pleasure and pain as the unrelenting thrusting continues. My hands press against the walls of the shed to hold myself taut, accepting everything he has to give. Wood scrapes against my knees, but the sensation of him moving inside me is so great I barely notice.

The blaze builds in my stomach as my climax approaches fast and furious. "Don't stop." My breathy plea floating through the cold air only seems to make him more aggressive. Whatever hurt him, whatever is plaguing his complicated mind, I'll take it, absorb it within me, and free him from the burden of it.

His palm comes down hard on my ass cheek, the sting of it eliciting a joyful cry. He gnarls like an animal in response. This is the rough, tawdry sex I've grown to expect from him. My legs become weak. The world starts to spin. My eyes jam shut as I come apart around him, exploding with the fire of a thousand suns.

The gratified wail of his name echoes through the yard, and Kade's incessant pounding comes to an abrupt halt. I still feel him, big and thick, riding high deep inside me as my insides shimmy and shake. He didn't come yet. Breathless and panting, I look back. His eyes lock on mine with a hard, frigid glare that turns my scalding desire to ice.

"Who's the one who makes you come?"

"You are."

Fingers bite into my hips so hard it hurts. "The only one?"

"Yes, Kade."

"Good. You only come because I let you. Don't forget it."

His body rips from mine, leaving me bare-assed, freezing in the wind and utterly confused. I hike up my tattered tights, watching him disappear into the house. He's mad at *me*? *Oh, hell no!* He's the one turning my life upside down, not the other way around.

The ground crunches underfoot as I march to my back door. He may be pissed, but now so am I. "What the hell was that?"

The door slams behind me as I storm into the house after him.

He hovers in the dining room as if he's waiting for me. As if he purposely left me out there, exposed and humiliated, expecting me to follow him.

The manipulative son of a bitch.

"You're mine, Ainsley. I told you already. I don't fucking share." He bites out the last bit through his teeth like a rabid beast. His hands twist and turn at his sides, and the veins in his neck bulge and throb. I've seen the change that comes over him when he's upset, but I've never seen him quite *this* twitchy before.

His tone fuels my angry fire. "Let's get something straight here, Kade. You don't own me . . ." My finger jams into his heaving chest as he looks down at me with a scowl. His intimidation tactics may work on everyone else, but they do not work on me. I know him too well. " . . . and I definitely don't like what you're implying. You'd better start talking or get the hell out of my house."

He doesn't move. His nostrils flare, and his irises slowly return to blue from black. "I saw you and Crocodile Dundee at the gallery. His hands were all over you."

"You came to my job?"

"You refused to talk to me, A. I needed to see you."

Now, it all makes sense. The crazy eyes, the savage chopping, the possessive way he took control when he saw me. He's jealous. He was channeling his aggression, and then I showed up.

"So you were marking your territory. Why not just piss a circle around me while you're at it?" The anger begins to rise in my esophagus like bile. His behavior was deplorable and completely unacceptable. "F.Y.I, Eric's presence at the gallery was strictly business. He is one of the artists being showcased at the fundraiser."

Kade doesn't say a word. He just stands there like a wounded child as I continue to berate him like one. "You cannot act like an animal every time another man comes near me! What the hell is wrong with you? How do you go from being the kindest, gentlest man I know to hate-fucking me in my own backyard? Where does all this hostility even come from?"

Defeated, he falls to his knees at my feet, wrapping his arms around my middle so tight it hurts to breathe. "Ainsley, I don't know what I'm doing anymore. My demons always seem to catch up to me no matter how far I run from them."

His damp hair flops in random directions on top of his head as I run my fingers through it. On his face, a picture show of emotions rotates one by one. "Kade, talk to me."

When he finally opens his mouth to speak, I'm unprepared for what he has to say.

Chapter 39

Kade

"**E**VERYTHING I'VE TOLD you about my family was nothing but lies."

Ever since the band took off, my life has been on display for all to see. Nothing is sacred. I've spent my entire career formulating the quick responses to questions about my past. The trick is to give enough of the flowery details that people want to hear so they don't notice that you've literally given them no real information. It's always worked, and it always will.

When Ainsley asked about my childhood, I gave her the same bullshit answer I always give. People love the Army brat story. They adore hearing how close my parents and I were and how their untimely death ultimately led me to success in their honor. I've polished it over the years like a smooth stone. So much so that I even believe it myself sometimes. Truth is, it's a fucking joke.

She looks at me with huge brown eyes waiting for answers. Wild hair falls around her heart-shaped face, framing her high cheekbones. Her lips are pursed into a perfect little pout. The burgundy lipstick she had on earlier is worn away, and the natural pink color stands out against the pale tone of her skin. She looks so innocent. I hate myself for violating her trust and losing my temper on the one person in this world I promised I'd never hurt.

"We moved around a lot, that part was true. But that was it . . ."

"Kade! Move! Move! Move!"

The Sergeant's Doberman style bark could be heard throughout the entire house. I spilled oil in the garage trying to grease my bike chain. My punishment is moving cinderblocks from one end of the yard to the other.

I'm hauling ass with a block under each arm, knowing if I don't get it done fast enough, he'll only make me do it again. Sometimes, he makes me carry them above my head and other times, straight out in front of me. Once, he even had me carry them with outstretched arms to the side, but a hairline fracture left me in a cast, a little setback that resulted in him calling me Katherine for the entire month. I'm told these punishments are meant to turn me into a man.

My mother hangs laundry from the line attached to the house while her husband stands close by with his arms crossed over his thick chest as their eleven-year-old son trips over his own absurdly large feet. I'm tall for my age but wiry and thin. Regaining my footing, I continue my hustle across the lawn.

The last block falls in the neat pile, and my arms fall weak and weary at my sides. I want to collapse onto the ground, but I turn toward him and wait to be excused. The Sergeant is still in his uniform, his hat pulled low over his shaved head, and his boots laced in immaculate rows. With a face devoid of emotion, he lifts the stopwatch as I sweat it out, wondering if my time was up to snuff. "Sufficient, private. Go clean the garage."

"Yes, sir." Physically exhausted to the point of passing out, I drag my body to the garage and begin cleaning up the small puddle of oil.

"Staff Sergeant Rodney Black was a militant son of a bitch

who demanded excellence. He ruled our home with an iron fist and a zero tolerance policy. His word was law."

"Dig a hole. Six feet wide and four feet deep."

I take the shovel from his hand without a word, seething inside as he sits back in a lawn chair and watches me push into the red Georgia dirt.

The punishments changed as I grew and became stronger. By the time I was sixteen, my back was powerful and my shoulders were broad. Years of backbreaking manual labor had sculpted my physique, making it muscular and firm. Hauling cinderblock was no longer strenuous enough. The old man had to get creative. Digging holes, chopping wood, flipping tractor tires . . . whatever the sadistic bastard could think of, he made me do.

Dirt flies out of the hole as I dig, knowing I have to get this done in a timely manner in order to avoid further punishment. It's hot, and my throat is so dry it burns, but I keep at it. Each time the shovel stabs the soil, I imagine it's a fist in the old man's face. The harder I dig, the better it feels.

By the time I'm done, the blood is rocketing through my veins, and I'm so pumped I feel like I can take on a bear. I stand on the edge and watch as he meticulously measures the proper four by six hole. "Get in."

"What?"

"Did I stutter, private? I said get in the hole!" A spooked flock of birds takes flight as his booming voice echoes off the trees. I jump in the hole and stand there waiting for my next instructions.

"Are you a homo or a woman?" he bellows loud enough that I'm sure the whole neighborhood could hear him. The old man always spoke in a stern Southern shout, as if commanding the troops instead of talking to his family.

My already rapid heartbeat jumps in my chest and begins thumping against my ribcage. Neither one, sir!" I shout back as expected.

"Didn't I give you explicit instructions to get your hair cut?"

"Yes, sir!" I spit out through my gritted teeth. The dirt sweating into my eyes is impossible to remove with my filthy hands.

"Didn't I give you the money to obtain said haircut?"

"Yes, sir!"

"Then why am I still looking at your shaggy ass standing in a hole, boy?" His smug face gives way to sarcastic laughter.

Something inside me snaps. The anger and humiliation that's been building inside me boils over into a river of rage flowing out of my body. It's aimed directly at the belligerent fuck standing in front of me. I've dug hundreds of holes, moved thousands of cinderblocks, and fulfilled every cruel and unusual punishment he thought to throw my way while he watched like a friggin' psychopath. No infraction was too minor. The abuse was always the same.

In one long leap, I jump out of the hole and tackle him to the ground without a second thought about the consequences. I'm already as tall as he is and nearly as wide. He falls like a tree, my fists coming down like the hammers of hell, bloodying his face and cracking his ribs.

The Sergeant gets in a few jabs, but it only serves to fuel the fire coursing through my veins as I unload a litany of punches. Each swing releases every last bit of anxiety, fear, and self-loathing I've carried around inside my gut for as long as I can remember. For the first time in my life, I feel free.

A cold blast of water whips me in the face, throwing me off my father, who's lying in a ball in the dirt. My mother hovers just a few feet away, aiming the hose at me like it's a gun. With hands in the air, I stand and surrender my fight. She drops the hose and runs to his aid.

"Looks like you were right, Dad. Your punishments made a man out of me after all." I spit in his direction, walk off the property, and never return.

"Every time someone gets in my way, all I see is cinderblocks and dirt. It all comes back, and the animosity returns with a vengeance."

Ainsley's eyes are so wide I can see the whites around her irises. She sits on the edge of her seat, inching closer to me in tiny increments as I tell her story after story. By the time I'm done, she may as well be in my lap. "You make it all go away. When I'm with you, I get a glimpse of the man I know I can be instead of the broken one I am." I run my thumb across her cheek. "I'm tired of feeling this way. I want to feel the way I do when I'm with you all the time."

Her eyes soften. I pull her off the chair and onto my knee, needing to feel her against me. I always thought sex and fighting were the greatest forms of escape, but I was wrong. This is. With her in my arms, everything is better.

The ringing of her phone breaks the heavy silence. She digs it from her coat pocket and looks down at the number. "It's Maxwell. . . ." I watch her brows crinkle as she listens then her eyes go wide and her lips part. "You're kidding . . . okay . . . yeah . . . I'll see you tomorrow afternoon. Thanks."

She disconnects the phone and stares at it for a second as she waits for whatever news to sink in. "His private investigator has been following Bob all week. You're not going to believe this."

Chapter 40

Ainsley

"THIS PRICK IS something else," Kade says. Sprawled out in a chair in Maxwell's office like he's king of the world, he flicks the photo he's holding back into the pile on the desk and rolls his eyes. I told him I could handle this on my own, but he insisted on coming with me.

I don't know why I'm surprised. Bob had been sleeping with Cami for years, right under my nose. I have no reason to believe he wouldn't do it again, yet here I am, staring at photos of him and his dental hygienist in utter disbelief. It's been over two years since I caught Bob and Cami in our bed, but seeing this is like reliving it all over again.

"I wonder how long this has been going on."

"I can't say for sure, but they seem very cozy together."

Maxwell sits behind his desk with the photos spread out between us. The sleeves on his crisp white dress shirt are rolled up his furry forearms, and I notice for the first time that he has a slight indentation on his bare left ring finger.

Acid burns a hole in my stomach. Charlene has been Bob's hygienist for years. I know her well. I swallow down the nagging feeling that he didn't just cheat on Cami with her, but me as well. "So what does this mean for the case?" A dull throbbing is beginning to form between my eyes.

"Well, it definitely shows his lack of commitment to family values. I mean his girlfriend is expecting, right?"

"Twins," I reply with a nod.

The thought of poor, pregnant Cami sitting home while Bob is out tapping his hygienist makes my heart ache. I can hear Jenny's voice in my mind saying Karma's a bitch, but I can't get on board with that. I don't forgive Cami for what she did, but I wouldn't wish this on anyone. "Do we threaten him with these or something?"

"I think it's best to save these as our ace in the hole to further sway the judge in our favor the day of the trial."

"No. Absolutely not." As delightful as it may be to see Bob suffer, these photos would destroy more than just him. His entire relationship with Cami would unravel. Shay already comes from one broken home. She loves Cami and is thrilled about the babies. I cannot allow my anger to steal her happiness away from her. When this comes out in the wash, it's going to be Bob's fault, not mine. "Keep digging. Find something else."

My lawyer looks at me as if I've gone mad. "Ms. Daniels, the affair builds a foolproof case against him. I implore you to reconsider."

"I'm not putting Shay through it again."

This is a constant cycle in Bob's life. He hasn't changed a bit since high school. It's evident he does not possess the ability to be a one-woman man; however, he can't be alone. The hygienist will just fall into Cami's place, followed by another woman, and another, until the trail of stepmother figures in my daughter's life is a mile long. It's not fair to her. I refuse to be the catalyst that sets that wheel in motion. "Either we use it against him privately, or we don't use it at all. I have faith in you to sway the judge without it."

Maxwell nods. "Okay, then. I'll build the case without it."

His Patek Philippe watch clinks on the desk as he collects the pile of photos and shoves them back into his file. I never asked Kade how much Maxwell was billing him for, but with a timepiece like that, I'm sure it's a hefty sum. I just hope he's worth it.

By the time we leave Maxwell's office, I'm drained. I deluded myself into believing Cami was the first, but now, I know he was never true to me, and it stings more than I care to admit. "Are you going back to the hotel?"

Kade stands outside the massive skyscraper with his hands in his pockets. The wind has kicked up, and the smell of winter is in the air. It won't be long before every tree is bare, and we're buried under a mountainous pile of snow. Considering my own icy behavior, I wonder if Kade will stick around long enough to see it. I'm a mess of up and down emotions these days. It's impressive that he hasn't split yet.

"Yeah, sweets, I guess I am."

I resolve to push Bob out of my mind as I begin to walk down the sidewalk. Focusing on shit I can't change won't do me any good at this point. The holidays are coming, and I'd rather focus my energy on the things I have rather than the things I've lost.

Kade jogs around to the street side and falls in line next to me. It reminds me of something my grandmother said to me once a long time ago about chivalry and the way a lady should be treated. *Never run out to a honking car, and never walk on the curb side of the road.* Thinking she's watching us makes me smile. We were close, and I miss her. She never came right out and said so, but she wasn't Bob's biggest fan. I bet she would have liked Kade.

"What's gotten you so happy all of a sudden?"

I rest my hand in the crook of his elbow and slow our brisk pace. "Do you want to spend Thanksgiving with me and my family next week?" Thoughts of my grandmother always remind me how short life is. All our drama aside, Kade shouldn't be alone on Thanksgiving. He should be with someone who cares about him. He's been alone for far too long already.

Chapter 41

Kade

I'M A SPASTIC bundle of nerves, which is an odd change for me. Usually I'm the one causing worry, not the other way around. Ainsley has this remarkable talent for making me feel things I've never felt before. Love, jealousy, heartbreak, redemption . . . and today: complete anxiety.

I drive to her house way earlier than I'm supposed to, but I can't sit still anymore. I'm always turned up to eleven. I've never been able to just relax and take it easy. The Sergeant's booming bark is a constant in my head. *Idle hands are the devil's workshop, boy! Get to work!* Ainsley is the only one who squelches that voice. I feel a sense of calm I can't explain when I'm around her.

The first time that I ever felt at ease was holding her against me in that hotel room after that awful interview with *Music Buzz*. She curled up next to me on the bed like a kitten, her little body nestled snugly under my arm. I was crazy about her from day one, but that was the moment I realized I couldn't live without her.

I ring the bell and wait for someone to answer. I hear two high-pitched voices, scurrying footsteps, and a series of clicks just before the door opens. The early afternoon sunlight filters into the doorway and catches on Shay's golden strands of hair. "Hi, Kade! Happy Thanksgiving! Mom's in the kitchen. She says come in."

"Happy Thanksgiving, kiddo."

The smell of food hangs in the air already, and I'm sure Ainsley has been cooking up a storm since early this morning. The door clicks closed, and Shay lifts her tiny fist in front of her. I smile and reciprocate, bopping my fist along with the countdown to our game. This time, on the count of three, I throw up two fingers and she keeps a tight fist. Rock beats scissors. "You're too good at this game!" I say tapping my fingertip on her nose. She grins.

The sight of Ainsley's bodacious rear end greets me in the doorway as I stroll into the kitchen. The woman has zero problems filling out a pair of jeans. "What are you doing up there?" My gaze travels up her stretching body from her knees on the countertop all the way to her pointed fingertips reaching into the gaping maw of the cabinet in front of her. The view stirs up all kinds of dirty in the back of my mind. Nothing on this planet is hotter than a thick, round ass with a tiny waist. Ainsley has both. "Let me help you before you get hurt."

"I'm fine! Just trying to get the stupid platter from the top—ow!" Her shriek echoes into the open cabinet as my teeth sink into the meaty part of her ass cheek. It was begging for it. I just couldn't help myself.

Her arm jets out behind her in a cliché mom swipe, but I swerve and duck, and she misses me completely. "See? Told you you'd get hurt."

"You're such a cocky asshole."

The look of shock on her face as she rubs her wounded cheek turns my chuckle to a cackle. My arm hooks around her middle, sweeping her off the counter and lowering her feet back to the floor.

Effortlessly, I pluck the turkey platter from the shelf and present it to her with a bow. "Your plate, my lady."

She rolls her eyes, snatching the platter from my hand. "You're like a big child. Why don't you go play with Shay for a while?"

"Aww," I placate, still trying to control my laughter. "Okay, I'm sorry. What else do you need help with? I'll be good, Scout's honor." One hand covers my heart, while the other one holds up three fingers.

"I find it very hard to believe you were ever a Boy Scout," she says flatly.

I steal an uncooked green bean from a bowl on the counter and snap it off between my teeth. "I was, actually, but I got kicked out for eating a Brownie."

Another eye roll. I'm two for two. She turns back to the counter with an *ugh*. "Just for that, I'm making you do the dishes." The quirking corners of her mouth assure me that her annoyed reaction is an act. She pretends I disgust her, but she secretly loves it.

I'm still grinning when I walk into the family room. The wooden coffee table in the center is covered with construction paper. Crayons litter the tabletop like a colorful array of fallen soldiers, tumbling out of a forgotten box laying on its side, while animated superheroes fight crime on the television ahead.

"Hey, kid. What are you making here?" I take a seat on the couch and watch as Shay folds a green piece of paper and slides her thumb across the edge, making a firm crease.

"Thanksgiving cards for Grammy and Pop-Pop."

Her teeny fist holds the crayon as it moves along the colored paper. She stops coloring for a minute to admire her work then goes right back to it. When she's done, she sets the crayon down and shows me with a triumphant grin.

"That's a nice turkey. I like the waddle."

"Thanks!" she beams, climbing onto the couch next to me.

My hands settle onto my lap, one resting on each knee. I'm not a hundred percent sure what to do with them, so I figure it's best to leave them in plain sight. "You don't have to be nervous around me. I like you."

"What makes you think I'm nervous?"

Shay lifts my hand, turning up my palm, and trailing her petite finger across it. "It's wet."

A smile grows on my face. A nine-year-old called me out for having sweaty palms. I like this kid. She's good at reading people. "Between us, I'm a little nervous about meeting your grandparents."

"Why?"

I glance back toward the kitchen, keeping my voice low so Ainsley can't hear me. "I guess because I don't have any family of my own. I want them to like me too."

"What happened to your family?" Shay looks like a cherub, all innocent and cute. Looking at her face, I feel my chest begin to tighten. I'm starting to grow attached to her.

"They weren't nice."

"Like my dad isn't nice?"

Ouch. "Your dad loves you."

"Not as much as my mom does." She settles back into the couch before adding, "She loves you, too, you know."

"Shay, clean up this mess and bring it upstairs, okay?" Ainsley's voice from behind us startles me, and I wonder how long she's been standing there. An old man groan escapes my chest as I push myself off the couch. All this sitting around is prematurely aging me.

Shay listens to her mother and sweeps all the paper into a pile and shoves the crayons back in the box. She breezes by us, disappearing down the hall. Taking advantage of our brief moment alone, I pull Ainsley against me. The delicious smell of her skin makes me hungry for more than just turkey.

"By the way, Happy Thanksgiving, big guy." Her breath tickles my neck, and my jeans begin to tighten. I silently remind my dick that it's not playtime. Not only is there a kid in the house, but Ainsley's parents are on their way over. As if that's not enough of a buzzkill, she still has me idling on yellow.

"Right back at ya, sweets."

My hands roll down her back. Her burnt orange sweater is soft to the touch, and the color is an amazing accent to her chocolate eyes. Delicate curls frame her face. She always tries to tame it down, but I love when her hair is wild like this. I want nothing more than to brush it back and lay a kiss on her pink lips that would transform us back from limbo to lovers, but before I get the chance, the doorbell rings. *It's showtime.*

Ainsley stays wrapped in my embrace, pushing herself up on tiptoes and plants a kiss on my freshly shaven chin. "Here we go." She untangles herself and jaunts off to answer the door. I stay leaned against the wall in the family room.

Voices filter in from the foyer, and footsteps scuffle on the hardwood floor. I uncross my arms and shove my hands in my pockets. Why am I so nervous? I have no trouble shaking my ass in front of millions of screaming fans, but standing here in Ainsley's living room, I'm attacked by a serious case of stage fright.

Ainsley returns to the family room, followed by a woman so identical to her, I have to blink twice. They have the same slight build, deep chocolate eyes, and pouty little lips, except her mother's are turned down in an accurately lined red scowl.

"Ainsley, dear, this hair." She starts smoothing down Ainsley's wild tendrils. Meanwhile, her own short, curly bob is sculpted and shellacked into place neat and precise. The severe crease in her dress pants sends a chill down my spine. She reminds me of my father.

Ainsley slaps her mother's hand away like she's swatting a

fly and leans in closer to her dad. "Kade, these are my parents, Carol and John Romano."

"Mr. and Mrs. Romano, it's nice to meet you." I extend my hand, and her father shakes it.

Her old man is quite the opposite of his wife. His silver hair and beard are combed neat, but not too neat. He stands casually in his polo shirt and jeans with his arm around his daughter and nothing but pride in his rich dark eyes. I see the same look in Ainsley every time she looks at Shay. She may look just like her mother, but she's daddy's little girl all the way.

"Glad to meet you, Kade, but call me John. Mr. Romano is my dad."

"What's this Mr. Romano crap?" We're interrupted by a gravelly voice followed by an elderly man with a cane shuffling into the family room. "Bill Romano, good to meet ya, son." He rests on his cane and offers me his free hand. "Big fucker, ain't ya?"

"Pop!" Ainsley's eyes go wide, but so does her smile. "Excuse my grandfather, he has no filter."

"Who needs a filter when you're eighty?" I shake his waiting hand and smile. I like the guy already. "Well, where am I sittin'?"

"Come on, Pop. You can sit at the table. Dinner's almost ready."

I trail behind as the family follows Ainsley into the dining room. Her dad and grandfather seem pretty cool, but the fact that her mother didn't say two words to me does not go unnoticed.

Chapter 42

Ainsley

"EVERYTHING WAS DELICIOUS, sweetheart. I'm stuffed." My father leans back in his chair, rubbing his round belly. He says he's done, but that's his tell. I guarantee he'll fit at least two pieces of pie down his throat before the day is over.

The table is scattered with empty plates and half-full serving dishes. It boggles my mind how it takes two days to prepare the meal, but only thirty minutes to pick it clean. "Shay, come help." I rise from the table and start gathering bowls to trek back into the kitchen. Shay follows suit, going around the room collecting the dinner plates.

A presence fills the space behind me as I begin the task of cleaning up the leftover feast. Kade's solid arms slide around my waist. I twist around so we're face to face. Well, face to chest anyway. "You seem to be hitting it off with my grandfather. I think you've finally met your foul-mouthed match," I say, looking up into his gorgeous blue eyes. They've changed. The biting fierceness that shone through has been replaced by a soft, warm glow.

Kade was the topic of conversation through most of dinner. My parents fired off question after question in rapid succession; from where he grew up to what it's like being in a band.

Naturally, my grandpa only wanted to know about the women.

Rich laughter wraps around me like silk. "He is pretty great." Grabbing the newly scraped plates, he places them in the sink. "Your dad's a nice guy, too. Pretty sure your mom hates my guts, though." The water rushes out of the faucet. Kade begins rinsing the plates and filing them in an orderly row in the dishwasher.

I gave him plenty of forewarning that my mom was a tough nut to crack. I nearly choked when she asked why a grown man would choose "the playboy lifestyle" instead of raising a family, but Kade handled himself with grace. His answer was spot-on, with no hesitation, as if he'd been holding it in his bag of tricks all along.

When I finally settle down, I intend for it to be forever. It's not a choice you make lightly.

"Don't take offense to it. She hates everyone who's not Bob." I empty the leftover stuffing into a Tupperware container and hand him the empty bowl. "She despises Jenny, always has. Blames her partly for ruining my marriage."

"That's twisted. Jenny didn't put Bob's dick in the nanny."

I snort. His joke is crude, but it's also the truth. Getting divorced sucked, and I really could have used my mom's support. I can still hear her nagging voice in my head telling me it was all my fault Bob cheated on me. The constant feeling that I wasn't good enough festered in my gut like a cancer. I really thought that maybe if I'd tried harder, Bob wouldn't have sought out the affection of another woman, but that's bull. It didn't matter what I did—I would never have been enough for him.

"I just don't get it. What is it about him she loves so much?"

A blast of cold hits me in the face as I push everything around in the fridge. "She's old-fashioned. She expected me to turn a blind eye to the affair and continue on as if nothing happened." The refrigerator door closes with a wisp as I move on to the next task. "The truth is insignificant. It only matters how you're perceived."

I lean against the counter and watch as Kade begins scrubbing out the turkey pan. His sleeves are rolled up his thick forearms, and his shoulders are hunched over the sink, causing his already fitted shirt to stretch across his muscular back. It's just so . . . real.

Whenever I tried to picture this exact scenario last year, I couldn't see past the star persona, but now, that other guy is like a faded memory. Kade sat at my dining room table, laughing with my family and enjoying a meal I made. He could be anyone. A mechanic, a lawyer, a businessman. The Stone Cold God of Rock is gone, replaced with a guy who blends into my life like watercolors.

The television suddenly blasts from the family room where my hard of hearing grandfather is watching what's left of the football game. "I can finish up here. Why don't you go keep Pop-Pop company?"

He dries his hands on a dishtowel and chucks it on the counter. "You sure?"

"Yeah. We're pretty much done anyway. Go ahead."

The dishwasher hums and whirs to life; water tings against the china as the wash cycle starts. He drops a kiss on my head and saunters off through the kitchen.

The heavenly aromas of warm pie and coffee fill the room as I finish wiping down the counter. The house is quiet, save for the grinding of the coffeemaker and the sports stats blaring from the television. I wander through the kitchen to join my family, but what I find causes me to stop in my tracks.

Kade is sprawled out on the couch, sandwiched between my grandfather and Shay; my three favorite people passed out in a tryptophan coma, side by side. Shay's body is a tiny ball, snuggled against Kade as she dozes, mouth open, drooling onto his shirt. Warmth spreads throughout my chest, and my eyes mist over. Dessert is ready, but this is much sweeter than pie.

I quietly pad out of the room to find my cell phone. I need to snap a photo to remember this classic hallmark moment. The rapid blinking of the blue light in the corner catches my eye. I have at least half a dozen missed calls and a few voice-mails. Before I even have a chance to check who called, the musical ringtone plays loudly in my hand.

Why is Cami calling me?

"Ainsley, thank God!" she sobs in my ear. "Do you know where Bob is?" Her voice is breathy and strained.

"It's Thanksgiving. I'd assume he's with you." My finger twirls in one of the curls hanging over my shoulder. Why would she think I have any idea where Bob is?

"We had a fight and he left." She lets out a long, drawn-out whine, panting in my ear. "His phone is going direct to voice-mail every time I call." Another whine floats out of the receiver, followed by more rapid panting. "I think I'm in labor. The babies are coming, and I can't find him!"

This is not happening.

My grip tightens on the phone. This should not be my problem. Bob divorced me to be with her. I am the last person she should be calling when he runs off. Part of me wants to hang up the phone and walk away from this, but I can't do that. I don't have it in me to turn my back on a woman who's obviously frightened and coming to me for help. As much as it kills me to do so, I will help her because she's the mother to Shay's brothers. "Sit tight. I'm on my way."

Chapter 43

Kade

"**K**ADE, WAKE UP."
My head pops up off the couch, and my eyes blink in rapid succession. My head is still foggy from a nap I didn't realize I was taking as Ainsley squats on the floor in front of me, steadying herself with my knees.

"Cami's in labor. Bob took off. I gotta go."

"Wait . . . what?" It takes a split second to register what she said. Shay dozes on my side like a sweet angel tucked under my arm. I untangle from her, trying my best not to wake her before following Ainsley into the hall. "Bob took off?"

"They had a fight, and he's not answering his phone. I have to take her to the hospital. I can't just leave her."

Hearing her say it pisses me off. Bob's level of bullshit knows no boundaries. Who runs out on their pregnant girlfriend on Thanksgiving then doesn't answer her calls?

I throw open the closet door and grab my coat. "We both know where he is, A. I'm going to go get that fucker and bring him to where he belongs."

"I don't know if that's a good idea. Maxwell gave explicit instructions to keep the two of you apart."

"He did. But I can't let Bob miss the birth of his children because he's a cheating, lying douchebag. I have her name. I'll look up her address on the way." Before she can protest any further, I turn to walk out the door.

A Google search uncovers one Charlene Mackelravy within a ten-mile radius. I click on the link and find a Facebook page confirming it's her. I can't believe this. It's like he can sense when Ainsley is having a good day and does everything in his power to screw it up royally. I swear it's a gift.

Thirty minutes later, I'm sitting in the car in front of a two-story apartment complex. Many of the bricks on the building are missing or cracked. Rows of blue doors and air conditioning units file past as I walk down the damaged walkway until I find the one I'm looking for. I knock and a busty brunette answers, her V-neck sweater cut so low you can practically see her stomach. Before Ainsley, I might have thought this chick was hot, but now, all I see is trash.

"I'm looking for Bob Daniels." Straight and to the point. I'm not here for small talk.

She eyes me up for a second, the tall stranger at her door looking for her boyfriend, and then cocks her head to the side like she might know me. The proverbial light bulb switches on over her head when she finally registers who exactly is standing on her welcome mat. "Oh my gosh . . . are you . . . ?" *Great. Another fucking fangirl.*

I flash her The Grin and rest my hand on the doorframe. "In the flesh, sweetheart. Now, be a peach and go fetch Bob, will ya?" She looks up at me in awe while I walk two fingers midair, reminding her to move in the nicest way possible.

"'scuse me," she simpers and backs away from the door. I probably shouldn't have laid it on so thick, but you catch more flies with honey. That, and I get a kick out of rendering Bob's girl speechless.

The door opens again, and Bob stands there like a deer in headlights. "What the . . . ?" He pokes his head out of the apartment and looks left and right, I assume trying to make sure we're alone. "How . . . ? What . . . ?" *My presence works on more than just fangirls, I see.*

"You are a sad, sorry excuse for a human being, but you don't need me telling you what you already know. While you're in here screwing your hygienist, your girlfriend is at the hospital giving birth to your children. You might want to get your ass over there."

I turn to leave. My goal was to tell him Cami was in labor, and now that I have, my work here is done. I have no need to look at his annoying face anymore. "Does Cami know I'm here?"

I spin back around to face him, stepping into his personal space as he backs away from me. "Nope, and you can thank Ainsley for that. She had the opportunity to use this affair against you but refused." His back hits the wall, and I tower over him.

"Why?"

"Because, unlike you, ruining the lives of others isn't high on her list of priorities. Remember that when you're sitting beside her in court next month." I turn on my heel and storm away. After everything he's done to her, she still insists on helping him. It speaks volumes for what kind of person she is.

Brisk footsteps fall in line behind me as I approach my car. "Hey!" I stop and wait as Bob jogs my way. "Thanks."

"Don't thank me, man. Just do the right thing." I slide into the driver's seat and close the door on this nonsense once and for all.

Chapter 44

Ainsley

I READ THE text and push the phone back in my pocket with a sigh of relief. Bob's on his way. As soon as he gets here, I can remove myself from this bizarre situation and attempt to salvage what is left of this ruined holiday. I hate Bob, but I hate myself more for being the sap who always picks up the pieces when he's inexplicably absent.

"Thanks for being here, Ainsley. You're a pal."

The rhythmic beeping of machines fills the dead air as Cami lies in the hospital bed. When I got to her house earlier, she was a sopping mess of tears and amniotic fluid. A trail of towels lined the floor where she walked from room to room, afraid Bob would be upset if she ruined the hardwood. She moaned and cried, doubled over in pain as contraction after contraction wracked her body. As soon as she settled in, they administered an epidural, and her shrill yelping subsided along with the pain, leaving nothing but uncomfortable silence between us.

"Let's not pretend we're friends, okay? I'm here because you needed my help. Nothing more." Her honey-colored eyes fill with fresh tears, and I shove aside any guilt that arises from having been too harsh.

"I'm sorry about the way things happened. I never meant to hurt you." Her weepy pout reminds me of the day I found her in bed with my husband. She'd been an honorary part of our family for years. She'd been on vacations with us, spent holidays with us. She wasn't just my nanny. She was the little sister I never had. A betrayal like that isn't something you can come back from.

I flip through the expired issue of *People* on my lap, not dignifying her apology with a response. Feeling her eyes on me, I pretend to be enthralled in the latest Kardashian drama. She expects me to absolve her of her crime, but I'm not giving her the satisfaction. My being here should be enough to appease her. We don't need to fill the time with meaningful conversation.

"Bob and I were fighting over you."

I tear my gaze away from the glossy page, and my eyes fix on hers. "What about me?"

She takes a deep breath and lets the air trickle back out. "This ridiculous lawsuit. His constant concern about what you're doing and who you're doing it with." A tear falls down her cheek, and she swipes it away with the flick of her finger. "He still wants you. I'm just his consolation prize."

I remember being in Cami's shoes, the agonizing feeling that I wasn't good enough weighing me down until I could barely move. Bob is the kind of man who gets better looking as he ages. Over the years, his football player build and thick blond hair would always turn many heads. Adding doctor to his name only added to his appeal.

My love for him bordered on obsession, so much so that I would do anything to make him happy, but he never was. He was always searching for the greener grass. The whole time we were together, I was convinced I was the problem, but now, I know I wasn't. Bob's constant need for perfection in all aspects of his life will always be a brick that drowns him slowly. He doesn't really want me. He's fixated on me because he knows for the first time in fifteen years that I don't want him.

I have no words of comfort to offer. She's with a man who can't possibly love her because he's incapable of it, and she will always feel less than worthy as a result. Looking at Cami now, I see she is a lot like I was. Naïve enough to believe all his lies, and full of faith that I could love him enough for the both of us.

Bob's panicked burst into the delivery room startles my thoughts. "Cami, baby, I'm sorry." He runs to her bedside like a doting lover, full of apologies and kisses. She'll forgive and forget because the alternative is too terrifying to fathom. It's not until you're staring at the relationship in your rearview mirror, miles after you've driven away from it, that you realize the truth. Loving Bob is lonelier than being alone.

"Good luck, Cami," I say, collecting my things and heading for the exit. She's going to need it in more ways than she realizes.

* * *

I CHUCK MY coat and purse on the bench as the door clicks behind me. I plop down next to them, pulling off my boots and kicking them into the corner. The house is quiet, and I'm grateful my parents have gone. I feel a slight sense of guilt leaving Kade to babysit Shay, but the disastrous events of the evening have left me too mentally drained to deal with my mother right now.

The faint hum of the television calls to me from the family room. It flickers in the dimly lit space, making everything seem that much more surreal. Kade's immense frame stretches out over the loveseat, causing it to appear small by comparison. His forearm is tucked under his head. One foot hangs off the arm, the other rests on the floor. When he sees me approach, he kicks himself up to a sitting position. "Hey, sweets. How'd it go?"

I shrug, letting out a deep sigh. "I need a big glass of wine first then we'll compare war stories. Where's Shay?"

"Shay's in bed. I told her you'd come up when you got home."

I push myself up the stairs to check on my daughter. Shay is just a tiny lump in the corner of her bed. Her arm hangs off the edge, breaking free from the tightly tucked blanket around her.

"Shay, baby. I'm home." I insert a stray lock of hair behind her ear and run a knuckle down her soft cheek.

Drowsy eyes flutter open then close again. "Am I a big sister yet?" she asks in a listless, quiet voice.

"Not yet. Soon. Go back to sleep." I drop a soft kiss on her temple and close the door behind me as I exit.

Kade waits for me at the bottom of the stairs with a wine glass in hand. My heart catapults at the sight of him. Being with Cami was a stark reminder of the insecure person I was as Mrs. Bob Daniels. I loathe that woman. I've been denying relationships for fear that I'll become her again, but now, I know that was Bob's manipulated way to keep me tied to him. That was never me at all.

I peer down at the beautiful man below and realize he's made me feel more loved in a month than Bob ever had in all our years together. Kade is not without his faults, but above all, he's been there for me when I needed him. I didn't even have to ask. He simply inserted himself into my insane life and shouldered some of the burden so I didn't have to do it alone.

My feet move with a mind of their own. I run down the steps, crashing into him, lips first. His hand splays across my back pulling my body against his. My fingers get lost in his hair as our tongues dance together in twirling harmony.

I pull away, righting myself on the bottom step where I'm standing, but his arm stays circled around my waist holding our hips close together. "What was that for?"

"I'm just finally realizing what I'm thankful for."

Chapter 45

Kade

ANSLEY STEPS OUT onto the stoop as I pull up in front of her house. I get out of the car and stop short. The full moon is a spotlight behind her, creating an otherworldly glow that turns her white lace dress into a beacon in the dark. It shines through her unruly mass of curls and kisses her smooth skin.

She slides her arms into a black leather jacket as she comes down the steps. My eyes follow her body as she glides toward me, her sky-high heels giving her the illusion of having legs for days. "Why are you looking at me like that?"

"You're too good to be true." I wrap my hands around her slender waist and pull her against me as I lean on the car. "Sometimes, I just can't believe you're real."

A sexy smirk curls along her dark red lips. "I assure you I'm real, and I'm all yours." Her fingers rest in the hollow of my exposed throat while her other hand grabs my loosely fastened tie, letting it glide through her fingers. "Broke out the big guns, huh?"

"What can I say? I'm a classy motherfucker."

I open the car door to help her in then jog to the other side. A quiet rock ballad plays through the speaker. The sound of her humming along is as pleasing as the music itself. The night has only just begun, and it's already awesome.

The night is unusually warm as we stroll through the city en route to the gallery. The place is lit up like a Christmas tree. We're one of the first to arrive, and she does a quick tour, making sure everything is in its place and all the vendors are doing their jobs. She scurries around the gleaming hardwood floors on her nude-colored stilts commanding attention. She's impressive. My usually sweet Ainsley is no nonsense when it comes to her job, and it shows. The exhibit she put together is extraordinary.

Before long, the place begins to fill, and I can feel the eyes and hear the whispers. Ainsley threads her hand in mine. "Come on. People want to meet you. Let's socialize." She leads me through the room, stopping to greet the folks she knows. Charming the pants off people is an art form in its own right, one I've honed like a science. I can work a room like it's my job.

Eyes stab me in the back from the corner of the room. The Aussie Fuck. He hangs in the corner, pretending not to notice me. It's cool. I get it. A month ago, I was the guy vying for Ainsley's affection and plotting his demise. The tables have turned, and the best man won.

He catches her eye and waves, but the look on his face is less than pleased. She waves back and slides her hand into mine giving it a tight squeeze, letting him know her choice is made. When he turns back toward his own date, I realize I was a jerk to think he was a better fit for her. He gave her up way too easily. The guy who deserves her is the one who's willing to fight for her.

"Ainsley, the caterer needs you." A young girl with Peter Pan hair comes running up to us in a panic. Her corduroy skirt is a total throwback to the Marcia Brady days.

"Oh sure, Robin. Be right there. Excuse me, Kade."

Ainsley runs off, leaving me standing there alone. The main

area is teeming with people and tuxedoed wait staff carrying trays of hors d'oeuvres. I wander around the quieter parts of the gallery, eying the various pieces placed systematically about. Most of it is beautiful, some of it is strange, but one in particular holds me hostage.

In the simplest terms, it's a sleeping man in a bed, but it's anything but simple. The details on the black and white picture are so lifelike and intense they appear to jump off the wall. As if the man is lying right in front of me, not drawn on the canvas.

The wild dark hair is a stark contrast against the white background. It conceals most of the man's profile, but the artist clearly defines the straight nose and angular jaw. The man's Herculean back and shoulders are severe compared to the soft backdrop of the bed. His lower half is swathed in a bed sheet with one athletic leg peeking out. But it's the arms that hold my attention. Black patterns swirl around the thick ribbons of muscle expertly recreated on the paper. My mouth drops open with a shocked gasp.

I'm staring at a portrait of myself.

Goose bumps prickle my flesh as I move in to get a better look. My eyes trace every line and curve until I see what I'm looking for. In the tiniest area, hugging the arch of the foot, is the artist's signature: *A. Daniels.*

"I sat in the room and watched you sleep until my ride arrived." Her heels echo through the quiet hall of the gallery as she approaches. I stand stock-still with my eyes glued to the charcoal drawing on the wall. Her drawing. "I committed this image to my memory thinking it was the last time I'd ever catch this glimpse of you again. Even now, when I close my eyes, I still see it. I didn't want to leave you, Kade. I had to. When you told me you loved me, I was too hurt, too damaged to accept it."

With my defenses down, I turn to face her. "And how do

you feel now?"

"I'm not fully mended. Not sure if I ever will be. But I'm ready to take the leap again. I'm ready to love you, to let you love me." She takes my hand, resting it on top of the soft lace covering her chest. "You have my heart, Kade. Don't break it."

Chapter 46

Ainsley

THE HOUSE IS dark when Kade and I enter through the front door, save for the lonely overhead light illuminating the entryway. The minute the door clicks closed, he pulls me against him. The leather of my jacket crinkles in his embrace. My lips land in the hollow of his throat as I tug at the loosely fixed knot around his neck and slide the tie from his collar.

He turned many heads tonight, and I'm sure it had less to do with the fame and everything to do with the dress clothes tailored to fit his body, highlighting his broad shoulders and long legs in a way that compels a woman to look twice. Thing is, he didn't even notice the stolen glances. He kept his attention focused on me, watching with his intense blue gaze like I was the only woman in the room.

He slides my coat off my shoulders, relieving me of its weight and dropping it on the bench next to his. Smoldering blue eyes watch me as I head for the stairs. "You runnin' away, sweets?"

"Not anymore."

I pause on the bottom step and reach for him. Now that I've admitted my feelings out loud, I can hardly contain them. The floodgates on my heart are fully open, and I feel like I'm bursting at the seams. I love him with a passion that burns so brightly it's blinding. It didn't matter how much distance I put between us, how much I fought against my feelings, or the fear lodged in my gut that someday I wouldn't be enough for him. I can't hide it anymore. I don't want to.

Kade takes my hand and follows me to my room. My heart beats so fast I can hardly contain it, just like it did our first night together. His lips brush against mine with a tentative sweetness that makes me melt against him the minute they touch. We shared a hundred kisses, a thousand heated glances, but not one of them compares to this moment right here, right now. I've broken down my barrier. Opened myself up to him. And from this moment on, nothing will be the same.

He glides the zipper on my dress open. With a feather-light touch, he slides his hands up my arms then pulls the straps down. The airy material whirls off my hips. I work the buttons on his shirt, taking the time to run my hands over the strong curves of his body. His abdominal muscles contract when I trace the viciously yummy V that disappears beneath his waistband.

His lips land on mine again as he glides his tongue into my mouth just enough to send me over the edge. I'm ravenous for more, but he keeps it soft and slow. One hand rests on my back while the other slides under my knees as he lifts me off the floor. The move is so intimate, so possessive, that when he lies me on my bed and settles between my legs, I'm trembling. Emotions overflow so fast they bubble over the rim. "Say it again, please," he says, stroking the hair off my forehead with tenderness.

"Say what?" I tighten around him, holding him so close that I can feel every inch of his body against my naked skin.

A low growl vibrates against my neck, his voice hoarse with desire. "That you love me."

"I love you, Kade," I say, arching my back as his pelvis presses against mine. His erection is a hard, thick bulge inside his pants, rubbing against the soft damp cotton of my underwear.

The strong muscles in his back ripple as he moves down my body with the agility of a panther. His breath is hot against me. He pushes my legs apart with his hands and sears his burning mouth over my panties, making them even wetter with his tongue. His thumbs hook in the slim lace band around my waist. Licking his lips, he maintains eye contact as he pulls them slowly down my legs then drops his head between my thighs again.

My head falls to the side as light pixies dance behind my eyelids. There are no words between us now. Just a series of pants and grunts, and the sound of his swirling tongue tasting me like a dainty dessert. A raspy gasp tumbles from my mouth as he pushes two fingers inside me all the way to the knuckle and back out again, hooking them just so as if coaxing the orgasm out of me.

A surge of energy rockets through my body, but Kade's free hand digs into my hip, holding me to the mattress. I bite down hard on my lip, tasting a trickle of blood on my tongue.

He sits up, pulling the belt from his pants and inching them down his hips until his cock springs free, then pushes himself into me while the orgasm still blossoms in my body. His hips move with slow and steady power, slipping between my thighs in an easy, determined tempo that pulls me under his riptide, immersing me in his wild river of ecstasy until I'm gasping and holding on for dear life.

Another orgasm crests over me, but instead of a blinding jolt of fire, I'm consumed by a delectable plateau that doesn't quit rolling through me until I'm wrung out and panting from exhaustion.

Being fucked by Kade Black is nothing short of spectacular,

but I have no words to describe the feeling of him making love to me like this. He doesn't say a word, and he doesn't have to. I see everything I need reflected in is soulful blue eyes. I'm the only one.

Chapter 47

Kade

MUSIC IS IN my soul. I hear it everywhere. It's in the wind rustling through the trees and the rumbling of the cars on the street. One rhythmic beat rolls right into the next, during even the simplest of everyday things. Ainsley's body is no different. The unparalleled harmony of her screams and whimpers as she shudders in my arms is like an orchestra. The sweet fluid gushing between her thighs is an ovation. It's a private concert only for me. I'm the conductor and the audience.

I run my hands along her cotton skin, caressing every inch that lays before me. My lips travel the same path, worshiping her. She stirs and smiles in her sleepy haze, like she's being awakened from a dream. My mouth moves softly over each breast and down her arms. I trail up each leg and across her stomach. Her fingers sink into my hair as I kiss her neck, her jaw, her lips.

"You're insatiable," she says, her voice thick with exhaustion.

I suppose I am, but Ainsley makes me feel things I've never felt before. I don't have to pretend when I'm with her. She doesn't want me for the sake of the rock star fantasy—she just wants *me*. Hearing the words I love you falling from her beautiful lips was like a shot of adrenaline. Even now, it races through my bloodstream, making me feel invincible.

I give in and roll to the side, allowing her to bask in her post-orgasmic coma. She scoots to face me. Her silhouette is a perfect panorama of dips and hills. My hand sweeps down the smooth curves from her shoulder, into the low valley of her waist, and up over the steep summit of her hip. "I just want to hear you scream my name one more time." I smirk, gliding down her ass cheek and bringing her leg over mine.

A slow, seductive smile curls on her lips. One eye peeks open, and the other one follows when she catches me looking. She slides on top of me, pushing me to my back and sitting on my thighs. Her heat radiates at the base of my groin, and I drag her higher onto my shaft.

"What do you plan to do with me now?" she asks with a head tilt and a raised eyebrow. Two adorable pink circles stand out on each cheek, a remnant from our recent lovemaking. Her big doe eyes appear innocent, but her hips pulsate with the savvy of an alley cat, covering me with slick wetness.

"Whatever I want."

My back leaves the mattress. When I grab her head to crush our lips together, my cock sticks up hard and ready between us. Her hand closes around the base with a gentle squeeze. The pressure increases. She pumps her fist once . . . twice . . . three times.

Frustration gets the best of me. I lean back on my palms as the jerk of her hand picks up speed, but it's not what I want to sate my needs. Her other hand slides between us, fondling my nuts. My head rolls back, reeling in the absolute perfection of her grasp. "Whatever *you* want, huh? Seems *I'm* the one who's got you by the balls."

Goddamn. A chick like her is every man's fantasy—an angel on the street and a vixen in the bedroom. How anyone would let her go is beyond me. She's smart, talented, and sexy as hell. When we first met, she seemed so demure. I expected a kept woman who was used to missionary with the lights off. I thought pushing her to her limits would be a fun challenge. She's not the same timid woman I met all those months ago. She was a quick study, rising to every challenge, and meeting me toe to toe.

Her tongue leaves a glistening trail of saliva up my chest as her hands tug in impeccable unison. I fall to the bed. My dick is purple and throbbing in her tight fist, which is now moving with the power of a freight train. My head pushes into the mattress, fingers dig hard into her thighs, teeth clench, and breath gasps out in rugged grunts. I'm staggering along the edge of exploding in her palm, when all I feel around me is sweltering hotness.

The air rushes from my lungs as her body glides down my cock inch by inch. Her inner walls clench and unclench, but she sits like a stone, watching my irritation grow with delight.

"Ainsley, baby, you're killing me." A shit-eating grin spreads across her face. Forget vixen, this woman is the devil.

I thrust my hips, and she bounces hard, her mouth turning into a small ring as a playful "oh" bolts from her lips. The heels of her palms dig into my chest for leverage as her body begins its slow roll. Her ass goes in a tight circle, causing her tits to face the sky with every rotation. I lie back, resting my hands on her swiveling hips, while enjoying the view of her riding me in unbridled, naked glory.

When she leans back, I feel myself rake against her insides. I grasp her hips and push. Her face turns toward the ceiling; sharp nails make ten tiny divots in my pecs, and a jolt of heat rockets between her legs. "You like that." It's a statement, not a question.

"Mmmhmm," she whines, and I pull her forward and push again. The serpentine circling becomes a fierce, steady grind.

Her lips part in an earnest sneer as she lurches back and forth, guided by my firm grip dragging her along.

The soaking proof of her pleasure covers me, slippery and wet, adding to the intense friction created by our grating bodies. Spasms clench around me. Her moans become a whining urgent chant over and over. " . . . ohmygodohmygodohmygod . . ." I catch her as she collapses on top of me, heaving and drooling onto my chest with gasping sobs.

Her body turns rigid under my touch, and her breath stutters with a satisfied sensitivity felt all over her skin. Every orgasm she has is like a religious experience. She's taken over, possessed by pleasure only I'm able to give her. My cock throbs while I wait for her to recover. I need more of her.

"Hold on, sweets."

Grabbing her ass with both hands, I slam her limp body onto the mattress still embedded deep inside. Her legs, once wrapped around me, splay out on my shoulders.

I fall forward, caging her in with my hands and knees, driving into her full-force and smacking hard against her ass. Her body vaults off the bed with a gasp. The slapping sounds of skin rival the guttural growls resonating from my chest.

The flush on her cheeks spreads to her chest and her fingers grip my forearms like a vice. She clasps her hands behind my neck, pulling her back off the bed, watching as I drive into her again and again.

"You like watching me fuck you?"

"I love it. Fuck me harder. I want to watch you make me come." Her dirty mouth is my undoing. Her pussy clenches, and I pulse inside her. The thick ropes of muscle in my arms and neck tighten as I release my climax along with her.

Her legs fall from my shoulders. We ride out our mutually shared orgasm cradled in each other's embrace. Our bodies, sticky and trembling from exertion, cling together so tight no air can pass between us.

She looks up at me with eyes so dark I lose myself in them. My hand finds hers, pressing her fingers to my lips and to my chest. Every heartbeat has her name in it. It says "I love you" when my mouth can't seem to, although I'm not sure love is even the right word anymore. My feelings for her are beyond that. She's the other half of me.

* * *

MY BODY IS wrapped around her as if my life depends on it. She peels my arm away, but her leg is held captive between mine. Memories of our past trickle into my mind. I'm on a crappy pull-out bed in the back of a moving bus, but I've never felt more comfortable.

She wriggles her lower half, trying to free her imprisoned limb, and my arm slides around her again. "You keep wigglin' your ass like that, you're gonna get more than you bargained for, sweets."

"Yeah, yeah, keep threatening, big man. Gimme my leg. You're like a furnace." I loosen my grip as she rolls over, pushing the covers down to cool off her slick back. "You always smell so good," she mumbles, burrowing her face in my chest. Sunlight filters in through her sheer bedroom curtains, splattering our bodies in shards of brightness. Last night was incredible, but waking up next to her is still my favorite.

"Let's just stay in bed all day." I roll onto my back taking her along. She slides on top of me and sits, pushing my arms up and holding them above my head. Visions of her riding me last night flood my brain. I can definitely go for a little more of that.

Who am I kidding? I can go for a lot more of that.

A shrill ringing arises from the pocket of my discarded pants for the second time that morning. "Somebody better be dead."

It's only seven o'clock in California. Who the hell is even awake yet?

"May as well check it. I need a shower anyway."

"What's the point? I'm just going to get you dirty again." I smack her ass and grind her back and forth on my growing erection. Her bottom lip disappears between her teeth, and an impish "mmm" sound comes out as my phone chimes again.

She drops a kiss to my nose. "Check it. Then come join me." I watch her saunter to the bathroom, taking her fine ass with her. I love her body, but that ass is priceless.

Jamming my thumb on the screen, I swipe upward to check the messages that keep flooding in. The number is blocked, and there's no text. Just photos.

I stand, pacing the room in a small circle next to the bed as I flick through half a dozen photos of Ainsley and me from last night. The first couple are tame—she and I holding hands walking into the house, a chaste peck on her cheek by the car—but the last few would put me in jail for murder if I knew who sent them. Whoever took these went to great lengths to get Ainsley in a compromising position. And she is. Bent in half. With me on top of her.

Fuck.

Ainsley's going to lose her shit. We aren't even supposed to be together, but here's proof of it in black and white, and I don't know where they came from. The tabloids are going to have a field day over this one. Not to mention Bob.

After everything that's happened, how do I turn around and tell her this? She handed me her heart and told me explicitly not to break it, but this is going to kill her. I need to get this taken care of before the media shit-storm happens. I fire off a series of texts to Vic, demanding his assistance with this headache before joining Ainsley in the shower.

The bathroom is thick with steam when I enter. Mouthwash

burns my mouth as I watch her distorted view through the frosted panes of glass, trying to come up with the best way to break the news before stepping in next to her.

Saturated hair hangs straight down her back. She raises her face toward the spray as it cascades down the graceful line of her body. *Goddamn.* She's gorgeous dry, but she's breathtaking when she's wet.

The clean scent of soap surrounds me. I grab her waist, dropping my lips to her neck and her head falls to the side. Slick skin glides through my hands as she turns to face me. "Everything okay?"

The water rushes all around her. Long lashes stick together creating little black spikes around each wide round eye. I don't have the heart to tell her. Not yet. Maybe I can fix it before anyone ever has to know. "Yep. Everything is great."

Chapter 48

Ainsley

THE SKY HAS changed from blue to purple by the time we leave my room in search of food. We stayed tangled up in a tight knot under the covers for the majority of the day, but Kade didn't seem much like himself. He assured me that everything is fine, but the permanent crease on his forehead tells me otherwise. He's been quiet, controlled. Not one hundred percent there. Whoever was on the other end of the phone today upset him. I just wish I knew what was up.

I slap the button on the radio in the kitchen before pulling out containers of Thanksgiving leftovers. Some random rock song croons from the speaker, while Kade grabs an apple and takes a bite. Sweet juice trickles down his chin, and he wipes it away with the back of his hand.

My feet leave the ground as he picks me up and sets me on the counter in front of him. His hands brace on the cabinet behind me. "I thought you were hungry?" The look on his face is conflicted. He seems almost . . . pissed off. We literally had sex all day, yet he's still so tense. It's weird.

His fruit-flavored tongue invades my mouth without answering my question. Hands roam under my shirt then reach for my panties. "Wait, wait. Kade, stop."

I slide off the counter putting some space between us. My

body is weak and sore, but damn if the idea of kitchen sex doesn't turn me on. Still, I can't just continue to ignore whatever this is anymore. "You haven't been yourself since this morning. Stop mounting me like an animal and tell me what's wrong."

"I told you a hundred times, I'm fine." When I avoid his reach, he gives me an incredulous look. *No* isn't a word he's used to hearing, especially from women, but I'm not backing down. If we're going to be in a relationship together, he needs to open up to me. Sex is not a solver of problems; it's a distraction from them.

Text messages blow up my phone two seconds after I plug it into the charger. It skitters across the counter, vibrating like a miniature earthquake. I reach for it, but Kade grabs it first. "Don't."

"Excuse me?"

"Just trust me on this one, sweets."

Pushing him aside, I grab my phone, and my heart begins flapping against my ribs like a hummingbird. "What the hell is this?" The question is rhetorical. I know exactly what it is. Picture after picture of Kade and me having sex. Not the nice kind you see in romantic movies either, the kind you see on late night cable.

Breathe, Ainsley, breathe. Everything is going to be fine.

I stay facing away from him, fixated on a spot on the wall in front of me, torturing myself with the images now emblazoned in my memory forever. "Relax, A. Vic is already working on it," Kade says, taking my elbow in his hand. "No one else is going to see these, I promise."

It hits me like a rock. He knew about this. "Are you kidding me right now?" I turn to face him, my arm still clutched in his grasp. Usually, any piece of his skin that touches mine causes a definite reaction, this time included. The only difference is right now that feeling is disgust. "You got these this morning, didn't you?" I wrench myself from his grip and back away.

"It's not a big deal, Ainsley. I've had this shit happen to me before, and Vic always takes care of it. No harm, no foul."

"No harm, no foul!" My voice has taken on that annoying high-pitched tone I hate, but I can't help it. I'm furious and on the verge of an all-out panic attack. "We aren't even supposed to be seeing each other, Kade! Do you have any idea what would happen to my life if these got out? If Bob saw these? Shay? I'm a suburban art curator, not a fucking porn star!"

The tears I've been holding back plummet out of my eyes into the palms of my hands. "Do you understand how creepy this is? In order for these to be taken, someone was sitting outside my window. Someone sat in a tree waiting for us to come home to use these disgusting pictures as blackmail."

"Yeah." He flinches, jamming his hands in his hair. "I know."

Talk about an eye opener. A life with Kade will always be like this. We'll always be watched, hounded, and followed. Fame isn't a gift; it's a curse. "I can't live like this! Go home, Kade. Go back to California. Get as far away from me as possible." I run up the stairs and slam the door to my bedroom.

"Come on, Ainsley. Open the door. Don't be like this." His voice pleads with me. I can feel his presence on the other side of the door, oozing underneath and puddling around me. I feel so pathetic. Half of me still wants to open that door and fling my arms around him even after all this. The other half wants him to leave and never return so that I can have some semblance of my normal life back.

Bob had to be behind this. When Kade showed up at Charlene's house, he knew he was caught. He knew I had something on him, so he needed to retaliate. It's classic Bob 101. Always have the upper hand. I'm a stupid, selfish woman, and my actions are going to lead to the worst possible outcome.

I let my desire get in the way of my brain. Maxwell told me to stay away from Kade, and in the eleventh hour, I proved how weak I am and ran right back to him.

No. I'm strong now, goddammit.

Standing from the floor, I collect Kade's belongings one by one. The suffocating smell of him rises off each piece as I pile them into my arms before opening the door. Last time I ran without a word, but this time, I'm facing it head-on. A forearm rests on either side of the richly stained woodwork as he stands there looking like he's bleeding from the inside. "Ainsley . . ."

"You told me once that you didn't want me tainted by your life. Well, I've been tainted. If you love me, give me a chance to raise my daughter the right way." Using his love for me against him is a low blow, but it's the only way to get him to listen.

"I'm taking care of this."

"I know you are. But it's too much. I can't have this in my life, or in Shay's life. Goodbye, Kade." I dump the pile of clothes into his arms, remaining stoic as he walks away from me for the second time.

Watching from the window, my gaze follows him as far as it possibly can. I crane my neck to catch the last glimpse of him as he walks out of my line of sight, ripping my heart out a little more with each step.

The first time he left was nothing compared to now. Losing him a second time feels like my skin is being peeled away. I'm irreparably damaged. Like a vase that's fallen on the ground— sure, my pieces can be glued together to give the illusion that I'm whole, but one tiny tap could smash me to dust.

I was doing fine before he came back here. He charged into my life like a bull in a china shop, shattering everything I had. I can't possibly be glued together again. There are far too many broken pieces this time.

Chapter 49

Kade

AINSLEY IS THE only thing I can think about as I unlock the door to my house and let myself in. Everything is exactly how I left it. You'd never know the housekeeper was here except for the newly stocked refrigerator. Vic must have told her I was coming home. She made some meals and left them in containers for me. That old woman's a peach. I should feel relieved to be home after so many weeks away, but instead, I feel like I've lost a limb.

I've been around some unstable women in my lifetime, but Ainsley takes the cake. She lost her damn mind last night. Yeah, it was bad, but her reaction was totally uncalled for. It was just a few pictures.

I barely have time to settle in before my cell phone is blowing up in my pocket. *Banger. Of course.*

"Dude, I just walked in the door. Can't a guy take a piss without being pestered?"

"You're home, bro? What happened?"

My hand runs over my face. "She chucked my ass to the curb. Again."

"She threw you out?" Jen's voice rings shrill through the phone, allowing me no time to answer my friend. "What do you mean she threw you out? What the hell did you do to her, Kade?"

"Control your lady, *Lance*. I didn't do shit. Someone snapped a few lewd photos of us and texted them to her. She went all *Exorcist* on my ass when she saw them."

I hear Jen in the background grumbling about chauvinism, and I smirk at the irony. After all, Ainsley was the one with the upper hand as she was crushing my heart into dust. "Great, she's not answering her phone. I'm gonna kill that asshole."

"Chill out, baby." Banger's voice is muffled, but I can hear the Georgia drawl he can't seem to shake punctuated in the syllables of his term of endearment. Years of being in California have leveled it out considerably, but every now and again, it resurfaces as a constant reminder of where we came from.

Jen's continued yapping becomes progressively quieter. A door clicks, and I no longer hear her at all. "So what now?"

"Fuck it; I'm done with this shit. There's a reason I don't do relationships."

The line is so silent that I pull the phone away from my ear to see if I've lost the call.

After a few minutes of contemplation, he finally talks. "After over a year of pining for this babe, you're giving up just like that, huh?"

"She told me to go! What am I supposed to do?"

"Same thing you did before. Give her a rest then go back out there guns blazing. Y'all fight like pit bulls and hump like bunnies. It's what makes you guys good together. You're both firecrackers."

Ever since we were kids, Banger has been the yin to my yang. He's the calm when I'm the storm, the logic when I'm irrational. I don't appreciate that quality in him nearly enough. He's a good guy to have in my corner.

"I don't know, man. Maybe she's right. What if she and the

kid are better off without me? I'm moody, arrogant, jealous . . ." An unexpected shot hits me in the chest when I mention Shay. The girl's gotten inside my heart just like her mother.

I have to get them back.

"And she loves you anyway, man. I don't know what kind of magic voodoo shit she's cast, but she changed you. Do not make a permanent decision based on a temporary emotion."

Banger's right. I'm not the same selfish bastard I was before she came along. For all my "I don't share" bullshit, I not only found one person I want to share my life with, I found two.

I should have busted through the damn door, kissed her until her lips were raw, and told her what she meant to me. I made a promise to myself that I wasn't going to walk away from her again, but the first time shit got hard, that's exactly what I did. I'm a fighter down to my very essence, but I didn't fight for us. "That's some insightful shit. When did you turn into Mr. Miyagi, dude?"

"Oh, Kadeney-San," he jokes in a garbled Miyagi-esque impersonation. "You're not a quitter, man. But since you're here, let's cut our next album and get the hell outta this cesspool of a state. Ya dig?"

* * *

MY EYES ARE bleary with sleep deprivation and overwork. I feel like I've just gone to bed when the alarm on my phone starts blasting through the room. Ainsley's case is today. I despise myself for not hopping on a plane to be there. The thought of her sitting in that courtroom to face that asshole alone makes me want to punch something, only I'm too exhausted to even move my arms.

She's set to appear at ten, which is seven a.m. California time. I'd set my alarm for six hoping to catch her before she goes. It's been over a week since I've heard her voice. I've not stopped working since the minute I got home except to sleep and wash the sweat off, but it's done little to ease my mind and strip away the burden I feel for having left her high and dry. The album is terrible, and I don't even care. My only goal right now is to get it finished and get back.

With a heavy hand, I slap the screen of my phone to hit the snooze button. Just ten more minutes of sleep, and then I'll call her.

My phone stirs me awake again, only this time, it's skittering across the nightstand with the annoying buzzing sound I set it to while I'm working. My face still mashed into the pillow, I pick it up with a garbled hello. "It's ten o'clock, dude. Where the hell are you?"

I shoot up in my bed and look at the clock. I must have turned off the alarm instead of hitting snooze. Not only did I miss Ainsley before court, but I also slept through our nine a.m. call time at the studio.

Goddammit!

My arm moves on its own accord and hurls my phone against the wall. Plastic explodes, shattering it into a hundred pieces on contact. Instantly, I realize what I've done. *How am I going to call Ainsley now?*

I rub my eyes, attempting to relieve the stress building behind them. Once again, I let my anger overshadow the parts of my brain that control logic, but I don't have a lot of time to sit and stew over it. I jump out of bed and get my ass to the studio to get to work.

Chapter 50

Ainsley

"WHAT DO YOU mean you're pregnant?" The look on Bob's face isn't quite what I anticipated when I imagined telling him our good news. We are going to be parents. "You're supposed to be barren. Isn't that what you told me?"

The word *barren* makes me wince. It seems so hateful coming out of him. Polycystic ovarian syndrome and endometriosis—that was the diagnosis for all the problems that have assaulted my insides since puberty started as a teenager. In laymen's terms, my periods suck and getting pregnant on my own would be damn near impossible.

"Well, yeah, I thought so, too, but I'm pregnant. We're pregnant. Look." Bob's brows crease as he plucks the strip from my fingers and looks at the word pregnant written across the front. This particular test is the last one of three. I didn't trust those little pink lines. What if they were wrong? What if the test was faulty? No, I needed to be one-hundred percent sure. When the word came up clear as a bell on the fancy digital test, there was no mistaking it. I was, indeed, pregnant.

Bob hands the strip back to me and runs his fingers through his blond hair. "How could you let an accident like this happen, Ainsley?"

Tears threaten, but I don't want to let them fall. We're not children anymore. Bob just graduated dental school, and I'm a semester shy of finishing my degree. This isn't an accident; it's a surprise. One I was ecstatic about until ten minutes ago. "You were there too, ya know. I didn't knock myself up."

He rolls his eyes and turns away, his hands still holding the hair off his forehead like he can't believe this is happening. "I guess you expect me to marry you now."

The tears I'd been holding slowly begin to fall. "I expect nothing from you, Bob, and I'm having this baby with or without you."

A bout of nausea hits me so hard I feel dizzy. After five years together, I assumed that was where we were headed. Call me old-fashioned, but I'd longed for marriage and children since I was a little kid playing baby dolls in my bedroom, and I'd wanted those things with Bob.

I run into the bathroom in his tiny studio apartment, the one he moved into after one year in the dorm because he couldn't get along with his roommate, and yack up the contents of my stomach into the outdated pink toilet.

Humiliation. That's what I'm feeling, in addition to nausea. I thought Bob saw a future with me. I thought we'd be together. But I'm pregnant and alone on a dirty tile floor, regurgitating my lunch and crying like a loser.

The whisper of his sneakers pads across the floor as Bob enters the bathroom. "I'm sorry, Bob," I sob. "I didn't think this would happen."

"It's okay, Ainsley. I was just surprised is all. You know I planned to marry you eventually. We may as well just do it now."

* * *

GOOD LUCK TODAY, lovie. Thinking about you. Everything is going to be fine! xo

I chuck my phone back into my purse without responding. Jenny has tried several times to get in touch with me, and I've ignored every attempt. I just can't talk to her. She represents a part of my life that's too painful to face, and I have enough drama to deal with today.

My head's in a fog as I get ready for court. The last time I was in a courtroom, I was losing my husband. Today, I may be losing my daughter. I curse myself as I compulsively check my phone again. As pathetic as it is, I'd hoped for a small something to show that he cared, but there's nothing from him, and I know there won't be. I haven't heard from Kade since he left. Can't say that I blame him. I've thrown him out twice now. How much do I expect the man to put up with?

The distance between us is like a phantom pain. The ache is everywhere. I can't sleep, yet I'm exhausted. My stomach is in a constant knot. I told myself it was because of the court case, but I know that's only part true. I miss him so much it hurts.

My appointment is scheduled for ten o'clock, but I arrive early. The house, much like the cavern of my chest, feels huge and empty. I can't stay there anymore waiting for the silence to swallow me whole. Over the past year, I've done many things alone, but I've never felt quite this lonely. He should be here.

You're a strong, independent woman. You can do this.

"Good morning, Ms. Daniels," Maxwell greets me in the lobby of the courthouse. His suit looks expensive and powerful. In our prior meetings, he was professional yet casual, but today he's polished from head to toe, right down to the blinding shine on his dress shoes. "Greg Warner arrived just a short time ago. Mr. Daniels isn't here yet. As soon as he arrives, we can get started."

The sloppy appearance of Bob's lawyer is surprising. His suit appears off the rack and is a size too small. The buttons on his jacket are screaming for release, stretched so tight across his round belly they're seconds from popping right off. In a life where he demands utter superiority above all else, Bob's attorney seems like a staggering choice.

I nod and take a seat. I can't speak for fear that the moment my mouth opens the river of tears I'd managed to keep at bay will flow and drown everyone in this room. There's nothing to do now but wait.

. . . and wait.

. . . and wait.

Maxwell glances nervously at his watch. It's almost ten thirty, and Bob still isn't here. Greg Warner paces in and out of the building, trying to call him but offers no update regarding his whereabouts. I cross my legs to control the bouncing of my knees. The idea of prolonging this any longer is agonizing. Now that we're here, I just want to get it over with. "What happens if he doesn't show up today?"

"The case will get thrown out, and everything will remain as is."

I want to believe that what happened on Thanksgiving changed Bob in some way. That he learned how important family is, or even that he realized I'm not as bad of a person as he thinks, but it's more fitting for his character to put me through all of this bullshit for nothing. No wonder his lawyer is a joke. He probably found the cheapest ambulance chaser he could find, knowing that he did not ever intend to show up. I should have known from the start that he didn't actually want Shay. He never did from day one.

An hour after we're supposed to appear, the judge calls a mistrial and sends us all home. Bob never surfaced or even answered a single call from his lawyer. He ignored the whole thing. His main goal was to get rid of Kade, and he succeeded. His horrifying photos made sure of that. There was no need to continue with this charade.

I pull my phone out of my bag and start to type a message. Victory is mine, but it doesn't feel complete unless I could share it with Kade. I want him to know my nightmare is over, and that everything is going to go back to normal. My thumb hovers over the send key as I look at the tiny thumbnail photos of his face next to all the other messages he'd sent over the past month, but I can't do it. If he cared to know, he would have asked.

The trial was coincidentally just like my relationship with Kade—a lot of useless energy expelled for nothing. I make a promise to myself that I'm going to move on from all of this. Shay is, and has always been, my first priority, and I allowed that to falter as Kade became more of a presence in our lives, but he's gone now.

He's gone.

I need to accept it.

Chapter 51

Ainsley

TORN GIFT WRAP litters just about every inch of my living room floor. Shay got me up at dawn this morning, excited to get downstairs to see if Santa came. I went overboard, as usual. I watch her from the couch, drinking my coffee as she sits near the tree on the floor tinkering with her new Kindle. One of these days, it will occur to her that Santa doesn't shop on Amazon, but today, she's still wide-eyed with Christmas wonderment, and I'm content to let the ruse continue. She may not be a baby anymore, but she'll always be my baby.

I drain my mug, yawning as I stand to get another cup. My family was over late last night for Christmas Eve, and now that the adrenaline of opening gifts has subsided, all I want to do is go back to bed. I plan to spend the whole day asleep. Bob will be coming to pick Shay up any minute to celebrate the holiday at his house, and the idea of spending another Christmas alone is too depressing to face.

The doorbell rings as I tip the carafe, and I miss the mug. Coffee puddles across the counter and trickles onto the floor in a steady stream. "Shit." I've been off my game, and it's becoming obvious to everyone around me. Even my friends at work have noticed the shift in my attitude lately. I blame it on holiday stress, but in reality, I still miss him.

It hurts just as bad as it did the day he left, if not worse. I lost not only my lover, but also my best friend, my favorite band, and my joy. If not for Shay, I might not be able to drag myself out of bed at all. Throwing him out was a stupid, impulsive decision that I should never have made, but hindsight is twenty-twenty.

The bell rings again while I'm sopping up the boiling hot mess. "I'm coming!" Tired, depressed, and annoyed, I can now add 'covered in coffee' to the list of things destroying my holiday glee. It's better that Shay goes to Bob's. I'm in a foul mood, and it seems to be getting worse by the minute. Being festive for her sake is exhausting in its own right.

I'm prepared to unleash the full force of my aggravation on my ex-husband, but the wind leaves my lungs when I see who's standing on my stoop.

Dressed all in black, he stands out against the snowy backdrop behind him. A knit hat is pulled low over his forehead, calling immediate attention to piercing blue eyes like the ghost of Christmas past coming back to haunt me.

"Kade . . ." The whisper of his name floats off my tongue into the cold morning air.

"Merry Christmas, beautiful."

I stand frozen, drinking in the sight of him. His cheeks and nose are pink from the cold, and each breath blows out in big white puffs. I haven't heard from him in a month, yet here he is in the flesh. I'd spent countless hours fantasizing all the things I'd say should I ever get the opportunity, but now that he's here, my brain can't seem to get my mouth to function.

"This month without you has been torture, Ainsley."

I blink my eyes, still half expecting him to vanish into thin air. My heart slams against my chest so hard, I swear I'm about to lose consciousness. My head screams at me to tell him to leave, that it's too late, and what's done is done, but my heart wants to pull him into this house and kiss him until I can no longer breathe.

"Don't leave me hanging, sweets. Say something."

My mouth opens, and I force myself to speak. There are a hundred things I want to say, but only one seems to make it out. "What took you so long?"

There's an old saying: If you love something, set it free, if it comes back, it's meant to be. He came back to me, just as he said he would. No matter what happens, Kade will always come after me, and I'll always want him to. We belong together.

The last time we were in this exact situation, I pushed my heart aside and listened to my head. Not a day has gone by that I don't regret that choice. Neither of us is perfect. We're both hardheaded, jealous idiots who've each made mistakes in this relationship, but I don't want to make another one.

Grasping the lapels on his jacket, I pull him toward me. His lips are frozen, but the warmth from his mouth spreads throughout my entire body. A gust of wind blows through the open door, whipping my hair around us. Kade runs his fingers through it, smoothing it back and cradling my face in his hands, as he kicks the door closed with his boot. "I missed you so much, A. I'm never going to leave you again." His lips move against my face, dropping determined kisses all over me.

A horn blast comes from outside. I can make out the sight of a mangled red blob through the thick decorative glass panel in my front door. Bob's here. "Shay! Dad's here!"

Shay bounds in from the family room, spritely and energetic as usual. "Kade!"

He squats down to her level as she runs toward him, flinging her arms around his neck. "Hey, kiddo." The soft look on his face as he embraces my daughter engulfs me. Adoration reflects in his deep blue eyes. "I missed you."

"We missed you, too!"

She whispers something in his ear. His dazzling smile widens, and his eyes crinkle in the corners. "Thanks, kid. I appreciate that. And I won't," he says with a wink.

"I got your back!" She returns his wink and smiles.

The horn blows outside a second time. Shay kisses me before grabbing the coat and bag waiting for her on the bench. "Hold up a sec." Kade's fingertips lightly grip Shay's wrist before she walks out the door. She turns back toward him as he pulls a tiny sliver of silver from his pocket. "I'm sorry I didn't wrap it," he says, working the delicate clasp with his thick fingers. "Merry Christmas, Shay."

Christmas lights glint off the chain as she holds up her wrist to inspect it. Three tiny charms hang against her skin: a rock, a pair of scissors, and a piece of paper. She smiles, fingering the charms. "This is awesome! Thanks, Kade!" she says, wrapping her arms around him a second time.

He holds her just a little tighter than before, his lids drifting closed. Tears fill my eyes. Shay's fondness for him is no surprise, but the way he loves her back melts my heart.

"Bye, Mom. I'll see you next week." Shay gives me a quick kiss and hug.

"I love you, baby. Have fun." With an ache in my heart, I watch as she trots down the walk to her father's car. It's been two years, but every time she goes, I still feel like a little piece of me goes with her.

"I have something for you, too, but you have to come with me." My lips part to say something, but he rests his fingertips against them. "Trust me."

"I'll always trust you, Kade."

My insides are teeming with intrigue as we pull away from my house. I can't imagine what he has to show me, but I don't have to wait long.

He pulls into a gated community on the other side of town. Looming high above the rest of the city, Fairfax Gardens is a community in and of itself. A black wrought-iron fence surrounds the neighborhood, and the only way in and out is through the guarded main gates.

I'm shocked when Kade pulls up and the gate opens like magic. I admire each property as he weaves around the quiet roads. Exquisite holiday decorations adorn each meticulous landscape. In all the years I've lived in this town, I've never been up here. It's beautiful.

The car swings into a driveway belonging to a giant brick and vinyl-sided house at the end of a cul-de-sac. It's a colonial-style home, but calling it that is far too modest. It's enormous. The various peaks add a beautiful architectural detail, as does the clean modern porch along the front. "Whose house is this?"

A devilish gleam twinkles in his eye as he cuts the engine and steps out of the car. I follow him out, allowing him to lead me up the cobblestone walkway by hand. I feel self-conscious and underdressed in my yoga pants and sneakers. I don't even have any makeup on. Had I known we were going to be visiting someone, I would have taken more time to get ready.

Kade unlocks the door and pulls me inside. Dark hardwood floors stretch as far as the eye can see, leading into an ultra-modern kitchen in the back. A two-sided fireplace sits off to the side separating what appears to be living space and a dining area. It's hard to tell, though, because the house is totally empty.

Now, I'm really confused.

"Are you going to let me in on the secret or what?" My voice echoes through the huge open space, giving off the illusion that I'm shouting, and my snow-soaked sneakers squeak along the clean floors as I wander further into the house.

"You're an incredible woman, Ainsley Daniels. When I came

here last month, the only thing I wanted was you, but after being here, I realized I was wrong." A surprised look must have registered on my face. He walks up to where I'm standing and rests his palm on my cheek. "I don't just want you, I want all of it."

"I don't think I understand."

"You, Shay, the house in the suburbs . . . It turns out the life you've built—the one I've spent my whole life running from— is exactly the one I want."

My eyes gaze around the empty house again. "Are you saying this house . . ."

"I bought this house for us, A. I may have accomplished everything I've dreamed of, but without you, it means nothing."

A tear rolls down my cheek. For the second time this morning, I'm speechless. "What about the band?"

His lip curls into a cocky side grin as he turns toward the gorgeous picture window in front of the house. "You see that house down there?" He pulls me close and points down the street. My gaze follows his finger to a large house in the crook of the cul-de-sac. "That one is Banger's."

My head snaps toward him with wide eyes. "Banger and Jenny are moving here too?"

"Yep! And Konner, JJ, Vic . . . the band is officially relocating. We don't need to live in L.A. to make music. We only need each other. We broke ties with RatBird, and we're starting our own label in New York."

More tears cascade down my cheeks. It's all too good to be true. I'm going to have everyone I love right here where they belong. "You really are full of surprises, aren't you?" I choke out between sobs. "You're not the only one, though. I have a surprise of my own."

"What do you mean?" he asks, cocking his head.

"I'm pregnant."

Every ounce of blood drains from his expressionless face. I'm prepared for this, and I will raise this baby alone. "Starting to rethink this whole plan, huh?"

I square my shoulders, preparing for him to blow up. To yell, curse, accuse me of lying. Anything. But I'm shocked when he falls to his knees at my feet. His hand covers my still-flat stomach, admiring it like a precious artifact before pressing his lips against it. "Mine," he whispers letting his fingers graze across my belly button. "All three of you."

With shaky hands, he reaches into the pocket of his coat and pulls out a tiny black box. "I was going to wait until the time was right, but I can't think of a better time than this."

A sharp breath stabs my lungs. "What the hell are you doing?" I take a step back. "No. No. I'm not accepting another bullshit shotgun proposal."

Tucking the little box into his palm, he grabs me by the hips and pulls me back. "A. You are the most stubborn and hardheaded woman I've ever known. From the moment I met you, you've done nothing but drive me crazy in every conceivable way. You're always challenging me, always making me work overtime to prove the way I feel about you, and you know what?" He pauses, wetting his lips. "I wouldn't have it any other way. I fuckin' love you, Ainsley Daniels. If you tell me no, that's fine. I get it. But you know I'll never give up." His mouth curls into a lascivious grin. "I always get what I want."

"You're such a cocky asshole," I say with a half-smile.

"I am. But I'm *your* cocky asshole."

Epilogue

Kade

"**K**ADE, THE BRIDE is ready for you."

Jenny's voice filters into the room, but just as quickly as she appeared, she's gone. It doesn't matter, though. My girl is beckoning for me, and I'll run to her side just like I always do. I was wrapped around her finger from the minute I looked into her huge brown eyes, and she knows it.

"Can I come in?" I say, knocking lightly on the door. The last time I was in a tuxedo like this was Banger and Jen's wedding. It seems like only yesterday, but so much has happened since then. It's crazy how fast the time goes.

"Yeah, I'm about as ready as I'll ever be," she calls through the door.

Dressed in white, she's like an angel so lovely I can hardly hold back the emotion blooming in my chest and filling my eyes with dampness. "You look beautiful." These years in the 'burbs have made me soft. The first thirty-three years of my life, I was a hardcore, arrogant ass who cared about no one but myself and my music, but that's not me anymore. Now, I'm the guy who records dance recitals and makes pancakes on Sunday mornings. You know what, though? Standing in front of her and seeing the hope and love in her eyes, I wouldn't change any of it for the world. I thought I knew what love was, but I had no idea until she entered my life.

"Don't make me cry. I'm nervous enough!" The overflowing charm bracelet on her wrist jingles as she lifts her arm to hand me a necklace. "Can you help me with this?" She holds up the thick golden curtain that rests over her bare shoulders so I can fasten the delicate chain around her neck. The clasp is tiny, and my hands are shaking.

She turns to face me, and I smile. Her freckles are hidden beneath a layer of professional makeup, and her teeth are even and straight now, but all I see when I look at her is that same gap-toothed little girl who, just like her mother, stole my heart the day I met her. "Jeff's a lucky guy, kiddo."

Laughter and squealing emanate from the hall, followed by a bang on the wall and the deep rumble of male voices. I open the door to investigate. "Ahem," I say loud enough to break up the threesome of teenagers—two boys and one girl—standing too close for my comfort.

"Oh . . . uh . . . hey Kade, we . . . uh . . . didn't realize you were in there." He runs his fingers through his sandy hair, while the other one backs away from the girl like she's poisonous. These two fuckers are just as sneaky as their old man was, and I trust them as far as I can throw them.

"Clearly. Stella, get in here."

Razor-sharp blue eyes glint from beneath a wild mane of curly black hair. "Jesus, Dad, we were just talking. Take a chill pill," she says, stalking into the bridal suite. She's as pretty as her mother is, but as snarky and mean as I am. A combination the boys seem to love but is going to put me in an early grave.

"You're banned from fraternizing with anyone who bears the last name Daniels, especially those identical putzes."

She rolls her eyes and smacks her over-glossed lips. "Whatever. Mom's last name is Daniels."

"What's the problem with my last name?" Ainsley asks as she strolls into the room bogged down by a box full of bouquets bigger than she is.

I take the box from her arms, and she shakes them out, releasing the tension. "It's not Black," I add without missing a beat.

"It doesn't need to be. I know you're not going anywhere."

I must have proposed at least a hundred times over the past sixteen years, and each time she's shot me down. 'Marry me, Ainsley' is going to be written on my tombstone. The closest I ever came to getting a yes was when three-year-old Stella asked on my behalf. It's a game between us now. I'll never give up, and she'll never give in.

She's a tough cookie, my Ainsley, but she's not wrong. There is nowhere else I'd rather be than right here. I love her today even more than I did back then. She's just as beautiful, sweet, and stubborn as she ever was. And just as delicious.

"You almost ready to go, kid? It's about that time," I say, offering my hand to Shay. Today, I have the honor of walking her down the aisle. It's one I didn't expect, but one I'll gladly accept. It's been six years since Bob died. He suffered a massive heart attack not long after marrying wife number three. Shay was devastated, even though her time with him diminished substantially after he and Cami split.

Growing up, we idolize our parents. We blindly love them, because we don't know anything else. It broke my heart when Shay had that moment of clarity and saw Bob for who he was. A lonely shell of a man who had a hard time loving anyone because he couldn't stand himself. I know he loved her, though. In his own way.

"Can you guys give me a minute alone with Kade?"

"I'll see you down there, my beautiful girl." Ainsley gives Shay a quick hug before she, Stella, and the handful of young girls in identical blue dresses leave the room, closing the door behind them. The heavy satin of Shay's gown makes a swooshing sound as she walks to the couch in the corner and sits. "I want to thank you."

"Don't thank me, kid. I'm more than happy to foot the bill on this shindig. You deserve it."

"I'm not talking about the wedding," she says, taking my hand in hers. "My entire life changed the second you walked into it. Most people only get to have one dad, but I was lucky enough to have two." Red rings form around her eyes, and she pauses, giving the corners a dainty dab with a Kleenex.

"Do you remember what I said to you the day you gave me this?" She fingers the charms dangling from her wrist. The chain has been replaced, but the tiny rock, paper, and scissors are still attached, along with an airplane, a Superman emblem, a slice of pizza, and a dozen others. One for every year I've known her. A collage of her favorite things always with her, even when I can't be.

My mind drifts back to that Christmas. The year I almost lost them both forever. Her bubblegum-scented breath on my cheek and her squeaky little whisper in my ear saying she put in a good word for me. *Please don't give up on us.* "Of course, I do, baby. I'll never forget, and I'll never give up."

"And for that, I say thank you."

★ ★ ★

Ainsley

I'M A BLUBBERING mess as Shay and Kade come down the aisle. Glowing light seems to radiate all around her from the beauty she exudes. She's grown up into such an amazing woman, and I couldn't be more proud.

Turns out, Shay's fascination with superheroes morphed

into an obsession with flying. I used to joke about her becoming a flight attendant, but I wasn't prepared for her to announce she was joining the Air Force. The pain I felt watching her leave for basic training was so great I didn't think it would ever heal. But Kade held me as I cried, reminding me that kids grow up and leave. I couldn't keep her forever, no matter how much I wanted to. Shay had wings, and it was her time to fly. Years later, she told me the only reason she had the courage to follow her dream was due to the strong example I'd set for her growing up.

Now, I'm watching my baby get married, and I'm a puddle of unmanageable emotion. Jeff's pulled his cap low over his head, but I can see the love in his face when he looks at her, and I know he's going to make her happy. It's all I ever wanted for her. Just to be happy and surrounded by people who love her.

Kade sits in his rightful seat by my side, trying to hide the glistening in his eyes. Family life has turned him from a grizzly bear to a teddy bear. Having daughters has certainly softened his jagged edges smooth and round, but the transition from Rock God to Step-Dad of the Year wasn't all peaches and cream. Kade was gone a lot at first. Out on the road with Black Diamond, touring and playing shows, working day and night to get the label started. Shay, Stella, and I were often alone in that huge house. Jenny and her son, Trent, would come for sleepovers and Kade would call and Skype, but it wasn't the same. I wanted my love. I wanted my family.

When he was home, Kade would put all of his energy into the girls. He was spreading himself too thin, insisting on being at every game, every recital, and every parent-teacher conference. He'd play a show on Saturday night, get home in the wee hours of the morning, and stay up so he wouldn't miss pancakes bright and early Sunday. It was too much, and it took its toll.

He withdrew from the band in teeny tiny increments and eventually stopped touring altogether. The media blamed me. They called me the next Yoko, but it was all his idea. Being with us was the most important thing to him, and it was time to move on. Besides, Black Diamond Records was thriving at that point. There was no need to spend months on the road anymore.

He threads our fingers as Shay and Jeff exchange their vows. I know what he's thinking. Another proposal is imminent—I can feel it. Sometimes, lavish events expertly carried out to plan, and other times, randomly asked while we're settling into bed at night. I'm still the only one who tells him no, and it still drives him crazy.

His blue eyes blaze, wicked and scheming, and I can't wait to see what he has in mind. It'd better be good because, after close to two decades together and hundreds of proposals, it's going to be the last one.

This time, I plan to say yes.

About the Author

J ANE ANTHONY IS a romance author, fist pumping Jersey girl, and hard rock enthusiast. She resides in the 'burbs of New Jersey with her husband and children. A lover of Halloween, vintage cars, & coffee, she's also a cornucopia of useless 80's knowledge and trivia. When not writing, she's an avid reader, concert goer, and party planner extraordinaire.

Jane loves hearing from her readers! Connect with her on these social media sites, and don't be too shy to say hello!

janeanthonyauthor.wixsite.com/romance
twitter.com/JAnthonyAuthor
facebook.com/JaneAnthonyAuthor
facebook.com/groups/JanesRomanceAddiction
instagram.com/janeanthonyauthor
pinterest.com/janeanthonyauth
tinyletter.com/janeanthonyauthor
goodreads.com/JaneAnthonyAuthor
amazon.com/author/janeanthony

Other novels by:
Jane Anthony

Secrets and Promises
"He was everything I desired except for
one thing I needed most: My brother's approval"

Coming January 2017
Chasing Casey
Austin Krehley was her first . . . AJ Morello is her forever.

Acknowledgements

AS I WRITE this, I'm chock full of bubbling emotion just having been able to make this book happen. This one almost killed me. And by that, I mean I think my friends would have murdered me if I changed my mind about it one more time! This manuscript has seen so many evolutions, it could be charted in a museum alongside the circle of life. What started as a simple novella about one woman's struggle to start over, turned into a year of sweat, tears, and so many rewrites even I had trouble keeping up. There were moments when I gave it up completely because I just couldn't look at it anymore. But Kade wants what he wants, and he was determined to be heard.

Before I get into all my professional thank yous, I need to drop the two names that were behind me all the way during this fiasco:

Stephanie H., you wore so many hats during this process—sounding board, soul soother, beta reader, and the wind beneath my wings. I drove you insane. I know you probably cringed seeing my name on your caller ID because it would just be another round of Kade and Ainsley bull-crap, but you always answered, and talked me down off every single ledge. In the end it was you who convinced me this book needed to be published. Your utter belief in me keeps me strong, even when I feel like my sanity is hanging on by a thread. I've said it before, and I'll keep saying it until my vocal chords cease to work, in which case, I'll write it: I couldn't accomplish any of this without you. You are truly my "Jenny" in every sense of the word. Long live Rod Strumwell!

Megan D., your help with those raw first drafts was vital to me getting my start as a writer. When I called you and said, "I'm thinking of writing a book inspired by you," your excitement and support is what drove me to continue. (Then again, I should probably be thanking whatshisface for being a douchebag.) I hope you loved how the story turned out! Much like you, Ainsley finally got her happy ending.

Now that my sob-fest is complete, there are so many other people to thank for having a hand in letting Kade loose on the world:

Nichole and Christine at Perfectly Publishable, you guys rock! Thanks for everything!

Cassy Roop at Pink Ink Designs, thank you so much for the amazing cover and teasers!

Jenny Sims at Editing4Indies, as usual, your proofreading skills astound the hell out of me!

My beta team—Jenny G., Devon C., Jillian V., Candice R., and Robin W.,—you guys all rock my friggin' socks off! The emails, the phone calls, the questions, the utter insanity . . . You put up with all of it! I would never even think of putting a book out without having it pass your eyes first! ("It's wanton, not wonton. That's soup!" haha!) I appreciate all your hard work and excitement from the bottom of my heart.

Thank you Ena and Amanda at Enticing Journeys for putting together another awesome blog tour. And also to ALL the bloggers who read, reviewed, and pimped out the book. You guys are the backbone of this industry. Without you, we'd be lost!

And saving the very best for last, THANK YOU to ALL of

my readers! All your kind words and comments make this non-sense worthwhile. I'm truly humbled by all of your support every day. I love each and every one of you!

Printed in Great Britain
by Amazon